THE SPORT OF
THE GODS

AND
OTHER ESSENTIAL
WRITINGS

PAUL LAURENCE DUNBAR

THE SPORT OF
THE GODS

AND
OTHER ESSENTIAL
WRITINGS

Edited and Introduced by
Shelley Fisher Fishkin and David Bradley

THE MODERN LIBRARY

NEW YORK

Published in the United States by Modern Library, an imprint of The Random
House Publishing Group, a division of Random House, Inc., New York.

MODERN LIBRARY and the TORCHBEARER Design are registered trademarks of
Random House, Inc.

LIBRARY OF CONGRESS CATALOGING-IN-PUBLICATION DATA
Dunbar, Paul Laurence, 1872–1906.
The sport of the gods: and other essential writings / edited
and introduced by Shelley Fisher Fishkin and David Bradley.
p. cm.
ISBN 978-0-8129-7279-5
1. African Americans—Literary collections.   I. Fishkin, Shelley Fisher.
II. Bradley, David.   III. Title.
PS1556.A4F57 2005

811'.4—dc22   2004061146

Printed in the United States of America

www.modernlibrary.com

CONTENTS

THE SPORT OF THE GODS
AND OTHER ESSENTIAL WRITINGS

PART ONE
POETRY

PART TWO
SHORT FICTION

PART THREE
NONFICTION

GENERAL INTRODUCTION

Shelley Fisher Fishkin and David Bradley

On May 1, 1893, in the White House, President Grover Cleveland pushed a button. A thousand miles away, on the far side of the Appalachians, the thirty-foot flywheel of a two-thousand-horsepower Corliss-Allis engine began to turn. The Chicago World's Columbian Exposition was under way.

The idea seemed simple: a celebration of the four hundredth anniversary of Columbus's discovery of America. But legendary show-man P. T. Barnum advised, "Make it the Greatest Show on Earth," adding, "There is only one place in the United States to hold [it] and that is New York City. No one appreciates or admires the enterprise and energy of our great Western cities more than I do, but . . . New York is our metropolis."

The citizens of trans-Appalachian America demurred. *Their* metropolis was Chicago, which, like the mythic phoenix, had arisen from the ashes of the Great Fire of 1871 to surpass Philadelphia and become the nation's Second City. They spent ten million dollars competing for the opportunity to demonstrate their enterprise and energy for the world. Their blow-hard, chest-thumping lobbying offended Eastern-ers, who extended the nickname "the Windy City" to the lobbyists. But the Windy City won.

The Exposition was intended to be an expression of the state of the art of American engineering, particularly trans-Appalachian engineering. The huge engine that responded to the president's distant hand was fabricated by the Allis Corporation of Milwaukee, Wisconsin, and provided power to the world's first "El"—for elevated, electric—train. The "Wheel-in-the-Sky" that lofted a thousand fairgoers at a time two hundred and fifty feet above Exposition grounds was designed and constructed by "a man born west of Chicago" named George Washington Ferris. The innovative alternating current electrical system, which, at nightfall, set the alabaster façades of the Exposition's Greek Revival buildings agleam, creating what would come to be known as the White City, had been built by Pittsburgh's Westinghouse Electric in daring challenge to Thomas Edison's direct current system, which General Electric was using to light New York's Broadway into the Great White Way.

But the Exposition was also intended to be an expression of the state of the art of American intellectual development. To this end, the organizers formed a "World's Congress Auxiliary," presenting an extensive program of lectures throughout the run of the Exposition, and contributed $200,000 to the construction of the Art Institute of Chicago, the better to provide elegant auditoria in which ideas might be "conspicuously displayed."

The Congress Auxiliary organized what it called a "World's Summer University," presenting nearly six thousand speeches by some four thousand different speakers over a thousand sessions. Henry Adams, a curmudgeonly and cynical critic if ever there was one, praised the overall program as "the first expression of American thought as a unity," and nearly a million people attended Congress Auxiliary presentations. Few probably expected academic papers to rival the Ferris Wheel or the Corliss-Allis engine for impact. But on July 12, a thirty-two-year-old professor of history at the University of Wisconsin named Frederick Jackson Turner presented a paper entitled "The Significance of the Frontier in American History." His ideas were not entirely original, owing much to the notions of another historian named Theodore Roosevelt, but his thesis was elegant:

> The existence of an area of free land, its continuous recession, and the advance of American settlement westward explains American development.

Turner's thesis meshed perfectly with the gears of the Exposition, and also with the desire to reunite the nation politically and mythologically after the Civil War. "When American history comes to be rightly viewed," Turner assured his audience, "it will be seen that the slavery question is an incident." Turner's replacement of the malignancy of slavery with the benignancies of geography "dazzled and delighted historians desperately seeking a theme," in the words of historian Daniel Boorstin, and his appearance at the Exposition would come, in the words of contemporary historian Richard Slotkin, "to symbolize a turning point in American history and historiography."

Unfortunately—and perhaps unintentionally—the Exposition was also an expression of the state of the art of American social attitudes, which included a profound and pervasive racial prejudice. This prejudice was not based on ignorance; on the contrary, it was based on social theories widely expounded by the most highly respected intellectuals in the nation, many of them professors at the nation's most august institutions.

One of these theories was "Social Darwinism," which held that the principles outlined by Charles Darwin in *On the Origin of Species by Means of Natural Selection* could also be applied to the cultural development of racial groups. That notion, suggested by Darwin's subtitle, *The Preservation of Favoured Races in the Struggle for Life,* had been expanded by Darwin's fellow Englishman Herbert Spencer, who coined the term "survival of the fittest." But Social Darwinism had found a strong American exponent in William Graham Sumner of Yale, who used Darwinist principles to justify laissez-faire capitalism, the "Protestant ethic," and unregulated competition for wealth and status, which, he argued, weeded out the less vigorous members of society. In Sumner's thinking, to be poor, uneducated, unempowered—indeed, to have been enslaved—indicated innate inferiority. Many educated Americans accepted this view.

Ironically, Darwin's ideas on the origin of species were less accepted, a theory called "polygeny" being much preferred. Polygeny explained the origin of humankind much in the manner of contemporary Creationism, but held that the various races, rather than having a single ancestor in the biblical Adam, were descended from different ancestors, and therefore were distinct species, with different physical, intellectual, and emotional capacities. This theory too had European origins, but in America it had become an issue not only of scientific truth but of intellectual independence. As Stephen Jay Gould described it:

> Ralph Waldo Emerson argued that intellectual emancipation should follow political independence. American scholars should abandon their subservience to European styles and theories. . . . In the early to mid-nineteenth century, the budding profession of American science organized itself to follow Emerson's advice. A collection of eclectic amateurs, bowing before the prestige of European theorists, became a group of professionals, with indigenous ideas and an internal dynamic that did not require constant fueling from Europe. The doctrine of polygeny acted as an important agent in this transformation, for it was one of the first theories of largely American origin that won the attention and respect of European scientists—so much so that Europeans referred to polygeny as the "American school" of anthropology. Polygeny had European antecedents . . . but Americans developed the data cited in its support and based a large body of research on its tenets.

The principal proponent of polygeny was Louis Agassiz, director of Harvard's Museum of Comparative Zoology. In 1850, amid the controversy over the Fugitive Slave Act, Agassiz combined polygeny with a line of logic from Thomas Jefferson and formulated the following opinion:

> It seems to us to be mock-philanthropy and mock-philosophy to assume that all races have the same abilities, enjoy the same powers, and show the same natural dispositions, and that in consequence of this equality they are entitled to the same position in human society. History speaks for itself. . . . This compact continent of Africa exhibits a population which has been in constant intercourse with the white race, which has enjoyed the benefit of the example of the Egyptian civilization, of the Phoenician civilization, of the Roman civilization, of the Arab civilization . . . and nevertheless there has never been a regulated society of black men developed on that continent. Does not this indicate in this race a peculiar apathy, a peculiar indifference to the advantages afforded by civilized society?

Four decades later, the Slavery Question had been answered, but Agassiz's opinion was being reiterated by America's foremost paleontologist, Edward Drinker Cope, of the University of Pennsylvania:

The highest race of man cannot afford to lose or even compromise the advantages it has acquired by hundreds of centuries of toil. . . . We cannot cloud or extinguish the fine nervous susceptibility, and the mental force, which cultivation develops in the continuation of the Indo-European, by the fleshy instincts, and dark mind of the African. Not only is the mind stagnated, and the life of mere living introduced in its stead, but the possibility of resurrection is rendered doubtful or impossible.

Today, these notions seem, at best, quirky and quaint—and more likely, infuriating. But in 1893 they did represent the state of the art of American thought. Accordingly, they were semiotically expressed throughout the Exposition.

To offer one enduring example, the Exposition saw the introduction of a new advertising icon: "Aunt Jemima," portrayed by forty-nine-year-old ex–Kentucky slave Nancy Green, who was hired by the R. T. Davis Milling Company to demonstrate a newfangled notion called "pancake mix"—the first ready-mix food sold commercially in America, which had been invented in Missouri in 1889. Green did not create the character—it was inspired by a song from a minstrel show—but she gave it life, flipping and serving thousands of pancakes while singing old songs and telling nostalgic-sounding tales of the plantation era, including the advertiser's legend about how she had been discovered in a cabin in Louisiana by a hungry Confederate general. The Davis Milling Company booth became so popular that special guards had to be hired to do crowd control, and at the Exposition's end, officials awarded Green a medal and proclaimed her "Pancake Queen." She was also offered a lifetime contract, which supported her for the next thirty years.

But less ironic instances abound. In the Transportation Building, which featured full-scale, fully functional facsimiles of Columbus's fleet and a thirty-foot-long model of a British warship, was also presented "A Bimba, or Canoe, from Banguella, Africa," which *The Dream City*, a widely distributed portfolio of commemorative engravings, described as

constantly surrounded by visitors, who could only with difficulty believe that it had been used as a canoe in an African river. There was no caulking, nor did it appear that any effort had even been made to keep the water from entering the boat, though the drying out of the small logs may have made a change in the sea-worthiness of the craft. . . . It is well held by the

philosophers that where man sleeps under a banana tree, to be awakened
for his dinner by the fall of a banana into his lap, he lets it go at that.... Yet
why these negroes should build a log canoe when they might use a wool-
skin or dug-out does not appear, either; and amid kyaks of Labrador,
caiques of the dardanelles, gondolas of Venice, bragazzas of the Adriatic,
phoenix-boats of Japan, bateaus of French pioneers, dug-outs, wool-skins
and what-not, this bimba seemed to be the worst boat at the World's Fair.

Art historian Michael Leja, who has analyzed the statuary commissioned by the organizers, concludes that even the official art

celebrated the ascension of "civilized" power over nature and "primitive"
peoples, and this contrast was staged in every field of endeavor.... Sometimes the organization of exhibits implied a hierarchy of races and nation-
alities, in which each represented a stage in the evolutionary process, as on
the midway in Chicago....

It was on that midway—more formally, the "Midway Plaisance," a
mile-long avenue that provided access and transition from the gritty
reality of Chicago to the ideal White City and other buildings of the
Exposition itself—that the worst examples of racism were to be found.

Originally, the Midway was to provide "dignified and decorous"
exhibitions of a diversity of cultures, as part of the "Expositions Department of Anthropology," headed by Frederic Ward Putnam, director of
the Smithsonian Institution. But the need to make a profit caused the
organizers to turn the Midway over to one Sol Bloom, whose mentor
was the by then late Barnum. Predictably, the Midway became a circus,
more precisely a carnival, where unsuspecting Americans were introduced to the snake charmer and the belly dancer—which, thanks to
the newly invented zipper, soon became a strip-tease, aka "hootchy-
kootch." *The Century* damned the Midway with ironic praise as "probably the greatest collection of 'fakes' the world has ever seen.... Here
was the greatest fakir of them all. I am proud to say that he was an
American." Observed *Harper's Weekly:* "One of the most comic things
connected with the Midway is that theoretically it is also a place for
scientific investigation."

Unfortunately, the humor was lost on the many gullible visitors, who
actually believed that paying thirty-five cents admission to "Blarney
Castle" entitled them to kiss the True Blarney Stone, and that "Dahomey

Village" (admission twenty-five cents) was an anthropological accuracy rather than a two-bit sideshow created by a Frenchman. Even historian (and Ohioan) Hubert Howe Bancroft, who produced a massive history of the Exposition, *The Book of the Fair,* succumbed to credulity, describing Dahomey Village as if it were one of the national exhibits:

> Dahomey has a village on the plaisance . . . its huts built in native fashion, with rough mud walls thatched with the bark and boughs of trees and with wooden floors and windows. . . . In one lives the village blacksmith, whose principal business is the sharpening of spear heads and the repairing of the spikes which protrude from Dahomean war-clubs. . . . Elsewhere a man is stooping over his embroidery; for in Dahomey this is the work of men, the women, if not nursing their babies, going forth to till the soil or to fight. . . . In the centre of the enclosure is the theatre, if such can be called a large, open shed, unwalled, with thatched roof and floor of rough planking. . . . At one end are grouped the musicians, all of them Dahomeans, all lean and lank, and all supremely hideous. They wear nose and earrings of metal, and as little clothing as decency permits, their dark, shining bodies showing the scars of many a hard fought battle. Seated on the platform is the king, a coal-black potentate, sleepy and fat, with thick, bush beard and head and jaws like a bull-dog. All day long he sits dozing with half-closed eyes and changeless expression of face, if his face can be said to have any expression save that of ferocity and lust . . . his majesty enjoys the music and dancing more perhaps than anything else in life, unless it be the cutting off of heads. The instruments are as grotesque as the performers. . . . Forward and backward passes this motley crew, brandishing war-clubs and grinning as only Dahomeans can grin. Louder and yet more loud grow the beating of drum, the blast of horn, and the clash of cymbal. Then the posturing begins; but in this there is nothing of the graceful or sensuous; simply a contortion and quivering of limb and body, with swinging of weapons as though nothing would delight them more than to kill and destroy. It is in truth a barbaric spectacle, and the more so as many of the performers are women, the amazons of western Africa, trained for the service of the king and esteemed as the choicest of his troops.

Richard Slotkin has described a visit to the Exposition in semiotic terms:

> Visitors to the fair entered an elaborately structured space. Those who followed the paths prefigured in the Exposition's map and program were engaged by symbols, displays and rituals that visualized the rapid course of American progress. . . . The centerpiece of the Exposition, and the

culmination of the typical itinerary, was the "White City," an architectural extravaganza in ersatz marble representing the pinnacle of Euro-American civilization, the original "alabaster city ... undimmed by human tears," [but] [t]he main road from the railroad station to this New Jerusalem lay through the "Midway Plaisance," a street lined with restaurants and souvenir shops, "kootch-dance" palaces side by side with exhibition pavilions and "villages" displaying the wares and folkways of other nations. . . . Moving up the Midway to the White City ... the visitor passed from ... displays of primitive savagery and exotic squalor to a utopia of dynamos and pillared façades. It was easy to construe the lesson implicit in the tour. More than one journalist observed that the exhibits featuring more "advanced" races ... tended to appear closer to the White City end of the Midway, while the non-White Dahomeans and American Indians appeared at the farthest remove from Utopia. "You have before you the civilized, the half-civilized and the savage worlds to choose from—or rather, to take one after the other," one journalist observed. The stroller "up" the Midway traces "the sliding scale of humanity" according to a Social-Darwinist program. Reporter Dentyon Snider advised his readers that, "undoubtedly the best way of looking at these races is to behold them in ascending scale, in the progressive movement. . . . In that way we move in harmony with the thought of evolution."

This overwhelming subtlety was expressed in the explicit insults common to the age. Black Americans had been denied jobs in building the White City and were denied work as members of the Exposition security force, the Columbian Guard. Eventually a hundred blacks were employed by the Exposition, but only as menials—restroom attendants and "chair men" who pushed visitors about the grounds in wheelchairs.

But despite its various expressions, the Social Darwinist/racist paradigm did not go uncontradicted. In early August the Congress Auxiliary presented an eight-day Congress on African Ethnology, which involved a number of prominent black Americans and native Africans. Although the original intent was both patronizing and colonialist—the opening address was delivered by a diplomat from Belgium, who insisted that "liberty and civilization had supplanted slavery and barbarism" thanks to his nation's colonial activities in the Congo—and although black speakers most often were presented off-site in churches and schools in the black community, contemporary historian Christopher Robert Reed has argued, not unconvincingly, that

For the American nation, this congress brought about a re-creation of the liberal arrangement between the races that originated in the abolitionist era. And, in its aftermath it represented a first dialogue in substantive interracial cooperation. Accordingly, well-educated blacks as well as the elite and middle class whites presented invited papers. Africans from the continent and from the Diaspora filled the black ranks, many being the most notable persons in their fields of endeavor—intellectually endowed, well-known and respected by members of both races. So, with enthusiasm, Caucasians from Europe, Africa and America collaborated in problem-solving based on African strengths rather than hand-wringing over African deficiencies. Significantly, what originated as an endeavor conceived by white American humanitarians, intellectuals, and foreign policy advocates to examine, validate, and perpetuate the most humane features of Great Power hegemony over the African continent, along with finding ways of eliminating the worst features of American racism, was to a great extent, and to their amazement, dominated rhetorically by the diasporan and continental Africans themselves.

The African Congress did air a number of emerging racial issues, including, as Bancroft reported:

Should the Afro-American colonize Africa, was among the topics considered, one of the speakers suggesting the formation of a chartered company, like that under which Virginia was colonized; but to this the sentiment of the congress was strongly opposed; for, as was stated, civilized negroes of the better class were needed where they were, to counteract the effect of poverty and illiteracy among others of their race.

Ironically, the proponent of immigration to Africa, a black man named Henry McNeal Turner, framed his argument in the context of the anthropological notions, when he (as Reed describes it)

launched into a peroration on the African origin of humankind.... "Revolting as the theory may appear to some present, I believe that all humanity started black—that black was the original color of mankind. That all of these white people present descended from black ancestors, however remotely in antiquity they may have existed."

A contradiction in keeping with the Columbian theme was to be found among the national pavilions. "Near the German building Hayti [*sic*] erected a model pavilion," wrote Bancroft, unable to escape the tendency to place the "primitive" in the context of the "civilized":

Above the main portico is the coat-of-arms, and below it, in gilt letters, the words Republique Haitienne, with the figures 1492, 1892, and 1804, the last referring to the acquisition of independence . . . in the centre a statue of "Reverie" by a native artist. Relics are freely displayed; among them the rapier of Toussaint L'Ouverture, while others refer to the Columbian era and to the aboriginal inhabitants, including one of the anchors lost from Columbus' flag-ship in 1493, the other being placed at the entrance to the convent of La Rabida. There are also portraits and busts of prominent men, as of the Haytian liberator, of the first president of the republic and of Frederick Douglass. . . . All that Hayti has contributed to the Fair is contained within her pavilion. . . .

The Dream City followed suit. The engraving of the Haitian Pavilion showed it with the comically phallic German Pavilion towering over it, while the caption captured the social context with emphatic, but probably unintentional, irony:

[T]he building portrayed in the engraving, which shows its proximity to the beautiful German House, was dedicated in the presence of an audience composed of Exposition officials and colored citizens of Chicago. Fred Douglas [*sic*] delivered the principal address. This structure was notable as expressing the civilization of a race long oppressed and last to receive its freedom. It was erected in the Southern colonial style. . . . A restaurant was kept in the southern part of this building, at which colored people found it agreeable to refresh themselves, for notwithstanding the protestations of the colored people and in defiance of the laws, the race line is still sharply drawn in the great Northern cities. It may thus be opined that the Haytien Building was a welcome addition to the group in Jackson Park.

Neither *The Book of the Fair* nor *The Dream City* mentions that anti-lynching crusader Ida B. Wells had a desk in the Haitian Pavilion, from which she distributed an eighty-page pamphlet protesting the racial discrimination at the Exposition, "The Reason Why the Colored American Is Not in the World's Columbian Exposition." But neither was able to ignore Frederick Douglass. In the half century since the publication of his *Narrative,* the statuesque Douglass had become a national icon, "the Sage of Anacostia."

Douglass had recently served as U.S. Consul General to Haiti, and Haitian president Florvil Hyppolite asked him to oversee the Pavilion. He soon became one of the most widely recognized and sought-out personages at the Exposition, holding court at the Haitian Pavilion and making speeches at the pavilions sponsored by the states of Vermont and Michigan.

Douglass himself was a critic of the Exposition. He not only gave Wells desk space, but issued the call for funds to support the printing of the pamphlet, to which he had contributed. He referred to the White City as a "whited sepulchre" and insisted Dahomey Village was a deliberate attempt "to exhibit the Negro as a repulsive savage." Yet he supported the idea of the Exposition itself, seeing it as an opportunity for an international audience to witness racial injustices in the nation and the world. When the Congress Auxiliary asked him to organize a special day for black Americans to attend the Exposition, Douglass agreed.

Special days were not unusual—the Exposition offered many such, dedicated to ethnic and geographic groups. But the announcement of "Colored American Day," scheduled for August 25, met with a problematical response. It was lampooned by the white press, which called it "Darkies' Day at the Fair." Many Negro leaders, including Wells, rejected the idea as "a sop to our pride," announced a boycott, and even criticized Douglass publicly for organizing the event. Some liberal whites applauded the idea, though it was felt necessary to remind the Negro masses to behave themselves and give foreign visitors a "good . . . impression of the colored race." Some Midway food vendors, out of personal prejudice or commercial concern that white customers would be kept away by an influx of blacks whom the vendors did not wish to serve, offered a special menu that included only fried chicken and watermelon.

But in the dignified auditorium of the Art Institute, an audience of twenty-five hundred witnessed black Americans issuing uncompromising challenges to the racist atmosphere outside. They heard the internationally famed Jubilee Singers of Tennessee's Fisk University perform Negro spirituals. They heard a virtuoso violin performance by Douglass's grandson, Joseph. They heard Douglass himself, in one of his last great speeches, declare the "Negro Problem" a chimera, and assert that "The true problem is . . . whether the American people have honesty enough, loyalty enough, honor enough, patriotism enough to live up to their own Constitution." They heard elocutionist Hallie Q. Brown of Ohio's Wilberforce College give a stirring rendition of George Boker's "The Black Regiment." And they heard an elevator operator from Dayton, Ohio, recite poems he himself had written. His name was Paul Laurence Dunbar.

He was but a boy, really, just turned twenty-one, with only a high school education. But he already had a modest regional reputation. In 1888 two of his poems had been published in the Dayton *Herald*. In 1891 his short story "The Tenderfoot" had been distributed by the A. N. Kellogg Syndicate, earning him six dollars. And in 1892 he had appeared before the annual meeting of the Western Association of Writers, convened in his hometown, to read a poem of welcome.

He had vanished abruptly, some thought suspiciously, from that gathering, though it was just that he had to get back to work. But one of the writers—J. N. Matthews, a poet, but one who did not sneer at on-spec journalism—sought him out and interviewed him, not without difficulty. Wrote Matthews:

> I found him seated in a chair on the lower landing hastily glancing at the July *Century*, and jotting down notes in a handy pencil tablet. Not having time to converse with me there, he invited me into the elevator, and during a few excursions from floor to floor, I gathered from him the following facts: His parents were both slaves, his father having escaped into Canada from the South. His mother is living in Dayton, and he is supporting her and himself on the pitiful sum of $4 per week. . . . [H]e stated he had been writing rhymes since he was 13. His favorite authors are Whittier and James Whitcomb Riley. . . .

Matthews's story of a black bird in a gilded elevator cage was published in the Indianapolis *Journal*, getting Dunbar some local notoriety, and into hot water with his employer, who disliked having his penuriousness exposed. Nor did Dunbar enjoy his fame; in November he wrote Matthews:

> [T]his publicity is disturbing me. It upsets me and makes me nervous. I feel like a man walking a slack rope above thousands of spectators, who knows himself as an amateur and is every moment expecting to fall.

But the story also got Dunbar a supportive letter from Riley, whose Hoosier dialect poems had made him the de facto poet laureate of the Midwest. It also got him a commitment from the editor of the

Chicago *News* to "in future . . . pay for my poetical contributions." Two weeks later, Dunbar was paid two dollars for a poem by yet another publication.

Encouraged by Riley and Matthews and the prospect of income from writing, Dunbar borrowed $125 to have his verses printed in a volume titled *Oak & Ivy.* The books were ready for the Christmas shopping season. He sold them in his elevator—hustled them, really. Word spread. Sales boomed. Dunbar was able to repay the loan before the year was out.

He went out on the road—Toledo, Detroit—reciting in Negro church basements and at the YMCA; he asked for money and sometimes got it, but read gratis when he had to, hoping to "find the means of securing a better situation," toting a satchel of books which he huckstered to Lane Seminary–type liberals and African Methodist Episcopal ladies' clubs and cigar-smoking juntos.

Meanwhile he moved ahead with prose, "trying to work into stories the old tales of the south that I have been hearing since childhood." He sent work out to newspapers and magazines but received only rejections, even from the Chicago *News.* He tried to stay positive, but lamented, "apparently no favorable outcome of my efforts is imminent." He'd begun to expect rejection.

So in the spring of 1893, like many others, white and black, he headed for Chicago, "in quest of work at which I can live. I make no pretensions to liking this place," he wrote Matthews, "I am here to make money. . . . As yet there is no opening for me, but I feel hopeful that there will be soon."

There was. Dunbar was one of the hundred black men hired by the Exposition. He wrote to his mother, Matilda,

> I have gone to work out at the World's Fair Grounds, at $10.50 a week. . . .
> My job is a soft snap. I help attend to a gentleman's toilet room . . .

He did not tell her that his first sight of the White City had so absorbed him that he forgot the Sabbath for the first time in his life, or of his disappointment that no newspaper would commission him to correspond about the Exposition. These things he confided only to Matthews, adding,

I would that I could make my living with my pen, but it seems that I am destined never to be able to do so, but "some say" who knows what may happen.

What happened was an introduction to Frederick Douglass, for whom he recited privately, then a job as Douglass's assistant at the Haitian Pavilion, then the acceptance of a poem by the Chicago *News*, and then the appearance at the World's Columbian Exposition before that audience of twenty-five hundred. In August 1893, Dunbar was indeed "a man walking a slack rope above thousands of spectators."

Historical hindsight is not 20/20. Past events viewed in the light of later knowledge lose their contemporary proportion. That which at the time seemed earth-shattering is forgotten; that which went unnoticed can loom large; that outcome which was not only unknown but seriously in doubt can seem almost predestined. In twenty years, the upstart alternating current would win out over direct. In twenty years, Turner's frontier hypothesis, written at the last minute, presented after five other, boring papers to a drowsing audience, would be the dominant paradigm of American history. In twenty years, Paul Laurence Dunbar not only would have come to make his living with his pen, but would be dubbed, by no lesser personage than Booker T. Washington, the "Poet Laureate of the Negro Race." He would also be dead.

Knowing, as we now do, that Dunbar would live fast, die young, leave a beautiful epitaph and a controversial legacy of artistic inspiration and political controversy, it is tempting to see him on the Exposition stage as already a powerful, influential, tragic figure—to see, as critic James D. Corrothers wrote decades later, "a youth, singing in the dawn . . . / Refining, as with great Apollo's fire, / His people's gift of song."

In fact, Dunbar's appearance was overshadowed by that of Frederick Douglass—and understandably so. Nor did it result in a "better situation." Perhaps it might have, as Douglass invited him to come to Washington. But Douglass was failing—Dunbar described him as "tottering into the room"—and seemingly impotent. After the Exposition, Dunbar returned to Dayton. There, newspaper reports of his activities had again brought unwelcome results. His "own people," he felt, saw his achievement as presumption and were "growing away from" him, and potential employers thought he no longer needed work—or more likely, preferred their employees obscure. He would make his living by his pen, but it would be less fulfilling a desire than a bowing to necessity: "It is not I, but these people," he wrote, "who have made up my mind for me that I must 'adopt literature as a profession.'" Nor would necessity mother success; though he dreamed of college, he would petition a potential patron:

> Could some of the money which was offered for my college course be sent me to relieve present embarrassments? I have no funds and no work, and a foreclosure is threatened on the little home I have been paying for through the Building and Loan Association.

Soon after, he would write: "There is only one thing left to be done, and I am too big a coward to do that."

Yet there was much prophecy in the vision of that dark, slender youth standing on the broad stage. He was a manifestation of a "New Negro"—born free and American, thanks to Constitutional amendments, grown to manhood before segregation became not merely local custom but the Law of the Land. The "growing away" he would lament was less a matter of publicity than of history, of psychology. His own people had known the lash, the leg irons; worse, they'd known their constant threat. He had not.

And yet he was not new. Slavery was not part of his experience, but it was part of his personal culture. It was in the minor-keyed spirituals sung movingly not only by the Fisk Singers, but by the congregation of the Eaker Street African Methodist Episcopal Church, where, at age twelve, he had given the first public recitation of his work. It was in those old tales he had been hearing since childhood, from his mother, father, uncles, and aunts. And if a verse in homage to black Union troops was to be read in Chicago, it should not have been a white Princetonian's paean, but Dunbar's ode to "The Colored Soldiers," for his father had been one of them, returning from the safety of Canada to help liberate his brothers, at the age of forty-seven.

But then he *was* new, not as a Negro, but as an American. Though it is doubtful that Frederick Jackson Turner had blacks in mind, Dunbar was a child of the Ohio Territory, the first trans-Appalachian frontier. His city, Dayton, was in its own way as windy as Chicago, a trading post with pretensions, the place where the cash register itself was invented. Though Turner and the Exposition's organizers might have been shocked to hear it, their theses and intentions were both embodied and anticipated in that slender youth upon the stage, for he had written, in his "Welcome Address to the Western Association of Writers":

> "Westward the course of empire takes its way,"—
> So Berkeley said, and so to-day
> The men who know the world still say.
> The glowing West, with bounteous hand,
> Bestows her gifts throughout the land,
> And smiles to see at her command
> Art, science, and the industries,—
> New fruits of new Hesperides.
> So, proud are you who claim the West
> As home land; doubly are you blest
> To live where liberty and health
> Go hand in hand with brains and wealth....

At the Exposition, Dunbar recited his "Columbian Ode," which many took as a poem written for the occasion, shaped to fit the Exposition's high-minded explicit rhetoric. It was an occasional poem ... and yet it was not. His words about trans-Appalachia expressed what he, as much as any man, believed: "The place that nurtured men of savage mien / Now teems with men of Nature's noblest types...." Though Social Darwinism denied it, Dunbar, as much as any man, fit that description. Though the Exposition's semiotic rhetoric denied it, Dunbar, as much as any man, belonged there.

One would like to leave it there. One cannot. For there was still that other, implicit rhetoric. On the Midway, the suckers P. T. Barnum said were born every minute were laughing at Dahomey Village, and the vendors were figuratively, and sometimes literally, forcing watermelon down black throats. The statuary screamed European supremacy. In the Transportation Building, that sad little boat sat high and dry while a replica of Columbus's flotilla rocked gently on the lake outside. While Aunt Jemima flipped flapjacks and told lies about old Louisiana, somewhere beyond the Exposition grounds Ida Wells was working on a new pamphlet to tell the truth about the 161 lynchings that had taken place in 1892, up from 113 in 1891, up from 85 in 1890.

Bancroft, in *The Book of the Fair*, wrote:

Among monuments marking the progress of civilization through the ages, the World's Columbian Exposition of 1893 will ever stand conspicuous. Gathered here are the forces which move humanity and make history, the ever-shifting powers that fit new thoughts to new conditions, and shape the destinies of mankind.

True, but with an irony Bancroft did not recognize. Nor, then, did young Paul Dunbar, singing in the dawn, with the day, both bright and dark, ahead.

———

The editors would like to thank Alana Noel Voth, Todd Dapremont, Jan Hafner, and Lauren McCoy for their assistance with researching and photocopying material for this book.

CHRONOLOGY

1872   June 27, born in Dayton, Ohio, to Joshua and Matilda Dunbar, the only black family living on Dayton's Howard Street.

1873   Parents separate.

1876   Mother petitions for divorce and receives custody of Paul.

1878   Writes first known poem, "An Easter Ode."

1884   Recites "An Easter Ode" at Eaker Street A.M.E. Church.

1885   Father dies (buried in Dayton National Cemetery).

1886   By his own account, "begins to write in earnest." In September, enters Dayton Central High School, the only black student in the class, and for some time, the only black in the school.

1888   First published poem, "Our Martyred Soldiers," appears in the Dayton *Herald*, followed by "On the River" in same publication.

1889   Contributes sketches and poems to *Westside News*, published by his friends Orville and Wilbur Wright.

1890   Edits the Dayton *Tattler* (printed by Orville and Wilbur Wright), publishes pieces including "Salutatory" and "Lager Beer"; serves as editor in chief of the *High School Times;* president of the Philomathean Literary Society.

1891   Sells first literary work, "The Tenderfoot," a Western dialect tale, to
        A. N. Kellogg Syndicate for six dollars; writes class song; graduates
        from Central High School; unable to find other job, works as eleva-
        tor operator at the Callahan Building, Dayton, earning four dollars
        a week.

1892   Writes and recites "Welcome Address" for the Western Association
        of Writers meeting in Dayton in June; completes first book of
        poems, *Oak & Ivy.*

1893   *Oak & Ivy* officially published in Dayton; sells book to passengers
        riding the elevator in the Callahan building; travels to Detroit and
        Toledo to give readings; travels to Chicago to seek work at World's
        Columbian Exposition (the first World's Fair); finds job cleaning
        mens' toilets; meets Frederick Douglass, who employs him as a clerk
        at the Haitian Exhibit at the fair; reads selections from his poems on
        Colored American Day at the fair; meets antilynching activist Ida B.
        Wells; begins work on the *Chicago Record* and writes for other news-
        papers.

1894   First contributions accepted by *Munsey's Magazine* and *The Century
        Magazine* (not published by *The Century* until 1895).

1895   Publishes first poem in *The Century,* "A Negro Love Song"; serves as
        editor of the Indianapolis *World,* a black newspaper; meets James
        Whitcomb Riley in Indianapolis; publishes second book of poems,
        Majors and Minors, which includes the first publication of "We Wear
        the Mask," "When Malindy Sings," and "An Ante-Bellum Sermon"
        (actually appears early 1896).

1896   Receives glowing review of *Majors and Minors* from William Dean
        Howells in *Harper's Weekly* on his birthday, prompting hundreds of let-
        ters and many orders for books; attends reception hosted by *The Cen-
        tury Magazine;* meets W.E.B. Du Bois; gives readings; publishes *Lyrics of
        Lowly Life* (all but 11 of the 105 poems previously published).

1897   Becomes engaged to Alice Ruth Moore; tours England giving public
        readings and recitations, and writes in London; returns to United
        States and takes job as assistant in Reading Room in the Library of
        Congress, Washington, D.C.; collaborates with composer Samuel
        Coleridge Taylor; publishes poems "At Candle-Lightin' Time" in
        The Century and "Little Brown Baby" in *Outlook.*

1898   Marries Alice Ruth Moore; publishes first novel, *The Uncalled,* and *Folks from Dixie,* a story collection that includes "Nelse Hatton's Vengeance," "At Shaft 11," and "The Ordeal at Mt. Hope"; collaborates with Will Marion Cook on *Clorindy, or the Origin of the Cakewalk;* publishes "The Race Question Discussed" in the Toledo *Journal* and other papers, inspired by the Wilmington race riots.

1899   Resigns from job at the Library of Congress to concentrate on writing and on public recitals; gives readings in Boston on program with Booker T. Washington and W.E.B. Du Bois to raise funds for Tuskegee Institute; is given honorary master of arts degree by Trustees of Atlanta University; falls ill with pneumonia and is diagnosed as having tuberculosis; travels to Colorado for his health, on doctors' advice; publishes *Lyrics of the Hearthside* (which includes "Sympathy") and the illustrated volume *Poems of Cabin and Field.*

1900   Attends conference of black farmers at Tuskegee; gives readings in Jacksonville, Florida, staying with James Weldon Johnson; visits the Catskills and Colorado for his health; continues to give recitations; returns to Washington, D.C.; publishes second story collection, *The Strength of Gideon and Other Stories* (which includes "The Ingrate," "One Man's Fortunes," "The Tragedy at Three Forks," and "Mr. Cornelius Johnson, Office-Seeker"), and second novel, *The Love of Landry;* publishes "Negro Life in Washington" in *Harper's Weekly* and "Is Higher Education for the Negro Hopeless?" in the *Philadelphia Times;* publishes short story "The Emancipation of Evalina Jones" in *The People's Monthly.*

1901   Writes Tuskegee Institute school song at Booker T. Washington's request; publishes illustrated collection of poems *Candle-Lightin' Time* and third novel, *The Fanatics;* publishes short story "The Lion Tamer" in *Smart Set.*

1902   Separates permanently from wife by mutual agreement; collaborates with Will Marion Cook; returns to Dayton to live with mother; publishes last novel, *The Sport of the Gods.*

1903   Gives readings in Kansas, Washington, Boston, New York, Baltimore, and Ohio; publishes poetry collection *Lyrics of Love and Laughter,* the illustrated poetry volume *When Malindy Sings,* story collection *In Old Plantation Days* (which includes "A Blessed Deceit"), and "The Fourth of July and Race Outrages" in *The New York Times.*

1904   Severity of illness increases; publishes story collection *The Heart of Happy Hollow* (which includes "The Mission of Mr. Scatters" and "The Lynching of Jube Benson") and illustrated poetry volume *L'il Gal.*

1905   Participates in President Theodore Roosevelt's inauguration parade; publishes poetry collection *Lyrics of Sunshine and Shadow* and illustrated poetry volume *Howdy, Honey, Howdy.*

1906   Publishes illustrated poetry volume *Joggin' Erlong;* February 9, dies of tuberculosis in Dayton at age thirty-three.

PART ONE

POETRY

INTRODUCTION

In 1781 Thomas Jefferson completed the first draft of what would come to be known as *Notes on the State of Virginia*. At inception, however, it was a collection of responses to a number of queries from a French aristocrat, François, Marquis de Barbé-Marbois, who served as secretary of the French legation to the United States between 1779 and 1785. Marbois' queries were wide-ranging, arising out of the science of the time, which had not yet coalesced into discrete disciplines, but instead mingled geology, geography, zoology, physiology, psychology, philosophy, biology, and botany under the rubric of "natural history," a proto-discipline that depended less on systematic investigation, and much less on experimentation, than on personal observation. Jefferson's responses, therefore, though wide-ranging and thorough, were essentially opinions allegedly supported by reason.

Jefferson gave a fairly complete and accurate description of the geography, geology, flora, fauna, population, and social organization of Virginia—a dispassionate, academic expression by a well-versed Man of Reason, which Jefferson purportedly was. But in the midst of his response to one query, Jefferson seemed to forget he was a member of the American Philosophical Society and became something altogether more agendaed.

The query read simply: "The administration of justice and description of the laws?"

Jefferson's response began, "The state is divided into counties. In every county are appointed magistrates, called justices of the peace ..." and continued with a long and tedious summary of Virginia's statutes governing everything from landholding to marriage and naturalization. The discussion became more interesting when Jefferson explained an ongoing revision of the codes intended to remove colonial vestiges, mentioning his own proffered amendment to the revision plan itself: a proposal to emancipate Negro slaves born in Virginia once they had reached majority, at which time, "they should be colonized to such place as the circumstances of the time should render most proper."

Although this would not have affected the legal status of slavery itself, applied only to blacks born in the future and would have given slave owners the right to work even those blacks for at least ten years, it was clear that this plan would eventually cause a labor shortage. This Jefferson proposed to remedy by sending "vessels at the same time to other parts of the world for an equal number of white inhabitants; to induce whom to migrate hither."

That all this seemed somewhat byzantine, Jefferson acknowledged in a rhetorical question:

> It will probably be asked, Why not retain and incorporate the blacks into the state, and thus save the expence of supplying, by importation of white settlers, the vacancies they will leave?

which he answered with a mordant prediction:

> Deep rooted prejudices entertained by the whites; ten thousand recollections, by the blacks, of the injuries they have sustained; new provocations; the real distinctions which nature has made; and many other circumstances, will divide us into parties, and produce convulsions which will probably never end but in the extermination of the one or the other race.

Jefferson then proceeded to enumerate the "real distinctions" of nature, laying out a series of canards that constitute a systematic codification, not of the laws of Virginia, but of the tropes of American racism. These included:

> They secrete less by the kidneys, and more by the glands of the skin, which gives them a very strong and disagreeable odour. ...

They are at least as brave, and more adventuresome. But this may perhaps proceed from a want of fore-thought, which prevents their seeing a danger till it be present. . . .

They are more ardent after their female: but love seems with them to be more an eager desire, than tender delicate mixture of sentiment and sensation. Their griefs are transient. . . .

In general, their existence appears to participate more of sensation than reflection. To this must be ascribed their disposition to sleep when abstracted from their diversions, and unemployed in labour. An animal whose body is at rest, and who does not reflect, must be disposed to sleep, of course.

In imagination they are dull, tasteless, and anomalous.

In music they are more generally gifted than the whites with accurate ears for tune and time, and they have been found capable of imagining a small catch. Whether they will be equal to the composition of a more extensive run of melody, or of complicated harmony, is yet to be proved.

However, the first trope Jefferson articulated was of particular interest:

The first difference that strikes us is that of colour. . . . And is this difference of no importance? Is it not the foundation of a greater or less share of beauty in the two races? Are not the fine mixtures of red and white, the expressions of every passion by greater or less suffusions of colour in the one, preferable to that eternal monotony, which reigns in the countenances, that immoveable veil of black which covers all the emotions of the other race? Add to these, flowing hair, a more elegant symmetry of form, their own judgement in favor of the whites, declared by their preference for them, as uniformly is the preference of the Oranootan for the black woman over those of his own species.

This was not merely an expression of personal aesthetics—an assertion that black is not, in fact, beautiful. The last part of the passage referred to a belief, seriously held by many educated Europeans, that given opportunity, African apes would come down out of the trees and force themselves on African females. Winthrop Jordan, in *White Over Black: American Attitudes Toward the Negro, 1550–1812,* explains this belief in psychological terms: "By forging a sexual link between Negroes and apes . . . Englishmen were able to give vent to their feelings that Negroes were a lewd, lascivious, and wanton people." Jefferson altered and extended the belief about the behavior of non-human animals to the behavior of human animals. What makes this curious—especially in the context of a discussion of the laws of Virginia—is that in discussing marriage elsewhere in his reply, Jefferson makes no mention of the anti-miscegenation laws, although such laws had been part of the Southern criminal codes, including Virginia's, for a hundred years. The existence and form of those laws made it quite clear that fully consensual sexual relationships between blacks of both genders and whites of both genders were so common that they had to be legally discouraged. But Jefferson turned that which was often a mutually consensual, albeit illegal, conjoining of black male and white female into something that was inevitably bestial rape, while making no mention of that other business, of white male masters coupling with black female slaves. It is not clear whether, at the time of this writing, Jefferson himself had engaged in such behavior, but he knew it existed. Yet rather than acknowledge the fact, or even the obvious implication, of the long-standing miscegenation laws, Jefferson chose to extend the European belief and suggest that the Negro male was as rapacious with respect to white females as was the "Oranootan" toward black females.

After listing these and other disparagements, Jefferson modestly summarized:

> I advance it therefore as a suspicion only, that the blacks, whether originally a distinct race, or made distinct by time and circumstances, are inferior to the whites in the endowments both of body and mind

and stated a conclusion in the form of another rhetorical question:

> Will not a lover of natural history then, one who views the gradations of all the races of animals with the eye of philosophy, excuse an effort to keep those in the department of man as distinct as nature has formed them? This unfortunate difference of colour, and perhaps of faculty, is a powerful obstacle to the emancipation of these people.

The *Notes* were published in England in 1787. A decade later, Jefferson was installed as president of the American Philosophical Society, the first scientific body in the nation, shortly after being elected vice president of the United States. Three years later, as he was in the process of becoming the nation's third president, he implicitly reiterated this position by publishing an appendix to the *Notes*. Thus, at the dawn of the nineteenth century, "Query XIV" constituted a public expression of American racial beliefs, articulated by one of the nation's most powerful intellectual authorities and its most powerful political authority.

At the end of the century, the notions expressed in Query XIV were palpable in the American reality. Jefferson's desire to deport American blacks to "such place as the circumstances of the time should render most proper" had been one motivation for his constitutionally questionable prosecution of the Louisiana Purchase, which had created much of the trans-Appalachian America celebrated at the Chicago Exposition. His mordant prediction of fatal conflicts between black and white in the South seemed by then to have come terribly true; certainly the terrorism called lynching seemed to fulfill the prophecy of "new provocations." Just who was being provoked was a question answered by Jefferson's conversion of consent to rape, since the justification most often given for lynching was that a black male had brought it on himself by "insulting" a white woman and any sexual contact between black male and white female was assumed to be rape, even if the woman claimed it was consensual. Meanwhile, Jefferson's more general disparagements were used to justify the increasing trend for states to pass laws requiring racial segregation, and the final thrust of his argument, that blacks, being inferior, were unworthy of political equality, justified the "grandfather clauses" and other stratagems being used to deny blacks the right to vote.

Not surprisingly, the arguments employed by blacks to attack disenfranchisement, segregation, and violence focused on the terms laid out in Query XIV. For example, Ida B. Wells's first pamphlet, "Southern Horrors," was not merely an exposé of incredible inhumanity, but an argument against a Jeffersonian implication. Many Americans, including many black Americans, accepted that the allegations of rape and attempted rape associated with lynching were true. Wells herself accepted that view, until she was prompted to begin systematic investigation. In "Southern Horrors" she presented documentary evidence—beginning with a case from Ohio—that the allegations were but a cover story for what was actually terrorism designed to achieve economic and political ends. She made the argument again in "A Red Record," but many still did not get the point; years later, Dunbar's friend, Toledo mayor Brand Whitlock, would object to Dunbar's use of the term "innocent" to refer to lynching victims in "The Haunted Oak."

Opposition to Query XIV also promoted more artistic literary activity, as one of Jefferson's disparagements was

> never yet could I find that a black had uttered a thought above the level of a plain narration. . . . Misery is often the parent of the most affecting touches in poetry. —Among the blacks is misery enough, God knows, but no poetry.

Jefferson had gone on to deny the significance of what, in 1781, was a well-known counterexample:

> Religion indeed has produced a Phyllis Whately [*sic*]; but it could not produce a poet. The compositions published under her name are below the dignity of criticism.

Jefferson's disparagement of Boston's Phillis Wheatley was essential to his general argument. Brought to Boston from Africa at the age of about six, she had learned quickly and well and soon produced poems that were so in keeping with the conventions of English poetry that it had been suspected that "the compositions published under her name" had in fact been written by someone else—which is to say, someone white. That they had not been was an evaluation made by the most prominent men of Boston, including John Hancock, co-signer, with Jefferson, of the Declaration of Independence. A volume of her verse, *Poems on Various Subjects Religious and Moral*, had been published in England in 1773. Marbois, the intended recipient of Jefferson's *Notes*, was well aware of her. In fact, he had written about Wheatley. His opinion of her work was not particularly favorable, however ("there is imagination, poetry, and zeal but no correctness nor order nor interest"). Jefferson's assertion that Wheatley's work was "below the dignity of criticism" was not evaluation, but desperation: her career, fairly judged, was evidence that tore his thesis to tatters.

The effect of Jefferson's disparagement was, in some ways, positive, as it encouraged black institutions, especially the churches and the schools, to pay more attention to art, particularly literature, than they might otherwise have. It was, for example, typical that Paul Laurence Dunbar's first public performance was the recitation of his "An Easter Ode" at Eaker Street African Methodist Episcopal Church, when he was about twelve, or that many of his early professional recitations and sales of his poetry collection *Oak & Ivy* took place under the auspices of church groups. While ministers and parishioners may not have known about Query XIV, they understood that a literary text produced by a black person was not merely an artistic expression, but evidence. The black intelligentsia did know about Query XIV, and they welcomed literary efforts as demonstration that either Jefferson had been wrong about black capability or, if he had been right, he was right no longer.

But this also placed certain expectations on the writers and the texts, specifically, that what was produced be acceptable in the sight of the white critical establishment—that the work be above "the dignity of criticism." The result was that literature produced by blacks was viewed in a complicated light. As Winthrop Jordan put it, "From the very first, Negro Literature was chained to the issue of racial equality." This fact has had an ongoing effect not only on black American literature, but on the criticism of black American literature. Certainly it has had an effect on critical statements about Dunbar.

By the time Dunbar appeared at the World's Columbian Exposition, many black writers had produced texts good enough to confound Jefferson. But there were logical problems. The greatest body of black writing was the "slave narratives," many of which had been produced with the assistance of white "editors," which complicated their use as evidence of equality. (It is no accident that the full title of Frederick Douglass's first book was *Narrative of the Life of Frederick Douglass, an American Slave, Written by Himself.*)

An additional problem was that many of the black writers were of mixed blood. This made it possible to argue—as many did—that it was this admixture of European blood that enabled them to write. In Europe, this rationalization was used to dismiss the challenge to white cultural superiority presented by the Russian Pushkin and the Frenchman Dumas. In America, it was used to dismiss the challenge to white political supremacy presented by Douglass, Harriet Jacobs, Charlotte Forten, F. E. Watkins, and Dunbar's fellow Ohioan Charles W. Chesnutt.

But Dunbar was what in his time was called a "pure black"—meaning that his parentage was pure freed slave, with no white master lurking in the woodpile. While the faces of men like Douglass and Booker T.

Washington and the young Harvard Ph.D. and Wilberforce professor W.E.B. Du Bois showed clearly the presence of Caucasian genes, Dunbar's complexion was dark, his features negroid.

The importance of this was made explicit by a white Toledo physician, H. A. Tobey, one of Dunbar's earliest supporters. Tobey read *Oak & Ivy* and invited Dunbar, sight unseen, to read at the Toledo State Hospital, of which Tobey was superintendent. At his first sight of Dunbar, Tobey exclaimed, "Thank God, he's black!" later adding, "Whatever genius he may have cannot be attributed to the white blood he may have in him."

This importance was reiterated by William Dean Howells in his introduction to Dunbar's first commercially published volume, *Lyrics of Lowly Life*, as Howells spoke of his earlier review of *Majors and Minors:*

> In my criticism of his book I had alleged Dumas in France, and I had forgetfully failed to allege the far greater Pushkin of Russia; but these were both mulattoes, who might have been supposed to derive their qualities from white blood vastly more artistic than ours. . . . So far as I could remember, Paul Dunbar was the only man of pure African blood and of American civilization to feel the negro life aesthetically and express it lyrically.

But while Dunbar's dark skin made him an anti–Query XIV poster child, it complicated his life and critical reception.

It complicated his life because he fell in love with a beautiful, talented young woman who happened to be light-skinned and came from a light-skinned family who harbored serious color prejudice; this inhibited their courtship, forced them to wed in secret, and may have hastened the failure of their marriage—certainly it figured in some of their arguments.

It complicated his career because Dunbar did not simply write poetry, or even recite it—he *performed* it. Early in his career he was paid little or nothing for the performance per se, but profited only from the sale of books. In other words, he sold volumes of poetry by selling individual poems in recitation, much like a modern recording artist touring in support of a CD. This was not a problem when the poem was "Ere Sleep Comes Down to Soothe the Weary Eyes." When it was "A Negro Love Song" . . . there could be a problem. For Dunbar's dark skin suggested an association with the blackface tradition of the minstrel show.

One of his most successful early performances took place in August 1896, in Narragansett Pier, Rhode Island, a fashionable vacation spot for the rich and famous. That category included a number of Northern Democrats—which is to say, not the party of Lincoln—such as Harriet Rebecca Lane, the niece of the bachelor president James Buchanan, who, serving as his First Lady, began the tradition of inviting artists to the White House. It also included many Southerners—one of them the widow of Confederate president Jefferson Davis, for whom Dunbar gave a private reading.

His public appearance was in the main ballroom of the New Matthewson Hotel. Afterward he wrote to his mother, Matilda: "The southern people have eaten me up wonderfully . . . I have order[ed] another 200 hundred books . . ." But part of what was "eaten up" was a performance of "The Cornstalk Fiddle" to the accompaniment of the hotel orchestra, during which Dunbar reportedly "acted out the various figures of the country dance described." He may have recited also "A Negro Love Song," which, according to Gossie Hudson and Jay Martin, was not written as verse but as a "hambone"—a lyric sung (or read rapidly) to the rhythmic slapping of thigh and chest.

This is not to say that any of Dunbar's performances, in Narragansett Pier or elsewhere, were minstrel shows, or that he was pandering to racially conservative white taste. Indeed, it is probable that, young, dazzled by the opulence around him, excited by his apparently positive reception, and driven by the need to sell books, Dunbar did not realize how his performance might be perceived. But four years later he wrote the lyrics for a Christmas show, *Uncle Eph's Christmas: A One-Act Play with Music,* produced by and starring a famed black minstrel, Ernest Hogan. Dunbar was embarrassed by reviews that called him "prince of the coon song writers," and at the apparently vocal insistence of his wife, who was said to have seriously insulted the venerable Hogan, asked that his name be removed from the billing.

Public performance aside, most of Dunbar's poems were actually too good to be obvious counters to Query XIV. Surely the subtle irony of "An Ante-Bellum Sermon" rises "above the level of a plain narration," but for some readers the irony may prove too subtle. Indeed, many of Dunbar's poems were, and are, liable to misinterpretation because they are "persona poems"—cast in the first person, with the language coming not from the poet, but from an invented person—in other words, a fictional character.

The persona poem is analogous to a narrative written in the first person, and many a fiction writer has discovered to his shock that some readers assume that the first person narrator is really the author under pseudonym—or worse, the other way around. In many of Dunbar's poems such misidentification of author with speaker causes little confusion, and in some it is virtually impossible—obviously, Dunbar was neither a turkey nor an oak tree. But in a significant number, it was to present a troubling issue.

When Dunbar began writing, the persona poem was a well-established form. What made his poetry different, and eventually controversial, was his choice to use the personae of people he knew, loved, and respected, including black ex-slaves with little education. Having made that choice, he was forced, by the principle of verisimilitude, to write in dialect. As Mark Twain wrote in only seeming jest, the "rules governing literary art . . . require that when the personages of a tale deal in conversation, the talk shall sound like human talk, and be talk such as human beings would be likely to talk in the given circumstances." For Dunbar, then, to write in dialect was not a choice, but an imperative of artistic intent.

But thanks to Query XIV, dialect caused trouble.

Part of the problem was, again, contextual. The last quarter of the nineteenth century had seen the publication of a number of literary works in which white writers, many of them Southerners, made arguably insulting use of allegedly Negro dialect. One of the earliest was a young Mississippian, Irwin Russell, whose Negro dialect poems—with illustration—were a feature in *Scribner's Monthly* in the late 1870s. (One memorable line: "Fur whar you finds de nigger—dar's de banjo an' de 'possum!") Russell died in 1879, but his *Poems* was published posthumously, in 1888. Also published in 1888 was *Befo' de War: Echoes in Negro Dialect*, by Armistead Churchill Gordon and Thomas Nelson Page. Gordon was a poet, known for lines like "Mars' George, sometimes de b'ilin' tear / Fills up my eyes, / 'Count o' de mizery now, an' de change—." Page was a fiction writer, author of stories published in *The Century*, some of which were published collectively in 1887 in *In Ole Virginia, Marse Chan, and Other Stories*. Page is sometimes credited with founding the "moonlight and magnolia" tradition that celebrated the antebellum South.

But the most famous writer of dialect stories was Georgian Joel Chandler Harris, whose "Uncle Remus" books first appeared in 1881. The third, *Uncle Remus and His Friends,* appeared in 1892. Harris's claims that his tales were authentic provided some quasi-scholarly justification for expressions like

> In dem times we 'uz all an us black; we 'uz all niggers tergedder, en 'cordin' ter all de 'counts w'at I years fokes 'uz gittin' 'long 'bout ez well in dem days ez dey is now. But atter 'w'ile de news come dat dere wuz a pon' er water some'rs in de naberhood, w'ich ef dey'd git inter dey'd be wash off nice en w'ite, en den one un um, he fine de place en make er splange inter de pon', en come out w'ite ez a town gal. En den, bless grashus! w'en de fokes seed it, dey make a break fer de pon', en dem w'at wuz de soopless, dey got in fus' en dey come out w'ite; en dem w'at wuz de nex' soopless, dey got in nex', en dey come out merlatters; en dey wuz sech a crowd un um dat dey mighty nigh use de water up, w'ich w'en dem yuthers come long, de morest dey could do wuz ter paddle about wid der foots en dabble in it wid der han's. Dem wuz de niggers, en down ter dis day dey ain't no w'ite 'bout a nigger 'ceppin de pa'ms er der han's en de soles er der foot.

For obvious reasons, these expressions created a context in which Negro dialect in literature was regarded, initially at least, with suspicion, especially by blacks.

But context aside, a dialect is merely a consistent variation from a "standard" language, with unique but consistent pronunciation, grammar, accent, vocabulary, and idioms. Although one can associate a dialect with race, dialects are primarily associated with geographical region. (They can also be secondarily associated with class, education, and national origin.)

Usually, when a writer uses dialect, part of the intent is to create character—to convey a sense of the nature of the speaker by transcribing not only words, but the patterns and rhythms of speech. Dialect can also convey a sense of place and time, and to the extent that it can convey class, economic, and other associations, it can literally give a voice to persons who usually go unheard.

It was, in fact, this aspect of dialect that led Howells to praise those pieces . . . where he studies the moods and traits of his race in its own accent of our English. We call such pieces dialect pieces for want of some closer phrase, but they are really not dialect so much as delightful personal attempts and failures for the spoken language. In nothing is his essentially refined and delicate art so well shown as in these pieces which . . . describe the range between appetite and emotion, with certain lifts far beyond and above it, which is the range of the race. He reveals in these a finely ironical perception of the negro's limitations, with a tenderness for them which I think so very rare as to be almost quite new.

The problem with Howells's expressions, in both the introduction to *Lyrics of Lowly Life* and his earlier review of *Majors and Minors,* are laden with the racial assumptions embodied in Query XIV. But unlike Jefferson, Howells admits the counterevidence, allowing that there did exist an American Negro—a man "of pure African blood and of American civilization"—who was not only able to utter a thought above the level of a plain narration, but also able to show, convincingly, that "among the blacks" there was both misery and poetry.

It is sadly ironic, therefore, that Query XIV had a lasting warping effect on academic criticism of Dunbar's poetry. Joanne M. Braxton, in her introduction to a 1993 reprint edition of the *Complete Poetry* of 1913, summarized that criticism:

> The central debate concerning Dunbar's poetry had begun to emerge when his second collection, *Majors and Minors* . . . was reviewed by William Dean Howells in the June 27, 1896, issue of *Harper's Weekly.* Howells's review drew wide attention to Dunbar, but it also limited the appreciation of the work of the twenty-four-year-old poet by declaring that the "Minors" [Dunbar's plantation-dialect poems, constituting about a third of the volume] were his real strength, and that there was nothing "especially notable" in Dunbar's standard English verse "except for the Negro face of the author." . . . With these words, Howells dismissed Dunbar's traditional verse and set the direction for future Dunbar criticism, "a line," in the words of Benjamin Brawley, "slavishly adhered to by reviewers. . . ."

Braxton goes on to describe how, after the Great Migration and the growth of Harlem as a cultural center, the image of

> the "old Negro" of plantation literature was supplanted by thematic treatment of the urban Negro . . . [and] views of black nightlife, dance and

music, sexual freedom, and generally uninhibited behavior associated by many and some bourgeois blacks with a black urban underclass

that figured in the work of later black writers. She goes on to write:

> More than one critic has found Howells's assessment of Dunbar's dialect verse to be a fair one. While Dunbar protested the unfair trivialization of his "Majors" by literary critics of his generation, Charles T. Davis argues that no American poet, black or white, has approached Dunbar's success in using "the spoken language of the people as a medium." ... Davis suggests that Dunbar's own use of the term *Minors* to describe his dialect verse suggests "problems about the poet's attitude about the use of dialect." One of Dunbar's failings, Davis suggests, is that he "never fully understood that he had to make a decision" ... Dunbar, Davis contends, lacked self-assurance where his dialect poems were concerned: "... Because of his cultural ambivalence, Dunbar "could not bring himself to perform the act of will...." This confusion distinguishes Dunbar from the generation of Negro artists who followed him, who were bold in their claims about the artistic value of racialized cultural materials, where Dunbar remained apologetic.

As a summary of critical positions, Braxton's discussion is useful, accurate, and admirably concise. But it is a fundamental misapprehension that the title *Majors and Minors* corresponds to a distinction between non-dialect poems and dialect poems. What underlies this long-standing misapprehension is not just a misreading of the text, but a reaction-formation to Query XIV leading to the assumption that Dunbar must have been defensive about his use of dialect and "racialized cultural materials."

In fact, the volume as originally printed separates the non-dialect and dialect poems into sections, the first titled "Majors and Minors," the second titled "Humor and Dialect." Each section has its own decorative half-title page. With one exception, the poems included in the "Majors and Minors" section are written in plain or "high language" English, not dialect.

It is therefore clear that—contrary to critical supposition—the title "Majors and Minors" does not indicate that Dunbar considered dialect poems in general and Negro dialect poems in particular to be of "minor" importance (nor that, for that matter, he considered dialect necessarily humorous). The use of the terms "major" and "minor" seems rather to be a statement about the tone of the poems, their meaning akin to that in music, in which a minor key denotes melancholy, sadness, or solemnity. And Dunbar emphatically did refer to poems as music. The dedication reads, "As my first faint pipings were inscribed to her, I deem it fitting, as a further recognition of my love and obligation, that I should also dedicate these later songs to my mother."

To be fair, the idea that Dunbar was "apologetic" or culturally ambivalent, that he had "problems" of "attitude about the use of dialect," is suggested by language employed by Dunbar's friend and political ally W.E.B. Du Bois, who wrote in *The Souls of Black Folk:*

> This, then, is the end of his striving: to be a co-worker in the kingdom of culture, to escape both death and isolation, to husband and use his best powers and his latent genius. . . . The innate love of harmony and beauty that set the ruder souls of his people a-dancing and a-singing raised but confusion and doubt in the soul of the black artist; for the beauty revealed to him was the soul-beauty of a race which his larger audience despised, and he could not articulate the message of another people.

Surely this was a dilemma. The point is that Dunbar, like Du Bois, grappled with it. As one would expect from a young man who was not only personally and artistically maturing, but traveling away from his small-town Midwestern origins, Dunbar's understanding of the critical climate became more sophisticated. He was well aware of the dialect usages of Page and Harris. Early on, he complained that the Chicago *News* was interested only in his dialect poetry. He was thrilled with the attention and with the Howells review—which was, in fact, as complex and thoughtful as it was problematical—and the sales of *Majors and Minors* that it generated, and he was thrilled that Howells's personal and written introductions allowed him entrée into commercial publishing, yet he wrote soon after, "I see now very clearly that Mr. Howells has done me irrevocable harm in the dictum he has laid down regarding my dialect verse." He wrote the lyrics that earned him that "prince of the coon song writers" sobriquet before disavowing them, and he told James Weldon Johnson:

> You know, of course, that I didn't start as a dialect poet. I simply came to the conclusion that I could write it as well, if not better, than anybody else

I knew of, and that by doing so I should gain a hearing, and now they don't want me to write anything else.

And he wrote the bitter verse "The Poet," which is not a persona poem, but which can be accurately read as Dunbar's comment on the public and critical reception of his work. To assume that he did not understand, that he failed to resolve the issue in his own mind, is in its own way to condescend as surely as did Jefferson in Query XIV.

Nor is this the only way in which Query XIV has distorted critical view of Dunbar. For American criticism has generally accepted the assumption that critical opinion can be racialized as a simple matter of—to use Jordan's title—"white over black."

As Darwin Turner has pointed out:

> A surprising number of individuals who can identify Dunbar as a poet seem unaware that he wrote the majority of his poems in the most elegant nineteenth-century English which he could manage. Even fewer readers seem to recognize that Dunbar wrote not one but two distinctive varieties of dialect poetry. Well known ... is his use of "Negro" dialect; less frequently perceived is his creation of a "white" dialect suggesting the speech of residents of Kentucky, Ohio and Indiana. Failure to note Dunbar's careful distinction ... can result in amusing misinterpretations of Dunbar's poetry ... "Deacon Jones' Grievance" is sometimes read and discussed as a black churchman's protest. ... Actually, Dunbar is reported to have written the poem in memory of the complaints of a German music master. ...

In fact, the misperception is more complex than Turner notes. At various times, Dunbar attempted a number of other "white" dialects, including the Scottish, in "A Border Ballad," the one dialect piece that did appear in the "Majors and Minors" section, and the German American, in a very early poem, "Lager Beer," which was suggested by the immigrant population of Southwestern Ohio. More significantly, "the most elegant nineteenth-century English which he could manage" was itself a dialect, in the sense that nobody—except possibly a British dandy or a frog gone a-courtin'—spoke "in the most elegant nineteenth-century English." Dunbar used it in the same way he used other dialects—to give an effect to his poetry. At other times he wrote far more simply, as in "The Poet."

As Darwin Turner stated repeatedly, "emphasis upon [Dunbar] as a symbol has tended to obscure the actual image of the man and his work." What has been obscured is the extent to which Dunbar was a poet in the English tradition, an American poet, and most specifically, a trans-Appalachian one.

Some of Dunbar's finest poems can be read as responses to specific works of English poetry. For example, in 1770, poet, essayist, and dramatist Oliver Goldsmith published a long persona poem called "The Deserted Village," which he developed from an earlier essay, "The Revolution in Low Life." The poem describes the reaction of a wanderer returned to his native village to find

> Thy sports are fled, and all thy charms withdrawn;
> Amidst thy bowers the tyrant's hand is seen,
> And desolation saddens all thy green:
> One only master grasps the whole domain,
> And half a tillage stints thy smiling plain.
> No more thy glassy brook reflects the day,
> But, chok'd with sedges, works its weedy way;
> Along thy glades, a solitary guest,
> The hollow-sounding bittern guards its nest;
> Amidst thy desert walks the lapwing flies,
> And tires their echoes with unvaried cries;
> Sunk are thy bowers in shapeless ruin all,
> And the long grass o'ertops the mould'ring wall;
> And trembling, shrinking from the spoiler's hand,
> Far, far away, thy children leave the land.

Dunbar wrote a persona poem, "The Deserted Plantation," the expression of an aging black retainer who has remained on an abandoned plantation. Dunbar's poem is in dialect, but draws on many of the same tropes and images used by Goldsmith. It was published in *Lyrics of Lowly Life*.

A similar correspondence can be drawn between William Blake's "The Lamb":

> Little Lamb, who made thee?
> Dost thou know who made thee? . . .
> Little Lamb, I'll tell thee . . .
> He is callèd by thy name,
> For he calls himself a Lamb. . . .

and Dunbar's "Hymn" ("O li'l' lamb out in de col', / De Mastah call you to de fol'...")

A more poignant connection exists between Robert Louis Stevenson's autoepitaph "Requiem," the last lines of which actually appear on Stevenson's grave:

> Under the wide and starry sky,
> Dig the grave and let me lie.
> Glad did I live and gladly die,
>   And I laid me down with a will.
>
> This be the verse you grave for me:
> Here he lies where he longed to be;
> Home is the sailor, home from sea,
>   And the hunter home from the hill.

and Dunbar's own autoepitaph, a dialect persona poem called "A Death Song." These last lines grace his memorial in Dayton's Woodland Cemetery:

> Fu' I t'ink de las' long res'
> Gwine to soothe my sperrit bes'
> Ef I's layin' 'mong de t'ings I's allus knowed.

But as Howells noted, Dunbar was a product of American civilization. And if his dialect pieces were his most distinctive, they were also part of a significant and growing American tradition, whose practitioners included not only the likes of Thomas Nelson Page, but Samuel Langhorne Clemens—Mark Twain. Indeed, the "Explanatory" Twain inserted before the text proper of *Huckleberry Finn* could easily be applied to the corpus of Dunbar's work:

> In this book a number of dialects are used, to wit: the Missouri negro dialect; the extremest form of the backwoods Southwestern dialect; the ordinary "Pike-County" dialect; and four modified varieties of this last. The shadings have not been done in a hap-hazard fashion, or by guess-work; but pains-takingly, and with the trustworthy guidance and support of personal familiarity with these several forms of speech. I make this explanation for the reason that without it many readers would suppose that all these characters were trying to talk alike and not succeeding.

In 1889 Dunbar responded to a New York journalist who asked, "In the poetry written by negroes, which is the quality that will most appear, something native and African and in every way different from the verse of Anglo-Saxons, or something that is not unlike what is written by white people?"

> My dear sir, the predominating power of the African race is lyric. In that I should expect the writers of my people to excel. But, broadly speaking, their poetry will not be exotic or differ much from that of the whites.... You forget that for two hundred and fifty years the environment of the negro has been American, in every respect the same as that of all other Americans.

In evaluating Dunbar's expectation that black American writers would "excel" in the lyric, one must not forget Walt Whitman's words: "I hear America singing, the varied carols I hear... / Each singing what belongs to him or her and to none else."

Nor can one forget that one of Dunbar's favorite poets was James Whitcomb Riley—that in fact Dunbar wrote a dialect poem in homage to Riley, subtitled "From a Westerner's Point of View," which began:

> No matter what you call it,
>   Whether genius or art,
> He sings the simple songs that come
>   The closest to your heart.

This affinity can enrich and complicate the understanding of what some would say is one of Dunbar's most specifically racial poems, "We Wear the Mask," which opens:

> We wear the mask that grins and lies,
> It hides our cheeks and shades our eyes,—
> This debt we pay to human guile;
> With torn and bleeding hearts we smile,
> And mouth with myriad subtleties.

Peter Revell, author of a definitive book on Dunbar, calls this poem

> arguably the finest poem Dunbar produced, a moving cry from the heart of suffering. The poem anticipates, and presents in terms of passionate per-

sonal regret, the psychological analysis of the fact of blackness in Frantz Fanon's *Peau Noire, Masques Blancs,* with a penetrating insight into the reality of the black man's plight in America. . . . The poem is also an apologia for all that his own and succeeding generations would condemn in his work, for the grin of minstrelsy and the lie of the plantation tradition that Dunbar felt himself bound to adopt as part of the "myriad subtleties" required to find a voice and to be heard. The "subtleties" lead us to expect that honest feelings and judgments, when they occur, will be obliquely presented and may be difficult to apprehend, a point of view that many critics of Dunbar have not taken into account. It should be noted that the poem itself is "masked," its link to the black race, though obvious enough, not being openly stated. Yet in this one poem Dunbar left aside the falsity of dialect and the didacticism of his serious poems on black subjects and spoke from the heart.

Maybe so. But one dare not forget that Riley wrote a poem that began

> We are not always glad when we smile:
> Though we wear a fair face and are gay,
> And the world we deceive
> May not ever believe
> We could laugh in a happier way—
> Yet, down in the deeps of the soul,
> Ofttimes, with our faces aglow,
> There's an ache and a moan
> That we know of alone,
> And as only the hopeless may know.

Which is not to say that Dunbar was not referring to the angst of the American Negro; indeed, given the racial horrors of the era, it is hard to believe he did not have that somewhere in mind. But it is to say—as Revell admits—that that assumption is based on facts not evidenced by the text. And it is also to say that that assumption is subtly limiting.

One doubts that any critic would describe "We Wear the Mask" as a penetrating insight into the reality of the white man's plight in America—though there is no reason not to do so. ("If you prick us, do we not bleed?" asked Shylock the Jew.) One also doubts that any critic would describe Riley's poem as a penetrating insight into the reality of the black man's plight in America—though again, there is no reason not to do so. But most significantly, one also doubts that any critic would describe Riley's poem as a penetrating insight into the reality of the white man's plight in America; in the case of a white poet, the universality would be assumed.

Ironically, but perhaps not surprisingly, it seems it was Ohioans who saw Dunbar most clearly, despite their own arguable bias. Howells—who hailed from Martin's Ferry—called Dunbar's dialect poems "evidence of the essential unity of the human race, which does not think or feel black in one and white in another, but humanly in all." And Toledo mayor Brand Whitlock, who had objected to one of Dunbar's most political poems, "The Haunted Oak," wrote in eulogy:

> There was nothing foreign in Paul's poetry, nothing imported, nothing imitated: it was all original, native and indigenous. Thus he becomes not the poet of his own race alone—I wish I could make people see this—but the poet of you, and of me, and of all men everywhere.

LAGER BEER

I lafs und sings, und shumps aroundt.
    Und somedimes acd so gueer.
You ask me vot der matter ish?
    I'm filled mit lager peer.

I hugs mine child, und giss mine vife.
    Oh, my dey was so dear;
Bot dot ish ven, you know, mire friend,
    I'm filled mit lager peer.

Eleetion gomes, I makes mire speech,
    Mine het it vas so glear:
De beoples laf, und say ha, ha,
    He's filled mit lager peer.

De oder night I got me mad,
    De beoples run mit fear.
De bleeceman gome und took me down
    All filled mit lager peer.

Next day I gomes pefore de judge,
    Says he, "Eh heh, you're here!"
I gifs you yust five-fifty-five
    For trinking lager peer.

I took mine bocket book qvick oud,
    So poor I don't abbear;
Mine money all vas gone, mine friend
    Vas gone in lager peer.

Und den dey dakes me off to shail,
    To work mine sendence glear,
Und dere I shwears no more to be
    Filled oup mit lager peer.

Und from dot day I drinks no more,
    Yah, dat ish very gueer,
But den I found de tevil lifed
    In dot same lager peer.

PFFENBERGER DEUTZELHEIM

WELCOME ADDRESS

TO THE WESTERN ASSOCIATION OF WRITERS

"Westward the course of empire takes its way,"—
So Berkeley said, and so to-day
The men who know the world still say.
The glowing West, with bounteous hand,
Bestows her gifts throughout the land,
And smiles to see at her command
Art, science, and the industries,—
New fruits of new Hesperides.
So, proud are you who claim the West
As home land; doubly are you blest
To live where liberty and health
Go hand in hand with brains and wealth.
So here's a welcome to you all,
Whate'er the work your hands let fall,—
To you who trace on history's page
The footprints of each passing age;
To you who tune the laureled lyre
To songs of love or deeds of fire;
To you before whose well-wrought tale
The cheek doth flush or brow grow pale;
To you who bow the ready knee
And worship cold philosophy,—
A welcome warm as Western wine,
And free as Western hearts, be thine.
Do what the greatest joy insures,—
The city has no will but yours!

COLUMBIAN ODE

I.

Four hundred years ago a tangled waste
  Lay sleeping on the west Atlantic's side;
Their devious ways the Old World's millions traced
  Content, and loved, and labored, dared and died,
While students still believed the charts they conned,
  And revelled in their thriftless ignorance,
Nor dreamed of other lands that lay beyond
  Old Ocean's dense, indefinite expanse.

II.

But deep within her heart old Nature knew
  That she had once arrayed, at Earth's behest,
Another offspring, fine and fair to view,—
  The chosen suckling of the mother's breast.
The child was wrapped in vestments soft and fine,
  Each fold a work of Nature's matchless art;
The mother looked on it with love divine,
  And strained the loved one closely to her heart.
And there it lay, and with the warmth grew strong
  And hearty, by the salt sea breezes fanned,
Till Time with mellowing touches passed along,
  And changed the infant to a mighty land.

III.

But men knew naught of this, till there arose
  That mighty mariner, the Genoese,
Who dared to try, in spite of fears and foes,
  The unknown fortunes of unsounded seas.
O noblest of Italia's sons, thy bark
  Went not alone into that shrouding night!

O dauntless darer of the rayless dark,
   The world sailed with thee to eternal light!
The deer-haunts that with game were crowded then
   To-day are tilled and cultivated lands;
The schoolhouse tow'rs where Bruin had his den,
   And where the wigwam stood the chapel stands;
The place that nurtured men of savage mien
   Now teems with men of Nature's noblest types;
Where moved the forest-foliage banner green,
   Now flutters in the breeze the stars and stripes!

JUSTICE

Enthroned upon the mighty truth,
    Within the confines of the laws,
True Justice seeth not the man,
    But only hears his cause.

Unconscious of his creed or race,
She cannot see, but only weighs;
For Justice with unbandaged eyes
Would be oppression in disguise.

ODE TO ETHIOPIA

O Mother Race! to thee I bring
This pledge of faith unwavering,
   This tribute to thy glory.
I know the pangs which thou didst feel,
When Slavery crushed thee with its heel,
   With thy dear blood all gory.

Sad days were those—ah, sad indeed!
But through the land the fruitful seed
   Of better times was growing.
The plant of freedom upward sprung,
And spread its leaves so fresh and young—
   Its blossoms now are blowing.

On every hand in this fair land,
Proud Ethiope's swarthy children stand
   Beside their fairer neighbor;
The forests flee before their stroke,
Their hammers ring, their forges smoke,—
   They stir in honest labour.

They tread the fields where honour calls;
Their voices sound through senate halls
   In majesty and power.
To right they cling; the hymns they sing
Up to the skies in beauty ring,
   And bolder grow each hour.

Be proud, my Race, in mind and soul;
Thy name is writ on Glory's scroll
   In characters of fire.
High 'mid the clouds of Fame's bright sky
Thy banner's blazoned folds now fly,
   And truth shall lift them higher.

Thou hast the right to noble pride,
Whose spotless robes were purified
   By blood's severe baptism.
Upon thy brow the cross was laid,
And labour's painful sweat-beads made
   A consecrating chrism.

No other race, or white or black,
When bound as thou wert, to the rack,
   So seldom stooped to grieving;
No other race, when free again,
Forgot the past and proved them men
   So noble in forgiving.

Go on and up! Our souls and eyes
Shall follow thy continuous rise;
   Our ears shall list thy story
From bards who from thy root shall spring,
And proudly tune their lyres to sing
   Of Ethiopia's glory.

THE OL' TUNES

You kin talk about yer anthems
    An' yer arias an' sich,
An' yer modern choir-singin'
    That you think so awful rich;
But you orter heerd us youngsters
    In the times now far away,
A-singin' o' the ol' tunes
    In the ol'-fashioned way.

There was some of us sung treble
    An' a few of us growled bass,
An' the tide o' song flowed smoothly
    With its 'comp'niment o' grace;
There was spirit in that music,
    An' a kind o' solemn sway,
A-singin' o' the ol' tunes
    In the ol'-fashioned way.

I remember oft o' standin'
    In my homespun pantaloons—
On my face the bronze an' freckles
    O' the suns o' youthful Junes—
Thinkin' that no mortal minstrel
    Ever chanted sich a lay
As the ol' tunes we was singin'
    In the ol'-fashioned way.

The boys 'ud always lead us,
    An' the girls 'ud all chime in,
Till the sweetness o' the singin'
    Robbed the list'nin' soul o' sin;
An' I used to tell the parson
    'Twas as good to sing as pray,

When the people sung the ol' tunes
   In the ol'-fashioned way.

How I long ag'in to hear 'em
   Pourin' forth from soul to soul,
With the treble high an' meller,
   An' the bass's mighty roll;
But the times is very diff'rent,
   An' the music heerd to-day
Ain't the singin' o' the ol' tunes
   In the ol'-fashioned way.

Little screechin' by a woman,
   Little squawkin' by a man,
Then the organ's twiddle-twaddle,
   Jest the empty space to span,—
An' ef you should even think it,
   'Tisn't proper fur to say
That you want to hear the ol' tunes
   In the ol'-fashioned way.

But I think that some bright mornin',
   When the toils of life air o'er,
An' the sun o' heaven arisin'
   Glads with light the happy shore,
I shall hear the angel chorus,
   In the realms of endless day,
A-singin' o' the ol' tunes
   In the ol'-fashioned way.

AN ANTE-BELLUM SERMON

We is gathahed hyeah, my brothahs,
　　In dis howlin' wildaness,
Fu' to speak some words of comfo't
　　To each othah in distress.
An' we chooses fu' ouah subjic'
　　Dis—we'll 'splain it by an' by;
"An' de Lawd said, 'Moses, Moses,'
　　An' de man said, 'Hyeah am I.'"

Now ole Pher'oh, down in Egypt,
　　Was de wuss man evah bo'n,
An' he had de Hebrew chillun
　　Down dah wukin' in his co'n;
'Twell de Lawd got tiahed o' his foolin',
　　An' sez he: "I'll let him know—
Look hyeah, Moses, go tell Pher'oh
　　Fu' to let dem chillun go."

"An' ef he refuse to do it,
　　I will make him rue de houah,
Fu' I'll empty down on Egypt
　　All de vials of my powah."
Yes, he did—an' Pher'oh's ahmy
　　Wasn't wuth a ha'f a dime;
Fu' de Lawd will he'p his chillun,
　　You kin trust him evah time.

An' yo' enemies may 'sail you
　　In de back an' in de front;
But de Lawd is all aroun' you,
　　Fu' to ba' de battle's brunt.
Dey kin fo'ge yo' chains an' shackles
　　F'om de mountains to de sea;

But de Lawd will sen' some Moses
    Fu' to set his chillun free.

An' de lan' shall hyeah his thundah,
    Lak a blas' f'om Gab'el's ho'n,
Fu' de Lawd of hosts is mighty
    When he girds his ahmor on.
But fu' feah some one mistakes me,
    I will pause right hyeah to say,
Dat I'm still a-preachin' ancient,
    I ain't talkin' 'bout to-day.

But I tell you, fellah christuns,
    Things'll happen mighty strange;
Now, de Lawd done dis fu' Isrul,
    An' his ways don't nevah change,
An' de love he showed to Isrul
    Wasn't all on Isrul spent;
Now don't run an' tell yo' mastahs
    Dat I's preachin' discontent.

'Cause I isn't; I'se a-judgin'
    Bible people by deir ac's;
I'se a-givin' you de Scriptuah,
    I'se a-handin' you de fac's.
Cose ole Pher'oh b'lieved in slav'ry,
    But de Lawd he let him see,
Dat de people he put bref in,—
    Evah mothah's son was free.

An' dahs othahs thinks lak Pher'oh,
    But dey calls de Scriptuah liar,
Fu' de Bible says "a servant
    Is a-worthy of his hire."
An' you cain't git roun' nor thoo dat,
    An' you cain't git ovah it,

Fu' whatevah place you git in,
    Dis hyeah Bible too'll fit.

So you see de Lawd's intention,
    Evah sence de worl' began,
Was dat His almighty freedom
    Should belong to evah man,
But I think it would be bettah,
    Ef I'd pause agin to say,
Dat I'm talkin' 'bout ouah freedom
    In a Bibleistic way.

But de Moses is a-comin',
    An' he's comin', suah and fas'
We kin hyeah his feet a-trompin',
    We kin hyeah his trumpit blas'.
But I want to wa'n you people,
    Don't you git too brigity;
An' don't you git to braggin'
    'Bout dese things, you wait an' see.

But when Moses wif his powah
    Comes an' sets us chillun free,
We will praise de gracious Mastah
    Dat has gin us liberty;
An' we'll shout ouah halleluyahs,
    On dat mighty reck'nin' day,
When we'se reco'nised ez citiz'—
    Huh uh! Chillun, let us pray!

ERE SLEEP COMES DOWN TO SOOTHE THE WEARY EYES

Ere sleep comes down to soothe the weary eyes,
　　Which all the day with ceaseless care have sought
The magic gold which from the seeker flies;
　　Ere dreams put on the gown and cap of thought,
And make the waking world a world of lies,—
　　Of lies most palpable, uncouth, forlorn,
That say life's full of aches and tears and sighs,—
　　Oh, how with more than dreams the soul is torn,
Ere sleep comes down to soothe the weary eyes.

Ere sleep comes down to soothe the weary eyes,
　　How all the griefs and heartaches we have known
Come up like pois'nous vapors that arise
　　From some base witch's caldron, when the crone,
To work some potent spell, her magic plies.
　　The past which held its share of bitter pain,
Whose ghost we prayed that Time might exorcise,
　　Comes up, is lived and suffered o'er again,
Ere sleep comes down to soothe the weary eyes.

Ere sleep comes down to soothe the weary eyes,
　　What phantoms fill the dimly lighted room;
What ghostly shades in awe-creating guise
　　Are bodied forth within the teeming gloom.
What echoes faint of sad and soul-sick cries,
　　And pangs of vague inexplicable pain
That pay the spirit's ceaseless enterprise,
　　Come thronging through the chambers of the brain,
Ere sleep comes down to soothe the weary eyes.

Ere sleep comes down to soothe the weary eyes,
　　Where ranges forth the spirit far and free?

Through what strange realms and unfamiliar skies
　　Tends her far course to lands of mystery?
To lands unspeakable—beyond surmise,
　　Where shapes unknowable to being spring,
Till, faint of wing, the Fancy fails and dies
　　Much wearied with the spirit's journeying,
Ere sleep comes down to soothe the weary eyes.

Ere sleep comes down to soothe the weary eyes,
　　How questioneth the soul that other soul,—
The inner sense which neither cheats nor lies,
　　But self exposes unto self, a scroll
Full writ with all life's acts unwise or wise,
　　In characters indelible and known;
So, trembling with the shock of sad surprise,
　　The soul doth view its awful self alone,
Ere sleep comes down to soothe the weary eyes.

When sleep comes down to seal the weary eyes,
　　The last dear sleep whose soft embrace is balm,
And whom sad sorrow teaches us to prize
　　For kissing all our passions into calm,
Ah, then, no more we heed the sad world's cries,
　　Or seek to probe th' eternal mystery,
Or fret our souls at long-withheld replies,
　　At glooms through which our visions cannot see,
When sleep comes down to seal the weary eyes.

The Poet and His Song

A song is but a little thing,
And yet what joy it is to sing!
In hours of toil it gives me zest,
And when at eve I long for rest;
When cows come home along the bars,
    And in the fold I hear the bell,
As Night, the shepherd, herds his stars,
    I sing my song, and all is well.

There are no ears to hear my lays,
No lips to lift a word of praise;
But still, with faith unfaltering,
I live and laugh and love and sing.
What matters yon unheeding throng?
    They cannot feel my spirit's spell,
Since life is sweet and love is long,
    I sing my song, and all is well.

My days are never days of ease;
I till my ground and prune my trees.
When ripened gold is all the plain,
I put my sickle to the grain.
I labor hard, and toil and sweat,
    While others dream within the dell;
But even while my brow is wet,
    I sing my song, and all is well.

Sometimes the sun, unkindly hot,
My garden makes a desert spot;
Sometimes a blight upon the tree
Takes all my fruit away from me;
And then with throes of bitter pain
    Rebellious passions rise and swell;
But—life is more than fruit or grain,
    And so I sing, and all is well.

WHEN MALINDY SINGS

G'way an' quit dat noise, Miss Lucy—
  Put dat music book away;
What's de use to keep on tryin'?
  Ef you practise twell you're gray,
You cain't sta't no notes a-flyin'
  Lak de ones dat rants and rings
F'om de kitchen to de big woods
  When Malindy sings.

You ain't got de nachel o'gans
  Fu' to make de soun' come right,
You ain't got de tu'ns an' twistin's
  Fu' to make it sweet an' light.
Tell you one thing now, Miss Lucy,
  An' I'm tellin' you fu' true,
When hit comes to raal right singin',
  'Tain't no easy thing to do.

Easy 'nough fu' folks to hollah,
  Lookin' at de lines an' dots,
When dey ain't no one kin sence it,
  An' de chune comes in, in spots;
But fu' real melojous music,
  Dat jes' strikes yo' hea't and clings,
Jes' you stan' an' listen wif me
  When Malindy sings.

Ain't you nevah hyeahd Malindy?
  Blessed soul, tek up de cross!
Look hyeah, ain't you jokin', honey?
  Well, you don't know whut you los'.
Y' ought to hyeah dat gal a-wa'blin',
  Robins, la'ks, an' all dem things,

Heish dey moufs an' hides dey faces
   When Malindy sings.

Fiddlin' man jes' stop his fiddlin',
   Lay his fiddle on de she'f;
Mockin'-bird quit tryin' to whistle,
   'Cause he jes' so shamed hisse'f.
Folks a-playin' on de banjo
   Draps dey fingahs on de strings—
Bless yo' soul—fu'gits to move 'em,
   When Malindy sings.

She jes' spreads huh mouf and hollahs,
   "Come to Jesus," twell you hyeah
Sinnahs' tremblin' steps and voices,
   Timid-lak a-drawin' neah;
Den she tu'ns to "Rock of Ages,"
   Simply to de cross she clings,
An' you fin' yo' teahs a-drappin'
   When Malindy sings.

Who dat says dat humble praises
   Wif de Master nevah counts?
Heish yo' mouf, I hyeah dat music,
   Ez hit rises up an' mounts—
Floatin' by de hills an' valleys,
   Way above dis buryin' sod,
Ez hit makes its way in glory
   To de very gates of God!

Oh, hit's sweetah dan de music
   Of an edicated band;
An' hit's dearah dan de battle's
   Song o' triumph in de lan'.
It seems holier dan evenin'
   When de solemn chu'ch bell rings,

Ez I sit an' ca'mly listen
  While Malindy sings.

Towsah, stop dat ba'kin', hyeah me!
  Mandy, mek dat chile keep still;
Don't you hyeah de echoes callin'
  F'om de valley to de hill?
Let me listen, I can hyeah it,
  Th'oo de bresh of angel's wings,
 Sof' an' sweet, "Swing Low, Sweet Chariot,"
  Ez Malindy sings.

If I Could But Forget

If I could but forget
The fullness of those first sweet days,
When you burst sun-like thro' the haze
Of unacquaintance, on my sight,
And made the wet, gray day seem bright
While clouds themselves grew fair to see.
    And since, no day is gray or wet,
But all the scene comes back to me,
        If I could but forget.

If I could but forget
How your dusk eyes look into mine,
And how I thrilled as with strong wine
Beneath your touch; while sped amain
The quickened stream thro' ev'ry vein;
How near my breath fell to a gasp,
    When for a space our fingers met
In one electric vibrant clasp,
        If I could but forget.

If I could but forget
The months of passion and of pain,
And all that followed in their train—
Rebellious thoughts that would arise,
Rebellious tears that dimmed mine eyes,
The prayers that I might set love's fire
    Aflame within your bosom yet—
The death at last of that desire—
        If I could but forget.

Not They Who Soar

Not they who soar, but they who plod
Their rugged way, unhelped, to God
Are heroes; they who higher fare,
And, flying, fan the upper air,
Miss all the toil that hugs the sod.
'Tis they whose backs have felt the rod,
Whose feet have pressed the path unshod,
May smile upon defeated care,
    Not they who soar.

High up there are no thorns to prod,
Nor boulders lurking 'neath the clod
To turn the keenness of the share,
For flight is ever free and rare;
But heroes they the soil who've trod,
    Not they who soar!

THE COLORED SOLDIERS

If the muse were mine to tempt it
    And my feeble voice were strong,
If my tongue were trained to measures,
    I would sing a stirring song.
I would sing a song heroic
    Of those noble sons of Ham,
Of the gallant colored soldiers
    Who fought for Uncle Sam!

In the early days you scorned them,
    And with many a flip and flout
Said "These battles are the white man's,
    And the whites will fight them out."
Up the hills you fought and faltered,
    In the vales you strove and bled,
While your ears still heard the thunder
    Of the foes' advancing tread.

Then distress fell on the nation,
    And the flag was drooping low;
Should the dust pollute your banner?
    No! the nation shouted, No!
So when War, in savage triumph,
    Spread abroad his funeral pall—
Then you called the colored soldiers,
    And they answered to your call.

And like hounds unleashed and eager
    For the life blood of the prey,
Sprung they forth and bore them bravely
    In the thickest of the fray.
And where'er the fight was hottest,
    Where the bullets fastest fell,

There they pressed unblanched and fearless
    At the very mouth of hell.

Ah, they rallied to the standard
    To uphold it by their might;
None were stronger in the labors,
    None were braver in the fight.
From the blazing breach of Wagner
    To the plains of Olustee,
They were foremost in the fight
    Of the battles of the free.

And at Pillow! God have mercy
    On the deeds committed there,
And the souls of those poor victims
    Sent to Thee without a prayer.
Let the fulness of Thy pity
    O'er the hot wrought spirits sway
Of the gallant colored soldiers
    Who fell fighting on that day!

Yes, the Blacks enjoy their freedom,
    And they won it dearly, too;
For the life blood of their thousands
    Did the southern fields bedew.
In the darkness of their bondage,
    In the depths of slavery's night,
Their muskets flashed the dawning,
    And they fought their way to light.

They were comrades then and brothers,
    Are they more or less to-day?
They were good to stop a bullet
    And to front the fearful fray.
They were citizens and soldiers,
    When rebellion raised its head;

And the traits that made them worthy,—
    Ah! those virtues are not dead.

They have shared your nightly vigils,
    They have shared your daily toil;
And their blood with yours commingling
    Has enriched the Southern soil.
They have slept and marched and suffered
    'Neath the same dark skies as you,
They have met as fierce a foeman,
    And have been as brave and true.

And their deeds shall find a record
    In the registry of Fame;
For their blood has cleansed completely
    Every blot of Slavery's shame.
So all honor and all glory
    To those noble sons of Ham—
The gallant colored soldiers
    Who fought for Uncle Sam!

SHIPS THAT PASS IN THE NIGHT

Out in the sky the great dark clouds are massing;
    I look far out into the pregnant night,
Where I can hear a solemn booming gun
    And catch the gleaming of a random light,
That tells me that the ship I seek is passing, passing.

My tearful eyes my soul's deep hurt are glassing;
    For I would hail and check that ship of ships.
I stretch my hands imploring, cry aloud,
    My voice falls dead a foot from mine own lips,
And but its ghost doth reach that vessel, passing, passing.

O Earth, O Sky, O Ocean, both surpassing,
    O heart of mine, O soul that dreads the dark!
Is there no hope for me? Is there no way
    That I may sight and check that speeding bark
Which out of sight and sound is passing, passing?

WE WEAR THE MASK

We wear the mask that grins and lies,
It hides our cheeks and shades our eyes,—
This debt we pay to human guile;
With torn and bleeding hearts we smile,
And mouth with myriad subtleties.

Why should the world be over-wise,
In counting all our tears and sighs?
Nay, let them only see us, while
   We wear the mask.

We smile, but, O great Christ, our cries
To thee from tortured souls arise.
We sing, but oh the clay is vile
Beneath our feet, and long the mile;
But let the world dream otherwise,
   We wear the mask!

WHY FADES A DREAM?

Why fades a dream?
   An iridescent ray
Flecked in between the tryst
   Of night and day.
   Why fades a dream?—
Of consciousness the shade
Wrought out by lack of light and made
   Upon life's stream.
   Why fades a dream?

That thought may thrive,
   So fades the fleshless dream;
Lest men should learn to trust
   The things that seem.
   So fades a dream,
That living thought may grow
And like a waxing star-beam glow
   Upon life's stream—
   So fades a dream.

ACCOUNTABILITY

Folks ain't got no right to censuah othah folks about dey habits;
Him dat giv' de squir'ls de bushtails made de bobtails fu' de rabbits.
Him dat built de gread big mountains hollered out de little valleys,
Him dat made de streets an' driveways wasn't shamed to make de
      alleys.

We is all constructed diff'ent, d'ain't no two of us de same;
We cain't he'p ouah likes an' dislikes, ef we'se bad we ain't to blame.
Ef we'se good, we needn't show off, case you bet it ain't ouah doin'
We gits into su'ttain channels dat we jes' cain't he'p pu'suin'.

But we all fits into places dat no othah ones could fill,
An' we does the things we has to, big er little, good er ill.
John cain't tek de place o' Henry, Su an' Sally ain't alike;
Bass ain't nuthin' like a suckah, chub ain't nuthin' like a pike.

When you come to think about it, how it's all planned out it's
      splendid.
Nuthin's done er evah happens, 'dout hit's somefin' dat's intended;
Don't keer whut you does, you has to, an' hit sholy beats de dickens,—
Viney, go put on de kittle, I got one o' mastah's chickens.

THE DILETTANTE: A MODERN TYPE

He scribbles some in prose and verse,
  And now and then he prints it;
He paints a little,—gathers some
  Of Nature's gold and mints it.

He plays a little, sings a song,
  Acts tragic rôles, or funny;
He does, because his love is strong,
  But not, oh, not for money!

He studies almost everything
  From social art to science;
A thirsty mind, a flowing spring,
  Demand and swift compliance.

He looms above the sordid crowd—
  At least through friendly lenses;
While his mamma looks pleased and proud,
  And kindly pays expenses.

A NEGRO LOVE SONG

Seen my lady home las' night,
  Jump back, honey, jump back.
Hel' huh han' an' sque'z it tight,
  Jump back, honey, jump back.
Hyeahd huh sigh a little sigh,
Seen a light gleam f'om huh eye,
An' a smile go flittin' by—
  Jump back, honey, jump back.

Hyeahd de win' blow thoo de pine,
  Jump back, honey, jump back.
Mockin'-bird, was singin' fine,
  Jump back, honey, jump back.
An' my hea't was beatin' so,
When I reached my lady's do',
Dat I couldn't ba' to go—
  Jump back, honey, jump back.

Put my ahm aroun' huh wais',
  Jump back, honey, jump back.
Raised huh lips an' took a tase,
  Jump back, honey, jump back.
Love me, honey, love me true?
Love me well ez I love you?
An' she answe'd, " 'Cose I do"—
  Jump back, honey, jump back.

THE PARTY

Dey had a gread big pahty down to Tom's de othah night;
Was I dah? You bet! I nevah in my life see sich a sight;
All de folks f'om fou' plantations was invited, an' dey come,
Dey come troopin' thick ez chillun when dey hyeahs a fife an' drum.
Evahbody dressed deir fines'—Heish yo' mouf an' git away,
Ain't seen no sich fancy dressin' sence las' quah'tly meetin' day;
Gals all dressed in silks an' satins, not a wrinkle ner a crease,
Eyes a-battin', teeth a-shinin', haih breshed back ez slick ez grease;
Sku'ts all tucked an' puffed an' ruffled, evah blessed seam an' stitch;
Ef you'd seen 'em wif deir mistus, couldn't swahed to which was
      which.
Men all dressed up in Prince Alberts, swallertails 'u'd tek yo' bref!
I cain't tell you nothin' 'bout it, y' ought to seen it fu' yo'se'f.
Who was dah? Now who you askin'? How you 'spect I gwine to know?
You mus' think I stood an' counted evahbody at de do'.
Ole man Babah's house-boy Isaac, brung dat gal, Malindy Jane,
Huh a-hangin' to his elbow, him a-struttin' wif a cane;
My, but Hahvey Jones was jealous! seemed to stick him lak a tho'n;
But he laughed with Viney Cahteh, tryin' ha'd to not let on,
But a pusson would 'a' noticed f'om de d'rection of his look,
Dat he was watchin' ev'ry step dat Ike an' Lindy took.
Ike he foun' a cheer an' asked huh: "Won't you set down?" wif a smile,
An' she answe'd up a-bowin', "Oh, I reckon 'tain't wuth while."
Dat was jes' fu' style, I reckon, 'cause she sot down jes' de same,
An' she stayed dah 'twell he fetched huh fu' to jine some so't o' game;
Den I hyeahd huh sayin' propah, ez she riz to go away,
"Oh, you raly mus' excuse me, fu' I hardly keers to play."
But I seen huh in a minute wif de othahs on de flo',
An' dah wasn't any one o' dem a-playin' any mo';
Comin' down de flo' a-bowin' an' a-swayin' an' a-swingin',
Puttin' on huh high-toned mannahs all de time dat she was singin':
"Oh, swing Johnny up an' down, swing him all aroun',
Swing Johnny up an' down, swing him all aroun',
Oh, swing Johnny up an' down, swing him all aroun',

Fa' you well, my dahlin'."
Had to laff at ole man Johnson, he's a caution now, you bet—
Hittin' clost onto a hunderd, but he's spry an' nimble yet;
He 'lowed how a-so't o' gigglin', "I ain't ole, I'll let you see,
D'ain't no use in gittin' feeble, now you youngstahs jes' watch me,"
An' he grabbed ole Aunt Marier—weighs th'ee hunderd mo' er less,
An' he spun huh 'roun' de cabin swingin' Johnny lak de res'.
Evahbody laffed an' hollahed: "Go it! Swing huh, Uncle Jim!"
An' he swung huh too, I reckon, lak a youngstah, who but him.
Dat was bettah 'n young Scott Thomas, tryin' to be so awful smaht.
You know when dey gits to singin' an' dey comes to dat ere paht:

     "In some lady's new brick house,
  In some lady's gyahden.
      Ef you don't let me out, I will jump out,
  So fa' you well, my dahlin'."

Den dey's got a circle 'roun' you, an' you's got to break de line;
Well, dat dahky was so anxious, lak to bust hisse'f a-tryin';
Kep' on blund'rin' 'roun' an' foolin' 'twell he giv' one gread big jump,
Broke de line, an' lit head-fo'most in de fiahplace right plump;
Hit 'ad fiah in it, mind you; well, I thought my soul I'd bust,
Tried my best to keep f'om laffin', but hit seemed like die I must!
Y' ought to seen dat man a-scramblin' f'om de ashes an' de grime.
Did it bu'n him! Sich a question, why he didn't give it time;
Th'ow'd dem ashes and dem cindahs evah which-a-way I guess,
An' you nevah did, I reckon, clap yo' eyes on sich a mess;
Fu' he sholy made a picter an' a funny one to boot,
Wif his clothes all full o' ashes an' his face all full o' soot.
Well, hit laked to stopped de pahty, an' I reckon lak ez not
Dat it would ef Tom's wife, Mandy, hadn't happened on de spot,
To invite us out to suppah—well, we scrambled to de table,
An' I'd lak to tell you 'bout it—what we had—but I ain't able,
Mention jes' a few things, dough I know I hadn't orter,
Fu' I know 'twill staht a hank'rin' an' yo' mouf 'll 'mence to worter.
We had wheat bread white ez cotton an' a egg pone jes like gol',
Hog jole, bilin' hot an' steamin' roasted shoat an' ham sliced cold—
Look out! What's de mattah wif you? Don't be fallin' on de flo';

Ef it's go'n' to 'fect you dat way, I won't tell you nothin' mo'.
Dah now—well, we had hot chittlin's—now you's tryin' ag'in to fall,
Cain't you stan' to hyeah about it? S'pose you'd been an' seed it all;
Seed dem gread big sweet pertaters, layin' by de possum's side,
Seed dat coon in all his gravy, reckon den you'd up and died!
Mandy 'lowed "you all mus' 'scuse me, d' wa'n't much upon my
       she'ves,
But I's done my bes' to suit you, so set down an' he'p yo'se'ves."
Tom, he 'lowed: "I don't b'lieve in 'pologisin' an' perfessin',
Let 'em tek it lak dey ketch it. Eldah Thompson, ask de blessin'.'"
Wish you'd seed dat colo'ed preachah cleah his th'oat an' bow his head;
One eye shet, an' one eye open,—dis is evah wud he said:
"Lawd, look down in tendah mussy on sich generous hea'ts ez dese;
Make us truly thankful, amen. Pass dat possum, ef you please!"
Well, we eat and drunk ouah po'tion, 'twell dah wasn't nothin' lef,
An' we felt jes' like new sausage, we was mos' nigh stuffed to def!
Tom, he knowed how we'd be feelin', so he had de fiddlah 'roun',
An' he made us cleah de cabin fu' to dance dat suppah down.
Jim, de fiddlah, chuned his fiddle, put some rosum on his bow,
Set a pine box on de table, mounted it an' let huh go!
He's a fiddlah, now I tell you, an' he made dat fiddle ring,
'Twell de ol'est an' de lamest had to give deir feet a fling.
Jigs, cotillions, reels an' break-downs, cordrills an' a waltz er two;
Bless yo' soul, dat music winged 'em an' dem people lak to flew.
Cripple Joe, de ole rheumatic, danced dat flo' f'om side to middle,
Th'owed away his crutch an' hopped it, what's rheumatics 'ginst a
       fiddle?
Eldah Thompson got so tickled dat he lak to los' his grace,
Had to tek bofe feet an' hol' dem so's to keep 'em in deir place.
An' de Christuns an' de sinnahs got so mixed up on dat flo',
Dat I don't see how dey'd pahted ef de trump had chanced to blow.
Well, we danced dat way an' capahed in de mos' redic'lous way,
'Twell de roostahs in de bahnyard cleahed deir th'oats an' crowed
       fu' day.
Y' ought to been dah, fu' I tell you evahthing was rich an' prime,
An' dey ain't no use in talkin', we jes had one scrumptious time!

THE SPELLIN'-BEE

I never shall furgit that night when father hitched up Dobbin,
An' all us youngsters clambered in an' down the road went bobbin'
To school where we was kep' at work in every kind o' weather,
But where that night a spellin'-bee was callin' us together.
'Twas one o' Heaven's banner nights, the stars was all a glitter,
The moon was shinin' like the hand o' God had jest then lit her.
The ground was white with spotless snow, the blast was sort o' stingin';
But underneath our round-abouts, you bet our hearts was singin'.
That spellin'-bee had be'n the talk o' many a precious moment,
The youngsters all was wild to see jes' what the precious show
      meant,
An' we whose years was in their teens was little less desirous
O' gittin' to the meetin' so's our sweethearts could admire us.
So on we went so anxious fur to satisfy our mission
That father had to box our ears, to smother our ambition.
But boxin' ears was too short work to hinder our arrivin',
He jest turned roun' an' smacked us all, an' kep' right on a-drivin'.
Well, soon the schoolhouse hove in sight, the winders beamin'
      brightly;
The sound o' talkin' reached our ears, and voices laffin' lightly.
It puffed us up so full an' big 'at I'll jest bet a dollar,
There wa'n't a feller there but felt the strain upon his collar.
So down we jumped an' in we went ez sprightly ez you make 'em,
But somethin' grabbed us by the knees an' straight began to shake 'em.
Fur once within that lighted room, our feelin's took a canter,
An' scurried to the zero mark ez quick ez Tam O'Shanter.
'Cause there was crowds o' people there, both sexes an' all stations;
It looked like all the town had come an' brought all their relations.
The first I saw was Nettie Gray, I thought that girl was dearer
'N gold; an' when I got a chance, you bet I aidged up near her.
An' Farmer Dobbs's girl was there, the one 'at Jim was sweet on,
An' Cyrus Jones an' Mandy Smith an' Faith an' Patience Deaton.
Then Parson Brown an' Lawyer Jones were present—all attention,
An' piles on piles of other folks too numerous to mention.

The master rose an' briefly said: "Good friends, dear brother
      Crawford,
To spur the pupils' minds along, a little prize has offered.
To him who spells the best to-night—or 'tmay be 'her'—no tellin'—
He offers ez a jest reward, this precious work on spellin'."
A little blue-backed spellin'-book with fancy scarlet trimmin';
We boys devoured it with our eyes—so did the girls an' women.
He held it up where all could see, then on the table set it,
An' ev'ry speller in the house felt mortal bound to get it.
At his command we fell in line, prepared to do our dooty,
Outspell the rest an' set 'em down, an' carry home the booty.
'Twas then the merry times began, the blunders, an' the laffin',
The nudges an' the nods an' winks an' stale good-natured chaffin'.
Ole Uncle Hiram Dane was there, the clostest man a-livin',
Whose only bugbear seemed to be the dreadful fear o' givin'.
His beard was long, his hair uncut, his clothes all bare an' dingy;
It wasn't 'cause the man was pore, but jest so mortal stingy.
An' there he sot by Sally Riggs a-smilin' an' a-smirkin',
An' all his childern lef' to home a diggin' an' a-workin'.
A widower he was, an' Sal was thinkin' 'at she'd wing him;
I reckon he was wond'rin' what them rings o' hern would bring him.
An' when the spellin'-test commenced, he up an' took his station,
A-spellin' with the best o' them to beat the very nation.
An' when he'd spell some youngster down, he'd turn to look at Sally,
An' say: "The teachin' nowadays can't be o' no great vally."
But true enough the adage says, "Pride walks in slipp'ry places,"
Fur soon a thing occurred that put a smile on all our faces.
The laffter jest kep' ripplin' 'roun' an' teacher couldn't quell it,
Fur when he give out "charity" ole Hiram couldn't spell it.
But laffin' 's ketchin' an' it throwed some others off their bases,
An' folks 'u'd miss the very word that seemed to fit their cases.
Why, fickle little Jessie Lee come near the house upsettin'
By puttin' in a double "kay" to spell the word "coquettin'."
An' when it come to Cyrus Jones, it tickled me all over—
Him settin' up to Mandy Smith an' got sot down on "lover."
But Lawyer Jones of all gone men did shorely look the gonest,

When he found out that he'd furgot to put the "h" in "honest."
An' Parson Brown, whose sermons were too long fur toleration,
Caused lots o' smiles by missin' when they give out "condensation."
So one by one they giv' it up—the big words kep' a-landin',
Till me an' Nettie Gray was left, the only ones a-standin',
An' then my inward strife began—I guess my mind was petty—
I did so want that spellin'-book; but then to spell down Nettie
Jest sort o' went ag'in my grain—I somehow couldn't do it,
An' when I git a notion fixed, I'm great on stickin' to it.
So when they giv' the next word out—I hadn't orter tell it,
But then 'twas all fur Nettie's sake—I missed so's she could spell it.
She spelt the word, then looked at me so lovin'-like an' mello',
I tell you't sent a hunderd pins a-shootin' through a fello'.
O' course I had to stand the jokes an' chaffin' of the fello's,
But when they handed her the book I vow I wasn't jealous.
We sung a hymn, an' Parson Brown dismissed us like he orter,
Fur, la! he'd learned a thing er two an' made his blessin' shorter.
'Twas late an' cold when we got out, but Nettie liked cold weather,
An' so did I, so we agreed we'd jest walk home together.
We both wuz silent, fur of words we nuther had a surplus,
'Till she spoke out quite sudden like, "You missed that word on
      purpose."
Well, I declare it frightened me; at first I tried denyin',
But Nettie, she jest smiled an' smiled, she knowed that I was lyin'.
Sez she: "That book is yourn by right;" sez I: "It never could be—
I—I—you—ah——" an' there I stuck, an' well she understood me.
So we agreed that later on when age had giv' us tether,
We'd jine our lots an' settle down to own that book together.

DISCOVERED

Seen you down at chu'ch las' night,
  Nevah min', Miss Lucy.
What I mean? oh, dat's all right,
  Nevah min', Miss Lucy.
You was sma't ez sma't could be,
But you couldn't hide f'om me.
Ain't I got two eyes to see!
  Nevah min', Miss Lucy.

Guess you thought you's awful keen;
  Nevah min', Miss Lucy.
Evahthing you done, I seen;
  Nevah min', Miss Lucy.
Seen him tek yo' ahm jes' so,
When he got outside de do'—
Oh, I know dat man's yo' beau!
  Nevah min', Miss Lucy.

Say now, honey, wha'd he say?—
  Nevah min', Miss Lucy!
Keep yo' secrets—dat's yo' way—
  Nevah min', Miss Lucy!
Won't tell me an' I'm yo' pal—
I'm gwine tell his othah gal,—
Know huh, too, huh name is Sal;
  Nevah min', Miss Lucy!

THE DESERTED PLANTATION

Oh, de grubbin'-hoe's a-rustin' in de co'nah,
    An' de plow's a-tumblin' down in de fiel',
While de whippo'will's a-wailin' lak a mou'nah
    When his stubbo'n hea't is tryin' ha'd to yiel'.

In de furrers whah de co'n was allus wavin',
    Now de weeds is growin' green an' rank an' tall;
An' de swallers roun' de whole place is a-bravin'
    Lak dey thought deir folks had allus owned it all.

An' de big house stan's all quiet lak an' solemn,
    Not a blessed soul in pa'lor, po'ch, er lawn;
Not a guest, ner not a ca'iage lef' to haul 'em,
    Fu' de ones dat tu'ned de latch-string out air gone.

An' de banjo's voice is silent in de qua'ters,
    D' ain't a hymn ner co'n-song ringin' in de air;
But de murmur of a branch's passin' waters
    Is de only soun' dat breks de stillness dere.

Whah's de da'kies, dem dat used to be a-dancin'
    Evry night befo' de ole cabin do'?
Whah's de chillun, dem dat used to be a-prancin'
    Er a-rollin' in de san' er on de flo'?

Whah's ole Uncle Mordecai an' Uncle Aaron?
    Whah's Aunt Doshy, Sam, an' Kit, an' all de res'?
Whah's ole Tom de da'ky fiddlah, how's he farin'?
    Whah's de gals dat used to sing an' dance de bes'?

Gone! not one o' dem is lef' to tell de story;
    Dey have lef' de deah ole place to fall away.
Couldn't one o' dem dat seed it in its glory
    Stay to watch it in de hour of decay?

Dey have lef' de ole plantation to de swallers,
　　But it hol's in me a lover till de las';
Fu' I fin' hyeah in de memory dat follers
　　All dat loved me an' dat I loved in de pas'.

So I'll stay an' watch de deah ole place an' tend it
　　Ez I used to in de happy days gone by.
'Twell de othah Mastah thinks it's time to end it,
　　An' calls me to my qua'ters in de sky.

HYMN

O li'l' lamb out in de col',
De Mastah call you to de fol',
   O li'l' lamb!
He hyeah you bleatin' on de hill;
Come hyeah an' keep yo' mou'nin' still,
   O li'l' lamb!

De Mastah sen' de Shepud fo'f;
He wandah souf, he wandah no'f,
   O li'l' lamb!
He wandah eas', he wandah wes';
De win' a-wrenchin' at his breas',
   O li'l' lamb!

Oh, tell de Shepud whaih you hide;
He wants you walkin' by his side,
   O li'l' lamb!
He know you weak, he know you so';
But come, don' stay away no mo',
   O li'l' lamb!

An' af'ah while de lamb he hyeah
De Shepud's voice a-callin' cleah—
   Sweet li'l' lamb!
He answah f'om de brambles thick,
"O Shepud, I's a-comin' quick"—
   O li'l' lamb!

A DEATH SONG

Lay me down beneaf de willers in de grass,
Whah de branch'll go a-singin' as it pass.
   An' w'en I's a-layin' low,
    I kin hyeah it as it go
Singin', "Sleep, my honey, tek yo' res' at las'."

Lay me nigh to whah hit meks a little pool,
An' de watah stan's so quiet lak an' cool,
   Whah de little birds in spring,
    Ust to come an' drink an' sing,
An' de chillen waded on dey way to school.

Let me settle w'en my shouldahs draps dey load
Nigh enough to hyeah de noises in de road;
   Fu' I t'ink de las' long res'
    Gwine to soothe my sperrit bes'
Ef I's layin' 'mong de t'ings I's allus knowed.

THE POET AND THE BABY

How's a man to write a sonnet, can you tell,—
How's he going to weave the dim, poetic spell,—
    When a-toddling on the floor
    Is the muse he must adore,
And this muse he loves, not wisely, but too well?

Now, to write a sonnet, every one allows,
One must always be as quiet as a mouse;
    But to write one seems to me
    Quite superfluous to be,
When you've got a little sonnet in the house.

Just a dainty little poem, true and fine,
That is full of love and life in every line,
    Earnest, delicate, and sweet,
    Altogether so complete
That I wonder what's the use of writing mine.

SONNET

ON AN OLD BOOK WITH UNCUT LEAVES

Emblem of blasted hope and lost desire,
No finger ever traced thy yellow page
   Save Time's. Thou hast not wrought to noble rage
The hearts thou wouldst have stirred. Not any fire
Save sad flames set to light a funeral pyre
   Dost thou suggest. Nay,—impotent in age,
   Unsought, thou holdst a corner of the stage
And ceasest even dumbly to aspire.

How different was the thought of him that writ.
   What promised he to love of ease and wealth,
When men should read and kindle at his wit.
   But here decay eats up the book by stealth,
While it, like some old maiden, solemnly,
Hugs its incongruous virginity!

For the Man Who Fails

The world is a snob, and the man who wins
    Is the chap for its money's worth:
And the lust for success causes half of the sins
    That are cursing this brave old earth.
For it's fine to go up, and the world's applause
    Is sweet to the mortal ear;
But the man who fails in a noble cause
    Is a hero that's no less dear.

'Tis true enough that the laurel crown
    Twines but for the victor's brow;
For many a hero has lain him down
    With naught but the cypress bough.
There are gallant men in the losing fight,
    And as gallant deeds are done
As ever graced the captured height
    Or the battle grandly won.

We sit at life's board with our nerves highstrung,
    And we play for the stake of Fame,
And our odes are sung and our banners hung
    For the man who wins the game.
But I have a song of another kind
    Than breathes in these fame-wrought gales,—
An ode to the noble heart and mind
    Of the gallant man who fails!

The man who is strong to fight his fight,
    And whose will no front can daunt,
If the truth be truth and the right be right,
    Is the man that the ages want.
Tho' he fail and die in grim defeat,
    Yet he has not fled the strife,
And the house of Earth will seem more sweet
    For the perfume of his life.

THE GARRET

Within a London garret high,
Above the roofs and near the sky,
My ill-rewarding pen I ply
    To win me bread.
This little chamber, six by four,
Is castle, study, den, and more,—
Altho' no carpet decks the floor,
    Nor down, the bed.

My room is rather bleak and bare;
I only have one broken chair,
But then, there's plenty of fresh air,—
    Some light, beside.
What tho' I cannot ask my friends
To share with me my odds and ends,
A liberty my aerie lends,
    To most denied.

The bore who falters at the stair
No more shall be my curse and care,
And duns shall fail to find my lair
    With beastly bills.
When debts have grown and funds are short,
I find it rather pleasant sport
To live "above the common sort"
    With all their ills.

I write my rhymes and sing away,
And dawn may come or dusk or day:
Tho' fare be poor, my heart is gay,
    And full of glee.
Though chimney-pots be all my views;
'Tis nearer for the winging Muse,
So I am sure she'll not refuse
    To visit me.

LITTLE BROWN BABY

Little brown baby wif spa'klin' eyes,
  Come to yo' pappy an' set on his knee.
What you been doin', suh—makin' san' pies?
  Look at dat bib—you's ez du'ty ez me.
Look at dat mouf—dat's merlasses, I bet;
  Come hyeah, Maria, an' wipe off his han's.
Bees gwine to ketch you an' eat you up yit,
  Bein' so sticky an sweet—goodness lan's!

Little brown baby wif spa'klin' eyes,
  Who's pappy's darlin' an' who's pappy's chile?
Who is it all de day nevah once tries
  Fu' to be cross, er once loses dat smile?
Whah did you git dem teef? My, you's a scamp!
  Whah did dat dimple come f'om in yo' chin?
Pappy do' know yo—I b'lieves you's a tramp;
  Mammy, dis hyeah's some ol' straggler got in!

Let's th'ow him outen de do' in de san',
  We do' want stragglers a-layin' 'roun' hyeah;
Let's gin him 'way to de big buggah-man;
  I know he's hidin' erroun' hyeah right neah.
Buggah-man, buggah-man, come in de do',
  Hyeah's a bad boy you kin have fu' to eat.
Mammy an' pappy do' want him no mo',
  Swaller him down f'om his haid to his feet!

Dah, now, I t'ought dat you'd hug me up close.
  Go back, ol' buggah, you sha'n't have dis boy.
He ain't no tramp, ner no straggler, of co'se;
  He's pappy's pa'dner an' playmate an' joy.
Come to you' pallet now—go to yo' res';
  Wisht you could allus know ease an' cleah skies;
Wisht you could stay jes' a chile on my breas'—
  Little brown baby wif spa'klin' eyes!

SYMPATHY

I know what the caged bird feels, alas!
    When the sun is bright on the upland slopes;
When the wind stirs soft through the springing grass,
And the river flows like a stream of glass;
    When the first bird sings and the first bud opes,
And the faint perfume from its chalice steals—
I know what the caged bird feels!

I know why the caged bird beats his wing
    Till its blood is red on the cruel bars;
For he must fly back to his perch and cling
When he fain would be on the bough a-swing;
    And a pain still throbs in the old, old scars
And they pulse again with a keener sting—
I know why he beats his wing!

I know why the caged bird sings, ah me,
    When his wing is bruised and his bosom sore,—
When he beats his bars and he would be free;
It is not a carol of joy or glee,
    But a prayer that he sends from his heart's deep core,
But a plea, that upward to Heaven he flings—
I know why the caged bird sings!

AT CANDLE-LIGHTIN' TIME

When I come in f'om de co'n-fiel' aftah wo'kin' ha'd all day,
It's amazin' nice to fin' my suppah all erpon de way;
An' it's nice to smell de coffee bubblin' ovah in de pot,
An' it's fine to see de meat a-sizzlin' teasin'-lak an' hot.

But when suppah-time is ovah, an' de t'ings is cleahed away;
Den de happy hours dat foller are de sweetes' of de day.
When my co'ncob pipe is sta'ted, an' de smoke is drawin' prime,
My ole 'ooman says, "I reckon, Ike, it's candle-lightin' time."

Den de chillun snuggle up to me, an' all commence to call,
"Oh, say, daddy, now it's time to mek de shadders on de wall."
So I puts my han's togethah—evah daddy knows de way,—
An' de chillun snuggle closer roun' ez I begin to say:—

"Fus' thing, hyeah come Mistah Rabbit; don' you see him wo'k his
    eahs?
Huh, uh! dis mus' be a donkey,—look, how innercent he 'pears!
Dah's de ole black swan a-swimmin'—ain't she got a' awful neck?
Who's dis feller dat's a-comin'? Why, dat's ole dog Tray, I 'spec'!"

Dat's de way I run on, tryin' fu' to please 'em all I can;
Den I hollahs, "Now be keerful—dis hyeah las' 's de buga-man!"
An' dey runs an' hides dey faces; dey ain't skeered—dey's lettin' on:
But de play ain't raaly ovah twell dat buga-man is gone.

So I jes' teks up my banjo, an' I plays a little chune,
An' you see dem haids come peepin' out to listen mighty soon.
Den my wife says, "Sich a pappy fu' to give you sich a fright!
Jes' you go to baid, an' leave him: say yo' prayers an' say good-night."

WHEN DEY 'LISTED COLORED SOLDIERS

Dey was talkin' in de cabin, dey was talkin' in de hall;
But I listened kin' o' keerless, not a-thinkin' 'bout it all;
An' on Sunday, too, I noticed, dey was whisp'rin' mighty much,
Stan'in' all erroun' de roadside w'en dey let us out o' chu'ch.
But I didn't think erbout it twell de middle of de week,
An' my 'Lias come to see me, an' somehow he couldn't speak.
Den I seed all in a minute whut he'd come to see me for;—
Dey had 'listed colo'ed sojers, an' my 'Lias gwine to wah.

Oh, I hugged him, an' I kissed him, an' I baiged him not to go;
But he tol' me dat his conscience, hit was callin' to him so,
An' he couldn't baih to lingah w'en he had a chanst to fight
For de freedom dey had gin him an' de glory of de right.
So he kissed me, an' he lef' me, w'en I'd p'omised to be true;
An' dey put a knapsack on him, an' a coat all colo'ed blue.
So I gin him pap's ol' Bible, f'om de bottom of de draw',—
W'en dey 'listed colo'ed sojers an' my 'Lias went to wah.

But I thought of all de weary miles dat he would have to tramp,
An' I couldn't be contented w'en dey tuk him to de camp.
W'y, my hea't nigh broke wid grievin' twell I seed him on de street;
Den I felt lak I could go an' th'ow my body at his feet.
For his buttons was a-shinin', an' his face was shinin', too,
An' he looked so strong an' mighty in his coat o' sojer blue,
Dat I hollahed, "Step up, manny," dough my th'oat was so' an' raw,—
W'en dey 'listed colo'ed sojers an' my 'Lias went to wah.

Ol' Mis' cried w'en mastah lef' huh, young Miss mou'ned huh
      brothah Ned,
An' I didn't know dey feelin's is de ve'y wo'ds dey said
W'en I tol' 'em I was so'y. Dey had done gin up dey all;
But dey only seemed mo' proudah dat dey men had heerd de call.
Bofe my mastahs went in gray suits, an' I loved de Yankee blue,
But I t'ought dat I could sorrer for de losin' of 'em too;

But I couldn't, for I didn't know de ha'f o' whut I saw,
Twell dey 'listed colo'ed sojers an' my 'Lias went to wah.

Mastah Jack come home all sickly; he was broke for life, dey said;
An' dey lef' my po' young mastah some'rs on de roadside,—dead.
W'en de women cried an' mou'ned 'em, I could feel it thoo an' thoo,
For I had a loved un fightin' in de way o' dangah, too.
Den dey tol' me dey had laid him some'rs way down souf to res',
Wid de flag dat he had fit for shinin' daih acrost his breas'.
Well, I cried, but den I reckon dat's what Gawd had called him for
W'en dey 'listed colo'ed sojers an' my 'Lias went to wah.

A Plea

Treat me nice, Miss Mandy Jane,
   Treat me nice.
Dough my love has tu'ned my brain,
   Treat me nice.
I ain't done a t'ing to shame,
Lovahs all ac's jes' de same:
Don't you know we ain't to blame?
   Treat me nice!

Cose I know I's talkin' wild;
   Treat me nice;
I cain't talk no bettah, child,
   Treat me nice;
Whut a pusson gwine to do,
W'en he come a-cou'tin' you
All a-trimblin' thoo, and thoo?
   Please be nice.

Reckon I mus' go de paf
   Othahs do:
Lovahs lingah, ladies laff;
   Mebbe you
Do' mean all the things you say,
An' pu'haps some latah day
W'en I baig you ha'd, you may
   Treat me nice!

SOLILOQUY OF A TURKEY

Dey's a so't o' threatenin' feelin' in de blowin' of de breeze,
    An' I's feelin' kin' o' squeamish in de night;
I's a-walkin' 'roun' a-lookin' at de diffunt style o' trees,
    An' a-measurin' dey thickness an' dey height.
Fu' dey's somep'n mighty 'spicious in de looks de da'kies give,
    Ez dey pass me an' my fambly on de groun',
So it 'curs to me dat lakly, ef I caihs to try an' live,
    It concehns me fu' to 'mence to look erroun'.

Dey's a cu'ious kin' o' shivah runnin' up an' down my back,
    An' I feel my feddahs rufflin' all de day,
An' my laigs commence to trimble evah blessid step I mek;
    W'en I sees a ax, I tu'ns my head away.
Folks is go'gin' me wid goodies, an' dey's treatin' me wid caih,
    An' I's fat in spite of all dat I kin do.
I's mistrus'ful of de kin'ness dat's erroun' me evahwhaih,
    Fu' it's jes' too good, an' frequent, to be true.

Snow's a-fallin' on de medders, all erroun' me now is white,
    But I's still kep' on a-roostin' on de fence;
Isham comes an' feels my breas'bone, an' he hefted me las' night,
    An' he's gone erroun' a-grinnin' evah sence.
'Tain't de snow dat meks me shivah; 'tain't de col' dat meks me shake;
    'Tain't de wintah-time itse'f dat's 'fectin' me;
But I t'ink de time is comin', an' I'd bettah mek a break,
    Fu' to set wid Mistah Possum in his tree.

W'en you hyeah de da'kies singin', an' de quahtahs all is gay,
    'Tain't de time fu' birds lak me to be erroun';
W'en de hick'ry chips is flyin', an' de log's been ca'ied erway,
    Den hit's dang'ous to be roostin' nigh de groun'.
Grin on, Isham! Sing on, da'kies! But I flop my wings an' go
    Fu' de sheltah of de ve'y highest tree,
Fu' dey's too much close ertention—an' dey's too much fallin' snow—
    An' it's too nigh Chris'mus mo'nin' now fu' me.

TO A CAPTIOUS CRITIC

Dear critic, who my lightness so deplores,
Would I might study to be prince of bores,
Right wisely would I rule that dull estate—
But, sir, I may not, till you abdicate.

IN THE MORNING

'Lias! 'Lias! Bless de Lawd!
Don' you know de day's erbroad?
Ef you don' git up, you scamp,
Dey'll be trouble in dis camp.
T'ink I gwine to let you sleep
W'ile I meks yo' boa'd an' keep?
Dat's a putty howdy-do—
Don' you hyeah me, 'Lias—you?

Bet ef I come crost dis flo'
You won' fin' no time to sno'.
Daylight all a-shinin' in
W'ile you sleep—w'y hit's a sin!
Ain't de can'le-light enough
To bu'n out widout a snuff,
But you go de mo'nin' thoo
Bu'nin' up de daylight too?

'Lias, don' you hyeah me call?
No use tu'nin' to'ds de wall;
I kin hyeah dat mattuss squeak;
Don' you hyeah me w'en I speak?
Dis hyeah clock done struck off six—
Ca'line, bring me dem ah sticks!
Oh, you down, suh; huh! you down—
Look hyeah, don' you daih to frown.

Ma'ch yo'se'f an' wash yo' face,
Don' you splattah all de place;
I got somep'n else to do,
'Sides jes' cleanin' aftah you.
Tek dat comb an' fix yo' haid—
Looks jes' lak a feddah baid.

Look hyeah, boy, I let you see
You sha'n't roll yo' eyes at me.

Come hyeah; bring me dat ah strap!
Boy, I'll whup you 'twell you drap;
You done felt yo'se'f too strong,
An' you sholy got me wrong.
Set down at dat table thaih;
Jes' you whimpah ef you daih!
Evah mo'nin' on dis place,
Seem lak I mus' lose my grace.

Fol' yo' han's an' bow yo' haid—
Wait ontwell de blessin' 's said;
"Lawd, have mussy on ouah souls—"
(Don' you daih to tech dem rolls—)
"Bless de food we gwine to eat—"
(You set still—I *see* yo' feet;
You jes' try dat trick again!)
"Gin us peace an' joy. Amen!"

THE POET

He sang of life, serenely sweet,
    With, now and then, a deeper note.
    From some high peak, nigh yet remote,
He voiced the world's absorbing beat.

He sang of love when earth was young,
    And Love, itself, was in his lays.
    But ah, the world, it turned to praise
A jingle in a broken tongue.

THE FISHER CHILD'S LULLABY

The wind is out in its rage to-night,
   And your father is far at sea.
The rime on the window is hard and white
     But dear, you are near to me.
       Heave ho, weave low,
         Waves of the briny deep;
       Seethe low and breathe low,
         But sleep you, my little one, sleep, sleep.

The little boat rocks in the cove no more,
   But the flying sea-gulls wail;
I peer through the darkness that wraps the shore,
     For sight of a home set sail.
       Heave ho, weave low,
         Waves of the briny deep;
       Seethe low and breathe low,
         But sleep you, my little one, sleep, sleep.

Ay, lad of mine, thy father may die
   In the gale that rides the sea,
But we'll not believe it, not you and I,
     Who mind us of Galilee.
       Heave ho, weave low,
         Waves of the briny deep;
       Seethe low and breathe low,
         But sleep you, my little one, sleep, sleep.

THE PLANTATION CHILD'S LULLABY

Wintah time hit comin'
   Stealin' thoo de night;
Wake up in the mo'nin'
   Evah ting is white;
Cabin lookin' lonesome
   Stannin' in de snow,
Meks you kin' o' nervous,
   W'en de win' hit blow.

Trompin' back from feedin',
   Col' an' wet an' blue,
Homespun jacket ragged,
   Win' a-blowin' thoo.
Cabin lookin' cheerful,
   Unnerneaf de do',
Yet you kin' o' keerful
   W'en de win' hit blow.

Hickory log a-blazin'
   Light a-lookin' red,
Faith o' eyes o' peepin'
   R'om a trun'le bed,
Little feet a-patterin'
   Cleak across de flo';
Bettah had be keerful
   W'en de win' hit blow.

Suppah done an' ovah,
   Evah t'ing is still;
Listen to de snowman
   Slippin' down de hill.
Ashes on de fiah,
   Keep it wa'm but low.

What's de use o' keerin'
   Ef de win' do blow?

Smoke house full o' bacon,
   Brown an' sweet an' good;
Taters in de cellah,
   'Possum roam de wood;
Little baby snoozin'
   Des ez ef he know.
What's de use o' keerin'
   Ef de win' do blow?

THE FARM CHILD'S LULLABY

Oh, the little bird is rocking in the cradle of the wind,
    And it's bye, my little wee one, bye;
The harvest all is gathered and the pippins all are binned;
    Bye, my little wee one, bye;
The little rabbit's hiding in the golden shock of corn,
The thrifty squirrel's laughing bunny's idleness to scorn;
You are smiling with the angels in your slumber, smile till morn;
    So it's bye, my little wee one, bye.

There'll be plenty in the cellar, there'll be plenty on the shelf;
    Bye, my little wee one, bye;
There'll be goodly store of sweetings for a dainty little elf;
    Bye, my little wee one, bye.
The snow may be a-flying o'er the meadow and the hill,
The ice has checked the chatter of the little laughing rill,
But in your cosey cradle you are warm and happy still;
    So bye, my little wee one, bye.

Why, the Bob White thinks the snowflake is a brother to his song;
    Bye, my little wee one, bye;
And the chimney sings the sweeter when the wind is blowing strong;
    Bye, my little wee one, bye;
The granary's overflowing, full is cellar, crib, and bin,
The wood has paid its tribute and the ax has ceased its din;
The winter may not harm you when you're sheltered safe within;
    So bye, my little wee one, bye.

THE HAUNTED OAK

Pray why are you so bare, so bare,
    Oh, bough of the old oak-tree;
And why, when I go through the shade you throw,
    Runs a shudder over me?

My leaves were green as the best, I trow,
    And sap ran free in my veins,
But I saw in the moonlight dim and weird
    A guiltless victim's pains.

I bent me down to hear his sigh;
    I shook with his gurgling moan,
And I trembled sore when they rode away,
    And left him here alone.

They'd charged him with the old, old crime,
    And set him fast in jail:
Oh, why does the dog howl all night long,
    And why does the night wind wail?

He prayed his prayer and he swore his oath,
    And he raised his hand to the sky;
But the beat of hoofs smote on his ear,
    And the steady tread drew nigh.

Who is it rides by night, by night,
    Over the moonlit road?
And what is the spur that keeps the pace,
    What is the galling goad?

And now they beat at the prison door,
    "Ho, keeper, do not stay!
We are friends of him whom you hold within,
    And we fain would take him away

"From those who ride fast on our heels
    With mind to do him wrong;
They have no care for his innocence,
    And the rope they bear is long."

They have fooled the jailer with lying words,
    They have fooled the man with lies;
The bolts unbar, the locks are drawn,
    And the great door open flies.

Now they have taken him from the jail,
    And hard and fast they ride,
And the leader laughs low down in his throat,
    As they halt my trunk beside.

Oh, the judge, he wore a mask of black,
    And the doctor one of white,
And the minister, with his oldest son,
    Was curiously bedight.

Oh, foolish man, why weep you now?
    'Tis but a little space,
And the time will come when these shall dread
    The mem'ry of your face.

I feel the rope against my bark,
    And the weight of him in my grain,
I feel in the throe of his final woe
    The touch of my own last pain.

And never more shall leaves come forth
    On a bough that bears the ban;
I am burned with dread, I am dried and dead,
    From the curse of a guiltless man.

And ever the judge rides by, rides by,
    And goes to hunt the deer,

And ever another rides his soul
    In the guise of a mortal fear.

And ever the man he rides me hard,
    And never a night stays he;
For I feel his curse as a haunted bough,
    On the trunk of a haunted tree.

TO THE SOUTH

ON ITS NEW SLAVERY

Heart of the Southland, heed me pleading now,
Who bearest, unashamed, upon my brow
The long kiss of the loving tropic sun,
And yet, whose veins with thy red current run.

Borne on the bitter winds from every hand,
Strange tales are flying over all the land,
And Condemnation, with his pinions foul,
Glooms in the place where broods the midnight owl.

What art thou, that the world should point at thee,
And vaunt and chide the weakness that they see?
There was a time they were not wont to chide;
Where is thy old, uncompromising pride?

Blood-washed, thou shouldst lift up thine honored head,
White with the sorrow for thy loyal dead
Who lie on every plain, on every hill,
And whose high spirit walks the Southland still:

Whose infancy our mother's hands have nursed.
Thy manhood, gone to battle unaccursed,
Our fathers left to till th' reluctant field,
To rape the soil for what she would not yield;

Wooing for aye, the cold unam'rous sod,
Whose growth for them still meant a master's rod;
Tearing her bosom for the wealth that gave
The strength that made the toiler still a slave.

Too long we hear the deep impassioned cry
That echoes vainly to the heedless sky;

Too long, too long, the Macedonian call
Falls fainting far beyond the outward wall,

Within whose sweep, beneath the shadowing trees,
A slumbering nation takes its dangerous ease;
Too long the rumors of thy hatred go
For those who loved thee and thy children so.

Thou must arise forthwith, and strong, thou must
throw off the smirching of this baser dust.
Lay by the practice of this later creed,
And be thine honest self again indeed.

There was a time when even slavery's chain
Held in some joys to alternate with pain,
Some little light to give the night relief,
Some little smiles to take the place of grief.

There was a time when, jocund as the day,
The toiler hoed his row and sung his lay,
Found something gleeful in the very air,
And solace for his toiling everywhere.

Now all is changed, within the rude stockade,
A bondsman whom the greed of men has made
Almost too brutish to deplore his plight,
Toils hopeless on from joyless morn till night.

For him no more the cabin's quiet rest,
The homely joys that gave to labor zest;
No more for him the merry banjo's sound,
Nor trip of lightsome dances footing round.

For him no more the lamp shall glow at eve,
Nor chubby children pluck him by the sleeve;

No more for him the master's eyes be bright,—
He has nor freedom's nor a slave's delight.

What, was it all for naught, those awful years
That drenched a groaning land with blood and tears?
Was it to leave this sly convenient hell,
That brother fighting his own brother fell?

When that great struggle held the world in awe,
And all the nations blanched at what they saw,
Did Sanctioned Slavery bow its conquered head
That this unsanctioned crime might rise instead?

Is it for this we all have felt the flame,—
This newer bondage and this deeper shame?
Nay, not for this, a nation's heroes bled,
And North and South with tears beheld their dead.

Oh, Mother South, hast thou forgot thy ways,
Forgot the glory of thine ancient days,
Forgot the honor that once made thee great,
And stooped to this unhallowèd estate?

It cannot last, thou will come forth in might,
A warrior queen full armored for the fight;
And thou wilt take, e'en with thy spear in rest,
Thy dusky children to thy saving breast.

Till then, no more, no more the gladsome song,
Strike only deeper chords, the notes of wrong;
Till then, the sigh, the tear, the oath, the moan,
Till thou, oh, South, and thine, come to thine own.

PART TWO

SHORT FICTION

INTRODUCTION

Paul Laurence Dunbar sold his first story to a large newspaper syndicate in 1891 when he was working as an elevator boy in the Callahan Building in Dayton, Ohio. The A. N. Kellogg newspaper syndicate paid Dunbar six dollars for "The Tenderfoot," a Western tale set in a mining camp in an unnamed locale, narrated in credible Western vernacular by a white miner, about characters who were all white. It was the first literary work for which Dunbar was paid. Although Dunbar's first three novels would similarly feature casts of characters that were almost entirely white (his third novel included a black man as a minor figure), he began experimenting with writing scenes of black life in the short stories he published in magazines and newspapers in the late 1890s. (His editors flagged the racial dimension of the subject matter in subtitles like "A Character Sketch of Real Darkey Life in New York" or "A Darkey Dialect Story.") Dunbar found a ready market for these stories of black life in publications including *The Independent, Cosmopolitan, Current Literature,* and *The Saturday Evening Post*—journals whose predominantly white audiences' tastes had been prepared for these scenes by popular traditions of local color writing. Most of these early stories, however—and perhaps the majority of the nearly one hundred stories Dunbar wrote—are rather formulaic and not especially memorable. But the large number of rather pedestrian stories Dunbar churned out to earn money should not distract us from the handful of masterful or intriguing ones he managed to produce along the way.

The twelve stories reprinted here all aspire to transcend the trite formulas of magazine stories of the day and, to a large extent, succeed. Our eclectic selection includes stories from each of the four collections of stories Dunbar published—*Folks from Dixie* (1898), *The Strength of Gideon* (1900), *In Old Plantation Days* (1903), and *The Heart of Happy Hollow* (1904)—as well as a story that appeared in *The People's Monthly* in 1900 but that Dunbar did not include in any of these collections. They are set during the antebellum years, Reconstruction, and the post-Reconstruction era. They take place in rural Kentucky, a small city in Ohio, West Virginia mining country, urban Washington, D.C., and various unnamed locales in both the North and the South. And although one story ("The Ordeal at Mt. Hope") features all black characters and one ("The Lion Tamer") features characters who are all white, most of these stories focus on black-white interactions.

Whether he is depicting the psychology of a young white child in a slaveholding household near Lexington, Kentucky ("A Blessed Deceit"), or black and white miners in West Virginia ("At Shaft 11"), or a black college graduate in the Midwest ("One Man's Fortunes"), Dunbar creates believable characters about whom we come to care. He also limns communities—black communities in particular—with compassion and skill. He is as ready to celebrate a black community's potential ("The Ordeal at Mt. Hope") as he is ready to poke fun at its gullibility ("The Mission of Mr. Scatters"). In stories that range in tone from comic to sentimental to tragic to satirical, Dunbar gives us a cast that includes men, women, and children of a broad range of ages, classes, and walks of life. Taken together, this sampling of Dunbar's short fiction is impressive for its versatility, for its attentiveness to varieties of American vernacular, and for the freshness with which it explores a range of themes, including the functions of friendship, the dynamics of deceit, and the challenges of the continuing, necessary battle against racism.

Two of the best stories in this group, "The Ingrate" and "One Man's Fortunes," resonate with Dunbar's own experiences or those of his father. "The Ingrate," which was published in *New England Magazine* in August 1899 and later included in *The Strength of Gideon and Other Stories,* centers on a slave named Joshua Leckler, who, like Dunbar's father,

Joshua Dunbar, was a skilled plasterer on a Kentucky plantation who made his way to Canada and then enlisted as a Union soldier in the Civil War. Josh's master in the story, Mr. Leckler, decides to teach Josh to read, write, and "cipher" to avoid being cheated by Eckley, a white man to whom he "rents" Josh as a plasterer. Mr. Leckler does so in the name of "principle"—the principle being his ostensible desire not to allow Josh to be cheated out of the portion of the pay that he is saving to buy his freedom. The slaveowner remarks to his wife,

> "Now, of course, I should not care, the matter of a dollar or two being nothing to me; but it is a very different matter when we consider poor Josh." There was deep pathos in Mr. Leckler's tone. "You know Josh is anxious to buy his freedom, and I allow him a part of whatever he makes; so you see it's he that's affected. Every dollar that he is cheated out of cuts off just so much from his earnings, and puts further away his hope of emancipation."
>
> If the thought occurred to Mrs. Leckler that, since Josh received only about one-tenth of what he earned, the advantage of just wages would be quite as much her husband's as the slaves, she did not betray it. . . .

But if Mrs. Leckler is reluctant to expose her husband's bad faith in the matter, Dunbar is not. On the contrary, he satirizes Mr. Leckler's high regard for himself as a magnanimous and kind slaveholder with a deftness not unlike that with which Mark Twain had satirized slaveholder Percy Driscoll's analogous regard for his own magnanimity and kindness in *Pudd'nhead Wilson* five years earlier. Dunbar makes it clear that Mr. Leckler invokes "principle" only as a rationalization to cast his self-interested behavior in a noble light. When he finds that Josh has been able to recover two dollars in pay that Eckley had hoped to cheat him out of, Mr. Leckler is jubilant:

> Mr. Leckler heard the story with great glee. "I laid for him that time—the old fox." But to Mrs. Leckler he said: "You see, my dear wife, my rashness in teaching Josh to figure for himself is vindicated. See what he has saved for himself."
>
> "What did he save?" asked the little woman indiscreetly.
>
> Her husband blushed and stammered for a moment, and then replied, "Well, of course, it was only twenty cents saved to him, but to a man buying his freedom every cent counts; and after all, it is not the amount, Mrs. Leckler, it's the principle of the thing."

In fact, Mr. Leckler has no intention of letting his slave actually buy his freedom. We observe him thinking to himself that

> it would be many years before the slave could pay the two thousand dollars, which price he had set upon him. Should he approach that figure, Mr. Leckler felt it just possible that the market in slaves would take a sudden rise.

Like Joshua Dunbar, Joshua Leckler became possessed of the burning ambition to be free: "To own himself, to be master of his hands, feet, of his whole body—something would clutch at his heart as he thought of it; and the breath would come hard between his lips." But he slyly hid his aspirations from his master: "he met his master with an impassive face, always silent, always docile; and Mr. Leckler congratulated himself that so valuable and intelligent a slave meant discontent; but not so with Josh. Who more content than he? He remarked to his wife: 'You see, my dear, this is what comes of treating even a nigger right.'"

Needless to say, Josh's owner feels stunned and betrayed when Josh—"Oh, the ingrate, the ingrate!"—steals himself away to Canada one night with a forged pass, and later turns up as a sergeant on the roster of "Company F," a black regiment in the Union army. It is interesting that this story of the trickster-master tricked by the poker-faced trickster-slave prefigures one of Charles Chesnutt's most acclaimed stories, "The Passing of Grandison," which was published in *The Wife of His Youth and Other Stories of the Color Line* several months after Dunbar's story appeared in *New England Magazine* in 1899. Both stories satirize the self-serving rationalizations of "kind" slaveholders while limning the resourcefulness and cunning of slaves who used whatever limited freedom and knowledge of the world they were granted to make their way north to freedom.

Dunbar's own struggles against the color line take center stage in the story "One Man's Fortunes," which he published in his collection *The Strength of Gideon and Other Stories* in 1900 (he also reprinted "The Ingrate" in this collection). Indeed, this story is probably the most extended personal meditation we have from Dunbar on his response to his own ill-fated search for a job in Dayton after he graduated from high school. The protagonist of the story, Bertram Halliday, is a young black man who has just graduated from a state university in the Midwest. The story begins the night after commencement, when Halliday chats with two friends, one black (Webb Davis) and one white (Charlie McLean). The notion that black and white school classmates might have engaged in the kind of honest, freewheeling conversation Dunbar shares with us at the start of this story may well reflect some of the conversations he had had with black and white friends at Dayton's Central High School, where Dunbar received a superior education (one that may have been comparable, on some levels, to a first-year college course). Dunbar was close friends with white students such as Orville and Wilbur Wright as well as black students such as William "Bud" Burns.

When he was a student at Central High, Dunbar had been president of the school debating society, editor of the school newspaper, and author of the school song—clearly a star of his cohort. He contributed articles to a neighborhood newspaper run by his friends Orville and Wilbur Wright, and he had begun to publish a newspaper of his own, for the black community, on the printing press the Wright brothers had rigged up in their bicycle shop. Journalism and poetry came easily to him. He had a sense of humor and a ready wit, he was personable, and he was ambitious. He hit the pavement to look for a job after graduation in the spring of 1891, convinced that with his track record of talent and responsibility, some local newspaper or law office would surely hire him in some clerical position. He was offered one job. It was in the Callahan building—one of the more impressive office buildings in downtown Dayton. He was hired to run the elevator, at a salary of four dollars a week. Nobody wanted to hire a black man in Dayton for a non-menial job in 1891, no matter how good he was.

Echoing themes that had pervaded the popular fiction of Horatio Alger, community leaders and educators across the nation in the 1890s championed the idea of America as the land of opportunity, as a meritocracy that rewarded talent and hard work (one such motivational speech is referred to in "One Man's Fortunes"). But Dunbar's brutally honest story exposed the ways in which racism made a mockery of the ideals to which the nation was allegedly committed. Bert Halliday in "One Man's Fortunes" believes in those ideals as much as Dunbar himself did when he graduated from Central High, and only the tutelage of harsh experience could shake that faith. Dunbar himself actually may have retained more of a belief that individual excellence could overcome racist discrimination than his character Bert Halliday does. But this story remains a remarkably detailed and compelling indictment of the bitter obstacles faced by even the most talented, intelligent, modest, hard-working, and ambitious young black man during this era, and provides a unique perspective on Dunbar's insight into the systemic roots of the racism he battled on a personal level during the period following high school.

Bert Halliday recognizes, as did Dunbar, that despite his stellar success in school, "the battle of life was, in reality, just beginning" after graduation, and he knows that "for him the battle would be harder than for his white comrades." But he refuses to set out on his job search in his hometown in a pessimistic frame of mind:

> Looking at his own position, he saw himself the member of a race dragged from complacent savagery into the very heat and turmoil of a civilization for which it was in nowise prepared; bowed beneath a yoke to which its shoulders were not fitted, and then, without warning, thrust forth into a freedom as absurd as it was startling and overwhelming. And yet, he felt, as most young men must feel, an individual strength that would exempt him from the workings of the general law. His outlook on life was calm and unfrightened. Because he knew the dangers that beset his way, he feared them less. He felt assured because with so clear an eye he saw the weak places in his armor which the world he was going to meet would attack, and these he was prepared to strengthen. Was it not the fault of youth and self-confessed weakness, he thought, to go into the world always thinking of it as a foe? Was not this great Cosmopolis, this dragon of a thousand talons, kind as well as cruel? Had it not friends as well as enemies? Yes. That was it: the outlook of young men, of colored young men in particular, was all wrong—they had gone at the world in the wrong spirit. They had looked upon it as a terrible foeman and forced it to be one. He would do it, oh, so differently. He would take the world as a friend. . . .

Bert's white classmate Charlie McLean plans to go into his father's business. But he avers that what the future holds for his black friends Bert and Webb is much more exciting:

> "Why, man, if I could, I'd change places with you. . . . What is before you? Hardships, perhaps, and long waiting. But then, you have the zest of the fight, the joy of the action and the chance of conquering. Now what is before me,—me, whom you are envying? I go out of here into a dull counting-room. The way is prepared for me. Perhaps I shall have no hardships, but neither have I the joy that comes from pains endured. Perhaps I shall

have no battle, but even so, I lose the pleasure of the fight and the glory of winning. Your fate is infinitely to be preferred to mine."

Webb Davis calls him a "sentimental idiot" for not seeing that the scales are dreadfully weighted against young black men like himself and Halliday. Halliday, who has been quiet up to this point in the conversation, then launches into a discussion of the English poet William Ernest Henley's ability to imagine the mind overcoming all obstacles, and recites from memory Henley's famous poem "Invictus," which Henley wrote while hospitalized for tuberculosis in the 1870s ("I am the master of my fate, / I am the captain of my soul"). Davis makes fun of Halliday's idealism (you're so "hopelessly young," he laughs). But Halliday refuses to be swayed.

Like Dunbar, who expected to have no trouble finding a clerical job in a Dayton newspaper or law office after high school, Halliday returns to his hometown of Broughton having "settled upon law as a profession." He knew that he "needed money," but did not think working and pursuing his studies at the same time would be an obstacle. After all,

he knew several fellows who had been able to go into offices, and by collecting and similar duties make something while they studied. Webb Davis would have said, "but they were white," but Halliday knew what his own reply would have been: "What a white man can do, I can do."

The first sign that he may have misjudged his community comes when an acquaintance from high school corrects him "patronizingly" when he fails to address this young man "whom he had often met upon the football and baseball fields" as "Mister," and then persists in addressing Bert himself by his first name only.

Bert is incredulous when Mr. Featherton, a white lawyer who had taken an interest in him in high school, tries to discourage him from becoming a lawyer, telling him that black people don't have a lot of money to spend on lawyers. Bert responds,

"I should not cater for the patronage of my own people alone."

"Yes, but the time has not come when a white person will employ a colored attorney."

"Do you mean to say that the prejudice here at home is such that if I were as competent as a white lawyer a white person would not employ me?"

"I say nothing about prejudice at all. It's nature. They have their own lawyers; why should they go outside of their own to employ a colored man?"

"But I am of their own. I am an American citizen, there should be no thought of color about it."

"Oh, my boy, that theory is very nice, but State University democracy doesn't obtain in real life."

Mr. Featherton then "explains," "The sentiment of remorse and the desire for atoning which actuated so many white men to help Negroes right after the war has passed off without being replaced by that sense of plain justice which gives a black man his due, not because of, nor in spite of, but without consideration of his color." He then offers to help Bert get a job if he's willing to begin "at the bottom." Bert is elated until he finds out that rather than hiring him at the law office, Mr. Featherton plans to speak to the head waiter of a local hotel. Later that day Bert reads a sign announcing that this very same Mr. Featherton is giving a lecture the following week at the YMCA on "How a Christian young man can get on in the law."

After finding only menial jobs being offered to him, and taking a job as a janitor, Bert is pleasantly surprised when Mr. Featherton does offer him a clerical position in his office. Although it means a pay cut, Bert takes the job and throws himself into it, happy for the chance to get ahead in the field of his choice; he works just as hard at mobilizing support in the black community for Mr. Featherton's candidacy for a judgeship. But when Featherton discharges him immediately after the successful election, Bert realizes that he has been used "as a housemaid would use a lemon." He writes his old friend Webb Davis that he was right—and adds that he understands now "why the sleeping and dining-car companies are supplied by men with better educations than half the passengers whom they serve"—a circumstance that unfortunately would persist throughout much of the new century. "We have been taught that merit wins," he writes his friend. "But I have learned that the adages, as well as the books and formulas were made by and for others than us of the black race." It is Webb Davis and not Bert Halliday who closes the story with the comment, "A colored man has no business with ideals—not in *this* nineteenth century!" But it is hard to imagine that Dunbar, as frustrated as Bert in his own search for a job after graduation, did not share at least a part of Davis's cynicism.

The threat of unemployment for black men in the 1890s may have been a serious one, but not as life-threatening as the epidemic of racially motivated lynchings that swept the country during this era. According to historian John Hope Franklin, there were more than twenty-five hundred lynchings during the last sixteen years of the nineteenth century, and the majority of the victims were black. Journalist Ida B. Wells devoted her newspaper career to documenting the details of many of these lynchings, and the chilling topic was also the focus of turn-of-the-century fiction by Mark Twain and Theodore Dreiser, among others. Dunbar wrote about lynchings in three different genres: in his newspaper journalism (see "The Race Question Discussed" and "The Fourth of July and Race Outrages" in this volume); in his poem "The Haunted Oak," which is told from the perspective of a tree whose limbs are used to hang lynching victims; and in two short stories, "The Tragedy at Three Forks" (in *The Strength of Gideon*) and "The Lynching of Jube Benson" (in *The Heart of Happy Hollow*). Neither of these stories was published in a periodical, and both run counter to the upbeat, sentimental tone of most of the stories in the collections in which they appeared. "The Tragedy at Three Forks" takes place in a rural settlement in the valleys and hollows of central Kentucky, while "The Lynching of Jube Benson" is set in Virginia. Both stories center on the propensity of the white residents of each region to blame any dastardly unsolved crime on "the niggers." And both result in the lynching of innocent black men.

In "The Tragedy at Three Forks," the reader watches Jane Hunster, a poor white consumed with resentment over being snubbed by the wealthy Seliny Williams, stealthily sneak up to the Williamses' house during an exceptionally dark night with a can of kerosene, set it on fire, and speed away without being seen, muttering with satisfaction about having "fixed" her stuck-up rival by making it likely that next time they met she'd be "ez pore ez I am." Her plan works, and the family of one of the wealthiest farmers in the region becomes homeless. It is Jane's father who first voices

the popular sentiment by saying, "Look a here, folks, I tell you that's the work o' niggers, I kin see their hand in it."

"Niggers, o' course," exclaimed every one else. "Why didn't we think of it before? It's jest like 'em."

The county paper follows suit with a sulphurous account of the affair, under the scarehead:

A TERRIBLE OUTRAGE!
MOST DASTARDLY DEED EVER COMMITTED IN THE
HISTORY OF BARLOW COUNTY. A HIGHLY RE-
SPECTED, UNOFFENDING AND WELL-BE-
LOVED FAMILY BURNED OUT OF HOUSE
AND HOME. NEGROES! UN-
DOUBTEDLY THE PERPETRA-
TORS OF THE DEED!

Rumors, fantasies, and fictions prompt the town to scour the woods "in search of strange 'niggers.'" Two unlucky black men who happen to be passing through the area are summarily lynched by the "law-abiding citizens of Barlow County" who take their professions of innocence as signs of the customary "nigger stubbornness." Dunbar manages to be both inside the heads of poor whites and outside, sardonically commenting on the delusionary morality play that has been enacted. Following the lynching, "conservative editors wrote leaders about it in which they deplored the rashness of the hanging but warned the negroes that the only way to stop lynching was to quit the crimes of which they so often stood accused."

"The Lynching of Jube Benson" is written from a very different point of view. Amid the smoke clouds of after-dinner cigars in the Virginia library of Gordon Fairfax,

> Handon Gay, who was an ambitious young reporter, spoke of a lynching story in a recent magazine, and the matter of punishment without trial put new life into the conversation.
> "I should like to see a real lynching," said Gay rather callously.

His host, Fairfax, says blandly, "Well, I should hardly express it that way, but if a real, live lynching were to come my way, I should not avoid it." But another guest, a physician named Dr. Melville, dissents and tells a story that is both moving and chilling about the role he himself took in lynching a black man who had been a devoted servant of his fiancée, but whom he mistakenly believed to have murdered her.

When it was too late to undo what he had done, the doctor found incontrovertible proof that the real murderer was a white man who had blacked his face to avoid being identified. The doctor, he tells his friends, has sworn off lynchings forever.

Both of these stories flesh out the kinds of circumstances that a writer like Ida B. Wells tracked so tirelessly in her campaign against lynchings. Interestingly, to make the stories work, Dunbar had to tell them from the perspective of whites who had taken part in the lynchings. This strategy was bolder, and ultimately more successful, than the one that Theodore Dreiser hit upon, for example, in his story "Nigger Jeff," told from the perspective of a reporter covering a lynching. Despite the fact that the reporter and author are sympathetic to the murdered man and his family, the reader never gets inside the heads of the lynchers, and is therefore more at a loss to understand the psychological factors that helped bring this particular act of brutality about, and that contributed to the proliferation of "lynch law" in the South.

While no one would charge the Dunbar who wrote these anti-lynching stories with being an "Uncle Tom," other stories that took a less tragic and sardonic look at black-white relations have led some twentieth-century critics to dismiss him as a sentimental accommodationist, a black writer who catered to the prejudices of the white marketplace. But although some of Dunbar's short stories conform more than others to sentimental popular genres, it is a mistake to try to pin a reductive label on Dunbar. His work is more complex than that—and more interesting. On the surface, for example, Dunbar's story "Nelse Hatton's Vengeance" (which appeared in *Folks from Dixie*) resembles those hugely popular Plantation Tradition tales of ex-slaves who remain fiercely loyal to their former masters, even to the point of giving them hard-earned money. The plot involves an unkempt white man in rags turning up on the Ohio doorstep of Nelse Hatton, a hard-working, relatively prosperous black homeowner, to beg for food. He turns out to be Hatton's former master, now fallen on hard times. The story ends with Hatton giving his former master money to return to the old plantation to die. But therein the similarities to works by Plantation Tradition writers like Thomas Nelson Page end. For the reader watches Nelse Hatton, who still bears a scar from his master's lash, struggle with his anger. Hatton has the power to take revenge, and contemplates doing just that, but instead transcends his anger and attains a higher level of Christian virtue by transmuting it into forgiveness, in the process subverting the culture's hierarchy of racial inferiority in profound and memorable ways. Rather than imitating a tradition forged by Thomas Nelson Page here, Dunbar may be refining and extending a move made several years earlier by black writer Victoria Earle Matthews in her story "Aunt Lindy," prominently published in the *A.M.E. Church Review.* (The quarterly journal was widely read by church members, and since Dunbar and his mother were active members of the Wayman African Methodist Episcopal Church on Eaker Street in Dayton when this story came out, and since Matthews was writing a kind of story Dunbar would aspire to write, it is highly likely that he read it.) In Matthews's story, the ex-slave's anger and opportunity for revenge against her former master are deflected by the sound of hymn-singing from the church next door that makes its way to her before she executes the vengeance she contemplates. Dunbar lets the impulse to Christian forgiveness enter Nelse Hatton's head without the aid of hymns from a church next door, but the story is otherwise the same. The point is that we can view Dunbar reductively as slavishly imitating the Plantation Tradition only if we ignore alternative models—in this case black models—that he found more appealing.

Similarly, Dunbar's story "A Blessed Deceit" could be reductively summarized as a story about a slave child so devoted to his young master that he sacrifices his own safety to protect him, suffering severe burns when he rushes to put out flames that have accidentally engulfed his young master at a birthday party. Thomas Nelson Page might have written a story with that plot line. But he could not have written the complicated and subtle story that Dunbar did about the challenge of forging a black-white friendship under the skewed power relations mandated by slavery. "A Blessed Deceit," which appeared in *In Old Plantation Days,* records a friendship that began between two two-year-olds, one a slave (Lucius) and one the child of the master (Robert), and takes the children through the white child's first birthday party, at age six. Dunbar carefully paints a complex, mutually satisfying childhood friendship that acknowledges but also challenges the racial hierarchies that underpin it. "The little black was never allowed to forget that he was his Master Robert's servant," Dunbar writes, "but there is a democracy about childhood that oversteps all conventions, and lays low all barriers of caste. Down in the quarters, with many secret giggles, the two were dubbed, 'The Daniels twins.'"

Dunbar shares conversations the children have with each other about Robert's upcoming birthday party, capturing the children's distinctive cadences and voices with charm and skill. And with similar care, Dunbar shows Robert deceiving his parents in order to make sure that Lucius gets to attend his birthday party: the six-year-old white child is smart enough to know that the one argument that is sure to secure Lucius's presence when the cake is cut is the notion that Robert would like his beautifully attired, attentive little servant to enhance his status on this occasion—that he'd like to use him to "show off" to the other white children who have been invited. His father approves, proud that at age six his young aristocrat already has a sense of his proper place in the world. By the story's end, however, Robert has confessed his deception: he didn't want Lucius there for show; he wanted him there because he is his best friend.

Elsewhere in his work, Dunbar makes it clear that he is not blind to slavery's heinous oppressions. But this story makes it clear that he is also willing to imagine a moment when a white child used his wit and cunning (however disastrously it all turned out) to tear a rent in the curtain of caste and color that divided him from his black friend. Dunbar did not have to imagine a genuine friendship among equals who happened to be white and black. He had such a friendship with Orville Wright in high school. But imagining the possibility of such cross-racial friendships' having existed on the plantation was a different matter. "A Blessed Deceit" has been ignored by critics, probably because they had no idea what to make of it.

Dunbar focuses on less "blessed" forms of deceit in "The Mission of Mr. Scatters," a well-crafted story about a black community's willingness to be duped by a charming black confidence man. It was published in *The Heart of Happy Hollow* in 1904. There are shades of Mark Twain's "The Man That Corrupted Hadleyburg" in this tale about a mysterious stranger who disrupts a complacent community's equilibrium with the promise of great wealth. And the ingratiating stranger's knowledge of the community and his fake English accent remind one a bit of the duke and the king in the Wilks episode of *Huckleberry Finn,* while the ways in which the community responds to a man believed to be associated with great wealth is not unlike Twain's "Million-Pound Bank-Note." Rather than being imitative or derivative, however (we have no proof that Dunbar read Twain), Dunbar's story is fresh and distinctive. In its surprise ending, in which the black confidence man wins a "not guilty" verdict in a white courtroom by playing on the vanities of the white powers-that-be with a virtuosity that stuns his black victims, Dunbar demonstrates a gift for satire that Twain would have been likely to appreciate (we have no evidence, either, that Twain was familiar with this or any other story by Dunbar—although we do know that he read some of his poems).

Dunbar's skill as a satirist also informs "Mr. Cornelius Johnson, Office-Seeker" and "The Lion Tamer." "Mr. Cornelius Johnson," which appeared in *Cosmopolitan* before being reprinted in *The Strength of Gideon*, takes a mercilessly sardonic look at the fervent dreams and foolish self-delusion of a pompous, self-important black aspirant for a political appointment in Washington during Reconstruction. "The Lion Tamer," which ran in *The Smart Set* in 1901, but which Dunbar never included in a collection, takes a wry look at white high society. It depicts the deception of a standoffish white writer by a cunning fan determined to get the reluctant author to read his work at a party.

Sincerity and sympathy rather than satire characterize Dunbar's stance in "The Ordeal at Mt. Hope," a story about one man whose imagination and energy transform a struggling Southern black community, as well as in "At Shaft 11," a dramatic story about the tensions between striking white miners and the black workers brought in to replace them in a West Virginia coal town, both of which appeared in Dunbar's first collection of stories, *Folks from Dixie*.

Dunbar chose not to anthologize one of his most distinctive stories, "The Emancipation of Evalina Jones," which ran in *The People's Monthly* in 1900. The story is about psychological spousal abuse. It charts a black woman's dawning realization of her oppression, and her successful efforts to strike back and to deter her husband from continuing his offensive behavior. Dunbar shows himself sensitive to the nuances of a topic that feminists discussed, but that few others took particularly seriously: women's inequality within the family, and the psychological abuse that husbands often inflicted on their wives with impunity. The poor, uneducated black characters in this story who speak in dialect are presented with empathy and respect. As Evalina emancipates herself from the slavery that her marriage has become and forges a relationship with her husband built on greater respect and equality, Dunbar shows himself to be as skilled a critic of male privilege as he is a critic on other occasions of white privilege.

As a short story writer, Dunbar may not have hit home runs as frequently as his contemporaries Mark Twain or Charles Waddell Chesnutt. But he was definitely playing in the same league. The variety of subjects, tones, styles, and strategies represented in these stories suggests an artist of surprising range and ambition well worth our attention today.

THE INGRATE

I

Mr. Leckler was a man of high principle. Indeed, he himself had admitted it at times to Mrs. Leckler. She was often called into counsel with him. He was one of those large souled creatures with a hunger for unlimited advice, upon which he never acted. Mrs. Leckler knew this, but like the good, patient little wife that she was, she went on paying her poor tribute of advice and admiration. Today her husband's mind was particularly troubled,—as usual, too, over a matter of principle. Mrs. Leckler came at his call.

"Mrs. Leckler," he said, "I am troubled in my mind. I—in fact, I am puzzled over a matter that involves either the maintaining or relinquishing of a principle."

"Well, Mr. Leckler?" said his wife, interrogatively.

"If I had been a scheming, calculating Yankee, I should have been rich now; but all my life I have been too generous and confiding. I have always let principle stand between me and my interests." Mr. Leckler took himself all too seriously to be conscious of his pun, and went on: "Now this is a matter in which my duty and my principles seem to conflict. It stands thus: Josh has been doing a piece of plastering for Mr. Eckley over in Lexington, and from what he says, I think that city rascal has misrepresented the amount of work to me and so cut down the pay for it. Now, of course, I should not care, the matter of a dollar or two being nothing to me; but it is a very different matter when we consider poor Josh." There was deep pathos in Mr. Leckler's tone. "You know Josh is anxious to buy his freedom, and I allow him a part of whatever he makes; so you see it's he that's affected. Every dollar that he is cheated out of cuts off just so much from his earnings, and puts further away his hope of emancipation."

If the thought occurred to Mrs. Leckler that, since Josh received only about one-tenth of what he earned, the advantage of just wages would be quite as much her husband's as the slave's, she did not betray it, but met the naive reasoning with the question, "But where does the conflict come in, Mr. Leckler?"

"Just here. If Josh knew how to read and write and cipher——"

"Mr. Leckler, are you crazy!"

"Listen to me, my dear, and give me the benefit of your judgment. This is a very momentous question. As I was about to say, if Josh knew these things, he could protect himself from cheating when his work is at too great a distance for me to look after it for him."

"But teaching a slave——"

"Yes, that's just what is against my principles. I know how public opinion and the law look at it. But my conscience rises up in rebellion every time I think of that poor black man being cheated out of his earnings. Really, Mrs. Leckler, I think I may trust to Josh's discretion, and secretly give him such instructions as will permit him to protect himself."

"Well, of course, it's just as you think best," said his wife.

"I knew you would agree with me," he returned. "It's such a comfort to take counsel with you, my dear!" And the generous man walked out to the veranda, very well satisfied with himself and his wife, and prospectively pleased with Josh. Once he murmured to himself, "I'll lay for Eckley next time."

Josh, the subject of Mr. Leckler's charitable solicitations, was the plantation plasterer. His master had given him his trade, in order that he might do whatever such work was needed about the place; but he became so proficient in his duties, having also no competition among the poor whites, that he had grown to be in great demand in the country thereabout. So Mr. Leckler found it profitable, instead of letting him do chores and field work in his idle time, to hire him out to neighboring farms and planters. Josh was a man of more than ordinary intelligence; and when he asked to be allowed to pay for himself by working over-time, his master readily agreed,—for it promised more work to be done, for which he could allow the slave just what he pleased. Of course, he knew now that when the black man began to cipher this state of affairs would be changed; but it would mean such an increase of profit from the outside, that he could afford to give up his own little peculations. Anyway, it would be many years before the slave could pay the two thousand dollars, which price he had set upon him. Should he approach that figure, Mr. Leckler felt it just possible that the market in slaves would take a sudden rise.

When Josh was told of his master's intention, his eyes gleamed with pleasure, and he went to his work with the zest of long hunger. He proved a remarkably apt pupil. He was indefatigable in doing the tasks assigned him. Even Mr. Leckler, who had great faith in his plasterer's ability, marveled at the speed which he had acquired the three R's. He did not know that on one of his many trips a free Negro had given Josh the rudimentary tools of learning, and that since the slave had been adding to his store of learning by poring over signs and every bit of print that he could spell out. Neither was Josh so indiscreet as to intimate to his benefactor that he had been anticipated in his good intentions.

It was in this way, working and learning, that a year passed away, and Mr. Leckler thought that his object had been accomplished. He could safely trust Josh to protect his own interests, and so he thought that it was quite time that his servant's education should cease.

"You know, Josh," he said, "I have already gone against my prin-ciples and against the law for your sake, and of course a man can't stretch his conscience too far, even to help another who's being cheated; but I reckon you can take care of yourself now."

"Oh, yes, suh, I reckon I kin," said Josh.

"And it wouldn't do for you to be seen with any books about you now."

"Oh, no, suh, su't'n'ty not." He didn't intend to be seen with any books about him.

It was just now that Mr. Leckler saw the good results of all he had done, and his heart was full of a great joy, for Eckley had been building some additions to his house, and sent for Josh to do the plastering for him. The owner admonished his slave, took him over a few examples to freshen his memory, and sent him forth with glee. When the job was done, there was a discrepancy of two dollars in what Mr. Eckley offered for it and the price which accrued from Josh's measurements. To the employer's surprise, the black man went over the figures with him and convinced him of the incorrectness of the payment—and the additional two dollars were turned over.

"Some o' Leckler's work," said Eckley, "teaching a nigger to cipher! Close-fisted old reprobate—I've a mind to have the law on him."

Mr. Leckler heard the story with great glee. "I laid for him that time—the old fox." But to Mrs. Leckler he said: "You see, my dear wife, my rashness in teaching Josh to figure for himself is vindicated. See what he has saved for himself."

"What did he save?" asked the little woman indiscreetly.

Her husband blushed and stammered for a moment, and then replied, "Well, of course, it was only twenty cents saved to him, but to a man buying his freedom every cent counts; and after all, it is not the amount, Mrs. Leckler, it's the principle of the thing."

"Yes," said the lady meekly.

II

Unto the body it is easy for the master to say, "Thus far shalt thou go, and no farther." Gyves, chains and fetters will enforce that command. But what master shall say unto the mind, "Here do I set the limit of your acquisition. Pass it not"? Who shall put gyves upon the intellect, or fetter the movement of thought? Joshua Leckler, as custom denominated him, had tasted of the forbidden fruit, and his appetite had grown by what it fed on. Night after night he crouched in his lonely cabin, by the blaze of a fat pine brand, poring over the few books that he had been able to secure and smuggle in. His fellow servants alternately laughed at him and wondered why he did not take a wife. But Joshua went on his way. He had no time for marrying or for love; other thoughts had taken possession of him. He was being swayed by ambitions other than the mere fathering of slaves for his master. To him his slavery was deep night. What wonder, then, that he should dream, and that through the ivory gate should come to him the forbidden vision of freedom? To own himself, to be master of his hands, feet, of his whole body—something would clutch at his heart as he thought of it; and the breath would come hard between his lips. But he met his master with an impassive face, always silent, always docile; and Mr. Leckler congratulated himself that so valuable and intelligent a slave meant discontent; but not so with Josh. Who more content than he? He remarked to his wife: "You see, my dear, this is what comes of treating even a nigger right."

Meanwhile the white hills of the North were beckoning to the chattel, and the north winds were whispering to him to be a chattel no longer. Often the eyes that looked away to where freedom lay were filled with a wistful longing that was tragic in its intensity, for they saw the hardships and the difficulties between the slave and his goal and, worst of all, an iniquitous law—liberty's compromise with bondage, that rose like a stone wall between him and hope—a law that degraded every free-thinking man to the level of a slave-catcher. There it loomed up before him, formidable, impregnable, insurmountable. He measured it in all its terribleness, and paused. But on the other side there was liberty; and one day when he was away at work, a voice came out of the woods and whispered to him "Courage!"—and on that night the shadows beckoned him as the white hills had done, and the forest called to him, "Follow."

"It seems to me that Josh might have been able to get home tonight," said Mr. Leckler, walking up and down his veranda; "but I reckon it's just possible that he got through too late to catch a train." In the morning he said: "Well, he's not here yet; he must have had to do some extra work. If he doesn't get here by evening, I'll run up there."

In the evening, he did take the train for Joshua's place of employment, where he learned that his slave had left the night before. But where could he have gone? That no one knew, and for the first time it dawned upon his master that Josh had run away. He raged; he fumed; but nothing could be done until morning, and all the time Leckler knew that the most valuable slave on his plantation was working his way toward the North and freedom. He did not go back home, but paced the floor all night long. In the early dawn he hurried out, and the hounds were put on the fugitive's track. After some nosing around they set off toward a stretch of woods. In a few minutes they came yelping back, pawing their noses and rubbing their heads against the ground. They had found the trail, but Josh had played the old slave trick of filling his tracks with cayenne pepper. The dogs were soothed, and taken deeper into the wood to find the trail. They soon took it up again, and dashed away with low bays. The scent led them directly to a little wayside station about six miles distant. Here it stopped. Burning with the chase, Mr. Leckler hastened to the station agent. Had he seen such a Negro? Yes, he had taken the northbound train two nights before.

"But why did you let him go without a pass?" almost screamed the owner.

"I didn't," replied the agent. "He had a written pass, signed James Leckler, and I let him go on it."

"Forged, forged!" yelled the master. "He wrote it himself."

"Humph!" said the agent, "how was I to know that? Our niggers round here don't know how to write."

Mr. Leckler suddenly bethought him to hold his peace. Josh was probably now in the arms of some Northern abolitionist, and there was nothing to be done now but advertise; and the disgusted master spread his notices broadcast before starting for home. As soon as he arrived at his house, he sought his wife and poured out his griefs to her.

"You see, Mrs. Leckler, this is what comes of my goodness of heart. I taught that nigger to read and write, so that he could protect himself—and look how he uses his knowledge. Oh, the ingrate, the ingrate! The very weapon which I give him to defend himself against others he turns upon me. Oh, it's awful, awful! I've always been too confiding. Here's the most valuable nigger on my plantation gone—gone, I tell you—and through my own kindness. It isn't his value, though, I'm thinking so much about. I could stand his loss, if it wasn't for the principle of the thing, the base ingratitude he has shown me. Oh, if I ever lay hands on him again!" Mr. Leckler closed his lips and clenched his fist with an eloquence that laughed at words.

Just at this time, in one of the underground railway stations, six miles north of the Ohio, an old Quaker was saying to Josh: "Lie still—thee'll be perfectly safe there. Here comes John Trader, our local slave-catcher, but I will parley with him and send him away. Thee need not fear. None of thy brethren who have come to us have ever been taken back to bondage—Good-evening, Friend Trader!" and Josh heard the old Quaker's smooth voice roll on, while he lay back half smothering in a bag, among other bags of corn and potatoes.

It was after ten o'clock that night when he was thrown carelessly into a wagon and driven away to the next station, twenty-five miles to the northward. And by such stages, hiding by day and traveling by night, helped by a few of his own people who were blessed with freedom, and always by the good Quakers wherever found, he made his way into Canada. And on one never-to-be-forgotten morning he stood up, straightened himself, breathed God's blessed air, and knew himself free!

III

To Joshua Leckler this life in Canada was all new and strange. It was a new thing for him to feel himself a man and to have his manhood recognized by the whites with whom he came into free contact. It was new, too, this receiving the full measure of his worth in work. He went to his labor with a zest that he had never known before, and he took a pleasure in the very weariness it brought him. Ever and anon there came to his ears the cries of his brethren in the South. Frequently he met fugitives who, like himself, had escaped from bondage; and the harrowing tales that they told him made him burn to do something for those whom he had left behind him. But these fugitives and the papers he read told him other things. They said that the spirit of freedom was working in the United States, and already men were speaking out boldly in behalf of the manumission of the slaves; already there was a growing army behind that noble vanguard, Sumner, Phillips, Douglass, Garrison. He heard the names of Lucretia Mott and Harriet Beecher Stowe, and his heart swelled, for on the dim horizon he saw the first faint streaks of dawn.

So the years passed. Then from the surcharged clouds a flash of lightning broke, and there was the thunder of cannon and the rain of lead over the land. From his home in the North he watched the storm as it raged and wavered, now threatening the North with its awful power, now hanging dire and dreadful over the South. Then suddenly from out the fray came a voice like the trumpet tone of God to him: "Thou and thy brothers are free!" Free, free, with the freedom not cherished by the few alone, but for all that had been bound. Free, with the freedom not torn from the secret night, but open to the light of heaven.

When the first call for colored soldiers came, Joshua Leckler hastened down to Boston, and enrolled himself among those who were willing to fight to maintain their freedom. On account of his ability to read and write and his general intelligence, he was soon made an orderly sergeant. His regiment had already taken part in an engagement before the public roster of this band of Uncle Sam's niggers, as they were called, fell into Mr. Leckler's hands. He ran his eye down the column of names.

It stopped at that of Joshua Leckler, Sergeant, Company F. He handed the paper to Mrs. Leckler with his finger on the place:

"Mrs. Leckler," he said, "this is nothing less than a judgment on me for teaching a nigger to read and write. I disobeyed the law of my state and, as a result, not only lost my nigger, but furnished the Yankees with a smart officer to help them fight the South. Mrs. Leckler, I have sinned—and been punished. But I am content, Mrs. Leckler; it all came through my kindness of heart—and your mistaken advice. But, oh, that ingrate, that ingrate!"

MR. CORNELIUS JOHNSON, OFFICE-SEEKER

It was a beautiful day in balmy May and the sun shone pleasantly on Mr. Cornelius Johnson's very spruce Prince Albert suit of gray as he alighted from the train in Washington. He cast his eyes about him, and then gave a sigh of relief and satisfaction as he took his bag from the porter and started for the gate. As he went along, he looked with splendid complacency upon the less fortunate mortals who were streaming out of the day coaches. It was a Pullman sleeper on which he had come in. Out on the pavement he hailed a cab, and giving the driver the address of a hotel, stepped in and was rolled away. Be it said that he had cautiously inquired about the hotel first and found that he could be accommodated there.

As he leaned back in the vehicle and allowed his eyes to roam over the streets, there was an air of distinct prosperity about him. It was in evidence from the tips of his ample patent-leather shoes to the crown of the soft felt hat that sat rakishly upon his head. His entrance into Washington had been long premeditated, and he had got himself up accordingly.

It was not such an imposing structure as he had fondly imagined, before which the cab stopped and set Mr. Johnson down. But then he reflected that it was about the only house where he could find accommodation at all, and he was content. In Alabama one learns to be philosophical. It is good to be philosophical in a place where the proprietor of a

café fumbles vaguely around in the region of his hip pocket and insinu-
ates that he doesn't want one's custom. But the visitor's ardor was not
cooled for all that. He signed the register with a flourish, and bestowed a
liberal fee upon the shabby boy who carried his bag to his room.

"Look here, boy," he said, "I am expecting some callers soon. If they
come, just send them right up to my room. You take good care of me
and look sharp when I ring and you'll not lose anything."

Mr. Cornelius Johnson always spoke in a large and important tone.
He said the simplest thing with an air so impressive as to give it the
character of a pronouncement. Indeed, his voice naturally was round,
mellifluous and persuasive. He carried himself always as if he were
passing under his own triumphal arch. Perhaps, more than anything
else, it was these qualities of speech and bearing that had made him
invaluable on the stump in the recent campaign in Alabama. Whatever
it was that held the secret of his power, the man and principles for
which he had labored triumphed, and he had come to Washington to
reap his reward. He had been assured that his services would not be
forgotten, and it was no intention of his that they should be.

After a while he left his room and went out, returning later with
several gentlemen from the South and a Washington man. There is
some freemasonry among these office-seekers in Washington that
throws them inevitably together. The men with whom he returned
were such characters as the press would designate as "old wheel-
horses" or "pillars of the party." They all adjourned to the bar, where
they had something at their host's expense. Then they repaired to his
room, whence for the ensuing two hours the bell and the bellboy were
kept briskly going.

The gentleman from Alabama was in his glory. His gestures as he
held forth were those of a gracious and condescending prince. It was
his first visit to the city, and he said to the Washington man: "I tell you,
sir, you've got a mighty fine town here. Of course, there's no opportunity for anything like local pride, because it's the outsiders, or the
whole country, rather, that makes it what it is, but that's nothing. It's a
fine town, and I'm right sorry that I can't stay longer."

"How long do you expect to be with us, Professor?" inquired Col.
Mason, the horse who had bent his force to the party wheel in the
Georgia ruts.

"Oh, about ten days, I reckon, at the furthest. I want to spend some time sightseeing. I'll drop in on the Congressman from my district to-morrow, and call a little later on the President."

"Uh, huh!" said Col. Mason. He had been in the city for some time.

"Yes, sir, I want to get through with my little matter and get back home. I'm not asking for much, and I don't anticipate any trouble in securing what I desire. You see, it's just like this, there's no way for them to refuse us. And if any one deserves the good things at the hands of the administration, who more than we old campaigners, who have been helping the party through its fights from the time that we had our first votes?"

"Who, indeed?" said the Washington man.

"I tell you, gentlemen, the administration is no fool. It knows that we hold the colored vote down there in our vest pockets and it ain't going to turn us down."

"No, of course not, but sometimes there are delays——"

"Delays, to be sure, where a man doesn't know how to go about the matter. The thing to do, is to go right to the center of authority at once. Don't you see?"

"Certainly, certainly," chorused the other gentlemen.

Before going, the Washington man suggested that the newcomer join them that evening and see something of society at the capital. "You know," he said, "that outside of New Orleans, Washington is the only town in the country that has any colored society to speak of, and I feel that you distinguished men from different sections of the country owe it to our people that they should be allowed to see you. It would be an inspiration to them."

So the matter was settled, and promptly at 8:30 o'clock Mr. Cornelius Johnson joined his friends at the door of his hotel. The gray Prince Albert was scrupulously buttoned about his form, and a shiny top hat replaced the felt of the afternoon. Thus clad, he went forth into society, where he need be followed only long enough to note the magnificence of his manners and the enthusiasm of his reception when he was introduced as Prof. Cornelius Johnson, of Alabama, in a tone which insinuated that he was the only really great man his state had produced.

It might also be stated as an effect of this excursion into Vanity Fair, that when he woke the next morning he was in some doubt as to whether he should visit his Congressman or send for that individual to call upon him. He had felt the subtle flattery of attention from that section of colored society which imitates—only imitates, it is true, but better than any other, copies—the kindnesses and cruelties, the niceties and deceits, of its white prototype. And for the time, like a man in a fog, he had lost his sense of proportion and perspective. But habit finally triumphed, and he called upon the Congressman, only to be met by an under-secretary who told him that his superior was too busy to see him that morning.

"But——"

"Too busy," repeated the secretary.

Mr. Johnson drew himself up and said: "Tell Congressman Barker that Mr. Johnson, Mr. Cornelius Johnson, of Alabama, desires to see him. I think he will see me."

"Well, I can take your message," said the clerk, doggedly, "but I tell you now it won't do you any good. He won't see any one."

But, in a few moments an inner door opened, and the young man came out followed by the desired one. Mr. Johnson couldn't resist the temptation to let his eyes rest on the underling in a momentary glance of triumph as Congressman Barker hurried up to him, saying: "Why, why, Cornelius, how'do? Ah, you came about that little matter, didn't you? Well, well, I haven't forgotten you; I haven't forgotten you."

The colored man opened his mouth to speak, but the other checked him and went on: "I'm sorry, but I'm in a great hurry now. I'm compelled to leave town today, much against my will, but I shall be back in a week; come around and see me then. Always glad to see you, you know. Sorry I'm so busy now; good morning, good morning."

Mr. Johnson allowed himself to be guided politely, but decidedly, to the door. The triumph died out of his face as the reluctant good morning fell from his lips. As he walked away, he tried to look upon the matter philosophically. He tried to reason with himself—to prove to his own consciousness that the Congressman was very busy and could not give the time that morning. He wanted to make himself believe that he had not been slighted or treated with scant ceremony. But, try as he would, he continued to feel an obstinate, nasty sting that would not let him rest, nor forget his reception. His pride was hurt. The thought came to him to go at once to the President, but he had experience enough to know that such a visit would be vain until he had seen the dispenser of patronage for his district. Thus, there was nothing for him to do but to wait the necessary week. A whole week! His brow knitted as he thought of it.

In the course of these cogitations, his walk brought him to his hotel, where he found his friends of the night before awaiting him. He tried to put on a cheerful face. But his disappointment and humiliation showed through his smile, as the hollows and bones through the skin of a cadaver.

"Well, what luck?" asked Col. Mason, cheerfully.

"Are we to congratulate you?" put in Mr. Perry.

"Not yet, not yet, gentlemen. I have not seen the President yet. The fact is—ahem—my Congressman is out of town."

He was not used to evasions of this kind, and he stammered slightly and his yellow face turned brick-red with shame.

"It is most annoying," he went on, "most annoying. Mr. Barker won't be back for a week, and I don't want to call on the President until I have had a talk with him."

"Certainly not," said Col. Mason, blandly. "There will be delays." This was not his first pilgrimage to Mecca.

Mr. Johnson looked at him gratefully. "Oh, yes; of course, delays," he assented; "most natural. Have something."

At the end of the appointed time, the office-seeker went again to see the Congressman. This time he was admitted without question, and got the chance to state his wants. But somehow, there seemed to be innumerable obstacles in the way. There were certain other men whose wishes had to be consulted; the leader of one of the party factions, who, for the sake of harmony, had to be appeased. Of course, Mr. Johnson's worth was fully recognized, and he would be rewarded according to his deserts. His interests would be looked after. He should drop in again in a day or two. It took time, of course, it took time.

Mr. Johnson left the office unnerved by his disappointment. He had thought it would be easy to come up to Washington, claim and get what he wanted, and, after a glance at the town, hurry back to his home and his honors. It had all seemed so easy—before election; but now——

A vague doubt began to creep into his mind that turned him sick at heart. He knew how they had treated Davis, of Louisiana. He had heard how they had once kept Brotherton, of Texas—a man who had spent all his life in the service of his party—waiting clear through a whole administration, at the end of which the opposite party had come into power. All the stories of disappointment and disaster that he had ever heard came back to him, and he began to wonder if some one of these things was going to happen to him.

Every other day for the next two weeks, he called upon Barker, but always with the same result. Nothing was clear yet, until one day the bland legislator told him that considerations of expediency had compelled them to give the place he was asking for to another man.

"But what am I to do?" asked the helpless man.

"Oh, you just bide your time. I'll look out for you. Never fear."

Until now, Johnson had ignored the gentle hints of his friend, Col. Mason, about a boardinghouse being more convenient than a hotel. Now, he asked him if there was a room vacant where he was staying, and finding that there was, he had his things moved thither at once. He felt the change keenly, and although no one really paid any attention to it, he believed that all Washington must have seen it, and hailed it as the first step in his degradation.

For a while the two together made occasional excursions to a glittering palace down the street, but when the money had grown lower and lower Col. Mason had the knack of bringing "a little something" to their rooms without a loss of dignity. In fact, it was in these hours with the old man, over a pipe and a bit of something, that Johnson was most nearly cheerful. Hitch after hitch had occurred in his plans, and day after day he had come home unsuccessful and discouraged. The crowning disappointment, though, came when, after a long session that lasted even up into the hot days of summer, Congress adjourned and his one hope went away. Johnson saw him just before his departure, and listened ruefully as he said: "I tell you, Cornelius, now, you'd better go on home, get back to your business and come again next year. The clouds of battle will be somewhat dispelled by then and we can see clearer what to do. It was too early this year. We were too near the fight still, and there were party wounds to be bound up and little factional sores that had to be healed. But next year, Cornelius, next year we'll see what we can do for you."

His constituent did not tell him that even if his pride would let him go back home a disappointed applicant, he had not the means wherewith to go. He did not tell him that he was trying to keep up appearances and hide the truth from his wife, who, with their two children, waited and hoped for him at home.

When he went home that night, Col. Mason saw instantly that things had gone wrong with him. But here the tact and delicacy of the old politician came uppermost and, without trying to draw his story from him—for he had already divined the situation too well—he sat for a long time telling the younger man stories of the ups and downs of men whom he had known in his long and active life.

They were stories of hardship, deprivation and discouragement. But the old man told them ever with the touch of cheeriness and the note of humor that took away the ghastly hopelessness of some of the pictures. He told them with such feeling and sympathy that Johnson was moved to frankness and told him his own pitiful tale.

Now that he had some one to whom he could open his heart, Johnson himself was no less willing to look the matter in the face, and even during the long summer days, when he had begun to live upon his wardrobe, piece by piece, he still kept up; although some of his pomposity went, along with the Prince Albert coat and the shiny hat. He now wore a shiny coat and less showy head gear. For a couple of weeks, too, he disappeared, and as he returned with some money, it was fair to presume that he had been at work somewhere, but he could not stay away from the city long.

It was nearing the middle of autumn when Col. Mason came home to their rooms one day to find his colleague more disheartened and depressed than he had ever seen him before. He was lying with his head upon his folded arm, and when he looked up there were traces of tears upon his face.

"Why, why, what's the matter now?" asked the old man. "No bad news, I hope."

"Nothing worse than I should have expected," was the choking answer. "It's a letter from my wife. She's sick and one of the babies is down, but"—his voice broke—"she tells me to stay and fight it out. My God, Mason, I could stand it if she whined or accused me or begged me to come home, but her patient, long-suffering bravery breaks me all up."

Col. Mason stood up and folded his arms across his big chest. "She's a brave little woman," he said, gravely. "I wish her husband was as brave a man." Johnson raised his head and arms from the table where they were sprawled, as the old man went on: "The hard conditions of life in our race have taught our women a patience and fortitude which the women of no other race have ever displayed. They have taught the men less, and I am sorry, very sorry. The thing, that as much as anything else, made the blacks such excellent soldiers in the civil war was their patient endurance of hardship. The softer education of more prosperous days seems to have weakened this quality. The man who quails or weakens in this fight of ours against adverse circumstances would have quailed before—no, he would have run from an enemy on the field."

"Why, Mason, your mood inspires me. I feel as if I could go forth to battle cheerfully." For the moment, Johnson's old pomposity had returned to him, but in the next, a wave of despondency bore it down. "But that's just it; a body feels as if he could fight if he only had something to fight. But here you strike out and hit—nothing. It's only a contest with time. It's waiting—waiting—waiting!"

"In this case, waiting is fighting."

"Well, even that granted, it matters not how grand his cause, the soldier needs his rations."

"Forage," shot forth the answer like a command.

"Ah, Mason, that's well enough in good country; but the army of office seekers has devastated Washington. It has left a track as bare as lay behind Sherman's troopers." Johnson rose more cheerfully. "I'm going to the telegraph office," he said as he went out.

A few days after this, he was again in the best of spirits, for there was money in his pocket.

"What have you been doing?" asked Mr. Toliver.

His friend laughed like a boy. "Something very imprudent, I'm sure you will say. I've mortgaged my little place down home. It did not bring much, but I had to have money for the wife and the children, and to keep me until Congress assembles; then I believe that everything will be all right."

Col. Mason's brow clouded and he sighed.

On the reassembling of the two Houses, Congressman Barker was one of the first men in his seat. Mr. Cornelius Johnson went to see him soon.

"What, you here already, Cornelius?" asked the legislator.

"I haven't been away," was the answer.

"Well, you've got the hang-on, and that's what an office-seeker needs. Well, I'll attend to your matter among the very first. I'll visit the President in a day or two."

The listener's heart throbbed hard. After all his waiting, triumph was his at last.

He went home walking on air, and Col. Mason rejoiced with him. In a few days came word from Barker: "Your appointment was sent in today. I'll rush it through on the other side. Come up tomorrow afternoon."

Cornelius and Mr. Toliver hugged each other.

"It came just in time," said the younger man; "the last of my money was about gone, and I should have had to begin paying off that mortgage with no prospect of ever doing it."

The two had suffered together, and it was fitting that they should be together to receive the news of the long-desired happiness; so arm in arm they sauntered down to the Congressman's office about five o'clock the next afternoon. In honor of the occasion, Mr. Johnson had spent his last dollar in redeeming the gray Prince Albert and the shiny hat. A smile flashed across Barker's face as he noted the change.

"Well, Cornelius," he said, "I'm glad to see you still prosperous-looking, for there were some alleged irregularities in your methods down in Alabama, and the Senate has refused to confirm you. I did all I could for you, but——"

The rest of the sentence was lost, as Col. Mason's arms received his friend's fainting form.

"Poor devil!" said the Congressman. "I should have broken it more gently."

Somehow Col. Mason got him home and to bed, where for nine weeks he lay wasting under a complete nervous give-down. The little wife and the children came up to nurse him, and the woman's ready industry helped him to such creature comforts as his sickness demanded. Never once did she murmur; never once did her faith in him waver. And when he was well enough to be moved back, it was money that she had earned, increased by what Col. Mason, in his generosity of spirit, took from his own narrow means, that paid their second-class fare back to the South.

During the fever fits of his illness, the wasted politician first begged piteously that they would not send him home unplaced, and then he would break out in the most extravagant and pompous boasts about his position, his Congressman and his influence. When he came to himself, he was silent, morose, and bitter. Only once did he melt. It was when he held Col. Mason's hand and bade him good-bye. Then the tears came into his eyes, and what he would have said was lost among his broken words.

As he stood upon the platform of the car as it moved out, and gazed at the white dome and feathery spires of the city, growing into gray indefiniteness, he ground his teeth, and raising his spent hand, shook it at the receding view. "Damn you! damn you!" he cried. "Damn your deceit, your fair cruelties; damn you, you hard, white liar!"

NELSE HATTON'S VENGEANCE

It was at the close of a summer day, and the sun was sinking dimly red over the hills of the little Ohio town which, for convenience, let us call Dexter.

The people had eaten their suppers, and the male portion of the families had come out in front of their houses to smoke and rest or read the evening paper. Those who had porches drew their rockers out on them, and sat with their feet on the railing. Others took their more humble positions on the front steps, while still others, whose houses were flush with the street, went even so far as to bring their chairs out upon the sidewalk, and over all there was an air of calmness and repose save when a glance through the open doors revealed the housewives busy at their evening dishes, or the blithe voices of the children playing in the street told that little Sally Waters was a-sitting in a saucer or asserted with doubtful veracity that London Bridge was falling down. Here and there a belated fisherman came straggling up the street that led from the river, every now and then holding up his string of slimy, wiggling catfish in answer to the query "Wha' 'd you ketch?"

To one who knew the generous and unprejudiced spirit of the Dexterites, it was no matter of wonder that one of their soundest and most highly respected citizens was a colored man, and that his home should nestle unrebuked among the homes of his white neighbors.

Nelse Hatton had won the love and respect of his fellow-citizens by the straightforward honesty of his conduct and the warmth of his heart. Everybody knew him. He had been doing chores about Dexter,—cutting grass in summer, cleaning and laying carpets in the spring and fall, and tending furnaces in the winter,—since the time when, a newly emancipated man, he had passed over from Kentucky into Ohio. Since then through thrift he had attained quite a competence, and, as he himself expressed it, "owned some little propity." He was one among the number who had risen to the dignity of a porch; and on this evening he was sitting thereon, laboriously spelling out the sentences in the *Evening News*—his reading was a *post-bellum* accomplishment—when the oldest of his three children, Theodore, a boy of twelve, interrupted him with the intelligence that there was an "old straggler at the back door."

After admonishing the hope of his years as to the impropriety of applying such a term to an unfortunate, the father rose and sought the place where the "straggler" awaited him.

Nelse's sympathetic heart throbbed with pity at the sight that met his eye. The "straggler," a "thing of shreds and patches," was a man about his own age, nearing fifty; but what a contrast he was to the well-preserved, well-clothed black man! His gray hair straggled carelessly about his sunken temples, and the face beneath it was thin and emaciated. The hands that pulled at the fringe of the ragged coat were small and bony. But both the face and the hands were clean, and there was an open look in the bold, dark eyes.

In strong contrast, too, with his appearance was the firm, well-modulated voice, somewhat roughened by exposure, in which he said, "I am very hungry; will you give me something to eat?" It was a voice that might have spoken with authority. There was none of the beggar's whine in it. It was clear and straightforward; and the man spoke the simple sentence almost as if it had been a protest against his sad condition.

"Jes' set down on the step an' git cool," answered Nelse, "an' I'll have something put on the table."

The stranger silently did as he was bidden, and his host turned into the house.

Eliza Hatton had been quietly watching the proceedings, and as her husband entered the kitchen she said, "Look a-here, Nelse, you shorely ain't a-goin' to have that tramp in the kitchen a-settin' up to the table?"

"Why, of course," said Nelse; "he's human, ain't he?"

"That don't make no difference. I bet none of these white folks round here would do it."

"That ain't none of my business," answered her husband. "I believe in every person doin' their own duty. Put somethin' down on the table; the man's hungry. An' don't never git stuck up, 'Lizy; you don't know what our children have got to come to."

Nelse Hatton was a man of few words; but there was a positive manner about him at times that admitted of neither argument nor resistance.

His wife did as she was bidden, and then swept out in the majesty of wounded dignity, as the tramp was ushered in and seated before the table whose immaculate white cloth she had been prudent enough to change for a red one.

The man ate as if he were hungry, but always as if he were a hungry gentleman. There was something in his manner that impressed Nelse that he was not feeding a common tramp as he sat and looked at his visitor in polite curiosity. After a somewhat continued silence he addressed the man: "Why don't you go to your own people when you're hungry instead of coming to us colored folks?"

There was no reproof in his tone, only inquiry.

The stranger's eyes flashed suddenly.

"Go to them up here?" he said; "never. They would give me my supper with their hypocritical patronage and put it down to charity. You give me something to eat as a favor. Your gift proceeds from disinterested kindness; they would throw me a bone because they thought it would weigh something in the balance against their sins. To you I am an unfortunate man; to them I am a tramp."

The stranger had spoken with much heat and no hesitation; but his ardor did not take the form of offense at Nelse's question. He seemed perfectly to comprehend the motive which actuated it.

Nelse had listened to him with close attention, and at the end of his harangue he said, "You hadn't ought to be so hard on your own people; they mean well enough."

"My own people!" the stranger flashed back. "My people are the people of the South,—the people who have in their veins the warm, generous blood of Dixie!"

"I don't see what you stay in the North fur ef you don't like the people."

"I am not staying; I'm getting away from it as fast as I can. I only came because I thought, like a lot of other poor fools, that the North had destroyed my fortunes and it might restore them; but five years of fruitless struggle in different places out of Dixie have shown me that it isn't the place for a man with blood in his veins. I thought that I was reconstructed; but I'm not. My State didn't need it, but I did."

"Where're you from?"

"Kentucky; and that's where I'm bound for now. I want to get back where people have hearts and sympathies."

The colored man was silent. After a while he said, and his voice was tremulous as he thought of the past, "I'm from Kintucky, myself."

"I knew that you were from some place in the South. There's no mistaking our people, black or white, wherever you meet them. Kentucky's a great State, sir. She didn't secede; but there were lots of her sons on the other side. I was; and I did my duty as clear as I could see it."

"That's all any man kin do," said Nelse; "an' I ain't a-blamin' you. I lived with as good people as ever was. I know they wouldn't 'a' done nothin' wrong ef they'd 'a' knowed it; an' they was on the other side."

"You've been a slave, then?"

"Oh, yes, I was born a slave; but the War freed me."

"I reckon you wouldn't think that my folks ever owned slaves; but they did. Everybody was good to them except me, and I was young and liked to show my authority. I had a little black boy that I used to cuff around a good deal, altho' he was near to me as a brother. But sometimes he would turn on me and give me the trouncing that I deserved. He would have been skinned for it if my father had found it out; but I was always too much ashamed of being thrashed to tell."

The speaker laughed, and Nelse joined him. "Bless my soul!" he said, "ef that ain't jes' the way it was with me an' my Mas' Tom—"

"Mas' Tom!" cried the stranger; "man, what's your name?"

"Nelse Hatton," replied the Negro.

"Heavens, Nelse! I'm your young Mas' Tom. I'm Tom Hatton; don't you know me, boy?"

"You can't be—you can't be!" exclaimed the Negro.

"I am, I tell you. Don't you remember the scar I got on my head from falling off old Baldy's back? Here it is. Can't you see?" cried the stranger, lifting the long hair away from one side of his brow. "Doesn't this convince you?"

"It's you—it's you; 'tain't nobody else but Mas' Tom!" and the ex-slave and his former master rushed joyously into each other's arms.

There was no distinction of color or condition there. There was no thought of superiority on the one hand, or feeling of inferiority on the other. They were simply two loving friends who had been long parted and had met again.

After a while the Negro said, "I'm sure the Lord must 'a' sent you right here to this house, so's you wouldn't be eatin' off o' none o' these poor white people 'round here."

"I reckon you're religious now, Nelse; but I see it ain't changed your feeling toward poor white people."

"I don't know about that. I used to be purty bad about 'em."

"Indeed you did. Do you remember the time we stoned the house of old Nat, the white wood-sawyer?"

"Well, I reckon I do! Wasn't we awful, them days?" said Nelse, with forced contrition, but with something almost like a chuckle in his voice.

And yet there was a great struggle going on in the mind of this black man. Thirty years of freedom and the advantages of a Northern state made his whole soul revolt at the word "master." But that fine feeling, that tender sympathy, which is natural to the real Negro, made him hesitate to make the poor wreck of former glory conscious of his changed estate by using a different appellation. His warm sympathies conquered.

"I want you to see my wife and boys, Mas' Tom," he said, as he passed out of the room.

Eliza Hatton sat in her neatly appointed little front room, swelling with impotent rage.

If this story were chronicling the doings of some fanciful Negro, or some really rude plantation hand, it might be said that the "front room was filled with a conglomeration of cheap but pretentious furniture, and the walls covered with gaudy prints"—this seems to be the usual phrase. But in it the chronicler too often forgets how many Negroes were house-servants, and from close contact with their masters' families imbibed aristocratic notions and quiet but elegant tastes.

This front room was very quiet in its appointments. Everything in it was subdued except—Mrs. Hatton. She was rocking back and forth in a light little rocker that screeched the indignation she could not express. She did not deign to look at Nelse as he came into the room; but an acceleration of speed on the part of the rocker showed that his presence was known.

Her husband's enthusiasm suddenly died out as he looked at her; but he put on a brave face as he said,—

"'Lizy, I bet a cent you can't guess who that pore man in there is."

The rocker suddenly stopped its violent motion with an equally violent jerk, as the angry woman turned upon her husband.

"No, I can't guess," she cried; "an' I don't want to. It's enough to be settin' an on'ry ol' tramp down to my clean table, without havin' me spend my time guessin' who he is."

"But look a-here, 'Lizy, this is all different; an' you don't understand."

"Don't care how different it is, I do' want to understand."

"You'll be mighty su'prised, I tell you."

"I 'low I will; I'm su'prised already at you puttin' yourself on a level with tramps." This with fine scorn.

"Be careful, 'Lizy, be careful; you don't know who a tramp may turn out to be."

"That ol' humbug in there has been tellin' you some big tale, an' you ain't got no more sense 'an to believe it; I 'spect he's crammin' his pockets full of my things now. Ef you don't care, I do."

The woman rose and started toward the door, but her husband stopped her. "You mustn't go out there that way," he said. "I want you to go out, you an' the children; but I want you to go right—that man is the son of my ol' master, my young Mas' Tom, as I used to call him."

She fell back suddenly and stared at him with wide-open eyes.

"Your master!"

"Yes, it's young Mas' Tom Hatton."

"An' you want me an' the children to see him, do you?"

"Why, yes, I thought—"

"Humph! that's the slave in you yet," she interrupted. "I thought thirty years had made you free! Ain't that the man you told me used to knock you 'round so?"

"Yes, 'Lizy; but—"

"Ain't he the one that made you haul him in the wheelbar', an' whipped you because you couldn't go fast enough?"

"Yes, yes; but that—"

"Ain't he the one that lef' that scar there?" she cried, with a sudden motion of her hand toward his neck.

"Yes," said Nelse, very quietly; but he put his hand up and felt the long, cruel scar that the lash of a whip had left, and a hard light came into his eyes.

His wife went on: "An' you want to take me an' the children in to see that man? No!" The word came with almost a snarl. "Me an' my children are free born, an', ef I kin help it, they sha'n't never look at the man that laid the lash to their father's back! Shame on you, Nelse, shame on you, to want your children, that you're trying to raise independent,—to want 'em to see the man that you had to call 'master'!"

The man's lips quivered, and his hand opened and shut with a convulsive motion; but he said nothing.

"What did you tell me?" she asked. "Didn't you say that if you ever met him again in this world you'd—"

"Kill him!" burst forth the man; and all the old, gentle look had gone out of his face, and there was nothing but fierceness and bitterness there, as his mind went back to his many wrongs.

"Go on away from the house, 'Lizy," he said hoarsely; "if anything happens, I do' want you an' the children around."

"I do' want you to kill him, Nelse, so you'll git into trouble; but jes' give him one good whippin' for those he used to give you."

"Go on away from the house"; and the man's lips were tightly closed. She threw a thin shawl over her head and went out.

As soon as she had gone Nelse's intense feeling got the better of him, and, falling down with his face in a chair, he cried, in the language which the Sunday sermons had taught him, "Lord, Lord, thou hast delivered mine enemy into my hands!"

But it was not a prayer; it was rather a cry of anger and anguish from an overburdened heart. He rose, with the same hard gleam in his eyes, and went back toward the kitchen. One hand was tightly clenched till the muscles and veins stood out like cords, and with the other he unconsciously fingered the lash's scar.

"Couldn't find your folks, eh, Nelse?" said the white Hatton.

"No," growled Nelse; and continued hurriedly, "Do you remember that scar?"

"Well enough—well enough," answered the other, sadly; "and it must have hurt you, Nelse."

"Hurt me! yes," cried the Negro.

"Ay," said Tom Hatton, as he rose and put his hand softly on the black scar; "and it has hurt me many a day since, though time and time again I have suffered pains that were as cruel as this must have been to you. Think of it, Nelse; there have been times when I, a Hatton, have asked bread of the very people whom a few years ago I scorned. Since the War everything has gone against me. You do not know how I have suffered. For thirty years life has been a curse to me; but I am going back to Kentucky now, and when I get there I'll lay it down without a regret."

All the anger had melted from the Negro's face, and there were tears in his eyes as he cried, "You sha'n't do it, Mas' Tom,—you sha'n't do it."

His destructive instinct had turned to one of preservation.

"But, Nelse, I have no further hopes," said the dejected man.

"You have, and you shall have. You're goin' back to Kintucky, an' you're goin' back a gentleman. I kin he'p you, an' I will; you're welcome to the last I have."

"God bless you, Nelse—"

"Mas' Tom, you used to be jes' about my size, but you're slimmer now; but—but I hope you won't be mad ef I ak you to put on a suit o' mine. It's put' nigh brand-new, an'—"

"Nelse, I can't do it! Is this the way you pay me for the blows—"

"Heish your mouth; ef you don't I'll slap you down!" Nelse said it with mock solemnity, but there was an ominous quiver about his lips.

"Come in this room, suh"; and the master obeyed. He came out arrayed in Nelse's best and newest suit. The colored man went to a drawer, over which he bent laboriously. Then he turned and said: "This'll pay your passage to Kentucky, an' leave somethin' in your pocket besides. Go home, Mas' Tom,—go home!"

"Nelse, I can't do it; this is too much!"

"Doggone my cats, ef you don't go on—"

The white man stood bowed for a moment; then, straightening up, he threw his head back. "I'll take it, Nelse; but you shall have every cent back, even if I have to sell my body to a medical college and use a gun to deliver the goods! Good-bye, Nelse, God bless you! good-bye."

"Good-bye, Mas' Tom, but don't talk that way; go home. The South is changed, an' you'll find somethin' to suit you. Go home—go home; an' ef there's any of the folks a-livin', give 'em my love, Mas' Tom—give 'em my love—good-bye—good-bye!"

The Negro leaned over the proffered hand, and his tears dropped upon it. His master passed out, and he sat with his head bowed in his hands.

After a long while Eliza came creeping in.

"Wha' 'd you do to him, Nelse—wha' 'd you do to him?" There was no answer. "Lawd, I hope you ain't killed him," she said, looking fearfully around. "I don't see no blood."

"I ain't killed him," said Nelse. "I sent him home—back to the ol' place."

"You sent him home! how'd you send him, huh?"

"I give him my Sunday suit and that money—don't git mad, 'Lizy, don't git mad—that money I was savin' for your cloak. I couldn't help it, to save my life. He's goin' back home among my people, an' I sent 'em my love. Don't git mad an' I'll git you a cloak anyhow."

"Pleggone the cloak!" said Mrs. Hatton, suddenly, all the woman in her rising in her eyes. "I was so 'fraid you'd take my advice an' do somethin' wrong. Ef you're happy, Nelse, I am too. I don't grudge your master nothin'—the ol' devil! But you're jes' a good-natured, big-hearted, weak-headed ol' fool!" And she took his head in her arms.

Great tears rolled down the man's cheeks, and he said: "Bless God, 'Lizy, I feel as good as a young convert."

THE ORDEAL AT MT. HOPE

"And this is Mt. Hope," said the Rev. Howard Dokesbury to himself as he descended, bag in hand, from the smoky, dingy coach, or part of a coach, which was assigned to his people, and stepped upon the rotten planks of the station platform. The car he had just left was not a palace, nor had his reception by his fellow-passengers or his intercourse with them been of such cordial nature as to endear them to him. But he watched the choky little engine with its three black cars wind out of sight with a look as regretful as if he were witnessing the departure of his dearest friend. Then he turned his attention again to his surroundings, and a sigh welled up from his heart. "And this is Mt. Hope," he repeated. A note in his voice indicated that he fully appreciated the spirit of keen irony in which the place had been named.

The color scheme of the picture that met his eyes was in dingy blacks and grays. The building that held the ticket, telegraph, and train despatchers' offices was a miserably old ramshackle affair, standing well in the foreground of this scene of gloom and desolation. Its windows were so coated with smoke and grime that they seemed to have been painted over in order to secure secrecy within. Here and there a lazy cur lay drowsily snapping at the flies, and at the end of the station, perched on boxes or leaning against the wall, making a living picture of equal laziness, stood a group of idle Negroes exchanging rude badinage with their white counterparts across the street.

After a while this bantering interchange would grow more keen and personal, a free-for-all friendly fight would follow, and the newspaper correspondent in that section would write it up as a "race war." But this had not happened yet that day.

"This is Mt. Hope," repeated the new-comer; "this is the field of my labors."

Rev. Howard Dokesbury, as may already have been inferred, was a Negro,—there could be no mistake about that. The deep dark brown of his skin, the rich overfullness of his lips, and the close curl of his short black hair were evidences that admitted of no argument. He was a finely proportioned, stalwart-looking man, with a general air of self-possession and self-sufficiency in his manner. There was firmness in the set of his lips. A reader of character would have said of him, "Here is a man of solid judgment, careful in deliberation, prompt in execution, and decisive."

It was the perception in him of these very qualities which had prompted the authorities of the little college where he had taken his degree and received his theological training, to urge him to go among his people at the South, and there to exert his powers for good where the field was broad and the laborers few.

Born of Southern parents from whom he had learned many of the superstitions and traditions of the South, Howard Dokesbury himself had never before been below Mason and Dixon's line. But with a confidence born of youth and a consciousness of the personal power, he had started South with the idea that he knew the people with whom he had to deal, and was equipped with the proper weapons to cope with their shortcomings.

But as he looked around upon the scene which now met his eye, a doubt arose in his mind. He picked up his bag with a sigh, and approached a man who had been standing apart from the rest of the loungers and regarding him with indolent intentness.

"Could you direct me to the house of Stephen Gray?" asked the minister.

The interrogated took time to change his position from left foot to right and to shift his quid, before he drawled forth, "I reckon you's de new Mefdis preachah, huh?"

"Yes," replied Howard, in the most conciliatory tone he could command, "and I hope I find in you one of my flock."

"No, suh, I's a Babtist myse'f. I wa'n't raised up no place erroun' Mt. Hope; I'm nachelly f'om way up in Adams County. Dey jes' sent me down hyeah to fin' you an' to tek you up to Steve's. Steve, he's workin' today an' couldn't come down."

He laid particular stress upon the "today," as if Steve's spell of activity were not an everyday occurrence.

"Is it far from here?" asked Dokesbury.

"'Tain't mo' 'n a mile an' a ha'f by de shawt cut."

"Well, then, let's take the short cut, by all means," said the preacher.

They trudged along for a while in silence, and then the young man asked, "What do you men about here do mostly for a living?"

"Oh, well, we does odd jobs, we saws an' splits wood an' totes bundles, an' some of 'em raises gyahden, but mos' of us, we fishes. De fish bites an' we ketches 'em. Sometimes we eats 'em an' sometimes we sells 'em; a string o' fish'll bring a peck o' co'n any time."

"And is that all you do?"

"'Bout."

"Why, I don't see how you live that way."

"Oh, we lives all right," answered the man; "we has plenty to eat an' drink, an' clothes to wear, an' some place to stay. I reckon folks ain't got much use fu' nuffin' mo'."

Dokesbury sighed. Here indeed was virgin soil for his ministerial labors. His spirits were not materially raised when, some time later, he came in sight of the house which was to be his abode. To be sure, it was better than most of the houses which he had seen in the Negro part of Mt. Hope; but even at that it was far from being good or comfortable-looking. It was small and mean in appearance. The weather boarding was broken, and in some places entirely fallen away, showing the great unhewn logs beneath; while off the boards that remained the whitewash had peeled in scrofulous spots.

The minister's guide went up to the closed door, and rapped loudly with a heavy stick.

"G' 'way f'om dah, an' quit you' foolin'," came in a large voice from within.

The guide grinned, and rapped again. There was a sound of shuffling feet and the pushing back of a chair, and then the same voice saying: "I bet I'll mek you git away f'om dat do'."

"Dat's A'nt Ca'line," the guide said, and laughed.

The door was flung back as quickly as its worn hinges and sagging bottom would allow, and a large body surmounted by a face like a big round full moon presented itself in the opening. A broomstick showed itself aggressively in one fat shiny hand.

"It's you, Tom Scott, is it—you trif'nin'—" and then, catching sight of the stranger, her whole manner changed, and she dropped the broomstick with an embarrassed "'Scuse me, suh."

Tom chuckled all over as he said, "A'nt Ca'line, dis is yo' new preachah."

The big black face lighted up with a broad smile as the old woman extended her hand and enveloped that of the young minister's.

"Come in," she said. "I's mighty glad to see you—that no-'count Tom come put' nigh mekin' me 'spose myse'f." Then turning to Tom, she exclaimed with good-natured severity, "An you go 'long, you scoun'll you!"

The preacher entered the cabin—it was hardly more—and seated himself in the rush-bottomed chair which A'nt Ca'line had been industriously polishing with her apron.

"An' now, Brothah—"

"Dokesbury," supplemented the young man.

"Brothah Dokesbury, I jes' want you to mek yo'se'f at home right erway. I know you ain't use to ouah ways down hyeah; but you jes' got to set in an' git ust to 'em. You must'n't feel bad of things don't go yo' way f'om de ve'y fust. Have you got a mammy?"

The question was very abrupt, and a lump suddenly jumped up in Dokesbury's throat and pushed the water into his eyes. He did have a mother away back there at home. She was all alone, and he was her heart and the hope of her life.

"Yes," he said, "I've got a little mother up there in Ohio."

"Well, I's gwine to be yo' mothah down hyeah; dat is, ef I ain't too rough an' common fu' you."

"Hush!" exclaimed the preacher, and he got up and took the old lady's hand in both of his own. "You shall be my mother down here; you shall help me, as you have done to-day. I feel better already."

"I knowed you would"; and the old face beamed on the young one. "An' now jes' go out de do' dah an' wash yo' face. Dey's a pan an' soap an' watah right dah, an' hyeah's a towel; den you kin go right into yo' room, fu' I knows you want to be erlone fu' a while. I'll fix yo' suppah while you rests."

He did as he was bidden. On a rough bench outside the door, he found a basin and a bucket of water with a tin dipper in it. To one side, in a broken saucer, lay a piece of coarse soap. The facilities for copious ablutions were not abundant, but one thing the minister noted with pleasure: the towel, which was rough and hurt his skin, was, nevertheless, scrupulously clean. He went to his room feeling fresher and better, and although he found the place little and dark and warm, it too was clean, and a sense of its homeness began to take possession of him.

The room was off the main living room into which he had been first ushered. It had one small window that opened out on a fairly neat yard. A table with a chair before it stood beside the window, and across the room—if the three feet of space which intervened could be called "across"—stood the little bed with its dark calico quilt and white pillows. There was no carpet on the floor, and the absence of a washstand indicated very plainly that the occupant was expected to wash outside. The young minister knelt for a few minutes beside the bed, and then rising cast himself into the chair to rest.

It was possibly half an hour later when his partial nap was broken in upon by the sound of a gruff voice from without saying, "He's hyeah, is he—oomph! Well, what's he ac' lak? Want us to git down on ouah knees an' crawl to him? If he do, I reckon he'll fin' dat Mt. Hope ain't de place fo' him."

The minister did not hear the answer, which was in a low voice and came, he conjectured, from Aunt "Ca'line"; but the gruff voice subsided, and there was the sound of footsteps going out of the room. A tap came on the preacher's door, and he opened it to the old woman. She smiled reassuringly.

"Dat 'uz my ol' man," she said. "I sont him out to git some wood, so's I'd have time to post you. Don't you mind him; he's lots mo' ba'k dan bite. He's one o' dese little yaller men, an' you know dey kin be powahful contra'y when dey sets dey haid to it. But jes' you treat him nice an' don't let on, an' I'll be boun' you'll bring him erroun' in little er no time."

The Rev. Mr. Dokesbury received this advice with some misgiving. Albeit he had assumed his pleasantest manner when, after his return to the living room, the little "yaller" man came through the door with his bundle of wood.

He responded cordially to Aunt Caroline's, "Dis is my husband, Brothah Dokesbury," and heartily shook his host's reluctant hand.

"I hope I find you well, Brother Gray," he said.

"Moder't, jes' moder't," was the answer.

"Come to suppah now, bofe o' you," said the old lady, and they all sat down to the evening meal, of crisp bacon, well-fried potatoes, egg-pone, and coffee.

The young man did his best to be agreeable, but it was rather discouraging to receive only gruff monosyllabic rejoinders to his most interesting observations. But the cheery old wife came bravely to the rescue, and the minister was continually floated into safety on the flow of her conversation. Now and then, as he talked, he could catch a stealthy upflashing of Stephen Gray's eye, as suddenly lowered again, that told him that the old man was listening. But, as an indication that they would get on together, the supper, taken as a whole, was not a success. The evening that followed proved hardly more fortunate. About the only remarks that could be elicited from the "little yaller man" were a reluctant "oomph" or "oomph-uh."

It was just before going to bed that, after a period of reflection, Aunt Caroline began slowly: "We got a son"—her husband immediately bristled up and his eyes flashed, but the old woman went on; "he named 'Lias, an' we thinks a heap o' 'Lias, we does; but"—the old man had subsided, but he bristled up again at the word—"he ain't jes' whut we want him to be." Her husband opened his mouth as if to speak in defense of his son, but was silent in satisfaction at his wife's explanation: "'Lias ain't bad; he jes' ca'less. Sometimes he stays at home, but right sma't o' de time he stays down at"—she looked at her husband and hesitated—"at de colo'ed s'loon. We don't lak dat. It ain't no fitten place fu' him. But 'Lias ain't bad, he jes' ca'less, an' me an' de ol' man we 'membahs him in ouah pra'ahs, an' I jes' t'ought I'd ax you to 'membah him too, Brothah Dokesbury."

The minister felt the old woman's pleading look and the husband's intense gaze upon his face, and suddenly there came to him an intimate sympathy in their trouble and with it an unexpected strength.

"There is no better time than now," he said, "to take his case to the Almighty Power; let us pray."

Perhaps it was the same prayer he had prayed many times before; perhaps the words of supplication and the plea for light and guidance were the same; but somehow to the young man kneeling there amid those humble surroundings, with the sorrow of these poor ignorant people weighing upon his heart, it seemed very different. It came more fervently from his lips, and the words had a deeper meaning. When he arose, there was a warmth at his heart just the like of which he had never before experienced.

Aunt Caroline blundered up from her knees, saying, as she wiped her eyes, "Blessed is dey dat mou'n, fu' dey shall be comfo'ted." The old man, as he turned to go to bed, shook the young man's hand warmly and in silence; but there was a moisture in the old eyes that told the minister that his plummet of prayer had sounded the depths.

Alone in his own room Howard Dokesbury sat down to study the situation in which he had been placed. Had his thorough college training anticipated specifically any such circumstance as this? After all, did he know his own people? Was it possible that they could be so different from what he had seen and known? He had always been such a loyal Negro, so proud of his honest brown; but had he been mistaken? Was he, after all, different from the majority of the people with whom he was supposed to have all thoughts, feelings, and emotions in common?

These and other questions he asked himself without being able to arrive at any satisfactory conclusion. He did not go to sleep soon after retiring, and the night brought many thoughts. The next day would be Saturday. The ordeal had already begun,—now there were twenty-four hours between him and the supreme trial. What would be its outcome? There were moments when he felt, as every man, howsoever brave, must feel at times, that he would like to shift all his responsibilities and go away from the place that seemed destined to tax his powers beyond their capability of endurance. What could he do for the inhabitants of Mt. Hope? What was required of him to do? Ever through his mind ran that world-old question: "Am I my brother's keeper?" He had never asked, "Are these people my brothers?"

He was up early the next morning, and as soon as breakfast was done, he sat down to add a few touches to the sermon he had prepared as his introduction. It was not the first time that he had retouched it and polished it up here and there. Indeed, he had taken some pride in it. But as he read it over that day, it did not sound to him as it had sounded before. It appeared flat and without substance. After a while he laid it aside, telling himself that he was nervous and it was on this account that he could not see matters as he did in his calmer moments. He told himself, too, that he must not again take up the offending discourse until time to use it, lest the discovery of more imaginary flaws should so weaken his confidence that he would not be able to deliver it with effect.

In order better to keep his resolve, he put on his hat and went out for a walk through the streets of Mt. Hope. He did not find an encouraging prospect as he went along. The Negroes whom he met viewed him with ill-favor, and the whites who passed looked on him with unconcealed distrust and contempt. He began to feel lost, alone, and helpless. The squalor and shiftlessness which were plainly in evidence about the houses which he saw filled him with disgust and a dreary hopelessness.

He passed vacant lots which lay open and inviting children to healthful play; but instead of marbles or leap-frog or ball, he found little boys in ragged knickerbockers huddled together on the ground, "shooting craps" with precocious avidity and quarreling over the pennies that made the pitiful wagers. He heard glib profanity rolling from the lips of children who should have been stumbling through baby catechisms; and his heart ached for them.

He would have turned and gone back to his room, but the sound of shouts, laughter, and the tum-tum of a musical instrument drew him on down the street. At the turn of a corner, the place from which the noise emanated met his eyes. It was a rude frame building, low and unpainted. The panes in its windows whose places had not been supplied by sheets of tin were daubed a dingy red. Numerous kegs and bottles on the outside attested the nature of the place. The front door was open, but the interior was concealed by a gaudy curtain stretched across the entrance within. Over the door was the inscription, in straggling characters, "Sander's Place"; and when he saw half a dozen Negroes enter, the minister knew instantly that he now beheld the colored saloon which was the frequenting-place of his hostess's son 'Lias; and he wondered, if, as the mother said, her boy was not bad, how anything good could be preserved in such a place of evil.

The cries and boisterous laughter mingled with the strumming of the banjo and the shuffling of feet told him that they were engaged in one of their rude hoe-down dances. He had not passed a dozen paces beyond the door when the music was suddenly stopped, the sound of a quick blow followed, then ensued a scuffle, and a young fellow half ran, half fell through the open door. He was closely followed by a heavily built ruffian who was striking him as he ran. The young fellow was very much the weaker and slighter of the two, and was suffering great punishment. In an instant all the preacher's sense of justice was stung into sudden life. Just as the brute was about to give his victim a blow that would have sent him into the gutter, he felt his arm grasped in a detaining hold and heard a commanding voice,—"Stop!"

He turned with increased fury upon this meddler, but his other wrist was caught and held in a viselike grip. For a moment the two men looked into each other's eyes. Hot words rose to the young man's lips, but he choked them back. Until this moment he had deplored the possession of a spirit so easily fired that it had been a test of his manhood to keep from "slugging" on the football field; now he was glad of it. He did not attempt to strike the man, but stood holding his arms and meeting the brute glare with manly flashing eyes. Either the natural cowardice of the bully or something in his new opponent's face had quelled the big fellow's spirit, and he said doggedly: "Lemme go. I wasn't a-go'n' to kill him nohow, but ef I ketch him dancin' with my gal anymo', I'll—" He cast a glance full of malice at his victim, who stood on the pavement a few feet away, as much amazed as the dumbfounded crowd which thronged the door of "Sander's Place." Loosing his hold, the preacher turned, and, putting his hand on the young fellow's shoulder, led him away.

For a time they walked on in silence. Dokesbury had to calm the tempest in his breast before he could trust his voice. After a while he said: "That fellow was making it pretty hot for you, my young friend. What had you done to him?"

"Nothin'," replied the other. "I was jes' dancin' 'long an' not thinkin' 'bout him, when all of a sudden he hollered dat I had his gal an' commenced hittin' me."

"He's a bully and a coward, or he would not have made use of his superior strength in that way. What's your name, friend?"

"'Lias Gray," was the answer, which startled the minister into exclaiming,—

"What! are you Aunt Caroline's son?"

"Yes, suh, I sho is; does you know my mothah?"

"Why, I'm stopping with her, and we were talking about you last night. My name is Dokesbury, and I am to take charge of the church here."

"I thought mebbe you was a preachah, but I couldn't scarcely believe it after I seen de way you held Sam an' looked at him."

Dokesbury laughed, and his merriment seemed to make his companion feel better, for the sullen, abashed look left his face, and he laughed a little himself as he said: "I wasn't a-pesterin' Sam, but I tell you he pestered me mighty."

Dokesbury looked into the boy's face,—he was hardly more than a boy,—lit up as it was by a smile, and concluded that Aunt Caroline was right. 'Lias might be "ca'less," but he wasn't a bad boy. The face was too open and the eyes too honest for that. 'Lias wasn't bad; but environment does so much, and he would be if something were not done for him. Here, then, was work for a pastor's hands.

"You'll walk on home with me, 'Lias, won't you?"

"I reckon I mout ez well," replied the boy. "I don't stay erroun' home ez much ez I oughter."

"You'll be around more, of course, now that I am there. It will be so much less lonesome for two young people than for one. Then, you can be a great help to me, too."

The preacher did not look down to see how wide his listener's eyes grew as he answered: "Oh, I ain't fittin' to be no he'p to you, suh. Fust thing, I ain't nevah got religion, an' then I ain't well larned enough."

"Oh, there are a thousand other ways in which you can help, and I feel sure that you will."

"Of co'se, I'll do de ve'y bes' I kin."

"There is one thing I want you to do soon, as a favor to me."

"I can't go to de mou'nah's bench," cried the boy, in consternation.

"And I don't want you to," was the calm reply.

Another look of wide-eyed astonishment took in the preacher's face. These were strange words from one of his guild. But without noticing the surprise he had created, Dokesbury went on: "What I want is that you will take me fishing as soon as you can. I never get tired of fishing and I am anxious to go here. Tom Scott says you fish a great deal about here."

"Why, we kin' go dis ve'y afternoon," exclaimed 'Lias, in relief and delight; "I's mighty fond o' fishin', myse'f."

"All right; I'm in your hands from now on."

'Lias drew his shoulders up, with an unconscious motion. The preacher saw it, and mentally rejoiced. He felt that the first thing the boy beside him needed was a consciousness of responsibility, and the lifted shoulders meant progress in that direction, a sort of physical straightening up to correspond with the moral one.

On seeing her son walk in with the minister, Aunt "Ca'line's" delight was boundless. "La! Brothah Dokesbury," she exclaimed, "wha'd you fin' dat scamp?"

"Oh, down the street here," the young man replied lightly. "I got hold of his name and made myself acquainted, so he came home to go fishing with me."

"'Lias is pow'ful fon' o' fishin', hisse'f. I 'low he kin show you some mighty good places. Cain't you, 'Lias?"

"I reckon."

'Lias was thinking. He was distinctly grateful that the circumstances of his meeting with the minister had been so deftly passed over. But with a half idea of the superior moral responsibility under which a man in Dokesbury's position labored, he wondered vaguely—to put it in his own thought-words—"ef de preachah hadn't put' nigh lied." However, he was willing to forgive this little lapse of veracity, if such it was, out of consideration for the anxiety it spared his mother.

When Stephen Gray came in to dinner, he was no less pleased than his wife to note the terms of friendship on which the minister received his son. On his face was the first smile that Dokesbury had seen there, and he awakened from his taciturnity and proffered much information as to the fishing-places thereabout. The young minister accounted this a distinct gain. Anything more than a frowning silence from the "little yaller man" was gain.

The fishing that afternoon was particularly good. Catfish, chubs, and suckers were landed in numbers sufficient to please the heart of any amateur angler.

'Lias was happy, and the minister was in the best of spirits, for his charge seemed promising. He looked on at the boy's jovial face, and laughed within himself; for, mused he, "it is so much harder for the devil to get into a cheerful heart than into a sullen, gloomy one." By the time they were ready to go home Howard Dokesbury had received a promise from 'Lias to attend service the next morning and hear the sermon.

There was a great jollification over the fish supper that night, and 'Lias and the minister were the heroes of the occasion. The old man again broke his silence, and recounted, with infinite dryness, ancient tales of his prowess with rod and line; while Aunt "Ca'line" told of famous fish suppers that in the bygone days she had cooked for "de white folks." In the midst of it all, however, 'Lias disappeared. No one had noticed when he slipped out, but all seemed to become conscious of his absence about the same time. The talk shifted, and finally simmered into silence.

When the Rev. Mr. Dokesbury went to bed that night, his charge had not yet returned.

The young minister woke early on the Sabbath morning, and he may be forgiven that the prospect of the ordeal through which he had to pass drove his care for 'Lias out of mind for the first few hours. But as he walked to church, flanked on one side by Aunt Caroline in the stiffest of ginghams and on the other by her husband stately in the magnificence of an antiquated "Jim-swinger," his mind went back to the boy with sorrow. Where was he? What was he doing? Had the fear of a dull church service frightened him back to his old habits and haunts? There was a new sadness at the preacher's heart as he threaded his way down the crowded church and ascended the rude pulpit.

The church was stiflingly hot, and the morning sun still beat relentlessly in through the plain windows. The seats were rude wooden benches, in some instances without backs. To the right, filling the inner corner, sat the pillars of the church, stern, grim, and critical. Opposite them, and, like them, in seats at right angles to the main body, sat the older sisters, some of them dressed with good old-fashioned simplicity, while others yielding to newer tendencies were gotten up in gaudy attempts at finery. In the rear seats a dozen or so much beribboned mulatto girls tittered and giggled, and cast bold glances at the minister.

The young man sighed as he placed the manuscript of his sermon between the leaves of the tattered Bible. "And this is Mt. Hope," he was again saying to himself.

It was after the prayer and in the midst of the second hymn that a more pronounced titter from the back seats drew his attention. He raised his head to cast a reproving glance at the irreverent, but the sight that met his eyes turned that look into one of horror. 'Lias had just entered the church, and with every mark of beastly intoxication was staggering up the aisle to a seat, into which he tumbled in a drunken heap. The preacher's soul turned sick within him, and his eyes sought the face of the mother and father. The old woman was wiping her eyes, and the old man sat with his gaze bent upon the floor, lines of sorrow drawn about his wrinkled mouth.

All of a sudden a great revulsion of feeling came over Dokesbury. Trembling he rose and opened the Bible. There lay his sermon, polished and perfected. The opening lines seemed to him like glints from a bright cold crystal. What had he to say to these people, when the full realization of human sorrow and care and of human degradation had just come to him? What had they to do with firstlies and secondlies, with premises and conclusions? What they wanted was a strong hand to help them over the hard places of life and a loud voice to cheer them through the dark. He closed the book again upon his precious sermon. A something new had been born in his heart. He let his glance rest for another instant on the mother's pained face and the father's bowed form, and then turning to the congregation began, "Come unto me, all ye that labor and are heavy laden, and I will give you rest. Take my yoke upon you, and learn of me: for I am meek and lowly in heart: and ye shall find rest unto your souls." Out of the fullness of his heart he spoke unto them. Their great need informed his utterance. He forgot his carefully turned sentences and perfectly rounded periods. He forgot all save that here was the well-being of a community put into his hands whose real condition he had not even suspected until now. The situation wrought him up. His words went forth like winged fire, and the emotional people were moved beyond control. They shouted, and clapped their hands, and praised the Lord loudly.

When the service was over, there was much gathering about the young preacher, and handshaking. Through all 'Lias had slept. His mother started toward him; but the minister managed to whisper to her, "Leave him to me." When the congregation had passed out, Dokesbury shook 'Lias. The boy woke, partially sober, and his face fell before the preacher's eyes.

"Come, my boy, let's go home." Arm in arm they went out into the street, where a number of scoffers had gathered to have a laugh at the abashed boy; but Howard Dokesbury's strong arm steadied his steps, and something in his face checked the crowd's hilarity. Silently they cleared the way, and the two passed among them and went home.

The minister saw clearly the things which he had to combat in his community, and through this one victim he determined to fight the general evil. The people with whom he had to deal were children who must be led by the hand. The boy lying in drunken sleep upon his bed was no worse than the rest of them. He was an epitome of the evil, as his parents were of the sorrows, of the place.

He could not talk to Elias. He could not lecture him. He would only be dashing his words against the accumulated evil of years of bondage as the ripples of a summer sea beat against a stone wall. It was not the wickedness of this boy he was fighting or even the wrong-doing of Mt. Hope. It was the aggregation of the evils of the fathers, the grand-fathers, the masters and mistresses of these people. Against this what could talk avail?

The boy slept on, and the afternoon passed heavily away. Aunt Caroline was finding solace in her pipe, and Stephen Gray sulked in moody silence beside the hearth. Neither of them joined their guest at evening service.

He went, however. It was hard to face those people again after the events of the morning. He could feel them covertly nudging each other and grinning as he went up to the pulpit. He chided himself for the momentary annoyance it caused him. Were they not like so many naughty, irresponsible children?

The service passed without unpleasantness, save that he went home with an annoyingly vivid impression of a yellow girl with red ribbons on her hat, who pretended to be impressed by his sermon and made eyes at him from behind her handkerchief.

On the way to his room that night, as he passed Stephen Gray, the old man whispered huskily, "It's de fus' time 'Lias evah done dat."

It was the only word he had spoken since morning.

A sound sleep refreshed Dokesbury, and restored the tone to his overtaxed nerves. When he came out in the morning, Elias was already in the kitchen. He too had slept off his indisposition, but it had been succeeded by a painful embarrassment that proved an effectual barrier to all intercourse with him. The minister talked lightly and amusingly, but the boy never raised his eyes from his plate, and only spoke when he was compelled to answer some direct questions.

Howard Dokesbury knew that unless he could overcome this reserve, his power over the youth was gone. He bent every effort to do it.

"What do you say to a turn down the street with me?" he asked as he rose from breakfast.

'Lias shook his head.

"What! You haven't deserted me already?"

The older people had gone out, but young Gray looked furtively about before he replied: "You know I ain't fittin' to go out with you—aftah—aftah—yestiddy."

A dozen appropriate texts rose in the preacher's mind, but he knew that it was not a preaching time, so he contended himself with saying,—

"Oh, get out! Come along!"

"No, I cain't. I cain't. I wisht I could! You needn't think I's ashamed, 'cause I ain't. Plenty of 'em git drunk, an' I don't keer nothin' 'bout dat"—this in a defiant tone.

"Well, why not come along, then?"

"I tell you I cain't. Don't ax me no mo'. It ain't on my account I won't go. It's you."

"Me! Why, I want you to go."

"I know you does, but I musn't. Cain't you see that dey'd be glad to say dat—dat you was in cahoots wif me an' you tuk yo' dram on de sly?"

"I don't care what they say so long as it isn't true. Are you coming?"

"No, I ain't."

He was perfectly determined, and Dokesbury saw that there was no use arguing with him. So with a resigned "All right!" he strode out the gate and up the street, thinking of the problem he had to solve.

There was good in Elias Gray, he knew. It was a shame that it should be lost. It would be lost unless he were drawn strongly away from the paths he was treading. But how could it be done? Was there no point in his mind that could be reached by what was other than evil? That was the thing to be found out. Then he paused to ask himself if, after all, he were not trying to do too much,—trying, in fact, to play Providence to Elias. He found himself involuntarily wanting to shift the responsibility of planning for the youth. He wished that something entirely independent of his intentions would happen.

Just then something did happen. A piece of soft mud hurled from some unknown source caught the minister square in the chest, and spattered over his clothes. He raised his eyes and glanced about quickly, but no one was in sight. Whoever the foe was, he was securely ambushed.

"Thrown by the hand of a man," mused Dokesbury, "prompted by the malice of a child."

He went on his way, finished his business, and returned to the house.

"La, Brothah Dokesbury!" exclaimed Aunt Caroline, "what's de mattah 'f yo' shu't bosom?"

"Oh, that's where one of our good citizens left his card."

"You don' mean to say none o' dem low-life scoun'els——"

"I don't know who did it. He took particular pains to keep out of sight."

"'Lias!" the old woman cried, turning on her son, "wha' 'd you let Brothah Dokesbury go off by hisse'f fu'? Whyn't you go 'long an' tek keer o' him?"

The old lady stopped even in the midst of her tirade, as her eyes took in the expression on her son's face.

"I'll kill some o' dem damn——"

"'Lias!"

"'Scuse me, Mistah Dokesbury, but I feel lak I'll bus' ef I don't 'spress myse'f. It makes me so mad. Don't you go out o' hyeah no mo' 'dout me. I'll go 'long an' I'll brek somebody's haid wif a stone."

"'Lias! how you talkin' fo' de' ministah?"

"Well, dat's whut I'll do, 'cause I kin outh'ow any of 'em an' I know dey hidin'-places."

"I'll be glad to accept your protection," said Dokesbury.

He saw his advantage, and was thankful for the mud,—the one thing that without an effort restored the easy relations between himself and his protégé.

Ostensibly these relations were reversed, and Elias went out with the preacher as a guardian and protector. But the minister was laying his nets. It was on one of these rambles that he broached to 'Lias a subject which he had been considering for some time.

"Look here, 'Lias," he said, "what are you going to do with that big back yard of yours?"

"Oh, nothin'. 'Tain't no 'count to raise nothin' in."

"It may not be fit for vegetables, but it will raise something."

"What?"

"Chickens. That's what."

Elias laughed sympathetically.

"I'd lak to eat de chickens I raise. I wouldn't want to be feedin' de neighborhood."

"Plenty of boards, slats, wire, and a good lock and key would fix that all right."

"Yes, but whah'm I gwine to git all dem things?"

"Why, I'll go in with you and furnish the money, and help you build the coops. Then you can sell chickens and eggs, and we'll go halves on the profits."

"Hush, man!" cried 'Lias, in delight.

So the matter was settled, and, as Aunt Caroline expressed it, "Fu' a week er sich a mattah, you nevah did see sich ta'in' down an' buildin' up in all yo' bo'n days."

'Lias went at the work with zest, and Dokesbury noticed his skill with tools. He let fall the remark: "Say, 'Lias, there's a school near here where they teach carpentering; why don't you go and learn?"

"What I gwine to do with bein' a cyahpenter?"

"Repair some of these houses around Mt. Hope, if nothing more," Dokesbury responded, laughing; and there the matter rested.

The work prospered, and as the weeks went on, 'Lias' enterprise became the town's talk. One of Aunt Caroline's patrons who had come with some orders about work regarded the changed condition of affairs, and said, "Why, Aunt Caroline, this doesn't look like the same place. I'll have to buy some eggs from you; you keep your yard and henhouse so nice, it's an advertisement for the eggs."

"Don't talk to me nothin' 'bout dat ya'd, Miss Lucy," Aunt Caroline had retorted. "Dat 'long to 'Lias an' de preachah. Hit dey doin's. Dey done mos' nigh drove me out wif dey cleanness. I ain't nevah seed no sich ca'in' on in my life befo'. Why, my 'Lias done got right brigity an' talk about bein' somep'n'."

Dokesbury had retired from his partnership with the boy save in so far as he acted as a general supervisor. His share had been sold to a friend of 'Lias, Jim Hughes. The two seemed to have no other thought save of raising, tending, and selling chickens.

Mt. Hope looked on and ceased to scoff. Money is a great dignifier, and Jim and 'Lias were making money. There had been some sniffs when the latter had hinged the front gate and whitewashed his mother's cabin, but even that had been accepted now as a matter of course.

Dokesbury had done his work. He, too, looked on, and in some satisfaction.

"Let the leaven work," he said, "and all Mt. Hope must rise."

It was one day, nearly a year later, that "old lady Hughes" dropped in on Aunt Caroline for a chat.

"Well, I do say, Sis' Ca'line, dem two boys o' ourn done sot dis town on fiah."

"What now, Sis' Lizy?"

"Why, evah sence 'Lias tuk it into his haid to be a cyahpenter an' Jim 'cided to go 'long an' lu'n to be a blacksmif, some o' dese hyeah othah young people's been tryin' to do somep'n'."

"All dey wanted was a staht."

"Well, now will you b'lieve me, dat no-'count Tom Johnson done opened a fish sto', an' he has de boys an' men bring him dey fish all de time. He give 'em a little somep'n' fu' dey ketch, den he go sell 'em to de white folks."

"Lawd, how long!"

"An' what you think he say?"

"I do' know, sis'."

"He say ez soon 'z he git money enough, he gwine to dat school whah 'Lias an' Jim gone an' lu'n to fahm scientific."

"Bless de Lawd! Well, 'um, I don' put nothin' pas' de young folks now."

Mt. Hope had at last awakened. Something had come to her to which she might aspire,—something that she could understand and reach. She was not soaring, but she was rising above the degradation in which Howard Dokesbury had found her. And for her and him the ordeal had passed.

AT SHAFT 11

Night falls early over the miners' huts that cluster at the foot of the West Virginia mountains. The great hills that give the vales their shelter also force upon them their shadow. Twilight lingers a short time, and then gives way to that black darkness which is possible only to regions in the vicinity of high and heavily wooded hills.

Through the fast-gathering gloom of a mid-spring evening, Jason Andrews, standing in his door, peered out into the open. It was a sight of rugged beauty that met his eyes as they swept the broken horizon. All about the mountains raised their huge forms,—here bare, sharp, and rocky; there undulating, and covered with wood and verdure, whose various shades melted into one dull, blurred, dark green, hardly distinguishable in the thick twilight. At the foot of the hills all was in shadow, but their summits were bathed in the golden and crimson glory of departing day.

Jason Andrews, erstwhile foreman of Shaft 11, gazed about him with an eye not wholly unappreciative of the beauty of the scene. Then, shading his eyes with one brawny hand, an act made wholly unnecessary by the absence of the sun, he projected his vision far down into the valley.

His hut, set a little way up the mountain side, commanded an extended view of the road, which, leaving the slope, ran tortuously through the lower land. Evidently something that he saw down the road failed to please the miner, for he gave a low whistle and reentered the house with a frown on his face.

"I'll be goin' down the road a minute, Kate," he said to his wife, throwing on his coat and pausing at the door. "There's a crowd gathered down toward the settlement. Somethin' 's goin' on, an' I want to see what's up." He slammed the door and strode away.

"Jason, Jason," his wife called after him, "don't you have nothin' to do with their goin's-on, neither one way nor the other. Do you hear?"

"Oh, I'll take care o' myself." The answer came back out of the darkness.

"I do wish things would settle down some way or other," mused Mrs. Andrews. "I don't see why it is men can't behave themselves an' go 'long about their business, lettin' well enough alone. It's all on account o' that pesky walkin' delegate too. I wisht he'd 'a' kept walkin'. If all the rest o' the men had had the common sense that Jason has, he wouldn't never 'a' took no effect on them. But most of 'em must set with their mouths open like a lot o' ninnies takin' in everything that come their way, and now here's all this trouble on our hands."

There were indeed troublous times at the little mining settlement. The men who made up the community were all employees, in one capacity or another, of the great Crofton West Virginia Mining Co. They had been working on, contented and happy, at fair wages and on good terms with their employers, until the advent among them of one who called himself, alternately, a benefactor of humanity and a labor agitator. He proceeded to show the men how they were oppressed, how they were withheld from due compensation for their labors, while the employers rolled in the wealth which the workers' hands had produced. With great adroitness of argument and elaboration of phrase, he contrived to show them that they were altogether the most ill-treated men in America. There was only one remedy for the misery of their condition, and that was to pay him two dollars and immediately organize a local branch of the Miners' Labor Union. The men listened. He was so perfectly plausible, so smooth, and so clear. He found converts among them. Some few combated the man's ideas, and none among these more forcibly than did Jason Andrews, the foreman of Shaft 11. But the heresy grew, and the opposition was soon overwhelmed. There are always fifty fools for every fallacy. Of course, the thing to do was to organize against oppression, and accordingly, amid great enthusiasm, the union was formed. With the exception of Jason Andrews, most of the men, cowed by the majority opposed to them, yielded their ground and joined. But not so he. It was sturdy, stubborn old Scotch blood that coursed through his veins. He stayed out of the society even at the expense of the friendship of some of the men who had been his friends. Taunt upon taunt was thrown into his face.

"He's on the side of the rich. He's for capital against labor. He's in favor of supporting a grinding monopoly." All this they said in the ready, pat parlance of their class; but the foreman went his way unmoved, and kept his own counsel.

Then, like the falling of a thunderbolt, had come the visit of the "walking-delegate" for the district, and his command to the men to "go out." For a little time the men demurred; but the word of the delegate was law. Some other company had failed to pay its employees a proper price, and the whole district was to be made an example of. Even while the men were asking what it was all about, the strike was declared on.

The usual committee, awkward, shambling, hat in hand, and un comfortable in their best Sunday clothes, called upon their employers to attempt to explain the grievances which had brought about the present state of affairs. The "walking-delegate" had carefully prepared it all for them, with the new schedule of wages based upon the company's earnings.

The three men who had the local affairs of the company in charge heard them through quietly. Then young Harold Crofton, acting as spokesman, said, "Will you tell us how long since you discovered that your wages were unfair?"

The committee severally fumbled its hat and looked confused. Finally Grierson, who had been speaking for them, said: "Well, we've been thinkin' about it fur a good while. Especially ever sence, ahem——"

"Yes," went on Crofton, "to be plain and more definite, ever since the appearance among you of Mr. Tom Daly, the agitator, the destroyer of confidence between employer and employed, the weasel who sucks your blood and tells you that he is doing you a service. You have discovered the unfairness of your compensation since making his acquaintance."

"Well, I guess he told us the truth," growled Grierson.

"That is a matter of opinion."

"But look what you all are earnin'."

"That's what were in the business for. We haven't left comfortable homes in the cities to come down to this hole in the mountains for our health. We have a right to earn. We brought capital, enterprise, and energy here. We give you work and pay you decent wages. It is none of your business what we earn." The young man's voice rose a little, and a light come into his calm gray eyes. "Have you not been comfortable? Have you not lived well and been able to save something? Have you not been treated like men? What more do you want? What real grievance have you? None. A scoundrel and a sneak has come here, and for his own purposes aroused your covetousness. But it is unavailing, and," turning to his colleagues, "these gentlemen will bear me out in what I say,—we will not raise your wages one-tenth of one penny above what they are. We will not be made to suffer for the laxity of other owners, and if within three hours the men are not back at work, they may consider themselves discharged." His voice was cold, clear, and ringing.

Surprised, disappointed, and abashed, the committee heard the ultimatum, and then shuffled out of the office in embarrassed silence. It was all so different from what they had expected. They thought that they had only to demand and their employers would accede rather than have the work stop. Labor had but to make a show of resistance and capital would yield. So they had been told. But here they were, the chosen representatives of labor, skulking away from the presence of capital like felons detected. Truly this was a change. Embarrassment gave way to anger, and the miners who awaited the report of their committee received a highly colored account of the standoffish way in which they had been met. If there had been anything lacking to inflame the rising feelings of the laborers, this new evidence of the arrogance of plutocrats supplied it, and with one voice the strike was confirmed.

Soon after the three hours' grace had passed, Jason Andrews received a summons to the company's office.

"Andrews," said young Crofton, "we have noticed your conduct with gratitude since this trouble has been brewing. The other foremen have joined the strikers and gone out. We know where you stand and thank you for your kindness. But we don't want it to end with thanks. It is well to give the men a lesson and bring them to their senses, but the just must not suffer with the unjust. In less than two days the mine will be manned by Negroes with their own foreman. We wish to offer you a place in the office here at the same wages you got in the mine."

The foreman raised his hand in a gesture of protest. "No, no, Mr. Crofton. That would look like I was profiting by the folly of the men. I can't do it. I am not in their union, but I will take my chances as they take theirs."

"That's foolish, Andrews. You don't know how long this thing may last."

"Well, I've got a snug bit laid by, and if things don't brighten in time, why, I'll go somewhere else."

"We'd be sorry to lose you, but I want you to do as you think best. This change may cause trouble, and if it does, we shall hope for your aid."

"I am with you as long as you are in the right."

The miner gave the young man's hand a hearty grip and passed out.

"Steel," said Crofton the younger.

"Gold," replied his partner.

"Well, as true as one and as good as the other, and we are both right."

As the young manager had said, so matters turned out. Within two days several carloads of Negroes came in and began to build their huts. With the true racial instinct of colonization, they all flocked to one part of the settlement. With a wisdom that was not entirely instinctive, though it may have had its origin in the Negroes' social inclination, they built one large eating-room a little way from their cabin and up the mountain side. The back of the place was the bare wall of a sheer cliff. Here their breakfasts and suppers were to be taken, the midday meal being eaten in the mine.

The Negro who held Jason Andrews' place as foreman of Shaft 11, the best yielding of all the mines, and the man who seemed to be the acknowledged leader of all the blacks, was known as big Sam Bowles. He was a great black fellow, with a hand like a sledge-hammer, but with an open, kindly face and a voice as musical as a lute.

On the first morning that they went in a body to work in the mines, they were assailed by the jeers and curses of the strikers, while now and then a rock from the hand of some ambushed foe fell among them. But they did not heed these things, for they were expected.

For several days nothing more serious than this happened, but ominous mutterings foretold the coming storm. So matters stood on the night that Jason Andrews left his cabin to find out what was "up."

He went on down the road until he reached the outskirts of the crowd, which he saw to be gathered about a man who was haranguing them. The speaker proved to be "Red" Cleary, one of Daly's first and most ardent converts. He had worked the men up to a high pitch of excitement, and there were cries of, "Go it, Red, you're on the right track!" "What's the matter with Cleary? He's all right!" and, "Run the niggers out. That's it!" On the edge of the throng, half in the shadow, Jason Andrews listened in silence, and his just anger grew.

The speaker was saying, "What are we white men goin' to do? Set still an' let niggers steal the bread out of our mouths? Ain't it our duty to rise up like free Americans an' drive 'em from the place? Who dares say no to that?" Cleary made the usual pause for dramatic effect and to let the incontrovertibility of his argument sink into the minds of his hearers. The pause was fatal. A voice broke the stillness that followed his question, "I do!" and Andrews pushed his way through the crowd to the front. "There ain't anybody stealin' the bread out of our mouths, niggers ner nobody else. If men throw away their bread, why, a dog has the right to pick it up."

There were dissenting murmurs, and Cleary turned to his opponent with a sneer. "Humph, I'd be bound for you, Jason Andrews, first on the side of the bosses and then takin' up for the niggers. Boys, I'll bet he's a Republican!" A laugh greeted this sally. The red mounted into the foreman's face and made his tan seem darker.

"I'm as good a Democrat as any of you," he said, looking around, "and you say that again, Red Cleary, and I'll push the words down your throat with my fist."

Cleary knew his man and turned the matter off. "We don't care nothin' about what party you vote with. We intend to stand up for our rights. Mebbe you've got something to say ag'in that."

"I've got something to say, but not against any man's rights. There's men here that have known me and are honest, and they will say whether I've acted on the square or not since I've been among you. But there is right as well as rights. As for the niggers, I ain't any friendlier to 'em than the rest of you. But I ain't the man to throw up a job and then howl when somebody else gets it. If we don't want our hoe-cake, there's others that do."

The plain sense of Andrews' remarks calmed the men, and Cleary, seeing that his power was gone, moved away from the center of the crowd, "I'll settle with you later," he muttered, as he passed Jason.

"There ain't any better time than now," replied the latter, seizing his arm and drawing him back.

"Here, here, don't fight," cried some one. "Go on, Cleary, there may be something better than a fellow-workman to try your muscle on before long." The crowd came closer and pushed between the two men. With many signs of reluctance, but willingly withal, Cleary allowed himself to be hustled away. The crowd dispersed, but Jason Andrews knew that he had only temporarily quieted the turmoil in the breasts of the men. It would break out very soon again, he told himself. Musing thus, he took his homeward way. As he reached the open road on the rise that led to his cabin, he heard the report of a pistol, and a shot clipped a rock three or four paces in front of him.

"With the compliments of Red Cleary," said Jason, with a hard laugh. "The coward!"

All next day, an ominous calm brooded over the little mining settlement. The black workmen went to their labors unmolested, and the hope that their hardships were over sprang up in the hearts of some. But there were two men who, without being informed, knew better. These were Jason Andrews and big Sam, and chance threw the two together. It was as the black was returning alone from the mine after the day's work was over.

"The strikers didn't bother you any today, I noticed," said Andrews.

Sam Bowles looked at him with suspicion, and then, being reassured by the honest face and friendly manner, he replied: "No, not today, but there ain't no tellin' what they'll do tonight. I don't like no sich sudden change."

"You think something is brewing, eh?"

"It looks mighty like it, I tell you."

"Well, I believe that you're right, and you'll do well to keep a sharp lookout all night."

"I, for one, won't sleep," said the Negro.

"Can you shoot?" asked Jason.

The Negro chuckled, and, taking a revolver from the bosom of his blouse, aimed at the top of a pine tree which had been grazed by lightning, and showed white through the fading light nearly a hundred yards away. There was a crack, and the small space no larger than a man's hand was splintered by the bullet.

"Well, there ain't no doubt that you can shoot, and you may have to bring that gun of yours into action before you expect. In a case like this it's your enemy's life against yours."

Andrews kept on his way, and the Negro turned up to the large supper room. Most of them were already there and at the meal.

"Well, boys," began big Sam, "you'd just as well get it out of your heads that our trouble is over here. It's jest like I told you. I've been talkin' to the fellow that used to have my place,—he ain't in with the rest of the strikers,—an' he thinks that they're goin' to try an' run us out tonight. I'd advise you, as soon as it gets darklike, to take what things you want out o' yore cabins an' brings 'em up here. It won't do no harm to be careful until we find out what kind of a move they're goin' to make."

The men had stopped eating, and they stared at the speaker with open mouths. There were some incredulous eyes among the gazers, too.

"I don't believe they'd dare come right out an' do anything," said one.

"Stay in yore cabin, then," retorted the leader angrily.

There was no more demur, and as soon as night had fallen, the Negroes did as they were bidden, though the rude, ill-furnished huts contained little or nothing of value. Another precaution taken by the blacks was to leave short candles burning in their dwellings so as to give the impression of occupancy. If nothing occurred during the night, the lights would go out of themselves and the enemy would be none the wiser as to their vigilance.

In the large assembly room the men waited in silence, some drowsing and some smoking. Only one candle threw its dim circle of light in the center of the room, throwing the remainder into denser shadow. The flame flickered and guttered. Its wavering faintness brought out the dark strained faces in fantastic relief, and gave a weirdness to the rolling white eyeballs and expanded eyes. Two hours passed. Suddenly, from the window where big Sam and a colleague were stationed, came a warning "S-sh!" Sam had heard stealthy steps in the direction of the nearest cabin. The night was so black that he could see nothing, but he felt that developments were about to begin. He could hear more steps. Then the men heard a cry of triumph as the strikers threw themselves against the cabin doors, which yielded easily. This was succeeded from all parts by exclamations of rage and disappointment. In the assembly room the Negroes were chuckling to themselves. Mr. "Red" Cleary had planned well, but so had Sam Bowles.

After the second cry there was a pause, as if the men had drawn together for consultation. Then some one approached the citadel a little way and said: "If you niggers'll promise to leave here tomorrow morning at daylight, we'll let you off this time. If you don't, there won't be any of you to leave tomorrow."

Some of the blacks were for promising, but their leader turned on them like a tiger. "You would promise, would you, and then give them a chance to whip you out of the section! Go, all of you that want to; but as for me, I'll stay here an' fight it out with the blackguards."

The man who had spoken from without had evidently waited for an answer. None coming, his footsteps were heard retreating, and then, without warning, there was a rattling fusillade. Some of the shots crashed through the thin pine boarding, and several men were grazed. One struck the man who stood at big Sam's side at the window. The blood splashed into the black leader's face, and his companion sunk to the floor with a groan. Sam Bowles moved from the window a moment and wiped the blood drops from his cheek. He looked down upon the dead man as if the deed had dazed him. Then, with a few sharp commands, he turned again to the window.

Some overzealous fool among the strikers had fired one of the huts, and the growing flames discovered their foes to the little garrison.

"Put out that light," ordered big Sam. "All of you that can, get to the two front windows—you, Toliver, an' you, Moten, here with me. All the rest of you lay flat on the floor. Now, as soon as that light gets bright, pick out yore man,—don't waste a shot, now—fire!" Six pistols spat fire out into the night. There were cries of pain and the noise of scurrying feet as the strikers fled pell-mell out of range.

"Now, down on the floor!" commanded Sam.

The order came not a moment too soon, for an answering volley of shots penetrated the walls and passed harmlessly over the heads of those within. Meanwhile, some one seeing the mistake of the burning cabin had ordered it extinguished; but this could not be done without the workmen being exposed to the fire from the blacks' citadel. So there was nothing to do save to wait until the shanty had burned down. The dry pine was flaming brightly now, and lit up the scene with a crimson glare. The great rocks and the rugged mountain side, with patches of light here and there contrasting with the deeper shadows, loomed up threatening and terrible, and the fact that behind those boulders lay armed men thirsty for blood made the scene no less horrible.

In his cabin, farther up the mountain side, Jason Andrews had heard the shouts and firing, seen the glare of the burning cabin through his window, and interpreted it aright. He rose and threw on his coat.

"Jason," said his wife, "don't go down there. It's none of your business."

"I'm not going down there, Kate," he said; "but I know my duty and have got to do it."

The nearest telegraph office was a mile away from his cabin. Thither Jason hurried. He entered, and, seizing a blank, began to write rapidly, when he was interrupted by the voice of the operator, "It's no use, Andrews, the wires are cut." The foreman stopped as if he had been struck; then, wheeling around, he started for the door just as Crofton came rushing in.

"Ah, Andrews, it's you, is it?—and before me. Have you telegraphed for troops?"

"It's no use, Mr. Crofton, the wires are cut."

"My God!" exclaimed the young man, "what is to be done? I did not think they would go to this length."

"We must reach the next station and wire from there."

"But it's fifteen miles away on a road where a man is liable to break his neck at any minute."

"I'll risk it, but I must have a horse."

"Take mine. He's at the door,—God speed you." With the word, Jason was in the saddle and away like the wind.

"He can't keep that pace on the bad ground," said young Crofton, as he turned homeward.

At the center of strife all was still quiet. The fire had burned low, and what remained of it cast only a dull light around. The assailants began to prepare again for action.

"Here, some one take my place at the window," said Sam. He left his post, crept to the door and opened it stealthily, and, dropping on his hands and knees, crawled out into the darkness. In less than five minutes he was back and had resumed his station. His face was expressionless. No one knew what he had done until a new flame shot athwart the darkness, and at sight of it the strikers burst into a roar of rage. Another cabin was burning, and the space about for a hundred yards was as bright as day. In the added light, two or three bodies were distinguishable upon the ground, showing that the shots of the blacks had told. With deep chagrin the strikers saw that they could do nothing while the light lasted. It was now nearly midnight, and the men were tired and cramped in their places. They dared not move about much, for every appearance of an arm or a leg brought a shot from the besieged. Oh for the darkness, that they might advance and storm the stronghold! Then they could either overpower the blacks by force of numbers, or set fire to the place that held them and shoot them down as they tried to escape. Oh for darkness!

As if the Powers above were conspiring against the unfortunates, the clouds, which had been gathering dark and heavy, now loosed a down-pour of rain which grew fiercer and fiercer as the thunder crashed down from the mountains echoing and reechoing back and forth in the valley. The lightning tore vivid, zigzag gashes in the inky sky. The fury of the storm burst suddenly, and before the blacks could realize what was happening, the torrent had beaten the fire down, and the way between them and their enemies lay in darkness. The strikers gave a cheer that rose even over the thunder.

———

As the young manager had said, the road over which Jason had to travel was a terrible one. It was rough, uneven, and treacherous to the step even in the light of day. But the brave man urged his horse on at the best possible speed. When he was halfway to his destination, a sudden drop in the road threw the horse and he went over the animal's head. He felt a sharp pain in his arm, and he turned sick and dizzy, but, scrambling to his feet, he mounted, seized the reins in one hand, and was away again. It was half-past twelve when he staggered into the telegraph office. "Wire—quick!" he gasped. The operator who had been awakened from a nap by the clatter of the horse's hoofs, rubbed his eyes and seized a pencil and blank.

"Troops at once—for God's sake—troops at once—Crofton's mine riot—murder being done!" and then, his mission being over, nature refused longer to resist the strain and Jason Andrews swooned.

His telegram had been received at Wheeling, and another ordering the instant despatch of the nearest militia, who had been commanded to sleep in their armories in anticipation of some such trouble, before a physician had been secured for Andrews. His arm was set and he was put to bed. But, loaded on flat-cars and whatever else came handy, the troops were on their way to the scene of action.

While this was going on, the Negroes had grown disheartened. The light which had disclosed to them their enemy had been extinguished, and under cover of the darkness and storm they knew their assailants would again advance. Every flash of lightning showed them the men standing boldly out from their shelter.

Big Sam turned to his comrades. "Never say die, boys," he said. "We've got jest one more chance to scatter 'em. If we can't do it, it's hand to hand with twice our number. Some of you lay down on the floor here with your faces jest as clost to the door as you can. Now some more of you kneel jest above. Now above them some of you bend, while the rest stand up. Pack that door full of gun muzzles while I watch things outside." The men did as he directed, and he was silent for a while. Then he spoke again softly: "Now they're comin'. When I say 'Ready!' open the door, and as soon as a flash of lightning shows you where they are, let them have it."

They waited breathlessly.

"Now, ready!"

The door was opened, and a moment there-after the glare of the lightning was followed by another flash from the doorway. Groans, shrieks, and curses rang out as the assailants scampered helter-skelter back to their friendly rocks, leaving more of their dead upon the ground behind them.

"That was it," said Sam. "That will keep them in check for a while. If we can hold 'em off until daybreak, we are safe."

The strikers were now angry and sore and wet through. Some of them were wounded. "Red" Cleary himself had a bullet through his shoulder. But his spirits were not daunted, although six of his men lay dead upon the ground. A long consultation followed the last unsuccessful assault. At last Cleary said: "Well, it won't do any good to stand here talkin'. It's gettin' late, an' if we don't drive 'em out tonight, it's all up with us an' we'd jest as well be lookin' out fur other diggin's. We've got to crawl up as near as we can an' then rush 'em. It's the only way, an' what we ought to done at first. Get down on your knees. Never mind the mud—better have it under you than over you." The men sank down, and went creeping forward like a swarm of great ponderous vermin.

They had not gone ten paces when some one said, "Tsch! what is that?" They stopped where they were. A sound came to their ears. It was the labored puffing of a locomotive as it tugged up the incline that led to the settlement. Then it stopped. Within the room they had heard it, too, and there was as great suspense as without.

With his ear close to the ground, "Red" Cleary heard the tramp of marching men, and he shook with fear. His fright was communicated to the others, and with one accord they began creeping back to their hiding places. Then, with a note that was like the voice of God to the besieged, through the thunder and rain, a fife took up the strains of "Yankee Doodle" accompanied by the tum-tum of a sodden drum. This time a cheer went up from within the room,—a cheer that directed the steps of the oncoming militia.

"It's all up!" cried Cleary, and, emptying his pistol at the wood fort, he turned and fled. His comrades followed suit. A bullet pierced Sam Bowles' wrist. But he did not mind it. He was delirious with joy. The militia advanced and the siege was lifted. Out into the storm rushed the happy blacks to welcome and help quarter their saviors. Some of the Negroes were wounded, and one dead, killed at the first fire. Tired as the men were, they could not sleep, and morning found them still about their fires talking over the night's events. It found also many of the strikers missing besides those who lay stark on the hillside.

For the next few days the militia took charge of affairs. Some of the strikers availed themselves of the Croftons' clemency, and went back to work along with the blacks; others moved away.

When Jason Andrews was well enough to be moved, he came back. The Croftons had already told of his heroism, and he was the admiration of white and black alike. He has general charge now of all the Crofton mines, and his assistant and stanch friend is big Sam.

One Man's Fortunes

Part I

When Bertram Halliday left the institution which, in the particular part of the middle west where he was born, was called the state university, he did not believe, as young graduates are reputed to, that he had conquered the world and had only to come into his kingdom. He knew that the battle of life was, in reality, just beginning and, with a common sense unusual to his twenty-three years but born out of the exigencies of a none-too-easy life, he recognized that for him the battle would be harder than for his white comrades.

Looking at his own position, he saw himself the member of a race dragged from complacent savagery into the very heat and turmoil of a civilization for which it was in nowise prepared; bowed beneath a yoke to which its shoulders were not fitted, and then, without warning, thrust forth into a freedom as absurd as it was startling and overwhelming. And yet, he felt, as most young men must feel, an individual strength that would exempt him from the workings of the general law. His outlook on life was calm and unfrightened. Because he knew the dangers that beset his way, he feared them less. He felt assured because with so clear an eye he saw the weak places in his armor which the world he was going to meet would attack, and these he was prepared to strengthen. Was it not the fault of youth and self-confessed weakness, he thought, to go into the world always thinking of it as a foe? Was not this great Cosmopolis, this dragon of a thousand talons, kind as well as cruel? Had it not friends as well as enemies? Yes. That was it: the outlook of young men, of colored young men in particular, was all wrong—they had gone at the world in the wrong spirit. They had looked upon it as a terrible foeman and forced it to be one. He would do it, oh, so differently. He would take the world as a friend. He would even take the old, old world under his wing.

They sat in the room talking that night, he and Webb Davis and Charlie McLean. It was the last night they were to be together in so close a relation. The commencement was over. They had their sheepskins. They were pitched there on the bed very carelessly to be the important things they were,—the reward of four years digging in Greek and Mathematics.

They had stayed after the exercises of the day just where they had first stopped. This was at McLean's rooms, dismantled and topsy-turvy with the business of packing. The pipes were going and the talk kept pace. Old men smoke slowly and in great whiffs with long intervals of silence between their observations. Young men draw fast and say many and bright things, for young men are wise,—while they are young.

"Now, it's just like this," Davis was saying to McLean, "Here we are, all three of us turned out into the world like a lot of little sparrows pitched out of the nest, and what are we going to do? Of course it's easy enough for you, McLean, but what are my grave friend with the nasty black briar, and I, your humble servant, to do? In what wilderness are we to pitch our tents and where is our manna coming from?"

"Oh, well, the world owes us all a living," said McLean.

"Hackneyed, but true. Of course it does; but every time a colored man goes around to collect, the world throws up its hands and yells 'insolvent'—eh, Halliday?"

Halliday took his pipe from his mouth as if he were going to say something. Then he put it back without speaking and looked meditatively through the blue smoke.

"I'm right," Davis went on, "to begin with, we colored people haven't any show here. Now, if we could go to Central or South America, or some place like that,—but hang it all, who wants to go thousands of miles away from home to earn a little bread and butter?"

"There's India and the young Englishmen, if I remember rightly," said McLean.

"Oh, yes, that's all right, with the Cabots and Drake and Sir John Franklin behind them. Their traditions, their blood, all that they know makes them willing to go 'where there ain't no ten commandments and a man can raise a thirst,' but for me, home, if I can call it home."

"Well, then, stick it out."

"That's easy enough to say, McLean; but ten to one you've got some snap picked out for you already, now 'fess up, ain't you?"

"Well, of course I'm going in with my father, I can't help that, but I've got——"

"To be sure," broke in Davis, "you go in with your father. Well, if all I had to do was to step right out of college into my father's business with an assured salary, however small, I shouldn't be falling on my own neck and weeping tonight. But that's just the trouble with us; we haven't got fathers before us or behind us, if you'd rather."

"More luck to you, you'll be a father before or behind some one else; you'll be an ancestor."

"It's more profitable being a descendant, I find."

A glow came into McLean's face and his eyes sparkled as he replied: "Why, man, if I could, I'd change places with you. You don't deserve your fate. What is before you? Hardships, perhaps, and long waiting. But then, you have the zest of the fight, the joy of the action and the chance of conquering. Now what is before me,—me, whom you are envying? I go out of here into a dull counting-room. The way is prepared for me. Perhaps I shall have no hardships, but neither have I the joy that comes from pains endured. Perhaps I shall have no battle, but even so, I lose the pleasure of the fight and the glory of winning. Your fate is infinitely to be preferred to mine."

"Ah, now you talk with the voluminous voice of the centuries," bantered Davis. "You are but echoing the breath of your Nelsons, your Cabots, your Drakes and your Franklins. Why, can't you see, you sentimental idiot, that it's all different and has to be different with us? The Anglo-Saxon race has been producing that fine frenzy in you for seven centuries and more. You come, with the blood of merchants, pioneers and heroes in your veins, to a normal battle. But for me, my forebears were savages two hundred years ago. My people learn to know civilization by the lowest and most degrading contact with it, and thus equipped or unequipped I attempt an abnormal contest. Can't you see the disproportion?"

"If I do, I can also see the advantage of it."

"For the sake of common sense, Halliday," said David, turning to his companion, "don't sit there like a clam; open up and say something to convince this Don Quixote who, because he himself sees only windmills, cannot be persuaded that we have real dragons to fight."

"Do you fellows know Henley?" asked Halliday, with apparent irrelevance.

"I know him as a critic," said McLean.

"I know him as a name," echoed the worldly Davis, "but——"

"I mean his poems," resumed Halliday, "he is the most virile of the present-day poets. Kipling is virile, but he gives you the man in hot blood with the brute in him to the fore; but the strong masculinity of Henley is essentially intellectual. It is the mind that is conquering always."

"Well, now that you have settled the relative place in English letters of Kipling and Henley, might I be allowed humbly to ask what in the name of all that is good has that to do with the question before the house?"

"I don't know your man's poetry," said McLean, "but I do believe that I can see what you are driving at."

"Wonderful perspicacity, oh, youth!"

"If Webb will agree not to run, I'll spring on you the poem that seems to me to strike the keynote of the matter in hand."

"Oh, well, curiosity will keep me. I want to get your position, and I want to see McLean annihilated."

In a low, even tone, but without attempt at dramatic effect, Halliday began to recite:

> "Out of the night that covers me,
>   Black as the pit from pole to pole,
> I thank whatever gods there be
>   For my unconquerable soul!
>
> "In the fell clutch of circumstance,
>   I have not winced nor cried aloud.
> Under the bludgeonings of chance,
>   My head is bloody, but unbowed.
>
> "Beyond this place of wrath and tears
>   Looms but the horror of the shade,

And yet the menace of the years
    Finds, and shall find me, unafraid.

"It matters not how strait the gate,
    How charged with punishments the scroll,
I am the master of my fate,
    I am the captain of my soul."

"That's it," exclaimed McLean, leaping to his feet, "that's what I mean. That's the sort of a stand for a man to take."

Davis rose and knocked the ashes from his pipe against the window sill. "Well, for two poetry-spouting, poetry-consuming, sentimental idiots, commend me to you fellows. 'Master of my fate, captain of my soul,' be dashed! Old Jujube, with his bone-pointed hunting spear, began determining a couple of hundred years ago what I should be in this year of our Lord one thousand eight hundred and ninety-four. J. Webb Davis, senior, added another brick to this structure, when he was picking cotton on his master's plantation forty years ago."

"And now," said Halliday, also rising, "don't you think it fair that you should start out with the idea of adding a few bricks of your own, and all of a better make than those of your remote ancestor, Jujube, or that nearer one, your father?"

"Spoken like a man," said McLean.

"Oh, you two are so hopelessly young," laughed Davis.

Part II

After the two weeks' rest which he thought he needed, and consequently promised himself, Halliday began to look about him for some means of making a start for that success in life which he felt so sure of winning.

With this end in view he returned to the town where he was born. He had settled upon the law as a profession, and had studied it for a year or two while at college. He would go back to Broughton now to pursue his studies, but of course, he needed money. No difficulty, however, presented itself in the getting of this for he knew several fellows who had been able to go into offices, and by collecting and similar duties make something while they studied. Webb Davis would have said, "but they were white," but Halliday knew what his own reply would have been: "What a white man can do, I can do."

Even if he could not go to studying at once, he could go to work and save enough money to go on with his course in a year or two. He had lots of time before him, and he only needed a little start. What better place then, to go to than Broughton, where he had first seen the light? Broughton, that had known him, boy and man. Broughton, that had watched him through the common school and the high school, and had seen him go off to college with some pride and a good deal of curiosity. For even in middle west towns of such a size, that is, between seventy and eighty thousand souls, a "smart Negro" was still a freak.

So Halliday went back home because the people knew him there and would respect his struggles and encourage his ambitions.

He had been home two days, and the old town had begun to take on its remembered aspect as he wandered through the streets and along the river banks. On this second day he was going up Main street deep in a brown study when he heard his name called by a young man who was approaching him, and saw an outstretched hand.

"Why, how de do, Bert, how are you? Glad to see you back. I hear you have been astonishing them up at college."

Halliday's reveries had been so suddenly broken into that for a moment, the young fellow's identity wavered elusively before his mind and then it materialized, and his consciousness took hold of it. He remembered him, not as an intimate, but as an acquaintance whom he had often met upon the football and baseball fields.

"How do you do? It's Bob Dickson," he said, shaking the proffered hand, which at the mention of the name, had grown unaccountably cold in his grasp.

"Yes, I'm Mr. Dickson," said the young man, patronizingly. "You seem to have developed wonderfully, you hardly seem like the same Bert Halliday I used to know."

"Yes, but I'm the same Mr. Halliday."

"Oh—ah—yes," said the young man, "well, I'm glad to have seen you. Ah—good-bye, Bert."

"Good-bye, Bob."

"Presumptuous darky!" murmured Mr. Dickson.

"Insolent puppy!" said Mr. Halliday to himself.

But the incident made no impression on his mind as bearing upon his status in the public eye. He only thought the fellow a cad, and went hopefully on. He was rather amused than otherwise. In this frame of mind, he turned into one of the large office buildings that lined the street and made his way to a business suite over whose door was the inscription, "H. G. Featherton, Counselor and Attorney-at-Law." Mr. Featherton had shown considerable interest in Bert in his school days, and he hoped much from him.

As he entered the public office, a man sitting at the large desk in the center of the room turned and faced him. He was a fair man of an indeterminate age, for you could not tell whether those were streaks of gray shining in his light hair, or only the glint which it took on in the sun. His face was dry, lean and intellectual. He smiled now and then, and his smile was like a flash of winter lightning, so cold and quick it was. It went as suddenly as it came, leaving the face as marbly cold and impassive as ever. He rose and extended his hand, "Why—why— ah—Bert, how de do, how are you?"

"Very well, I thank you, Mr. Featherton."

"Hum, I'm glad to see you back, sit down. Going to stay with us, you think?"

"I'm not sure, Mr. Featherton; it all depends upon my getting something to do."

"You want to go to work, do you? Hum, well, that's right. It's work makes the man. What do you propose to do, now since you've graduated?"

Bert warmed at the evident interest of his old friend. "Well, in the first place, Mr. Featherton," he replied, "I must get to work and make some money. I have heard of fellows studying and supporting themselves at the same time, but I mustn't expect too much. I'm going to study law."

The attorney had schooled his face into hiding any emotion he might feel, and it did not betray him now. He only flashed one of his quick cold smiles and asked, "Don't you think you've taken rather a hard profession to get on in?"

"No doubt. But anything I should take would be hard. It's just like this, Mr. Featherton," he went on, "I am willing to work and to work hard, and I am not looking for any snap."

Mr. Featherton was so unresponsive to this outburst that Bert was ashamed of it the minute it left his lips. He wished this man would not be so cold and polite and he wished he would stop putting the ends of his white fingers together as carefully as if something depended upon it.

"I say the law is a hard profession to get on in, and as a friend I say that it will be harder for you. Your people have not the money to spend in litigation of any kind."

"I should not cater for the patronage of my own people alone."

"Yes, but the time has not come when a white person will employ a colored attorney."

"Do you mean to say that the prejudice here at home is such that if I were as competent as a white lawyer a white person would not employ me?"

"I say nothing about prejudice at all. It's nature. They have their own lawyers; why should they go outside of their own to employ a colored man?"

"But I am of their own. I am an American citizen, there should be no thought of color about it."

"Oh, my boy, that theory is very nice, but State University democracy doesn't obtain in real life."

"More's the pity, then, for real life."

"Perhaps, but we must take things as we find them, not as we think they ought to be. You people are having and will have for the next ten or a dozen years the hardest fight of your lives. The sentiment of remorse and the desire for atoning which actuated so many white men to help Negroes right after the war has passed off without being replaced by that sense of plain justice which gives a black man his due, not because of, nor in spite of, but without consideration of his color."

"I wonder if it can be true, as my friend Davis says, that a colored man must do twice as much and twice as well as a white man before he can hope for even equal chances with him? That white mediocrity demands black genius to cope with it?"

"I am afraid your friend has philosophized the situation about right."

"Well, we have dealt in generalities," said Bert, smiling, "let us take up the particular and personal part of this matter. Is there any way you could help me to a situation?"

"Well,—I should be glad to see you get on, Bert, but as you see, I have nothing in my office that you could do. Now, if you don't mind beginning at the bottom——"

"That's just what I expected to do."

"—Why, I could speak to the head waiter of the hotel where I stay. He's a very nice colored man and I have some influence with him. No doubt Charlie could give you a place."

"But that's a work I abhor."

"Yes, but you must begin at the bottom, you know. All young men must."

"To be sure, but would you have recommended the same thing to your nephew on his leaving college?"

"Ah—ah—that's different."

"Yes," said Halliday, rising, "it is different. There's a different bottom at which black and white young men should begin, and by a logical sequence, a different top to which they should aspire. However, Mr. Featherton, I'll ask you to hold your offer in abeyance. If I can find nothing else, I'll ask you to speak to the head waiter. Good morning."

"I'll do so with pleasure," said Mr. Featherton, "and good morning."

As the young man went up the street, an announcement card in the window of a publishing house caught his eye. It was the announcement of the next Sunday's number in a series of addresses which the local business men were giving before the YMCA. It read, "'How a Christian young man can get on in the law'—an address by a Christian lawyer—H. G. Featherton."

Bert laughed. "I should like to hear that address," he said. "I wonder if he'll recommend them to his head waiter. No, 'that's different.' All the addresses and all the books written on how to get on, are written for white men. We blacks must solve the question for ourselves."

He had lost some of the ardor with which he had started out but he was still full of hope. He refused to accept Mr. Featherton's point of view as general or final. So he hailed a passing car that in the course of a half hour set him down at the door of the great factory which, with its improvements, its army of clerks and employees, had built up one whole section of the town. He felt especially hopeful in attacking this citadel, because they were constantly advertising for clerks and their placards plainly stated that preference would be given to graduates of the local high school. The owners were philanthropists in their way. Well, what better chance could there be before him? He had graduated there and stood well in his classes, and besides, he knew that a number of his classmates were holding good positions in the factory. So his voice was cheerful as he asked to see Mr. Stockard, who had charge of the clerical department.

Mr. Stockard was a fat, wheezy young man, with a reputation for humor based entirely upon his size and his rubicund face, for he had really never said anything humorous in his life. He came panting into the room now with a "Well, what can I do for you?"

"I wanted to see you about a situation"—began Halliday.

"Oh, no, no, you don't want to see me," broke in Stockard, "you want to see the head janitor."

"But I don't want to see the head janitor. I want to see the head of the clerical department."

"You want to see the head of the clerical department!"

"Yes, sir, I see you are advertising for clerks with preference given to the high school boys. Well, I am an old high school boy, but have been away for a few years at college."

Mr. Stockard opened his eyes to their widest extent, and his jaw dropped. Evidently he had never come across such presumption before.

"We have nothing for you," he wheezed after awhile.

"Very well, I should be glad to drop in again and see you," said Halliday, moving to the door. "I hope you will remember me if anything opens."

Mr. Stockard did not reply to this or to Bert's good-bye. He stood in the middle of the floor and stared at the door through which the colored man had gone, then he dropped into a chair with a gasp.

"Well, I'm dumbed!" he said.

A doubt had begun to arise in Bertram Halliday's mind that turned him cold and then hot with a burning indignation. He could try nothing more that morning. It had brought him nothing but rebuffs. He hastened home and threw himself down on the sofa to try and think out his situation.

"Do they still require of us bricks without straw? I thought all that was over. Well, I suspect that I will have to ask Mr. Featherton to speak to his head waiter in my behalf. I wonder if the head waiter will demand my diploma. Webb Davis, you were nearer right than I thought."

He spent the day in the house thinking and planning.

PART III

Halliday was not a man to be discouraged easily, and for the next few weeks he kept up an unflagging search for work. He found that there were more Feathertons and Stockards than he had ever looked to find. Everywhere that he turned his face, anything but the most menial work was denied him. He thought once of going away from Broughton, but would he find it any better anywhere else, he asked himself? He determined to stay and fight it out there for two reasons. First, because he held that it would be cowardice to run away, and secondly, because he felt that he was not fighting a local disease, but was bringing the force of his life to bear upon a national evil. Broughton was as good a place to begin curative measures as elsewhere.

There was one refuge which was open to him, and which he fought against with all his might. For years now, from as far back as he could remember, the colored graduates had "gone South to teach." This course was now recommended to him. Indeed, his own family quite approved of it, and when he still stood out against the scheme, people began to say that Bertram Halliday did not want work; he wanted to be a gentleman.

But Halliday knew that the South had plenty of material, and year by year was raising and training her own teachers. He knew that the time would come, if it were not present, when it would be impossible to go South to teach, and he felt it to be essential that the North should be trained in a manner looking to the employment of her own Negroes. So he stayed. But he was only human and when the tide of talk anent his indolence began to ebb and flow about him, he availed himself of the only expedient that could arrest it.

When he went back to the great factory where he had seen and talked with Mr. Stockard, he went around to another door and this time asked for the head janitor. This individual, a genial Irishman, took stock of Halliday at a glance.

"But what d ye want to be doin' sich wurruk for, whin ye've been through school?" he asked.

"I am doing the only thing I can get to do," was the answer.

"Well," said the Irishman, "ye've got sinse, anyhow."

Bert found himself employed as an under janitor at the factory at a wage of nine dollars a week. At this, he could pay his share to keep the house going, and save a little for the period of study he still looked forward to. The people who had accused him of laziness now made a martyr of him, and said what a pity it was for a man with such an education and with so much talent to be employed menially.

He did not neglect his studies, but read at night, whenever the day's work had not made both brain and body too weary for the task.

In this way his life went along for over a year when one morning a note from Mr. Featherton summoned him to that gentleman's office. It is true that Halliday read the note with some trepidation. His bitter experience had not yet taught him how not to dream. He was not yet old enough for that. "Maybe," he thought, "Mr. Featherton has relented, and is going to give me a chance anyway. Or perhaps he wanted me to prove my mettle before he consented to take me up. Well, I've tried to do it, and if that's what he wanted, I hope he's satisfied." The note which seemed written all over with joyful tidings shook in his hand.

The genial manner with which Mr. Featherton met him reaffirmed in his mind the belief that at last the lawyer had determined to give him a chance. He was almost deferential as he asked Bert into his private office, and shoved a chair forward for him.

"Well, you've been getting on, I see," he began.

"Oh, yes," replied Bert, "I have been getting on by hook and crook."

"Hum, done any studying lately?"

"Yes, but not as much as I wish to. Coke and Wharton aren't any clearer to a head grown dizzy with bending over mops, brooms and heavy trucks all day."

"No, I should think not. Ah—oh—well, Bert, how should you like to come into my office and help around, do such errands as I need and help copy my papers?"

"I should be delighted."

"It would only pay you five dollars a week, less than what you are getting now, I suppose, but it will be more genteel."

"Oh, now that I have had to do it, I don't care so much about the lack of gentility of my present work, but I prefer what you offer because I shall have a greater chance to study."

"Well, then, you may as well come in on Monday. The office will be often in your charge, as I am going to be away a great deal in the next few months. You know I am going to make the fight for nomination to the seat on the bench which is vacant this fall."

"Indeed. I have not so far taken much interest in politics, but I will do all in my power to help you with both nomination and election."

"Thank you," said Mr. Featherton, "I am sure you can be of great service to me as the vote of your people is pretty heavy in Broughton. I have always been a friend to them, and I believe I can depend upon their support. I shall be glad of any good you can do me with them."

Bert laughed when he was out on the street again. "For value received," he said. He thought less of Mr. Featherton's generosity since he saw it was actuated by self-interest alone, but that in no wise destroyed the real worth of the opportunity that was now given into his hands. Featherton, he believed, would make an excellent judge, and he was glad that in working for his nomination his convictions so aptly fell in with his inclinations.

His work at the factory had put him in touch with a larger number of his people than he could have possibly met had he gone into the office at once. Over them, his naturally bright mind exerted some influence. As a simple laborer he had fellowshipped with them but they acknowledged and availed themselves of his leadership, because they felt instinctively in him a power which they did not have. Among them now he worked sedulously. He held that the greater part of the battle would be in the primaries, and on the night when they convened, he had his friends out in force in every ward which went to make up the third judicial district. Men who had never seen the inside of a primary meeting before were there actively engaged in this.

The *Diurnal* said next morning that the active interest of the hard-working, churchgoing colored voters, who wanted to see a Christian judge on the bench, had had much to do with the nomination of Mr. Featherton.

The success at the primaries did not tempt Halliday to relinquish his efforts on his employer's behalf. He was indefatigable in his cause. On the west side where the colored population had largely colonized, he made speeches and held meetings clear up to election day. The fight had been between two factions of the party and after the nomination it was feared that the defection of the party defeated in the primaries might prevent the ratification of the nominee at the polls. But before the contest was half over all fears for him were laid. What he had lost in the districts where the skulking faction was strong, he made up in the wards where the colored vote was large. He was overwhelmingly elected.

Halliday smiled as he sat in the office and heard the congratulations poured in upon Judge Featherton.

"Well, it's wonderful," said one of his visitors, "how the colored boys stood by you."

"Yes, I have been a friend to the colored people, and they know it," said Featherton.

It would be some months before His Honor would take his seat on the bench, and during that time, Halliday hoped to finish his office course.

He was surprised when Featherton came to him a couple of weeks after the election and said, "Well, Bert, I guess I can get along now. I'll be shutting up this office pretty soon. Here are your wages and here is a little gift I wish to add out of respect to you for your kindness during my run for office."

Bert took the wages, but the added ten dollar note he waved aside. "No, I thank you, Mr. Featherton," he said, "what I did, I did from a belief in your fitness for the place, and out of loyalty to my employer. I don't want any money for it."

"Then let us say that I have raised your wages to this amount."

"No, that would only be evasion. I want no more than you promised to give me."

"Very well, then accept my thanks, anyway."

What things he had at the office Halliday took away that night. A couple of days later he remembered a book which he had failed to get and returned for it. The office was as usual. Mr. Featherton was a little embarrassed and nervous. At Halliday's desk sat a young white man about his own age. He was copying a deed for Mr. Featherton.

PART IV

Bertram Halliday went home, burning with indignation at the treatment he had received at the hands of the Christian judge.

"He has used me as a housemaid would use a lemon," he said, "squeezed all out of me he could get, and then flung me into the street. Well, Webb was nearer right than I thought."

He was now out of everything. His place at the factory had been filled, and no new door opened to him. He knew what reward a search for work brought a man of his color in Broughton, so he did not bestir himself to go over the old track again. He thanked his stars that he, at least, had money enough to carry him away from the place and he determined to go. His spirit was quelled, but not broken.

Just before leaving, he wrote to Davis.

"My dear Webb!" the letter ran, "you, after all, were right. We have little or no show in the fight for life among these people. I have struggled for two years here at Broughton, and now find myself back where I was when I first stepped out of school with a foolish faith in being equipped for something. One thing, my eyes have been opened anyway, and I no longer judge so harshly the shiftless and unambitious among my people. I hardly see how a people, who have so much to contend with and so little to hope for, can go on striving and aspiring. But the very fact that they do, breeds in me a respect for them. I now see why so many promising young men, class orators, valedictorians and the like fall by the wayside and are never heard from after commencement day. I now see why the sleeping and dining-car companies are supplied by men with better educations than half the passengers whom they serve. They get tired of swimming always against the tide, as who would not? and are content to drift.

"I know that a good many of my friends would say that I am whining. Well, suppose I am, that's the business of a whipped cur. The dog on top can bark, but the under dog must howl.

"Nothing so breaks a man's spirit as defeat, constant, unaltering, hopeless defeat. That's what I've experienced. I am still studying law in a half-hearted way for I don't know what I am going to do with it when I have been admitted. Diplomas don't draw clients. We have been taught that merit wins. But I have learned that the adages, as well as the books and the formulas were made by and for others than us of the black race.

"They say, too, that our brother Americans sympathize with us, and will help us when we help ourselves. Bah! The only sympathy that I have ever seen on the part of the white man was not for the Negro himself, but for some portion of white blood that the colored man had got tangled up in his veins.

"But there, perhaps my disappointment has made me sour, so think no more of what I have said. I am going now to do what I abhor. Going South to try to find a school. It's awful. But I don't want any one to pity me. There are several thousands of us in the same position.

"I am glad you are prospering. You were better equipped than I was with a deal of materialism and a dearth of ideals. Give us a line when you are in good heart.

Yours,
Halliday.

"P.S.—Just as I finished writing I had a note from Judge Featherton offering me the court messengership at five dollars a week. I am twenty-five. The place was held before by a white boy of fifteen. I declined, 'Southward Ho!'"

Davis was not without sympathy as he read his friend's letter in a city some distance away. He had worked in a hotel, saved money enough to start a barber shop and was prospering. His white customers joked with him and patted him on the back, and he was already known to have political influence. Yes, he sympathized with Bert, but he laughed over the letter and jingled the coins in his pockets.

"Thank heaven," he said, "that I have no ideals to be knocked into a cocked hat. A colored man has no business with ideals—not in *this* nineteenth century!"

THE EMANCIPATION OF EVALINA JONES

Douglass Street was alive with people, and astir from one dirty end to the other. Flags were flying from houses, and everything was gay with life and color. Every denizen of Little Africa was out in the street. That is, every one except Evalina Jones, and even she came as far as the corner, when with banners flying, and the sound of the colored band playing "'Rastus on Parade," the "Hod-Carriers' Union," bright in their gorgeous scarlet uniforms, came marching down. It was a great day for Little Africa, the twenty-second of September, and they were celebrating the emancipation of their race. The crowning affair of the day was to be this picnic of the "Hod-Carriers' Union," at the Fair Grounds where there was to be a balloon ascension, dancing, feasting, and fireworks, with a speech by the Rev. Mr. Barnett, from Green County, a very famous orator, who had been in the legislature, and now aspired to be a Bishop.

Evalina looked on with eyes that sparkled with the life of the scene, until the last of the pageant had passed, and then the light died out of her face and she hurried back to her home as she saw a man coming toward her up the street. She was bending over her wash-tub when he came into the house.

"Got any money, Evalina?" he asked, leering at her.

"I got fifty cents, Jim, but what do you want with that?" she replied.

"Nevah you mind what I want with it, give it to me."

"But Jim, that's all I got to go to the picnic with, an' I been hu'yin' thoo so I could git sta'ted."

"Picnic," he said. "Picnic, I'll picnic you. You ain't goin' a step f'om this house. What's the mattah with you, ain't you got that washin' to finish?"

"Yes, but I kin get throo in time, an' I want to go Jim, I want to go. You made me stay home last yeah, an' yeah befo', and I'm jes' the same ez a slave, I am."

"You gi' me that money," he said menacingly. Evalina's hand went down into the pocket of her calico dress, and reluctantly drew forth a pitiful half dollar.

"Umph," said her worse half. "This is a pretty looking sum fu' you to have, pu'tendin' to wo'k all the time," and he lurched out of the door.

Evalina stopped only long enough to wipe a few tears from her eyes, and then she went stolidly on with her washing. She had been married to Jim for five years, and for that length of time he had bullied her, and made her his slave. She had been a bright, bustling woman, but he had killed all the brightness in her and changed her bustling activity into mere stolid slavishness. Cheerfully she bore it at first, for a little child had come to bless her life. But when, after two pain-ridden years, the little one had passed away, she took up her burden sullenly, and without relief. People knew that Jim abused her, but she never complained to them; she was close-mouthed and patient. The very firmness with which she set her mouth when things went particularly hard, indicated that she might have beat her husband at his own game, had she tried. But somehow she never tried. There was a remarkable reserve force about the woman, but it needed something strong, something thrilling, to stir it into action.

Now and again, as she bent over the tub, her tears fell and mingled with the suds. They fell faster as the image of the little grave, which she had worked so hard to have digged outside the confines of Potter's Field, would arise in her mind. Then a tap came at her door.

"Come in," she said. A woman entered, bright in an array of cheap finery.

"Howdy, Evalina," she said.

"Howdy, yo'se'f, Ca'line," was the response.

"Oh, I middlin'. Ain't you goin' to the picnic?"

"No, I reckon I ain't. I got my work to do. I ain't got no time fu' picnics."

"Why, La, chile, this ain't no day fu' wo'k—Celebration Day! Why, evahbody's goin'; I even see ol' Aunt Maria Green hobblin' out wid huh cane, an' ol' Uncle Jimmy Hunter."

"I reckon they got time," said Evalina; "I ain't."

She looked the woman over with an unfriendly eye. She knew that this creature who made of life so light and easy a thing, stood between her and any joy that she might have found in her bare existence. She knew that Jim liked Caroline Wilson, and compared his wife unfavorably with her. She looked at the flashy ribbons, and the brilliant hat, and then involuntarily glanced down at her own shabby gown, torn and faded and suds-splashed, and an anger, the heat of which she had never known before, came into her heart. Her throat grew dry and throbbed, but she said huskily,

"'Taint fu' me to go to picnics, it's fu' nice ladies what live easy, an' dress fine. I mus' wo'k an' dig an' scrub."

"Humph," said the other, "of co'se there's a diffunce in people."

"Well, that's one thng I kin thank Gawd fu'," said Evalina, with grim humor.

Caroline Wilson bridled. "I hope you ain't th'owin' out no slurs at me, Evalina Jones, cause I wants you to know I's a lady, myse'f."

"I ain't th'owin' out no slurs at nobody," said Evalina, slowly. "But all I kin say is thet ef that shoe fits you, put it on and waih it."

Her visitor was angry, and she showed it. She stood up, and the spirit of battle was strong in her. But she gave a glance first at her finery, and then at the strong arms which her hostess had placed akimbo as she looked at her, and she decided not to bring matters to an issue.

"Well, of co'se," temporized Caroline, "I'd like to see you go, but it ain't none o' my business. I allus got along wid my po' hu'ban' w'en he was livin'."

"Oh, I ain't 'sputin' that, I ain't 'sputin' that. They ain't no woman that knows you goin' 'ny you got wunnerful pow'rs fu' handlin' men."

"Well, I does know how to keep what I has."

"Yes, an' you knows how to git what you hasn't." The light was growing greatly in Evalina's eyes, and Caroline saw it. She wasn't a coward, not she. But she looked at her finery again. It did look so flimsy and delicate to her eyes; then she said, "I mus' be goin', goo'bye."

"Goo'bye. Well, ef I didn't have a min' to frail that ooman, I ain't hyeah," and Evalina went back to her work with a shaking head and a new spirit.

Some instinct drew her to the door, and feeling that she might at least avail herself of a little breathing space, she walked as far as the corner of the now entirely deserted street. It was good that she had come, for the sight that she saw there aroused the life in her that had lain dead for the five years that she had been Jim's wife. She stood at the corner, and gazed down at the street that ran at right angles. Her arms unconsciously went akimbo, and she grinned a half-mouthed grin, showing the white gleam of her upper teeth like a dog when someone has robbed him of his precious bone.

"Oom-hoomph, Ca'line," she said, "oom-humph, Jim, I caught you." There was no shade of the anger she felt in her heart expressed in her tones. They were dry, hard and even, but she grinned that dog-like grin which boded no good to Jim and Caroline, who, all unconscious of it, walked on down the street towards the Fair Grounds.

She was done by eleven o'clock. Then she put on the best dress she had, and even that best was shabby, for Jim "needed" most of her money, and went up town to see Mrs. Wharton, for whom she worked. Mrs. Wharton was a little woman, with a very large spirit.

"Why, Evalina," she said, when she saw the black woman, "why on earth aren't you at the picnic?"

"That's jes' what I come hyeah to talk to you about," was the reply.

"Well, do let me hear! If you didn't have the money, why didn't you come to me? That's just what I say about you, you never open your mouth when you need anything. You know I'd have helped you out," rushed on the little lady.

"'Taint that, 'taint that," replied Evalina, "I'd a spoke to you this week. 'Taint the money, Mis' Wharton, it's Jim."

"Jim, Jim, what's that great hulking lazybones got to do with your going to the picnic?"

"He says I ain't to go."

"Ain't to go! Well, we'll show him whether you're to go or not."

At this sign of encouragement, Evalina brightened up. "Mis' Wharton," she burst out, "you don't know what I been bearin' f'om that man, an' I ain't nevah said nothin', but I cain't hol' in any longer. I ain't got a decent thing to wear, an' this very day, Jim tuk my las' cent o' money, an' walked off to the Fair Grounds wid another ooman."

"Come into the sewing-room, Evalina," said Mrs. Wharton with sudden energy. "You'll go to that picnic, and if that brute interferes with you, I'll put him where the rain won't touch him."

In the sewing-room, where Mrs. Wharton led the bewildered and delighted Evalina, there was wonderful letting out of seams, piecing of short skirts, and stretching over of scanty folds. But the washer-woman came out from there smiling and happy, well dressed and spirited. Say not that clothes have nothing to do with the feeling of the average human being. She felt that she could meet a dozen Jims and out-face them all. The day of her awakening had come, and it had been like the awakening of a young giantess.

Jim was enjoying himself in a quadrille with Caroline when Evalina reached the dancing hall. He was just in the midst of a dashing faran-dole, much to the delight of the crowd, when he caught a glimpse of his wife arrayed in all her glory; he suddenly stopped. The people about thought he had paused for applause, and they gave it to him gen-erously, but he failed to repeat his antics. He was surprised out of a desire for their approval. He gazed at his slave, and she, his slave no longer, gazed back at him calmly. For the rest of that quadrille he proved a most spiritless partner, and at its close Caroline, with a toss of her head, yielded herself to some more desirable companion. Then, with a surprise which he could not suppress, struggling for expression on his lowering brow, Jim went over to Evalina.

"What you doin' out hyeah?" he said roughly.

"Enjoyin' myse'f, like you is," replied Evalina.

"Didn't I tell you not to come?"

"What diffunce do yo' tellin' make?"

"I show you what diffunce my tellin' make," he said threateningly.

"You ain't goin' to show me not a pleg-goned thing," was the reply which started him out of his senses, as Evalina started away on the arm of a partner, who had come to claim her for the next dance. Jim leaned up against a post to get his breath. He had expected Evalina to be scared, and she was not. There was some mistake, surely. This was not the Evalina whom he had known and married. Suddenly all of his tra-ditions had been destroyed, and his mind reached out for something to grasp and hold to, and found only empty air. Meanwhile his wife, all her youthful lightness seeming to have come back to her, was whirling away in the mazes of the dance, stepping out as he had seen her step, when she had charmed him years ago. He stood and looked at her dully. He hadn't even energy enough to seek another partner and so show his resentment.

When the dance was over, Jim went up to Evalina and said shame-facedly, "Well, sence you're out hyeah, folks are goin' to 'spec' us to dance togethah, I reckon?"

"Don't you min' folks," she said, "you jes' disapp'int 'em. Thaih's Ca'line ovah thaih waitin' fu' you," and she bowed graciously to a robust hod-carrier, who was on the other side asking "fu' de pleasure."

Jim could stand it no longer. He wandered out of the dance hall, and walked down by the horse stables alone, thinking of the change that had come to Evalina. He felt grieved, and a great wave of self-pity surged over him. His wife wasn't treating him right. He was a very much ill-used man.

Then it was time for the speaking, and he went back to the stand, to find his recreant wife the center of a number of women-folk, drawn about her by the unaccustomed fineness of her quiet gown. She was chatting, as he remembered she had chatted before he had discouraged all lightness of talk in her. When the speaker began there was no applause readier than her own. The Rev. Mr. Barnett was a very witty man. In fact, it was his wit, rather than his brains or his morals, that had sent him to the legislature; and when he scored a good point, Jim heard her laugh ring out, clear, high, and musical. He could not help but wonder. It dazed him. Evalina had not laughed before since her little one had died, and when the speaking was over she was on the floor again, without a glance for him.

"That's the way with women," he told himself. "Hyeah I is, walkin' 'roun' hyeah all alone, an' she don't pay no mo' 'tention to me then if I was a dog." So he wandered over to the place where they were selling drinks, but they would not give him credit there, and feeling worse abused than ever, he went back to stand a silent witness of his wife's pleasure.

Evalina did not approve of remaining until after dark at the Fair Grounds, when the rougher element began to come, so she left before Jim. She had finished her supper, and was sitting at the door when he came home. He passed her sullenly and went into the house, where he dropped into a chair. She was humming a light tune and paid no attention to him. Finally he said:

"You treated me nice to-day, didn't you? Dancin' 'roun' without payin' no 'tention to me, an' you my own lawful wife!"

This was too much for Evalina, it was too unjust. She got up and faced him, "Yo' own lawful wife," she said, "I don't reckon you thought o' that this mornin' when you tuk my las' cent, an' went out thaih wid Ca'line Wilson. Yo' lawful wife! You been treatin' me lak a wife, ain't you? This is the fust 'Mancipation Day I've had since I ma'ied you, but I want you to know I'se stood all I'se goin' to stan' f'om you, an' evah day's goin' to be 'Mancipation Day aftah this."

Jim was aghast. Rebellion cowed him. He wanted to be ugly, but he was crushed.

"I don't care nothin' 'bout Ca'line Wilson," he said.

"An' I don' care nothin' 'bout you," she retorted.

Jim's voice trembled. This was going too far. "That's all right, Evalina," he said, "that's all right. Mebbe I ain't no angel, but that ain't no way to talk to me; I's yo' husban'." He was on the verge of maudlin tears. Somewhere he had found credit, and his conquered condition softened Evalina.

"You ain't been very keerful how you talk to me," she said in an easier tone. "But thaih's one thing suttain, aftah this you got to walk straight,—you hyeah me! Want some supper?"

"Yes," said Jim humbly.

THE TRAGEDY AT THREE FORKS

It was a drizzly, disagreeable April night. The wind was howling in a particularly dismal and malignant way along the valleys and hollows of that part of Central Kentucky in which the rural settlement of Three Forks is situated. It had been "trying to rain" all day in a half-hearted sort of manner, and now the drops were flying about in a cold spray. The night was one of dense, inky blackness, occasionally relieved by flashes of lightning. It was hardly a night on which a girl should be out. And yet one was out, scudding before the storm, with clenched teeth and wild eyes, wrapped head and shoulders in a great blanket shawl, and looking, as she sped along like a restless, dark ghost. For her, the night and the storm had no terrors; passion had driven out fear. There was determination in her every movement, and purpose was apparent in the concentration of energy with which she set her foot down. She drew the shawl closer about her head with a convulsive grip, and muttered with a half sob, "'Tain't the first time, 'tain't the first time she's tried to take me down in comp'ny, but—" and the sob gave way to the dry, sharp note in her voice, "I'll fix her, if it kills me. She thinks I ain't her ekals, does she? 'Cause her pap's got money, an' has good crops on his lan', an' my pap ain't never had no luck, but I'll show 'er, I'll show 'er that good luck can't allus last. Pleg-take 'er, she's jealous, 'cause I'm better lookin' than she is, an' pearter in every way, so she tries to make me little in the eyes of people. Well, you'll find out what it is to be pore—to have nothin', Seliny Williams, if you live."

The black night hid a gleam in the girl's eyes, and her shawl hid a bundle of something light, which she clutched very tightly, and which smelled of kerosene.

The dark outline of a house and its outbuildings loomed into view through the dense gloom; and the increased caution with which the girl proceeded, together with the sudden breathless intentness of her conduct, indicated that it was with this house and its occupants she was concerned.

The house was cellarless, but it was raised at the four corners on heavy blocks, leaving a space between the ground and the floor, the sides of which were partly closed by banks of ashes and earth which were thrown up against the weather-boarding. It was but a few minutes' work to scrape away a portion of this earth, and push under the pack of shavings into which the mysterious bundle resolved itself. A match was lighted, sheltered, until it blazed, and then dropped among them. It took only a short walk and a shorter time to drop a handful of burning shavings into the hay at the barn. Then the girl turned and sped away, muttering: "I reckon I've fixed you, Seliny Williams, mebbe, next time you meet me out at a dance, you won't snub me; mebbe next time, you'll be ez pore ez I am, an'll be willin' to dance crost from even ole 'Lias Hunster's gal."

The constantly falling drizzle might have dampened the shavings and put out the fire, had not the wind fanned the sparks into too rapid a flame, which caught eagerly at shingle, board and joist until house and barn were wrapped in flames. The whinnying of the horses first woke Isaac Williams, and he sprang from bed at sight of the furious light which surrounded his house. He got his family up and out of the house, each seizing what he could of wearing apparel as he fled before the flames. Nothing else could be saved, for the fire had gained terrible headway, and its fierceness precluded all possibility of fighting it. The neighbors attracted by the lurid glare came from far and near, but the fire had done its work, and their efforts availed nothing. House, barn, stock, all, were a mass of ashes and charred cinders. Isaac Williams, who had a day before, been accounted one of the solidest farmers in the region, went out that night with his family—homeless.

Kindly neighbors took them in, and by morning the news had spread throughout all the country-side. Incendiarism was the only cause that could be assigned, and many were the speculations as to who the guilty party could be. Of course, Isaac Williams had enemies. But who among them was mean, ay, daring enough to perpetrate such a deed as this?

Conjecture was rife, but futile, until old 'Lias Hunster, who though he hated Williams, was shocked at the deed, voiced the popular sentiment by saying, "Look a here, folks, I tell you that's the work o' niggers, I kin see their hand in it."

"Niggers, o' course," exclaimed every one else. "Why didn't we think of it before? It's jest like 'em."

Public opinion ran high and fermented until Saturday afternoon when the county paper brought the whole matter to a climax by coming out in a sulphurous account of the affair, under the scarehead:

A TERRIBLE OUTRAGE!
MOST DASTARDLY DEED EVER COMMITTED IN THE
HISTORY OF BARLOW COUNTY. A HIGHLY RE-
SPECTED, UNOFFENDING AND WELL-BE-
LOVED FAMILY BURNED OUT OF HOUSE
AND HOME. NEGROES! UN-
DOUBTEDLY THE PERPETRA-
TORS OF THE DEED!

The article went on to give the facts of the case, and many more supposed facts, which had originated entirely in the mind of the correspondent. Among these facts was the intelligence that some strange negroes had been seen lurking in the vicinity the day before the catastrophe and that a party of citizens and farmers were scouring the surrounding country in search of them. "They would, if caught," concluded the correspondent, "be summarily dealt with."

Notwithstanding the utter falsity of these statements, it did not take long for the latter part of the article to become a prophecy fulfilled, and soon, excited, inflamed and misguided parties of men and boys were scouring the woods and roads in search of strange "niggers." Nor was it long, before one of the parties raised the cry that they had found the culprits. They had come upon two strange negroes going through the woods, who seeing a band of mounted and armed men, had instantly taken to their heels. This one act had accused, tried and convicted them.

The different divisions of the searching party came together, and led the negroes with ropes around their necks into the centre of the village. Excited crowds on the one or two streets which the hamlet boasted, cried "Lynch 'em, lynch 'em! Hang the niggers up to the first tree!"

Jane Hunster was in one of the groups, as the shivering negroes passed, and she turned very pale even under the sunburn that browned her face.

The law-abiding citizens of Barlow County, who composed the capturing party, were deaf to the admonitions of the crowd. They filed solemnly up the street, and delivered their prisoners to the keeper of the jail, sheriff, by courtesy, and scamp by the seal of Satan; and then quietly dispersed. There was something ominous in their very orderliness.

Late that afternoon, the man who did duty as prosecuting attorney for that county, visited the prisoners at the jail, and drew from them the story that they were farm-laborers from an adjoining county. They had come over only the day before, and were passing through on the quest for work; the bad weather and the lateness of the season having thrown them out at home.

"Uh, huh," said the prosecuting attorney at the conclusion of the tale, "your story's all right, but the only trouble is that it won't do here. They won't believe you. Now, I'm a friend to niggers as much as any white man can be, if they'll only be friends to themselves, an' I want to help you two all I can. There's only one way out of this trouble. You must confess that you did this."

"But Mistah," said the bolder of the two negroes, "how kin we 'fess, when we wasn' nowhahs nigh de place?"

"Now there you go with regular nigger stubbornness; didn't I tell you that that was the only way out of this? If you persist in saying you didn't do it, they'll hang you; whereas, if you own, you'll only get a couple of years in the 'pen.' Which 'ud you rather have, a couple o' years to work out, or your necks stretched?"

"Oh, we'll 'fess, Mistah, we'll 'fess we done it; please, please don't let 'em hang us!" cried the thoroughly frightened blacks.

"Well, that's something like it," said the prosecuting attorney as he rose to go. "I'll see what can be done for you."

With marvelous and mysterious rapidity, considering the reticence which a prosecuting attorney who was friendly to the negroes should display, the report got abroad that the negroes had confessed their crime, and soon after dark, ominous looking crowds began to gather in the streets. They passed and repassed the place, where stationed on the little wooden shelf that did duty as a doorstep, Jane Hunster sat with her head buried in her hands. She did not raise up to look at any of them, until a hand was laid on her shoulder, and a voice called her, "Jane!"

"Oh, hit's you, is it, Bud," she said, raising her head slowly, "howdy?"

"Howdy yoreself," said the young man, looking down at her tenderly.

"Bresh off yore pants an' set down," said the girl making room for him on the step. The young man did so, at the same time taking hold of her hand with awkward tenderness.

"Jane," he said, "I jest can't wait fur my answer no longer! you got to tell me to-night, either one way or the other. Dock Heaters has been a-blowin' hit aroun' that he has beat my time with you. I don't believe it, Jane, fur after keepin' me waitin' all these years, I don't believe you'd go back on me. You know I've allus loved you, ever sence we was little children together."

The girl was silent until he leaned over and said in pleading tones, "What do you say, Jane?"

"I hain't fitten fur you, Bud."

"Don't talk that-a-way, Jane, you know ef you jest say 'yes,' I'll be the happiest man in the state."

"Well, yes, then, Bud, for you're my choice, even ef I have fooled with you fur a long time; an' I'm glad now that I kin make somebody happy." The girl was shivering, and her hands were cold, but she made no movement to rise or enter the house.

Bud put his arms around her and kissed her shyly. And just then a shout arose from the crowd down the street.

"What's that?" she asked.

"It's the boys gittin' worked up, I reckon. They're going to lynch them niggers to-night that burned ole man Williams out."

The girl leaped to her feet, "They mustn't do it," she cried. "They ain't never been tried!"

"Set down, Janey," said her lover, "they've owned up to it."

"I don't believe it," she exclaimed, "somebody's jest a lyin' on 'em to git 'em hung because they're niggers."

"Sh—Jane, you're excited, you ain't well; I noticed that when I first come to-night. Somebody's got to suffer fur that house-burnin', an' it might ez well be them ez anybody else. You mustn't talk so. Ef people knowed you wuz a standin' up fur niggers so, it 'ud ruin you."

He had hardly finished speaking, when the gate opened, and another man joined them.

"Hello, there, Dock Heaters, that you?" said Bud Mason.

"Yes, it's me. How are you, Jane?" said the newcomer.

"Oh, jest middlin', Dock, I ain't right well."

"Well, you might be in better business than settin' out here talkin' to Bud Mason."

"Don't know how as to that," said his rival, "seein' as we're engaged."

"You're a liar!" flashed Dock Heaters.

Bud Mason half rose, then sat down again; his triumph was suffi-cient without a fight. To him "liar" was a hard name to swallow without resort to blows, but he only said, his flashing eyes belying his calm tone, "Mebbe I am a liar, jest ast Jane."

"Is that the truth, Jane?" asked Heaters, angrily.

"Yes, hit is, Dock Heaters, an' I don't see what you've got to say about it; I hain't never promised you nothin' shore."

Heaters turned toward the gate without a word. Bud sent after him a mocking laugh, and the bantering words, "You'd better go down, an' he'p hang them niggers, that's all you're good fur." And the rival really did bend his steps in that direction.

Another shout arose from the throng down the street, and rising hastily, Bud Mason exclaimed, "I must be goin', that yell means business."

"Don't go down there, Bud!" cried Jane. "Don't go, fur my sake, don't go." She stretched out her arms, and clasped them about his neck.

"You don't want me to miss nothin' like that," he said as he unclasped her arms; "don't you be worried, I'll be back past here." And in a moment he was gone, leaving her cry of "Bud, Bud, come back," to smite the empty silence.

When Bud Mason reached the scene of action, the mob had already broken into the jail and taken out the trembling prisoners. The ropes were round their necks and they had been led to a tree.

"See ef they'll do any more house-burnin'!" cried one as the ends of the ropes were thrown over the limbs of the tree.

"Reckon they'll like dancin' hemp a heap better," mocked a second.

"Justice an' pertection!" yelled a third.

"The mills of the gods grind swift enough in Barlow County," said the schoolmaster.

The scene, the crowd, the flaring lights and harsh voices intoxicated Mason, and he was soon the most enthusiastic man in the mob. At the word, his was one of the willing hands that seized the rope, and jerked the negroes off their feet into eternity. He joined the others with savage glee as they emptied their revolvers into the bodies. Then came the struggle for pieces of the rope as "keepsakes." The scramble was awful. Bud Mason had just laid hold of a piece and cut it off, when some one laid hold of the other end. It was not at the rope's end, and the other man also used his knife in getting a hold. Mason looked up to see who his antagonist was, and his face grew white with anger. It was Dock Heaters.

"Let go this rope," he cried.

"Let go yoreself, I cut it first, an' I'm a goin' to have it."

They tugged and wrestled and panted, but they were evenly matched and neither gained the advantage.

"Let go, I say," screamed Heaters, wild with rage.

"I'll die first, you dirty dog!"

The words were hardly out of his mouth before a knife flashed in the light of the lanterns, and with a sharp cry, Bud Mason fell to the ground. Heaters turned to fly, but strong hands seized and disarmed him.

"He's killed him! Murder, murder!" arose the cry, as the crowd with terror-stricken faces gathered about the murderer and his victim.

"Lynch him!" suggested some one whose thirst for blood was not yet appeased.

"No," cried an imperious voice, "who knows what may have put him up to it? Give a white man a chance for his life."

The crowd parted to let in the town marshal and the sheriff who took charge of the prisoner, and led him to the little rickety jail, whence he escaped later that night; while others improvised a litter, and bore the dead man to his home.

The news had preceded them up the street, and reached Jane's ears. As they passed her home, she gazed at them with a stony, vacant stare, muttering all the while as she rocked herself to and fro, "I knowed it, I knowed it!"

The press was full of the double lynching and the murder. Conservative editors wrote leaders about it in which they deplored the rashness of the hanging but warned the negroes that the only way to stop lynch-ing was to quit the crimes of which they so often stood accused. But only in one little obscure sheet did an editor think to say, "There was Salem and its witchcraft; there is the south and its lynching. When the blind frenzy of a people condemn a man as soon as he is accused, his enemies need not look far for a pretext!"

THE LION TAMER

Mrs. De Courcey-Hartwell—hyphen Hartwell, if you please, was a patron of the arts. Of course, envious people said she was a lion hunter; but this statement may be taken with a grain of salt when it is considered that those who made it were just on the outer edge, in fact, on the very fringe of that society of which the De Courcey-Hartwells formed the brilliant and resplendent center.

It is quite true that the lady in question had a somewhat inordinate fancy for people who had done something. But much may be forgiven one who has good manners, a better cook and a surpassing cellar. When, added to all this, one's family has been wealthy for a half-century—twenty years puts an American out of the class of the *nouveau riche*—all the arrows of criticism are turned.

The young men who went to Mrs. De Courcey-Hartwell's lectures, literary evenings and strange, unaccountable musicals were a little prone to laugh over the affairs; for a brief moment to envy the lion his share of the girls' adoring attention, and then to wander off to the smoking room, whence they would emerge, after the program, to congratulate their hostess on the success of her entertainment.

This devoted patron of the arts was not only fair, but was wise for the thirty-eight years to which she owned, and she was not fooled. She used to say to Archie Courtney, who was a famous shirker: "Ah, never mind, Archie, if the mental pabulum I have provided was not to your taste; take heart, supper is now on." So it came to pass that they separated her foibles from herself, and laughed at them, but never at her.

Mrs. De Courcey-Hartwell's husband was in leather, as his father and his grandfather—he had a grandfather—had been before him. He looked on complacently at his wife's artistic endeavors, ever ready to pay the bills, which, whatever the catechism may say, is man's highest duty, especially if that man be a husband. Some malicious gossips said that they were still in love with each other after fifteen years of married life. But most of their acquaintances were charitable enough to give them the benefit of the doubt, even though the fact that the husband enjoyed himself at his own home looked dark. Perhaps, however, it was only a pose, just because they were rich enough to be odd.

———

"Well, what has our hostess on for tonight?" asked Forsythe Brandon of Archie Courtney as they went bowling up the street; "is it a reformed burglar, a captured Mahatma or an African Prince?"

"Oh, chuck it!" said Archie, scornfully. "Why, old man, you're talking in your sleep."

"It can't be, it can't be; oh, don't tell me that it is a party without a lion!"

"Certainly not. Didn't you read your card?"

"No, I just glanced at it and saw that it was the De Courcey-Hartwells', knew that there would be something good to eat, cried 'My tablets, my tablets!' and here I am."

"Glutton."

"Oh, most worthy exemplar!"

Archie laughed.

"Well, it's a real card this time. We're invited to meet that new writer who has been making such a stir. Worthington is his name."

"Whew!" whistled Brandon; "you don't say! Why, I thought he was playing the high and mighty, scorning society and all that!"

"I suppose he has been, but they say his appearance tonight is all Tom Van Kleek's doing. He and Tom are as thick as thieves."

"A strange pair."

"I don't know whether it's the author's liking for the Van or for the man."

"Possibly the Van."

"I don't know; Van Kleek's rather a white chap."

Brandon murmured something about Whitechapel, but Archie could not countenance the remark, and immediately froze into unconsciousness.

———

Except for Tom Van Kleek it seems hardly possible that Worthington and Mrs. De Courcey-Hartwell could have met, the man and the woman were so dissimilar in character.

Worthington had come down from Canada a few years before, when his books began to succeed in the United States. He made good acquaintances, but went out very little. There was something of the freedom and breeziness of his own woods about him—something charming but untamable—and he did not talk about his Art. He loved nothing quite so much as to get into a disreputable smoking-jacket, through the pocket of which the fire from his old brier had burned a volcanic-looking hole, and to loll in slippered ease alone with a book or with a few choice spirits.

He did not pose, or seem to pose, save that he wore a great shock of unruly black hair. When his friends twitted him about this he told them, with a laugh, that he was "knot pated," and did not dare to wear his hair short. They smiled, and in revenge he had his hair cut, after which a committee waited upon him to beg him not to do it again. The chairman of this committee plainly told him that he looked like a phrenologist's specially prepared subject, and they were all sorry for two weeks. From that time his hair went unmolested and unremarked.

He was a sociable fellow, outside of society, easy and gracious. The boys called him Dick, but he was Richard Barry Worthington under his stories, poems and articles and on the title pages of the books that had made him famous. Literary men put in all the name they can, presumably to add weight to whatever they offer the heartless editor.

It was Dick, rather than Richard Barry, who entered Mrs. De Courcey-Hartwell's drawing room with Tom Van Kleek on the night when a few friends had been invited to meet him. Forsythe Brandon was standing beside Helen Archer.

"Heavens!" he exclaimed, "the man is well dressed!"

"Why, why not?"

"And he hasn't stumbled over his feet once."

"Mr. Brandon, aren't you ashamed of yourself?"

"Not in the least. Just look at that bow; and he didn't forget to speak to his hostess."

"I think you are very silly, and I do think he is in very good form."

"That's just it; that's what I resent. Don't you know it's very bad form for a genius to be in good form? He might, at least, have respected tradition enough to be shabby and have red hands—" And he sighed tragically.

Helen laughed, and moved away.

Much later in the evening Tom Van Kleek wandered disconsolately in from the smoking room, where the lion had taken refuge as in his lair; someone had mentioned a reading, and he had incontinently fled.

"What's the matter, Tom?" asked Millicent Martin. "You look like a hired mourner at a funeral."

"Don't joke, Millicent. I'm in an awful fix. You know I am partly responsible for Worthington's being here. But I'm afraid I've offended both him and our hostess. Everyone is expecting him to read something. Mrs. De Courcey-Hartwell sends me to feel him on the subject, and he absolutely refuses to do a thing."

"In other words," laughed Millicent, "the lion refuses to roar."

"Quite so."

"Where is he?"

"In the smoking room, yarning it with a lot of fellows."

"Oh, well, don't be disheartened. I'll help you out."

"Can you?"

"We'll try. Can you get him in? Say there is to be some reading. I'll do the rest. Mrs. De Courcey-Hartwell shall not be disappointed."

Millicent's eyes were twinkling as she made her way toward her hostess, and Tom Van Kleek went back into the smoking room with hope in his heart.

"Say, old man," he addressed Worthington, "come in with me. There's to be some doings, and they'll expect you. Oh, that's all right," he said, in answer to a questioning look; "they're not going to call on you to read."

"All right, I'll go, if I'm to be entertained," the author replied, bluntly, but with a smile in his eyes.

There was quite a little flutter when he re-entered the drawing room—the complacent sound of rustling silks.

The hostess was always very simple in her announcements. She said now only: "Miss Millicent Martin has kindly consented to recite for us."

There was faint patter of applause and a few disappointed looks. It was well that Worthington did not see the roguish look in Millicent's eyes as she began:

"I know that I am very daring, but in honor of the guest whom our hostess has so kindly invited us to meet"—here she bowed slightly to Worthington—"I will recite his exquisite poem, 'The Troubadour.'"

Worthington groaned in spirit, but his escape was cut off.

Millicent began. Her elocution was—well, bad; oh, but it was bad, and the author almost wept. When she was half through, he whispered, in an agonized voice: "Oh, Tom, Tom, don't let her do it again! I'll do anything; tell them I'll read. I'll do anything, but don't let that girl do it again!"

Van Kleek beamed. "Awfully good of you, old man!" he said, but Worthington only sighed.

When Millicent was done it fell to Van Kleek's lot to inform the assembled guests of the author's condescension. Then Worthington rose. He read well always, but tonight he was magnificent in his fury. He was defending himself against the insinuation of insipidity that the girl's interpretation had put upon his work, and all the fire and earnestness of his nature went into his rendition of the lines. The women from the halls and the men from the smoking room crowded the doorways, and there was a storm of applause as he sat down.

"I have always maintained that you should be called 'Militant,'" whispered Van Kleek as Millicent passed him.

As for Worthington, he was angry with himself, and altogether felt very much the fool. People had congratulated him until he was tired.

"I shall be spouting at afternoon teas next," he told his friend, savagely, when they were alone for a moment; but just then Millicent came up, and Tom moved guiltily away.

"I enjoyed it so much," she said, holding out her hand.

"Thank you."

She waited, smiling up into his face.

"And have you nothing to say of my work?"

"It—it—was charming," he stammered.

"Which, translated, means abominable."

He wondered why that girl should stand there laughing at him with her marvelous eyes. It annoyed him, and it pleased him. He answered:

"I am very, very sure you underrate yourself."

"Fie! Mr. Worthington, fie! I know it was abominable, because I tried to make it so."

He looked up quickly.

"I hope you will forgive me, for I have a confession to make. I am not heroic or self-sacrificing, and I want you to know that I can read better than I did, and that I felt what I read more deeply than I expressed. But—but—you are a lion, you know."

"Oh, am I?"

He was beginning to see, and the red mounted to his face.

"Yes," she said, "and you were very unsatisfactory; you would not roar, so I read badly, to compel you to read in self-defense. There!"

He struggled between anger and admiration at her audacity. The latter triumphed. He laughed a low, amused laugh. "If I am a lion, you are a lion tamer," he said. "May I come to see you some day?"

Her apprehensions fled, and she joined in his merriment.

"Will you promise not to be very fierce?"

"I promise to 'roar me as gently as a sucking dove.'"

"Then you may come," she said. "Good night, Sir Lion."

"Good night, my Lady Lion Tamer."

A Blessed Deceit

As Martha said, "it warn't long o' any sma'tness dat de rapscallion evah showed, but des 'long o' his bein' borned 'bout de same time ez young mastah dat Lucius got tuk into de big house." But Martha's word is hardly to be taken, for she had a mighty likely little pickaninny of her own who was overlooked when the Daniels were looking about for a companion for the little toddler, their one child. Martha might have been envious. However, it is true that Lucius was born about the same time that his young Master Robert was, and it is just possible that that might have had something to do with his appointment, although he was as smart and likely a little darky as ever cracked his heels on a Virginia plantation. Years after, people wondered why that black boy with the scarred face and hands so often rode in the Daniels' carriage, did so little work, and was better dressed than most white men. But the story was not told them; it touched too tender a spot in the hearts of all who knew. But memory deals gently with old wounds, and the balm of time softens the keenest sorrow.

Lucius first came to the notice of Mr. Daniels when as a two-year-old pickaninny he was rolling and tumbling in the sand about the quarters. Even then, he could sing so well, and was such a cheerful and good-natured, bright little scamp that his master stood and watched him in delight. Then he asked Susan how old he was, and she answered, "La, Mas' Stone, Lucius he 'bout two years old now, don't you ricollec'?

He born 'bout de same time dat little Mas' Robert came to you-alls."
The master's eyes sparkled, and he tapped the black baby on the head.
His caress was immediately responded to by a caper of enjoyment on
the youngster's part. Stone Daniels laughed aloud, and said, "Wash
him, Susan, and I'll send something down from the house by Lou, then
dress him, and send him on up." He turned away, and Susan, her heart
bounding with joy, seized the baby in her arms and covered his round
black body with kisses. This was a very easy matter for her to do, for he
only wore one pitiful shift, and that was in a sadly dilapidated condition. She hurried to fulfil her master's orders. There was no telling
what great glory might come of such a command. It was a most wonderful blue dress with a pink sash that Lou brought down from the
house, and when young Lucius was arrayed therein, he was a sight to
make any fond mother's heart proud. Of course, Lucius was rather a
deep brunette to wear such dainty colors, but plantation tastes are not
very scrupulous, and then the baby Robert, whose garments these had
been, was fair, with the brown hair of the Daniels, and was dressed
accordingly.

Half an hour after the child had gone to the big house, Susan
received word that he had been appointed to the high position of companion in chief, and amuser in general to his young master, and the
cup of her earthly joy was full. One hour later, the pickaninny and his
master were rolling together on the grass, throwing stones with the
vigorous gusto of two years, and the sad marksmanship of the same
age, and the blue dress and pink sash were of the earth, earthy.

"I tell you, Eliza," said Stone, "I think I've struck just about the right
thing in that little rascal. He'll take the best care of Robert, and I think
that playing like that out in the sunshine will make our little one
stronger and healthier. Why, he loves him already. Look at that out
there." Mrs. Daniels did look. The young scion of the Daniels house
was sitting down in the sand and gravel of the drive, and his companion
and care taker was piling leaves, gravel, dirt, sticks, and whatever he
could find about the lawn on his shoulders and head. The mother
shuddered.

"But don't you think, Stone, that that's a little rough for Robert,
and his clothes—oh my, I do believe he is jamming that stick down his
throat!"

"Bosh," said Stone, "that's the way to make a man out of him."

When the two children were brought in from their play, young Robert showed that he had been taken care of. He was scratched, he was bruised, but he was flushed and happy, and Stone Daniels was in triumph.

One, two, three years the companionship between the two went on, and the love between them grew. The little black was never allowed to forget that he was his Master Robert's servant, but there is a democracy about childhood that oversteps all conventions, and lays low all barriers of caste. Down in the quarters, with many secret giggles, the two were dubbed, "The Daniels twins."

It was on the occasion of Robert's sixth birthday that the pair might have been seen "codgin'" under the lilac bush, their heads very close together, the same intent look on both the black and the white face. Something momentous was under discussion. The fact of it was, young Master Robert was to be given his first party that evening, and though a great many children of the surrounding gentry had been invited, provision had not been made for the entertainment of Lucius in the parlor. Now this did not meet with Robert's views of what was either right or proper, so he had determined to take matters in his own hands, and together with his black confederate was planning an amendment of the affair.

"You see, Lucius," he was saying, "you are mine, because papa said so, and you was born the same time I was, so don't you see that when I have a birthday party, it is your birthday party too, and you ought to be there?"

"Co'se," said Lucius, with a wise shake of the head, and a very old look, "Co'se, dat des de way it look to me, Mas' Robert."

"Well, now, as it's your party, it 'pears like to me that you ought to be there, and not be foolin' 'round with the servants that the other company bring."

"Pears lak to me dat I oughter be 'roun' dah somewhah," answered the black boy.

Robert thought for awhile, then he clapped his little knee and cried, "I've got it, Lucius, I've got it!" His face beamed with joy, the two heads went closer together, and with many giggles and capers of amusement, their secret was disclosed, and the young master trotted off to the house, while Lucius rolled over and over with delight.

A little while afterwards Robert had a very sage and professional conversation with his father in the latter's library. It was only on state occasions that he went to Doshy and asked her to obtain an interview for him in that august place, and Stone Daniels knew that something great was to be said when the request came to him. It was immediately granted, for he denied his only heir nothing, and the young man came in with the air and mien of an ambassador bearing messages to a potentate.

What was said in that conversation, and what was answered by the father, it boots not here to tell. It is sufficient to say that Robert Daniels came away from the interview with shining eyes and a look of triumph on his face, and the news he told to his fellow conspirator sent him off into wild peals of pleasure. Quite as eagerly as his son had gone out to Lucius, Stone Daniels went to talk with his wife.

"I tell you, Eliza," he said, "there's no use talking, that boy of ours is a Daniels through and through. He is an aristocrat to his finger tips. What do you suppose he has been in to ask me?"

"I have no idea, Stone," said his wife, "what new and original thing this wonderful boy of ours has been saying now."

"You needn't laugh now, Eliza, because it is something new and original he has been saying."

"I never doubted it for an instant."

"He came to me with that wise look of his; you know it?"

"Don't I?" said the mother tenderly.

"And he said, 'Papa, don't you think as I am giving a party, an' my servant was born 'bout the same time as I was, don't you think he ought to kinder—kinder—be 'roun' where people could see him, as, what do you call it in the picture, papa?' 'What do you mean?' I said. 'Oh, you know, to set me off.' 'Oh, a background, you mean?' 'Yes, a background; now I think it would be nice if Lucius could be right there, so whenever I want to show my picture books or anything, I could just say, "Lucius, won't you bring me this, or won't you bring me that?" like you do with Scott.' 'Oh, but my son,' I said, 'a gentleman never wants to show off his possessions.' 'No, papa,' he replied, with the most quizzical expression I ever saw on a child's face, 'no, I don't want to show off. I just want to kinder indicate, don't you know, cause it's a birthday party, and that'll kinder make it stronger.'"

"Of course you consented?" said Mrs. Daniels.

"With such wise reasoning, how could a man do otherwise?" He replied, "Don't you see the child has glimmers of that fine feeling of social contrast, my dear?"

"I see," said Mrs. Daniels, "that my son Robert wants to have Lucius in the room at the party, and was shrewd enough to gain his father's consent."

"By the Lord!" said her husband, "but I believe you're right! Well, it's done now, and I can't go back on my word."

"The Daniels twins" were still out on the lawn dancing to the piping of the winds and throwing tufts of grass into the air and over their heads, when they were called in to be admonished and dressed. Peacock never strutted as did Lucius when, arrayed in a blue suit with shining brass buttons, he was stationed in the parlor near his master's chair. Those were the days when even children's parties were very formal and elegant affairs. There was no hurrying and scurrying then, and rough and tumble goings-on. That is, at first, there was not; when childhood gets warmed up though, it is pretty much the same in any period of the world's history. However, the young guests coming were received with great dignity and formality by their six-year-old host. The party was begun in very stately fashion. It was not until supper was announced that the stiffness and awe of the children at a social function began to wear off. Then they gathered about the table, cheerful and buoyant, charmed and dazzled by its beauty. There was a pretty canopy over the chair of the small host, and the dining-room and tables were decorated with beautiful candles in the silver candlesticks that had been heirlooms of the Daniels for centuries. Robert had lost some of his dignity, and laughed and chatted with the rest as the supper went on. The little girls were very demure, the boys were inclined to be a little boisterous. The most stately figure in the room was Lucius where he was stationed stiff and erect behind his master's chair. From the doorway, the elders looked on with enjoyment at the scene. The supper was nearly over, and the fun was fast and furious. The boys were unable longer to contain the animal spirits which were bubbling over, and there began surreptitious scufflings and nudges under the table. Someone near Robert suddenly sprang up, the cloth caught in his coat, two candles were tipped over straight into the little host's lap. The melted wax ran over him, and in a twinkle the fine frills and laces about him were a mass of flames. Instantly all was confusion, the children were shrieking and rushing pell-mell from the table. They crowded the room in frightened and confused huddles, and it was this that barred Stone Daniels as he fought his way fiercely to his son's side. But one was before him. At the first sign of danger to his young master, Lucius had sprung forward and thrown himself upon him, beating, fighting, tearing, smothering, trying to kill the fire. He grabbed the delicate linen, he tore at the collar and jacket; he was burning himself, his clothes were on fire, but he heeded it not. He only saw that his master was burning, burning before him, and his boy's heart went out in a cry, "Oh, Mas' Bob, oh, Mas' Bob!"

Somehow, the father reached his child at last, and threw his coat about him. The flames were smothered, and the unconscious child carried to his room. The children were hurried into their wraps and to their homes, and a messenger galloped away for the doctor.

And what of Lucius? When the heir of the Daniels was in danger of his life no one had time to think of the slave, and it was not until he was heard moaning on the floor where he had crept in to be by his master's bedside, that it was found out that he also was badly burned, and a cot was fixed for him in the same room.

When the doctor came in he shook his head over both, and looked very grave indeed. First Robert and then his servant was bound and bandaged, and the same nurse attended both. When the white child returned to consciousness his mother was weeping over him, and his father with face pale and drawn stood at the foot of the bed. "Oh, my poor child, my poor child!" moaned the woman; "my only one!"

With a gasp of pain Robert turned his face toward his mother and said, "Don't you cry, mamma; if I die, I'll leave you Lucius."

It was funny afterwards to think of it, but then it only brought a fresh burst of tears from the mother's heart, and made a strange twitching about the father's mouth.

But he didn't die. Lucius' caretaking had produced in him a robust constitution, and both children fought death and gained the fight. When they were first able to sit up—and Robert was less inclined to be parted from Lucius than ever—the young master called his father into the room. Lucius' chair was wheeled near him when the little fellow began:

"Papa, I want to 'fess somethin' to you. The night of the party I didn't want Lucius in for indicatin', I wanted him to see the fun, didn't I Lucius?"

Lucius nodded painfully, and said, "Uh-huh."

"I didn't mean to 'ceive you, papa, but you know it was both of our birthdays—and—er—" Stone Daniels closed his boy's mouth with a kiss, and turned and patted the black boy's head with a tender look on his face, "For once, thank God, it was a blessed deceit."

That is why in years later, Lucius did so little work and dressed like his master's son.

The Mission of Mr. Scatters

It took something just short of a revolution to wake up the sleepy little town of Miltonville. Through the slow, hot days it drowsed along like a lazy dog, only half rousing now and then to snap at some flying rumour, and relapsing at once into its pristine somnolence.

It was not a dreamless sleep, however, that held the town in chains. It had its dreams—dreams of greatness, of wealth, of consequence and of growth. Granted that there was no effort to realise these visions, they were yet there, and, combined with the memory of a past that was not without credit, went far to give tone to its dormant spirit.

It was a real spirit, too; the gallant Bourbon spirit of the old South; of Kentucky when she is most the daughter of Virginia, as was evidenced in the awed respect which all Miltonvillians, white and black alike, showed to Major Richardson in his house on the hill. He was part of the traditions of the place. It was shown in the conservatism of the old white families, and a certain stalwart if reflected self-respect in the older coloured inhabitants.

In all the days since the school had been founded and Mr. Dunkin's marriage to the teacher had raised a brief ripple of excitement, these coloured people had slumbered. They were still slumbering that hot August day, unmindful of the sensation that lay at their very doors, heedless of the portents that said as plain as preaching, "Miltonville, the time is at hand, awake!"

So it was that that afternoon there were only a few loungers, and these not very alert, about the station when the little train wheezed and puffed its way into it. It had been so long since anyone save those whom they knew had alighted at Miltonville that the loungers had lost faith, and with it curiosity, and now they scarcely changed their positions as the little engine stopped with a snort of disgust. But in an instant indifference had fled as the mist before the sun, and every eye on the platform was staring and white. It is the unexpected that always happens, and yet humanity never gets accustomed to it. The loafers, white and black, had assumed a sitting posture, and then they had stood up. For from the cars there had alighted the wonder of a stranger—a Negro stranger, gorgeous of person and attire. He was dressed in a suit of black cloth. A long coat was buttoned close around his tall and robust form. He was dead black, from his shiny top hat to his not less shiny boots, and about him there was the indefinable air of distinction. He stood looking about the platform for a moment, and then stepped briskly and decisively toward the group that was staring at him with wide eyes. There was no hesitation in that step. He walked as a man walks who is not in the habit of being stopped, who has not known what it is to be told, "Thus far shalt thou go and no further."

"Can you tell me where I can find the residence of Mr. Isaac Jackson?" he asked sonorously as he reached the stupefied loungers. His voice was deep and clear.

Someone woke from his astonishment and offered to lead him thither, and together the two started for their destination, the stranger keeping up a running fire of comment on the way. Had his companion been a close observer and known anything about the matter, he would have found the newcomer's English painfully, unforgivably correct. A language should be like an easy shoe on a flexible foot, but to one unused to it, it proves rather a splint on a broken limb. The stranger stalked about in conversational splints until they arrived at Isaac Jackson's door. Then giving his guide a dime, he dismissed him with a courtly bow, and knocked.

It was a good thing that Martha Ann Jackson had the innate politeness of her race well to the fore when she opened the door upon the radiant creature, or she would have given voice to the words that were in her heart: "Good Lawd, what is dis?"

"Is this the residence of Mr. Isaac Jackson?" in the stranger's suavest voice.

"Yes, suh, he live hyeah."

"May I see him? I desire to see him upon some business." He handed her his card, which she carefully turned upside down, glanced at without understanding, and put in her apron pocket as she replied:

"He ain't in jes' now, but ef you'll step in an' wait, I'll sen' one o' de chillen aftah him."

"I thank you, madam, I thank you. I will come in and rest from the fatigue of my journey. I have travelled a long way, and rest in such a pleasant and commodious abode as your own appears to be will prove very grateful to me."

She had been half afraid to invite this resplendent figure into her humble house, but she felt distinctly flattered at his allusion to the home which she had helped Isaac to buy, and by the alacrity with which the stranger accepted her invitation.

She ushered him into the front room, mentally thanking her stars that she had forced the reluctant Isaac to buy a bright new carpet a couple of months before.

A child was despatched to find and bring home the father, while Martha Ann, hastily slipping out of her work-dress and into a starched calico, came in to keep her visitor company.

His name proved to be Scatters, and he was a most entertaining and ingratiating man. It was evident that he had some important business with Isaac Jackson, but that it was mysterious was shown by the guarded way in which he occasionally hinted at it as he tapped the valise he carried and nodded knowingly.

Time had never been when Martha Ann Jackson was so flustered. She was charmed and frightened and flattered. She could only leave Mr. Scatters long enough to give orders to her daughter, Lucy, to prepare such a supper as that household had never seen before; then she returned to sit again at his feet and listen to his words of wisdom.

The supper progressed apace, and the savour of it was already in the stranger's nostrils. Upon this he grew eloquent and was about to divulge his secret to the hungry-eyed woman when the trampling of Isaac's boots upon the walk told him that he had only a little while longer to contain himself, and at the same time to wait for the fragrant supper.

Now, it is seldom that a man is so well impressed with a smooth-tongued stranger as is his wife. Usually his hard-headedness puts him on the defensive against the blandishments of the man who has won his better half's favour, and, however honest the semi-fortunate individual may be, he despises him for his attainments. But it was not so in this case. Isaac had hardly entered the house and received his visitor's warm hand-clasp before he had become captive to his charm. Business, business—no, his guest had been travelling and he must be both tired and hungry. Isaac would hear of no business until they had eaten. Then, over a pipe, if the gentleman smoked, they might talk at their ease.

Mr. Scatters demurred, but in fact nothing could have pleased him better, and the open smile with which he dropped into his place at the table was very genuine and heartfelt. Genuine, too, were his praises of Lucy's cooking; of her flaky biscuits and mealy potatoes. He was pleased all through and he did not hesitate to say so.

It was a beaming group that finally rose heavily laden from the supper table.

Over a social pipe a little later, Isaac Jackson heard the story that made his eyes bulge with interest and his heart throb with eagerness.

Mr. Scatters began, tapping his host's breast and looking at him fixedly, "You had a brother some years ago named John." It was more like an accusation than a question.

"Yes, suh, I had a brothah John."

"Uh, huh, and that brother migrated to the West Indies."

"Yes, suh, he went out to some o' dem outlandish places."

"Hold on, sir, hold on, I am a West Indian myself."

"I do' mean no erfence, 'ceptin' dat John allus was of a rovin' disper-sition."

"Very well, you know no more about your brother after his depar-ture for the West Indies?"

"No, suh."

"Well, it is my mission to tell you the rest of the story. Your brother John landed at Cuba, and after working about some years and living frugally, he went into the coffee business, in which he became rich."

"Rich?"

"Rich, sir."

"Why, bless my soul, who'd 'a evah thought that of John? Why, suh, I'm sho'ly proud to hyeah it. Why don't he come home an' visit a body?"

"Ah, why?" said Mr. Scatters dramatically. "Now comes the most painful part of my mission. 'In the midst of life we are in death.'" Mr.

Scatters sighed, Isaac sighed and wiped his eyes. "Two years ago your brother departed this life."

"Was he saved?" Isaac asked in a choked voice. Scatters gave him one startled glance, and then answered hastily, "I am happy to say that he was."

"Poor John! He got an' me lef'."

"Even in the midst of our sorrows, however, there is always a ray of light. Your brother remembered you in his will."

"Remembered me?"

"Remembered you, and as one of the executors of his estate,"—Mr. Scatters rose and went softly over to his valise, from which he took a large square package. He came back with it, holding it as if it were something sacred,—"as one of the executors of his estate, which is now settled, I was commissioned to bring you this." He tapped the package. "This package, sealed as you see with the seal of Cuba, contains five thousand dollars in notes and bonds."

Isaac gasped and reached for the bundle, but it was withdrawn. "I am, however, not to deliver it to you yet. There are certain formalities which my country demands to be gone through with, after which I deliver my message and return to the fairest of lands, to the Gem of the Antilles. Let me congratulate you, Mr. Jackson, upon your good fortune."

Isaac yielded up his hand mechanically. He was dazed by the vision of this sudden wealth.

"Fi' thousan' dollahs," he repeated.

"Yes, sir, five thousand dollars. It is a goodly sum, and in the meantime, until court convenes, I wish you to recommend some safe place in which to put this money, as I do not feel secure with it about my person, nor would it be secure if it were known to be in your house."

"I reckon Albert Matthews' grocery would be the safes' place fu' it. He's got one o' dem i'on saftes."

"The very place. Let us go there at once, and after that I will not encroach upon your hospitality longer, but attempt to find a hotel."

"Hotel nothin'," said Isaac emphatically. "Ef my house ain't too common, you'll stay right thaih ontwell co't sets."

"This is very kind of you, Mr. Jackson, but really I couldn't think of being such a charge upon you and your good wife."

"'Taint no charge on us; we'll be glad to have you. Folks hyeah in Miltonville has little enough comp'ny, de Lawd knows."

Isaac spoke the truth, and it was as much the knowledge that he would be the envy of all the town as his gratitude to Scatters that prompted him to prevail upon his visitor to stay.

Scatters was finally persuaded, and the men only paused long enough in the house to tell the curiosity-eaten Martha Ann the news, and then started for Albert Matthews' store. Scatters carried the precious package, and Isaac was armed with an old shotgun lest anyone should suspect their treasure and attack them. Five thousand dollars was not to be carelessly handled!

As soon as the men were gone, Martha Ann started out upon her rounds, and her proud tongue did for the women portion of Miltonville what the visit to Matthews' store did for the men. Did Mrs. So-and-So remember brother John? Indeed she did. And when the story was told, it was a "Well, well, well! he used to be an ol' beau o' mine." Martha Ann found no less than twenty women of her acquaintance for whom her brother John seemed to have entertained tender feelings.

The corner grocery store kept by Albert Matthews ˮas the general gathering-place for the coloured male population of the town. It was a small, one-roomed building, almost filled with barrels, boxes, and casks.

Pride as well as necessity had prompted Isaac to go to the grocery just at this time, when it would be quite the fullest of men. He had not calculated wrongly when he reckoned upon the sensation that would be made by his entrance with the distinguished-looking stranger. The excitement was all the most hungry could have wished for. The men stared at Jackson and his companion with wide-open eyes. They left off chewing tobacco and telling tales. A half-dozen of them forgot to avail themselves of the joy of spitting, and Albert Matthews, the proprietor, a weazened little brown-skinned man, forgot to lay his hand upon the scale in weighing out a pound of sugar.

With a humility that was false on the very face of it, Isaac introduced his guest to the grocer and the three went off together mysteriously into a corner. The matter was duly explained and the object of the visit told. Matthews burned with envy of his neighbour's good fortune.

"I do' reckon, Mistah Scatters, dat we bettah let de othah folks in de sto' know anything 'bout dis hyeah bus'ness of ouahs. I got to be 'sponsible fu dat money, an' I doesn't want to tek no chances."

"You are perfectly right, sir, perfectly right. You are responsible, not only for the money itself, but for the integrity of this seal which means the dignity of government."

Matthews looked sufficiently impressed, and together they all went their way among the barrels and boxes to the corner where the little safe stood. With many turnings and twistings the door was opened, the package inclosed and the safe shut again. Then they all rose solemnly and went behind the counter to sample something that Matthews had. This was necessary as a climax, for they had performed, not a mere deed, but a ceremonial.

"Of course, you'll say nothing about this matter at all, Mr. Matthews," said Scatters, thereby insuring publicity to his affair.

There were a few introductions as the men passed out, but hardly had their backs turned when a perfect storm of comment and inquiry broke about the grocer's head. So it came to pass, that with many mysterious nods and headshakings, Matthews first hinted at and then told the story.

For the first few minutes the men could scarcely believe what they had heard. It was so utterly unprecedented. Then it dawned upon them that it might be so, and discussion and argument ran rife for the next hour.

The story flew like wildfire, there being three things in this world which interest all sorts and conditions of men alike: great wealth, great beauty, and great love. Whenever Mr. Scatters appeared he was greeted with deference and admiration. Any man who had come clear from Cuba on such an errand to their fellow-townsman deserved all honour and respect. His charming manners confirmed, too, all that preconceived notions had said of him. He became a social favourite. It began with Mr. and Mrs. Dunkin's calling upon him. Then followed Alonzo Taft, and when the former two gave a reception for the visitor, his position was assured. Miltonville had not yet arisen to the dignity of having a literary society. He now founded one and opened it himself with an address so beautiful, so eloquent and moving that Mr. Dunkin bobbed his head dizzy in acquiescence, and Aunt Hannah Payne thought she was in church and shouted for joy.

The little town had awakened from its long post-bellum slumber and accepted with eagerness the upward impulse given it. It stood aside and looked on with something like adoration when Mr. Scatters and Mrs. Dunkin met and talked of ineffable things—things far above the ken of the average mortal.

When Mr. Scatters found that his mission was known, he gave up further attempts at concealing it and talked freely about the matter. He expatiated at length upon the responsibility that devolved upon him and his desire to discharge it, and he spoke glowingly of the great government whose power was represented by the seal which held the package of bonds. Not for one day would he stay away from his beloved Cuba, if it were not that that seal had to be broken in the presence of the proper authorities. So, however reluctant he might be to stay, it was not for him to shirk his task: he must wait for the sitting of court.

Meanwhile the Jacksons lived in an atmosphere of glory. The womenfolk purchased new dresses, and Isaac got a new wagon on the strength of their good fortune. It was nothing to what they dreamed of doing when they had the money positively in hand. Mr. Scatters still remained their guest, and they were proud of it.

What pleased them most was that their distinguished visitor seemed not to look down upon, but rather to be pleased with, their homely fare. Isaac had further cause for pleasure when his guest came to him later with a great show of frank confidence to request the loan of fifty dollars.

"I should not think of asking even this small favour of you but that I have only Cuban money with me and I knew you would feel distressed if you knew that I went to the trouble of sending this money away for exchange on account of so small a sum."

This was undoubtedly a mark of special confidence. It suddenly made Isaac feel as if the grand creature had accepted and labelled him as a brother and an equal. He hastened to Matthews' safe, where he kept his own earnings; for the grocer was banker as well.

With reverent hands they put aside the package of bonds and together counted out the required half a hundred dollars. In a little while Mr. Scatters' long, graceful fingers had closed over it.

Mr. Jackson's cup of joy was now full. It had but one bitter drop to mar its sweetness. That was the friendship that had sprung up between the Cuban and Mr. Dunkin. They frequently exchanged visits, and sat long together engaged in conversation from which Isaac was excluded.

This galled him. He felt that he had a sort of proprietary interest in his guest. And any infringement of this property right he looked upon with distinct disfavour. So that it was with no pleasant countenance that he greeted Mr. Dunkin when he called on a certain night.

"Mr. Scatters is gone out," he said, as the old man entered and deposited his hat on the floor.

"Dat's all right, Isaac," said Mr. Dunkin slowly, "I didn't come to see de gent'man. I come to see you."

The cloud somewhat lifted from Isaac's brow. Mr. Dunkin was a man of importance and it made a deal of difference whom he was visiting.

He seemed a little bit embarrassed, however, as to how to open conversation. He hummed and hawed and was visibly uneasy. He tried to descant upon the weather, but the subject failed him. Finally, with an effort, he hitched his chair nearer to his host's and said in a low voice, "Ike, I reckon you has de confidence of Mistah Scatters?"

"I has," was the proud reply, "I has."

"Hum! uh! huh! Well—well—has you evah loant him any money?"

Isaac was aghast. Such impertinence!

"Mistah Dunkin," he began, "I considah——"

"Hol' on, Ike!" broke in Dunkin, laying a soothing hand on the other's knee, "don' git on yo' high hoss. Dis hyeah's a impo'tant mattah."

"I ain't got nothin' to say."

"He ain't never tol' you 'bout havin' nothin' but Cubian money on him?"

Isaac started.

"I see he have. He tol' me de same thing."

The two men sat staring suspiciously into each other's faces.

"He got a hun'ed an' fifty dollahs f'om me," said Dunkin.

"I let him have fifty," added Jackson weakly.

"He got a hun'ed an' fifty dollahs f'om thews. Dat's how I come to git 'spicious. He tol' him de same sto'y."

Again that pregnant look flashed between them, and they both rose and went out of the house.

They hurried down to Matthews' grocery. The owner was waiting for them there. There was solemnity, but no hesitation, in the manner with which they now went to the safe. They took out the package hastily and with ruthless hands. This was no ceremonial now. The seal had no longer any fears for them. They tore it off. They tore the wrappers. Then paper. Neatly folded paper. More wrapping paper. Newspapers. Nothing more. Of bills or bonds—nothing. With the debris of the mysterious parcel scattered about their feet, they stood up and looked at each other.

"I nevah did believe in furriners nohow," said Mr. Dunkin sadly.

"But he knowed all about my brothah John."

"An' he sho'ly did make mighty fine speeches. Maybe we's missed de money." This from the grocer.

Together they went over the papers again, with the same result.

"Do you know where he went to-night, Ike?"

"No."

"Den I reckon we's seed de las' o' him."

"But he lef' his valise."

"Yes, an' he lef' dis," said Dunkin sternly, pointing to the paper on the floor. "He sho'ly is mighty keerless of his valybles."

"Let's go git de constable," said the practical Matthews.

They did, though they felt that it would be unavailing.

The constable came and waited at Jackson's house. They had been there about half an hour, talking the matter over, when what was their surprise to hear Mr. Scatters' step coming jauntily up the walk. A sudden panic of terror and shame seized them. It was as if they had wronged him. Suppose, after all, everything should come right and he should be able to explain? They sat and trembled until he entered. Then the constable told him his mission.

Mr. Scatters was surprised. He was hurt. Indeed, he was distinctly grieved that his friends had had so little confidence in him. Had he been to them anything but a gentleman, a friend, and an honest man? Had he not come a long distance from his home to do one of them a favour? They hung their heads. Martha Ann, who was listening at the door, was sobbing audibly. What had he done thus to be humiliated? He saw the effect of his words and pursued it. Had he not left in the care of one of their own number security for his integrity in the shape of the bonds?

The effect of his words was magical. Every head went up and three pairs of flashing eyes were bent upon him. He saw and knew that they knew. He had not thought that they would dare to violate the seal around which he had woven such a halo. He saw that all was over, and, throwing up his hands with a despairing gesture, he bowed graciously and left the room with the constable.

All Miltonville had the story next day, and waited no less eagerly than before for the "settin' of co't."

To the anger and chagrin of Miltonvillians, Fox Run had the honour and distinction of being the county seat, and thither they must go to the sessions; but never did they so forget their animosities as on the day set for the trial of Scatters. They overlooked the pride of the Fox Runners, their cupidity and their vaunting arrogance. They ignored the indignity of showing interest in anything that took place in that village, and went in force, eager, anxious, and curious. Ahorse, afoot, by ox-cart, by mule-wagon, white, black, high, low, old, and young of both sexes invaded Fox Run and swelled the crowd of onlookers until, with pity for the very anxiety of the people, the humane judge decided to discard the now inadequate court-room and hold the sessions on the village green. Here an impromptu bar was set up, and over against it were ranged the benches, chairs, and camp-stools of the spectators.

Every man of prominence in the county was present. Major Richardson, though now retired, occupied a distinguished position within the bar. Old Captain Howard shook hands familiarly with the judge and nodded to the assembly as though he himself had invited them all to be present. Former Judge Durbin sat with his successor on the bench.

Court opened and the first case was called. It gained but passing attention. There was bigger game to be stalked. A hog-stealing case fared a little better on account of the intimateness of the crime involved. But nothing was received with such awed silence as the case of the State against Joseph Scatters. The charge was obtaining money under false pretences, and the plea "Not Guilty."

The witnesses were called and their testimony taken. Mr. Scatters was called to testify in his own defence, but refused to do so. The prosecution stated its case and proceeded to sum up the depositions of the witnesses. As there was no attorney for the defence, the State's attorney delivered a short speech, in which the guilt of the defendant was plainly set forth. It was as clear as day. Things looked very dark for Mr. Scatters of Cuba.

As the lawyer sat down, and ere the case could be given to the jury, he rose and asked permission of the Court to say a few words.

This was granted him.

He stood up among them, a magnificent, strong, black figure. His eyes swept the assembly, judge, jury, and spectators with a look half amusement, half defiance.

"I have pleaded not guilty," he began in a low, distinct voice that could be heard in every part of the inclosure, "and I am not guilty of the spirit which is charged against me, however near the letter may touch me. I did use certain knowledge that I possessed, and the seal which I happened to have from an old government position, to defraud—that is the word, if you will—to defraud these men out of the price of their vanity and their cupidity. But it was not a long-premeditated thing. I was within a few miles of your town before the idea occurred to me. I was in straits. I stepped from the brink of great poverty into the midst of what you are pleased to deem a greater crime."

The Court held its breath. No such audacity had ever been witnessed in the life of Fox Run.

Scatters went on, warming to his subject as he progressed. He was eloquent and he was pleasing. A smile flickered over the face of Major Richardson and was reflected in the features of many others as the speaker burst forth:

"Gentlemen, I maintain that instead of imprisoning you should thank me for what I have done. Have I not taught your community a lesson? Have I not put a check upon their credulity and made them wary of unheralded strangers?"

He had. There was no disputing that. The judge himself was smiling, and the jurymen were nodding at each other.

Scatters had not yet played his trump card. He saw that the time was ripe. Straightening his form and raising his great voice, he cried: "Gentlemen, I am guilty according to the letter of the law, but from that I appeal to the men who make and have made the law. From the hard detail of this new day, I appeal to the chivalry of the old South which has been told in story and sung in song. From men of vindictiveness I appeal to men of mercy. From plebeians to aristocrats. By the memory of the sacred names of the Richardsons"—the Major sat bolt upright and dropped his snuffbox—"the Durbins"—the ex-judge couldn't for his life get his pince-nez on—"the Howards"—the captain openly rubbed his hands—"to the memory that those names call up I appeal, and to the living and honourable bearers of them present. And to you, gentlemen of the jury, the lives of whose fathers went to purchase this dark and bloody ground, I appeal from the accusation of these men, who are not my victims, not my dupes, but their own."

There was a hush when he was done. The judge read the charge to the jury, and it was favourable—very. And—well, Scatters had taught the darkies a lesson; he had spoken of their families and their traditions, he knew their names, and—oh, well, he was a good fellow after all—what was the use?

The jury did not leave their seats, and the verdict was acquittal.

Scatters thanked the Court and started away; but he met three ominous-looking pairs of eyes, and a crowd composed of angry Negroes was flocking toward the edge of the green.

He came back.

"I think I had better wait until the excitement subsides," he said to Major Richardson.

"No need of that, suh, no need of that. Here, Jim," he called to his coachman, "take Mr. Scatters wherever he wants to go, and remember, I shall hold you responsible for his safety."

"Yes, suh," said Jim.

"A thousand thanks, Major," said the man with the mission.

"Not at all, suh. By the way, that was a very fine effort of yours this afternoon. I was greatly moved by it. If you'll give me your address I'll send you a history of our family, suh, from the time they left Vuhginia and before."

Mr. Scatters gave him the address, and smiled at the three enemies, who still waited on the edge of the green.

"To the station," he said to the driver.

THE LYNCHING OF JUBE BENSON

Gordon Fairfax's library held but three men, but the air was dense with clouds of smoke. The talk had drifted from one topic to another much as the smoke wreaths had puffed, floated, and thinned away. Then Handon Gay, who was an ambitious young reporter, spoke of a lynching story in a recent magazine, and the matter of punishment without trial put new life into the conversation.

"I should like to see a real lynching," said Gay rather callously.

"Well, I should hardly express it that way," said Fairfax, "but if a real, live lynching were to come my way, I should not avoid it."

"I should," spoke the other from the depths of his chair, where he had been puffing in moody silence. Judged by his hair, which was freely sprinkled with gray, the speaker might have been a man of forty-five or fifty, but his face, though lined and serious, was youthful, the face of a man hardly past thirty.

"What, you, Dr. Melville? Why, I thought that you physicians wouldn't weaken at anything."

"I have seen one such affair," said the doctor gravely, "in fact, I took a prominent part in it."

"Tell us about it," said the reporter, feeling for his pencil and notebook, which he was, nevertheless, careful to hide from the speaker.

The men drew their chairs eagerly up to the doctor's, but for a minute he did not seem to see them, but sat gazing abstractedly into the fire, then he took a long draw upon his cigar and began:

"I can see it all very vividly now. It was in the summer time and about seven years ago. I was practicing at the time down in the little town of Bradford. It was a small and primitive place, just the location for an impecunious medical man, recently out of college.

"In lieu of a regular office, I attended to business in the first of two rooms which I rented from Hiram Daly, one of the more prosperous of the townsmen. Here I boarded and here also came my patients—white and black—whites from every section, and blacks from 'nigger town,' as the west portion of the place was called.

"The people about me were most of them coarse and rough, but they were simple and generous, and as time passed on I had about abandoned my intention of seeking distinction in wider fields and determined to settle into the place of a modest country doctor. This was rather a strange conclusion for a young man to arrive at, and I will not deny that the presence in the house of my host's beautiful young daughter, Annie, had something to do with my decision. She was a beautiful young girl of seventeen or eighteen, and very far superior to her surroundings. She had a native grace and a pleasing way about her that made everybody that came under her spell her abject slave. White and black who knew her loved her, and none, I thought, more deeply and respectfully than Jube Benson, the black man of all work about the place.

"He was a fellow whom everybody trusted; an apparently steady-going, grinning sort, as we used to call him. Well, he was completely under Miss Annie's thumb, and would fetch and carry for her like a faithful dog. As soon as he saw that I began to care for Annie, and anybody could see that, he transferred some of his allegiance to me and became my faithful servitor also. Never did a man have a more devoted adherent in his wooing than did I, and many a one of Annie's tasks which he volunteered to do gave her an extra hour with me. You can imagine that I liked the boy and you need not wonder any more than as both wooing and my practice waxed apace, I was content to give up my great ambitions and stay just where I was.

"It wasn't a very pleasant thing, then, to have an epidemic of typhoid break out in the town that kept me going so that I hardly had time for the courting that a fellow wants to carry on with his sweetheart while he is still young enough to call her his girl. I fumed, but duty was duty, and I kept to my work night and day. It was not that Jube proved how invaluable he was as a coadjutor. He not only took messages to Annie, but brought sometimes little ones from her to me, and he would tell me little secret things that he had overheard her say that made me throb with joy and swear at him for repeating his mistress's conversation. But best of all, Jube was a perfect Cerberus, and no one on earth could have been more effective in keeping away or deluding the other young fellows who visited the Dalys. He would tell me of it afterward, chuckling softly to himself. 'An', Doctah, I say to Mistah Hemp Stevens, "'Scuse us, Mistah Stevens, but Miss Annie, she des gone out," an' den he go outer de gate lookin' moughty lonesome. When Sam Elkins come, I say, "Sh, Mistah Elkins, Miss Annie, she done tuk down," an' he say, "What, Jube, you don' reckon hit de——" Den he stop an' look skeert, an' I say, "I feared hit is, Mistah Elkins," an' sheks my haid ez solemn. He goes outer de gate lookin' lak his bes' frien' done daid, an' all de time Miss Annie behine de cu'tain ovah de po'ch des' a laffin' fit to kill.'

"Jube was a most admirable liar, but what could I do? He knew that I was a young fool of a hypocrite, and when I would rebuke him for these deceptions, he would give way and roll on the floor in an excess of delighted laughter until from very contagion I had to join him—and, well, there was no need of my preaching when there had been no beginning to his repentance and when there must ensue a continuance of his wrongdoing.

"This thing went on for over three months, and then, pouf! I was down like a shot. My patients were nearly all up, but the reaction from overwork made me an easy victim of the lurking germs. Then Jube loomed up as a nurse. He put everyone else aside, and with the doctor, a friend of mine from a neighboring town, took entire charge of me. Even Annie herself was put aside, and I was cared for as tenderly as a baby. Tom, that was my physician and friend, told me all about it afterward with tears in his eyes. Only he was a big, blunt man and his expressions did not convey all that he meant. He told me how my nigger had nursed me as if I were a sick kitten and he my mother. Of how fiercely he guarded his right to be the sole one to 'do' for me, as he called it, and how, when the crisis came, he hovered, weeping, but hopeful, at my bedside, until it was safely passed, when they drove him, weak and exhausted, from the room. As for me, I knew little about it at the time, and cared less. I was too busy in my fight with death. To my chimerical vision there was only a black but gentle demon that came and went, alternating with a white fairy, who would insist on coming in on her head, growing larger and larger and then dissolving. But the pathos and devotion in the story lost nothing in my blunt friend's telling.

"It was during the period of a long convalescence, however, that I came to know my humble ally as he really was, devoted to the point of abjectness. There were times when for very shame at his goodness to me, I would beg him to go away, to do something else. He would go, but before I had time to realize that I was not being ministered to, he would be back at my side, grinning and pottering just the same. He manufactured duties for the joy of performing them. He pretended to see desires in me that I never had, because he liked to pander to them, and when I became entirely exasperated, and ripped out a good round oath, he chuckled with the remark, 'Dah, now, you sholy is gittin' well. Nevah did hyeah a man anywhaih nigh Jo'dan's sho' cuss lak dat.'

"Why, I grew to love him, love him, oh, yes, I loved him as well—oh, what am I saying? All human love and gratitude are damned poor things; excuse me, gentlemen, this isn't a pleasant story. The truth is usually a nasty thing to stand.

"It was not six months after that that my friendship to Jube, which he had been at such great pains to win, was put to too severe a test.

"It was in the summer again, and as business was slack, I had ridden over to see my friend, Dr. Tom. I had spent a good part of the day there, and it was past four o'clock when I rode leisurely into Bradford. I was in a particularly joyous mood and no premonition of the impending catastrophe oppressed me. No sense of sorrow, present or to come forced itself upon me, even when I saw men hurrying through the almost deserted streets. When I got within sight of my home and saw a crowd surrounding it, I was only interested sufficiently to spur my horse into a jog trot, which brought me up to the throng, when something in the sullen, settled horror in the men's faces gave me a sudden, sick thrill. They whispered a word to me, and without a thought, save for Annie, the girl who had been so surely growing into my heart, I leaped from the saddle and tore my way through the people to the house.

"It was Annie, poor girl, bruised and bleeding, her face and dress torn from struggling. They were gathered round her with white faces, and, oh, with what terrible patience they were trying to gain from her fluttering lips the name of her murderer. They made way for me and I knelt at her side. She was beyond my skill, and my will merged with theirs. One thought was in our minds.

"'Who?' I asked.

"Her eyes half opened, 'That black———' She fell back into my arms dead.

"We turned and looked at each other. The mother had broken down and was weeping, but the face of the father was like iron.

"'It is enough,' he said; 'Jube has disappeared.' He went to the door and said to the expectant crowd, 'She is dead.'

"I heard the angry roar without swelling up like the noise of a flood, and then I heard the sudden movement of many feet as the men separated into searching parties, and laying the dead girl back upon her couch, I took my rifle and went out to join them.

"As if by intuition the knowledge had passed among the men that Jube Benson had disappeared, and he, by common consent, was to be the object of our search. Fully a dozen of the citizens had seen him hastening toward the woods and noted his skulking air, but as he had grinned in his old good-natured way, they had, at the time, thought nothing of it. Now, however, the diabolical reason of his slyness was apparent. He had been shrewd enough to disarm suspicion, and by now was far away. Even Mrs. Daly, who was visiting with a neighbor, had seen him stepping out a back way, and had said with a laugh, 'I reckon that black rascal's a-running off somewhere.' Oh, if she had only known.

"'To the woods! To the woods!' that was the cry, and away we went, each with the determination not to shoot, but to bring the culprit alive into town, and then to deal with him as his crime deserved.

"I cannot describe the feelings I experienced as I went out that night to beat the woods for this human tiger. My heart smoldered within me like a coal, and I went forward under the impulse of a will that was half my own, half some more malignant power's. My throat throbbed dryly, but water nor whiskey would not have quenched my thirst. The thought has come to me since that now I could interpret the panther's desire for blood and sympathize with it, but then I thought nothing. I simply went forward, and watched, watched with burning eyes for a familiar form that I had looked for as often before with such different emotions.

"Luck or ill-luck, which you will, was with our party, and just as dawn was graying the sky, we came upon our quarry crouched in the corner of a fence. It was only half light, and we might have passed, but my eyes had caught sight of him, and I raised the cry. We leveled our guns and he rose and came toward us.

"'I t'ought you wa'n't gwine see me,' he said sullenly, 'I didn't mean no harm.'

"'Harm!'

"Some of the men took the word up with oaths, others were ominously silent.

"We gathered around him like hungry beasts, and I began to see terror dawning in his eyes. He turned to me, 'I's moughty glad you's hyeah, doc,' he said, 'you ain't gwine let 'em whup me.'

"'Whip you, you hound,' I said, 'I'm going to see you hanged,' and in the excess of my passion I struck him full on the mouth. He made a motion as if to resent the blow against even such odds, but controlled himself.

"'W'y, doctah,' he exclaimed in the saddest voice I have ever heard, 'w'y, doctor! I ain't stole nuffin' o' yo'n, an' I was comin' back. I only run off to see my gal, Lucy, ovah to de Centah.'

"'You lie!' I said, and my hands were busy helping the others bind him upon a horse. Why did I do it? I don't know. A false education, I reckon, one false from the beginning. I saw his black face glooming there in the half light, and I could only think of him as a monster. It's tradition. At first I was told that the black man would catch me, and when I got over that, they taught me that the devil was black, and when I had recovered from the sickness of that belief, here were Jube and his fellows with faces of menacing blackness. There was only one conclusion: This black man stood for all the powers of evil, the result of whose machinations had been gathering in my mind from childhood up. But this has nothing to do with what happened.

"After firing a few shots to announce our capture, we rode back into town with Jube. The ingathering parties from all directions met us as we made our way up to the house. All was very quiet and orderly.

There was no doubt that it was as the papers would have said, a gathering of the best citizens. It was a gathering of stern, determined men, bent on a terrible vengeance.

"We took Jube into the house, into the room where the corpse lay. At sight of it, he gave a scream like an animal's and his face went the color of storm-brown water. This was enough to condemn him. We divined, rather than heard, his cry of 'Miss Ann, Miss Ann, oh, my God, doc, you don't t'ink I done it?'

"Hungry hands were ready. We hurried him out into the yard. A rope was ready. A tree was at hand. Well, that part was the least of it, save that Hiram Daly stepped aside to let me be the first to pull upon the rope. It was lax at first, and I felt the quivering soft weight resist my muscles. Other hands joined, and Jube swung off his feet.

"No one was masked. We knew each other. Not even the culprit's face was covered, and the last I remember of him as he went into the air was a look of sad reproach that will remain with me until I meet him face to face again.

"We were tying the end of the rope to a tree, where the dead man might hang as a warning to his fellows, when a terrible cry chilled us to the marrow.

"'Cut 'im down, cut 'im down, he ain't guilty. We got de one. Cut him down, fu' Gawd's sake. Here's de man, we foun' him hidin' in de barn!'

"Jube's brother, Ben, and another Negro, came rushing toward us, half dragging, half carrying a miserable-looking wretch between them. Someone cut the rope and Jube dropped lifeless to the ground.

"'Oh, my Gawd, he's daid, he's daid!' wailed the brother, but with blazing eyes he brought his captive into the center of the group, and we saw in the full light the scratched face of Tom Skinner—the worst white ruffian in the town—but the face we saw was not as we were accustomed to see it, merely smeared with dirt. It was blackened to imitate a Negro's.

"God forgive me; I could not wait to try to resuscitate Jube. I knew he was already past help, so I rushed into the house and to the dead girl's side. In the excitement they had not yet washed or laid her out. Carefully, carefully, I searched underneath her broken finger nails. There was skin there. I took it out, the little curled pieces, and went with it to my office.

"There, determinedly, I examined it under a powerful glass, and read my own doom. It was the skin of a white man, and in it were embedded strands of short, brown hair or beard.

"How I went out to tell the waiting crowd I do not know, for something kept crying in my ears, 'Blood guilty! Blood guilty!'

"The men went away stricken into silence and awe. The new prisoner attempted neither denial nor plea. When they were gone I would have helped Ben carry his brother in, but he waved me away fiercely, 'You he'ped murder my brotha, you dat was *his* frien', go 'way, go 'way! I'll tek him home myse'f.' I could only respect his wish, and he and his comrade took up the dead man and between them bore him up the street on which the sun was now shining full.

"I saw the few men who had not skulked indoors uncover as they passed, and I—I—stood there between the two murdered ones, while all the while something in my ears kept crying, 'Blood guilty! Blood guilty!' "

The doctor's head dropped into his hands and he sat for some time in silence, which was broken by neither of the men, then he rose, saying, "Gentlemen, that was my last lynching."

PART THREE

NONFICTION

INTRODUCTION

Anyone inclined to view Paul Laurence Dunbar as an apologist for the South or as a white-identified "Uncle Tom" would be quickly disabused of that view by reading the caustic, eloquent attacks on white racism that Dunbar published in newspapers. In "The Race Question Discussed," for example, written the week after the end of the Spanish-American War, in which black troops had acquitted themselves with honor, and shortly after the 1898 election-related anti-black massacre in Wilmington, North Carolina, Dunbar excoriates white hypocrisy with an irony as searing and dramatic as that of Mark Twain at his mordant best: "The new attitude may be interpreted as saying: 'Negroes, you may fight for us, but you may not vote for us. You may prove a strong bulwark when the bullets are flying, but you must stand from the line when the ballots are in the air." Unmasking what he refers to as white America's "acts of sophistry," Dunbar exposes the unstated attitude underlying the violence his white countrymen condoned in Wilmington: "The whites are stronger than the blacks. Why not then say to them openly: 'We don't like you; we do not want you in certain places. Therefore when we please we will kill you.'"

One would be hard-pressed to find any journalist—black or white—voicing a more scathing condemnation of racism in 1898. That this twenty-six-year-old black writer whose living depended largely on the patronage of white readers had the courage to write such a piece for a white newspaper syndicate is remarkable. *McClure's Magazine* (which had originally commissioned it) evidently found it too outspoken. But a number of newspapers picked it up, including the Toledo, Ohio, *Journal,* and it was widely reprinted. That Dunbar would be more remembered a century later for a rollicking feel-good poem like "The Party" than for an article like this one is unfortunate. For Dunbar's journalism provides key insights into both the writer himself and the world his writing entered.

Dunbar first tried his hand at journalism in high school, where he became editor in chief of the school newspaper at Dayton's Central High, a school in which he was one of only a handful of black students. One can see signs of the militance of the Toledo *Journal* article quoted above in an editorial Dunbar wrote for the first issue of the *Tattler,* the black community newspaper he published while still in high school. "Bear in mind that the agitation of *deeds* is tenfold more effectual than the agitation of *words.* For your own sake, for the sake of Heaven and the race, stop saying and go to doing." Dunbar had high hopes for the *Tattler,* which his friend Orville Wright printed on his homemade printing press in the bicycle shop down the street from Dunbar's house in Dayton. At the time Dunbar launched the *Tattler,* there were hundreds of newspapers written by and for African Americans and supported by black communities across the nation. An article Dunbar published several years later, "Of Negro Journals," makes it clear that Dunbar was well aware of the important role that black newspapers had played in the United States since the first was published in 1827. It was not surprising, perhaps, that this bright teenager sought to make a place for himself in this tradition. But he soon learned a lesson many an editor of a black newspaper would painfully learn: the economics of the newspaper business in a poor community can be punishing. Dunbar's *Tattler* soon went out of business for lack of funds.

Although Dunbar worked as editor of another black newspaper for several months in 1895, the Indianapolis *World,* most of his journalism ran in mainstream newspapers and periodicals. Since Dunbar earned a living from his writing, and mainstream publications could pay for articles more readily than black newspapers could, this should not surprise us. But it is likely that some of these pieces were reprinted in black newspapers around the country as well. That phenomenon is difficult to track, however, since turn-of-the-century black newspapers are generally not digitized or indexed yet and are therefore hard to search, as well as often hard to locate. All of the extant articles by Dunbar appeared in white-run publications such as the *Chicago Record,* the *Independent,* the *Columbus Dispatch,* the *Denver Post, Harper's Weekly,* the *Philadelphia Times,* the *Chicago Tribune, The Saturday Evening Post,* and *The New York Times.* With the exception of some high school journalism and a few reports for the *Chicago Record* on the 1893 World's Columbian Exposition, all of the articles that we have address aspects of being black and American at the turn of the century.

The pieces Dunbar wrote for these publications entered an ongoing cultural conversation about African Americans in the nation's media, one which Dunbar sought to shape in constructive ways. Sometimes a piece was a direct response to an article by a white writer that angered him. This was the case with "Is Higher Education for the Negro Hopeless?" which ran in the *Philadelphia Times* on June 10, 1900. Charles Dudley Warner, one of the country's leading writers and editors, had recently published a widely discussed essay entitled "The Education of the Negro" in which he asserted that in contemporary America, the net effect of higher education for African Americans had been detrimental to society. It had been a mistake, Warner opined, to try to teach a liberal arts curriculum to African Americans in institutions of higher learning. Echoing some of the views expressed by Booker T. Washington, Warner wrote that industrial training was more suited to "the negro race" at this moment in time.

Dunbar minced no words in challenging Warner's legitimacy as a commentator on this issue, calling the article, by one of the country's leading writers, "the work of one who speaks without authority." Dunbar argued that Warner's analysis, "founded upon observation of the South from a car window," was "not borne out by the facts." Black colleges, Dunbar noted, had raised the moral, social, and industrial level of the communities in which they were situated. The notion that higher education would discourage a people's inclination to work hard was hogwash: "I believe I know my own people pretty thoroughly," Dunbar wrote. "I know them in all classes, the high and the low, and I have yet to see any young man or young woman who had the spirit of work in them before, driven from labor by a college education."

Dunbar then refuted Warner's main example—New Orleans— point by point, noting specific positive developments in that city which

were directly related to the spread of higher education. He also chal-
lenged Warner's appraisal of black politicians in New Orleans, whom
Dunbar had found to be "men of high intelligence, clean morality, and
undisputed ability.... I say this out of no partisan or racial feeling, but
because I know and think that Mr. Warner does not know or has not
met these men." Dunbar also reminded his readers that critics like
Warner ignored the continuing impact of prejudice and discrimination in shaping the fate of African Americans:

> If, in the Northern cities, as he says, the Negro has been crowded out of the
> many occupations by the more vigorous races, was it because of their vigor,
> or because of the prejudice which preferred the alien to the citizen? Was it
> the vigor of the foreign miners in Illinois that drove the Negroes from their
> work, or the prejudice of a narrow people which allowed it?

Dunbar then deftly refuted Warner's efforts to use "statistics to
prove the increase of Negro criminality." With arguments that anticipate ones that are still, alas, both necessary and apt today, Dunbar
maintains,

> Statistics may prove anything, but in this case especially they are inade-
> quate. No one has the right to base any conclusions about Negro criminal-
> ity upon the number of prisoners in the jails and other places of restraint.
> Even in the North the prejudice against the Negro reverses the precedents
> of law, and every one accused is looked upon as guilty until he is proven
> innocent. In the South it is worse. Taking into account that some of the
> offenses for which a white boy would be reprimanded and released would
> send a Negro to the chain gang or the jail, it is easy to see how the percent-
> age of criminals is raised. A fight upon the street, picking up coal, with the
> accusation of throwing it off the cars, brawling generally, what with white
> boys would be called children's fights land the black boy in jail, and so the
> percentage of criminals increase....

Dunbar is lacerating when he writes that "Mr. Warner's ill-advised
article has done the Negro, who has looked to him as a friend, unutterable harm, more harm really than he knows. It is a pitiful thing, altogether. He has observed badly or been misinformed...." It is noteworthy
that Dunbar was unafraid to risk alienating white writers by challenging one of the leading white commentators of the day this bluntly in a
major mainstream newspaper. Few if any of his peers had the confi-

dence or the clout to circulate a critique this assertive to as broad a general audience.

Dunbar had been championing higher education for African Americans well before answering this attack on it by Warner. Although he recognized the value of industrial education, and in later years would pen some favorable pieces about Booker T. Washington, Dunbar feared that too great an emphasis on industrial education could constrict the size of the canvas on which African Americans could paint their lives. In "Our New Madness," for example, published in 1898 in *The Independent,* Dunbar wrote that

> while the high and sublime object of teaching may be to produce an able, thinking carpenter, with the power of enjoying the higher intellectual pleasures of life, is it not likely that what will be produced from this new people will be a carpenter with a steady hand—and I do not decry that— but with a mind out of which is shut all appreciation for the beauty of art, science, and literature.

"There has been here, of late, too great an insistence upon manual training for the negro," Dunbar wrote. The black man demonstrated during slavery, "when he was the plantation blacksmith and carpenter and shoemaker," that he knew how to work with his hands.

> But his intellectual capacity is still in doubt. Any attempt at engaging in pursuits where his mind is employed is met by an attitude that stigmatizes his effort as presumption. Then if the daring one succeeds, he is looked upon as a monster. He is put into the same category with the "two-headed boy" and the "bearded lady." There has not, in the history of the country, risen a single intellectual black man whose pretensions have not been sneered at, laughed at, and then lamely wondered at. . . .

Little had changed on this front in the half century that had passed since the fugitive slave Frederick Douglass had felt obligated to demonstrate his intellectual capacity to the white race by publishing a first-rate newspaper. The negro, Dunbar wrote, still needed to prove his "intellectuality" to whites who continued to "[take] it for granted that [the Negro] ought not to work with his head." Such a view "flatters and satisfies [white people's] self-complacency," Dunbar wrote. But these views should not deter African Americans from seeking a proper balance in their lives—a blend of "industry, commerce, art, science, and letters, of materialism and idealism, of utilitarianism and beauty!" For Dunbar held a view somewhat akin to Du Bois's idea of the role of the "talented tenth," the minority within the black community who would use their education and intellectual talents to leaven the whole. As he put it in "The Negro as an Individual" (1902),

> the chief value of the Negro schools of the South is not in the hundreds upon hundreds of colored boys and girls which they turn out each year with more or less knowledge of the classics or the handicrafts, but the few bright particular stars which may be held up as beacons for the whole race....

Dunbar himself was one of the brightest stars of the race when he wrote this, and although he was the product not of a Southern college but of a Northern high school, he recognized the importance of the excellent, if relatively brief, education he had received.

Dunbar may have reserved his sharpest criticism for those who ignored or condoned white racism, and who would deny black people the opportunities to develop to their fullest capacity, but he was also outspoken on the mistakes so many of his fellow African Americans made in their life choices. In "The Negroes of the Tenderloin" (1895), he expressed his sadness over "the crowds of idle, shiftless Negroes" thronging the Tenderloin district of New York, "great, naughty, irresponsible children," as he called them, "deceived by the glare and glitter of the city streets," men whose "highest ideal is a search for pleasure" and who "think they have found it when they indulge in vice." Dunbar felt pity and despair for these brethren drawn to the city from the country who "have given up the fields for the gutters," who "have forgotten to laugh and have learned to sneer." Much of this pity and despair would find its way into *Sport of the Gods*. Dunbar saw no simple solution to the problem: "It is probably wrong to introduce a problem and then to suggest no specific remedy, but I confess that I can see no practicable one now."

On some level he felt the problem lay in the continuing mass migration of Southern blacks to Northern cities. But while in 1895 Dunbar could say that he would rather that more of his brothers and sisters remain on the farm than migrate to the city, by 1899, in "The

Hapless Southern Negro," he made it clear that remaining in primitive rural poverty was hardly an answer. Here Dunbar, writing from Denver, where he had gone for his health, championed the advantages of migrating to the West. "The West, the great and generous West, has extended her hands to every nation and said: 'Come and be free.' She has not refused the pauper from Europe; she has not turned back the criminal from the East. Could she then say no to her poor black brother, who has been in the family for two hundred fifty years and whose blood and whose sweat have gone to give to the South whatever wealth it possesses today?" The Exodusters, former slaves who had left the rural South for Kansas during the decades following the breakdown of Reconstruction, had followed a similar dream. However idealistic Dunbar's view of the West may have been, he was not alone among his contemporaries in viewing the West as a place that held out more opportunities to African Americans at the turn of the century than did the North or the South.

Nor was Dunbar the first African American writer to find that a sojourn in England clarified his understanding of the condition of African Americans in the United States. In "England as Seen by a Black Man" (1897), published in *The Independent,* Dunbar expresses the palpable sense of relief that came with being in a place in which anti-black racism did not throw obstacles in his path on a daily basis:

> It would be an inestimable blessing if a number of Negroes from every State in the Union could live abroad for a few years, long enough to cool in their blood the fever-heat of strife. Here where there is so much opposition to his development, and, remember, I do not assert that is always conscious and intentional, the black man practices defense until it grows into aggression. Remove him from his surroundings, take away the barrier against which he is constantly pushing, and he will return to the perpendicular—to the upright.

Dunbar's insight into the invisible toll that pushing against "opposition to his development" takes on African Americans (however unconscious that racism may be) is a theme that echoes throughout black letters in the twentieth century. Relieved during his stay in England of the burden of dealing with that opposition on a daily basis (if he encountered racism there, it was much less blatant and noxious than the forms he encountered in America), Dunbar was free to appreciate qualities in his surroundings that transcended issues of race—such as the importance and orderliness of family life that he observed among the English. (The fact that he was courting Alice Ruth Moore at the time he published this piece may have influenced his inclination to extol the joys of harmonious family life.) He also seems to have admired "the British subject's contentment with his lot in life," and felt that a measure of that sort of contentment would benefit his fellow African Americans—a view he would contradict in other articles he wrote. One might uncharitably turn Dunbar's criticism of Warner on Dunbar himself and say that his views of English life may have been founded upon observation "from a car window." Be that as it may, what one takes from this piece is Dunbar's own sense of relief—and, yes, contentment—at being in a place where race did not determine the world's responses to a man, "[M]erit is not discouraged there on account of color, neither is it taken for granted because one is black." Frederick Douglass had enjoyed a similar vacation from virulent racial prejudice and stereotyping during his own stay in England two generations before.

While he did not hesitate to excoriate wrong-headed white writers who presumed to prescribe cures for the ills of black people, or misguided black folks who chased evanescent pleasures in Northern cities, Dunbar also wrote articles celebrating positive aspects of African American life. In "Negro Music," for example, published in the *Chicago Record* in 1899, Dunbar dryly notes, "Foreign critics have said that these plantation songs were the only original music that America has produced. This is a mis-statement, for America has not produced even these; she has only taken what Africa has given her." But Dunbar acknowledges, "It is said, and generally conceded to be true, that the negro is ashamed of his music. If it be so, it is a shame to be rebuked and one which he must overcome, for he has the most beautiful melodies of any in the world. They are his by inheritance and it is for him to make the best use of his rich legacy."

And while Dunbar would be the last to say that the social life of the black elite of Washington, D.C., deserved to inspire as much pride as the black spiritual, Dunbar recognized that drawing the curtain open on a rather glittering world that was largely invisible to white America could counter the image that the majority of African Americans lived the degraded existence of those he profiled in his article on the Tenderloin. The articles Dunbar wrote on black social life in the nation's capital in the *Baltimore News* in 1900 ("Negro Life in Washington") and in *The Saturday Evening Post* in 1901 ("Negro Society in Washington") implicitly responded to the view that "negro society in the city" is simply "a caricature of white society" (as an article in *The Chautauquan* had put it). These pieces, the second of which is the longest article Dunbar ever published in a newspaper or magazine, limned a world of black wealth and refinement which was probably completely unknown to these publications' predominantly white readership.

In the first of these pieces, Dunbar shows an awareness of the range of classes that Washington's black community included, recording snippets of interview material in a form designed to convey the rhythms of the vernacular of uneducated Southern speakers. These portraits would have been more familiar to readers of the *Baltimore News* than the sketches that followed of men and women with money and taste and leisure—and the propensity to combine all three in a lively and satisfying social life that any middle-class white American might envy. Dunbar maintains a certain degree of distance from this world, noting that the black people immersed in it probably take it too seriously and white people dismiss it too readily as amusing and inconsequential. He concludes by saying that "negro life in Washington is a promise rather than a fulfillment. But it is worthy of note for the really excellent things which are promised." Along the way, however, he also manages to convey some of the milestones already achieved, mentioning that members of Washington's black community "have taken their degrees from Cambridge, Oxford, Edinburgh, Harvard, Yale, Cornell, Wellesley, and a score of minor colleges"—a roster of achievement that relatively few white communities could rival.

In his extended profile of this community in *The Saturday Evening Post,* Dunbar gives white America something they were not likely to find elsewhere: a candid glimpse of prosperous, educated black America at play. While newspapers were more likely to feature a black murderer than a black millionaire (a point Dunbar made elsewhere in his journalism), here Dunbar depicts a cosmopolitan world of wealth, refinement, and intricate social hierarchies, with respect—as well as a measure of bemused distance. This world in which black doctors, judges, businessmen, diplomats, and their families organized balls, musical gatherings, athletic contests, and literary societies was a far cry from the degraded, anomic black urban life that Dunbar himself had profiled in his article on the Tenderloin. But one was as much a part of contemporary black America as the other. And Dunbar realized that sharing the portrait of this educated, economically successful black community with white readers could help break down the stereotypes that bolstered white racism.

———

None of Dunbar's earlier pieces—with the possible exception of "The Race Question Discussed"—attacked white racism with the force, power, and precision of "The Fourth of July and Race Outrages," which ran in *The New York Times* on July 10, 1903, and was widely reprinted around the country. Anyone inclined to view Dunbar as a conciliationist captive of the white book-buying public on whom he depended for his living would do well to read this scathing, seething, and effective jeremiad, a piece that echoes (on an unconscious if not a conscious level) Frederick Douglass's famous speech on July 5, 1852, "What to the Slave is the Fourth of July?"

Dunbar begins by noting the irony of the country's sending "a protest to Russia" on the occasion of the most recent massive pogrom there, while ignoring the "bloody deeds" perpetrated on its own black citizens at home. But rather than launch a frontal attack on the myopic powers that be, Dunbar slyly focuses his criticism on his fellow African Americans' unthinking or naïve willingness to celebrate a holiday honoring freedom while their own freedom is violated at every turn. As the litany of heinous conditions builds to a new crescendo in every paragraph, Dunbar's ironic refrain—"and we celebrate"—takes on ever more bitter power with each repetition.

> The papers are full of the reports of peonage in Alabama. A new and more dastardly slavery there has arisen to replace the old. For the sake of reenslaving the Negro, the Constitution has been trampled under feet, the rights of man have been laughed out of court, and the justice of God has been made a jest and we celebrate.
>
> Every wire, no longer in the South alone, brings us news of a new hanging or a new burning, some recent outrage against a helpless people . . . and we celebrate.
>
> Like a dark cloud, pregnant with terror and destruction, disenfranchisement has spread its wings over our brethren of the South. Like the

same dark cloud, industrial prejudice glooms above us in the North. We may not work save when the new-come foreigner refuses to, and then they, high prized above our sacrificial lives, may shoot us down with impunity. And yet we celebrate.

With citizenship discredited and scorned, with violated homes and long unheeded prayers, with bleeding hands uplifted, still sore and smarting from long beating at the door of opportunity, we raise our voices and sing, "My Country, 'Tis of Thee"; we shout and sing while from the four points of the compass comes our brothers' unavailing cry, and so we celebrate. . . .

As W.E.B. Du Bois would put it in his 1935 book *Black Reconstruction*, the slave went free, stood a few brief minutes in the sun, and then went back again into slavery. By the 1960s, this understanding of the post-Reconstruction era, the period we now know as "the Nadir" in American race relations, would be generally accepted by historians. But in 1903, when Dunbar wrote this article, his hard-hitting indictment of his country's betrayals of its ideals was particularly bold and brazen. In 1903, the evils he related were topics that historians, as well as the majority of white Americans, preferred to ignore, deny, or repress, championing instead national narratives of progress and reconciliation that had little to do with the realities experienced daily by African Americans. And that he made his case not in some obscure provincial journal but in *The New York Times* was all the more striking. Dunbar may have written poetry that sold, but he was far from a sellout. On the contrary, he used the bully pulpit he had earned as a popular poet to remind his countrymen of some hard truths they preferred to forget. If there were a canon of compelling anti-racist writing by Americans, at least two of Dunbar's newspaper articles—"The Race Question Discussed" and "The Fourth of July and Race Outrages"—would deserve a permanent place of honor there.

SALUTATORY

Dayton with her sixty thousand inhabitants, among which are numbered five thousand colored people, has for a long time demanded a paper, representative of the energy and enterprise of our citizens. It is this long-felt want which the *Tattler* now aspires to fill. Her mission shall be to encourage and assist the enterprises of the city, to give our young people a field in which to exercise their literary talents, to champion the cause of right, and to espouse the principles of honest republicanism. The desire which is the guiding star of our existence is that some word may be dropped in our columns, which shall reach the hearts of our colored voters and snatch them from the brink of that yawning chasm—paid democracy.

There are materials to make a successful newspaper in this city, if they can only be combined and utilized. And we must ask the co-operation of a generous public, in our attempt to do this. Every one can give us some aid: first by subscribing to the paper; for local pride if nothing else should prompt you to do this; next by advertising; and thirdly by contributing. You should subscribe first because knowing as you do that a city having so many colored inhabitants as Dayton should support a newspaper, you would feel it your duty; then because it will benefit you by keeping you posted on all current matters. The literaries shall be represented and all the lodges shall find their notices readily published by us, and we shall have items of interest from many other cities. Why you should advertise with us, can be told in few words, because *it is money in your pockets.*

Grocers, blacksmiths, restaurateurs, all should advertise, and boarding house keepers should not forget that the paper will go out of town and their "ads" will be noticed in other cities so that when people come from those towns here, they will know where to stop. So advertise and advertise soon.

Lastly, contribute because there is no better way for ambitious young men and young ladies to bring themselves before the public than by writing for a live newspaper.

With these few introductory words, the *Dayton Tattler* makes its initial bow to the public, demanding the recognition which is its right.

———

A great mistake that has been made by editors of the race is that they only discuss one question, the race problem. This no doubt is important, but a quarter of a century of discussion of one question has worn it thread-bare; we may venture to assert without fear of refutation, that no new idea has been presented upon this subject for the last ten years, and yet it is hacked at, and tossed about until one is almost prone to say, that more harm than good is being done. We do not counsel you, debaters, writers, and fellow editors, to throw away your opinions on this all important question; on the contrary we deem it one worthy of constant thought. But the time has come when you should act your opinions out, rather than write them. Your cry is, "we must agitate, we must agitate." So you must but bear in mind that the agitation of *deeds* is tenfold more effectual than the agitation of *words.* For your own sake, for the sake of Heaven and the race, stop saying, and go to doing. Find other things than this one question to talk about; the political field teems with abundant material. Give us a variety and cease feeding your weary readers on an unbroken diet of the race problem.

(DAYTON) *TATTLER,* DEC. 13, 1890, VOL. 1, NO. 1.

OF NEGRO JOURNALS

Special to the Chicago Record.

DAYTON, O., JUNE 22.—For one to dilate upon the important part which journalism has taken in the uplifting of mankind would be an ungrateful, because an unnecessary, task. The power of the press has been too long known and too universally acknowledged for one at this late day to lay upon his shoulders the burden of proving its reality. The freedom of the press has ever been closely allied to the prosperity of the people and a living proof of the statement is in the American nation. From these facts it has come to be an accepted principle to judge the general progress of a people by the character and tone of its press.

If this standard be a true one it may not be amiss to look into negro journalism as a very considerable entity in the discussion of the black man's advancement.

Even a cursory glance over the past history of his journalistic achievements will show that the negro's newspaper, crude and faulty as it may have been, has not merely kept pace with his evolutions, but rather led the way. It was the voice of an oppressed people uplifted through *Freedom's Journal*, the *Ram's Horn* and the *North Star* that awakened pubic opinion and paved—albeit with jagged rocks—the way to emancipation. However feeble the efforts, however incapable the projectors, however brief the existence of many of those ante-bellum journals, they, at least, had a worthy *causa vivendi,* which is more than can be said of some of their successors.

AFTER USES FOR THESE PAPERS

They were actuated by a stern purpose that was their producer and preserver. They were knights errant arrayed against the dragon Slavery, to whose ferocity many of them were sacrificed. When he was finally laid low, it would have been fair to suppose that this separate and distinct press had no further call for existence, but not so. As soon as the head of Slavery was cut off the negro found that the monster was like Hydra, and that there were a dozen more very aggressive heads newly arisen that needed destroying. In the emergency five papers arose for every head. Subsequently this proposition has been maintained, which accounts for the 250 papers published by colored people in the United States today.

But it has been a question in the minds of some as to whether the colored newspaper has not increased in quantity rather than in quality. Indeed, a few have had the temerity to assert that the old journals were better edited and impressed the reader more deeply than the modern papers. But this is a delusion which the different circumstances surrounding the two publications make natural. The old journals were more impressive, not because they were better edited but because they brimmed with but one purpose, and that a purpose which was alive in the heart of every friendly reader. They discussed but one question, and that a question which was agitating the mind of every unfriendly reader. They called forth more attention because they were rarer. More of the white race read them than read negro journals now, because they were the first shoots of an intellectual growth in a people who were popularly supposed to be incapable of any such development, and as such were novelties.

PAPERS READ ONLY BY BLACKS

It is one of the disadvantages that the negro journal has to encounter in its protest against national wrongs that it is generally read only by the wronged race. It does not reach the people whom it would affect. So confined is its scope that its labors become fruitless. For it is constantly presenting the sad truth to people who already know it and flaunting crimes and outrages in the faces of people who never think of committing them. If a white man takes [i.e. subscribes to] a colored man's paper it is generally, as he expresses it, for the purpose of "helping him along" and he never for an instant supposes that there is or can be anything in it to interest him. But is this true? And if it is true where does the fault rest?

People of intelligent tastes have pleasures in common and there should be no reason why an intelligent, fair-minded white man should not enjoy the same paper that gives pleasure to a black man of like temperament and accomplishments. But the fact of the matter is this: The negro newspaper is too often not a paper designed for general reading. It is too closely a chronicle of unimportant personal facts, unrelieved by the less confined interest of an editorial column. In picking up a strange paper it is to the editorial column that one instinctively turns and if a dearth be found there little hope can be entertained for the rest of the paper. Again, the colored newspaper is not literary; it seldom publishes a story or poem, and a review is almost an unknown feature.

Intelligent colored men read and tolerate these papers because the papers are in closer contact with the people whose doings they chronicle. But what possible interest can the white friend of the race, who pays for a year's subscription, have in the fact that "Miss Peggy Wilson of Plum Tree Center gave a taffy-pull last week"? It is this attention to minute and personal details that precludes any general circulation of the colored man's newspaper.

Partisan Leaning of the Press

Another fault of the colored man's journalism lies in the fact that your negro newspaper is nothing if not partisan. Every petty journal that is started launches out upon the stormy sea of politics—poor, frail craft on a main where so many stauncher vessels are wrecked. Every little sheet, it matters not how insignificant, must needs raise its voice in the affairs of government and throw its featherweight of influence in the scales to help turn the balance one way or the other. The space that might contain some story or poem that would inspire the young reader to do or be something is given over to twaddle about the merits of the candidate for sheriff. The column that might be filled with helpful household hints to the girls whose mothers have so lately come from toiling in the cotton fields, is devoted to exploiting the merits of the man who wants to be county prosecutor. The black race in America is hungry for right, knowledge, and valuable information. And oh, negro editors, they "ask you for bread and you give them a stone." Is it fair to them or best for yourselves?

It is an unfortunate fact that the average colored editor is poor enough to be in the range of temptation. And too often the silver of some candidate, which crosses his palm makes him to prophesy good that never comes and to hide evil that is present.

I do not write as a malicious croaker, but as one deeply interested in the development of the best that is in the negro. And I dare to say that the negro press has not accomplished the best that it could have done; that it has not supplied the wants of its people; that it has given them wrong aspirations and fostered wrong tastes in them.

MEN REGARDED AS SUCCESSFUL

The man who through subserviency to party succeeds in securing a janitorship in a public building is of more weight in the race and more highly respected than he who through constant study and hard labor seeks to put and succeeds in putting himself on an intellectual level with his white brother. The aspirations of the race are too entirely dependent upon a political line, and that it is so is the fault of the negro press, for it has preached politics to the exclusion of science, art and literature.

There is a certain prominent negro journal which supplements its statement of terms with the announcement that all poetical contributions must be accompanied by payment for publication at regular advertising rates. Rare encouragement, indeed, for that proverbially impecunious class, the poets.

"But," some optimistic brother remarks, "look at the training the numerous correspondents of these papers secure." But is this training a fact? Real training consists in having one's faults corrected and one's mistakes set right. But nine-tenths of the negro editors pass the communications of their correspondents without correction and allow them to go forth in cold type with all their imperfections on their head.

The correspondent reads it just as he wrote it, and supposes that it must have been right and "the last state of that man is worse than the first."

It is not to be imagined, though, that these papers, faulty as they are, have accomplished no good. Far from it. They have taught their people the use and the importance of their suffrage, and if they have misguided it, it is because the privilege was so new. They have at every opportunity impressed upon their readers the fact that they were citizens and if they have said more of loyalty to party than of loyalty to country it is because they looked upon the two as synonymous.

They have made mistakes, but they will live to profit by them, for an institution of which a spirit like Douglass's was one of the pioneers cannot fail.

God has given them a message to deliver and they will correct their faults and live up to the "high source of their endowment."

Chicago Record, June 22, 1894.

England as Seen by a Black Man

Nothing could be more significant than the word "impressions," when speaking of England from a Negro's point of view. For "impressed" he is, from the time he sets foot on English soil until he is again upon his native shores. He may not set down the new sensations which he is experiencing as so many separate estimates of a people and a condition, but when he is home again, all that he has seen and heard crystallizes in the changed environment. In so far as he is like other men in his nature and condition, he is similarly affected by what he sees and hears about him. He is astounded by the evidences of age which surround him. He is bewildered by the magnitude of the greatest city in the world. Her temples and her taverns, her homes and her hedges, the places where Romance has blossomed and the spots where History has made her abiding-place—all these stir him to broader views and higher thoughts. But more than by all these, more than is possible to the average man, is he impressed by the new conditions with which he comes into contact.

The Negro who takes a right view of the matter must realize that it is not so much what he has lost in coming home as it is what he has learned in being away, that is of value. To be sure, it is a great thing to have been accepted upon the basis of worth alone; to have found a people who do not assert color as a badge of degradation. But it is more to have learned that an unmistakably great people look upon the black race in America with hope, interest, and admiration. It is a good thing to have been accepted upon terms of equality in excellent English families; but it is of infinitely more importance to have come away from contact with this institution, which has been at the very foundation of British power, with some ideas to inform and elevate Negro family life. This latter seems to me to be a point of especial importance.

The beauty and perfection of a pure family life is one thing which, say what we will, the Negro needs greatly to learn. I must confess that no phase of English social observance struck me more forcibly than this.

It seems to me that we Americans, of whatever caste or complexion, hold too lightly the ties of relationship. More and more are our natures taking on the Gallic character, in which the distinguishing trait is not a love of family. Our whole tendency is to the glorification of the individual. I wish I could have taken some of my black brothers who have come to the North and prospered, and in prosperity forgotten the parental cabin in Kentucky or Virginia or Tennessee, into the heart of a typical middle-class English household. I would want them to see how, with these people, the good of the whole is the primal thing, and how all work together harmoniously for the best ends.

I would have some of those whom I hear exclaiming against marriage and the "bother" of children go into these families and, apart from any ethical consideration, just witness the simple delight of such an association. The father with his sturdy sons grouped about him, the mother in the midst of her healthful, hearty daughters—great, strong, big families; they are kingdoms in themselves.

An incidental point in this same matter which will force itself upon the observer's mind is the manner in which an English boy is trained. I like his reverence for authority, a feeling that is inculcated at the very beginning of his life. He knows how to obey.

Against this view, some one may urge the highhanded violations of which the young English aristocrat has been guilty, their open defiance of law on account of their position; but I do not feel that they are representative either of the whole English people, or of the best English people. I do not believe that a nation is any more fairly represented by her highest than by her lowest. Park Place and Berkeley Square are no more England than is Whitechapel. It is the great middle-class, the bone and sinew of the country, which is the true index of the national tendency; and the way a middle-class boy is trained is a thing to be admired and imitated. The youngster believes that he is a citizen of the greatest country on earth. To him, the world is composed of England, her possessions, and a few other countries. But he looks through all the intervening stages of society up to the one who is the epitome of all the power and glory of his country.

Everywhere he turns he sees the ramifications of this power and glory, which he always refers to the source. So, while he grows up with a pride in his land, with a sturdy independence, yet his strongest emotions are tempered by an earnest and deep-rooted respect for authority.

After considering the boy in his home, I can understand the spirit of the Englishman in the field. The attitude of the youth toward his parents, to me, interprets Balaklava.

I am a little afraid that it is too often taken as an indication of commendable spirit when one of our boys smashes his slate and kicks his governess. It is, without doubt, spirit of a kind. It is true that there are some few geniuses, a necessity of whose being it is that they be a law unto themselves; but it will not do for a whole nation. Indeed, most of us poor mortals need governing. We are clay and must have the potter's hand. On the voyage home I remember being told by a genial Western American that his little son was a perfect aristocrat, and, in support of his statement, he related to me how his young heir would show his extreme contempt for servants and people below his class. He was delighted at the child's early recognition of his own superiority. To my mind, feeling as I do the danger which menaces us from the very feeling of our independence, it was a serious fault that needed speedy correction. The proud father, tho, had the grace to add; "But that boy of mine will get out of all that before he is through with these American public schools." Perhaps he will.

Here again, in this matter of obedience, of respect for authority and submission to control, the point of view of a black man comes in. I believe that it is Mr. Fortunate who so wisely says that what the Negro needs is not so much leaders as the ability to follow when he is led. This is true, and with a reason. For so long a time he was the sole obeying party that when he did come to have command of his own affairs a violent reaction took place, and he stoutly objected to being led or commanded by anybody. He seemed to think that the highest evidence of a state of freedom was a refusal to obey superiors. He recognized vaguely that the genius of American civilization is the equality of all men; and he reduced the principle to his own ideas and said: "I am as good as anybody else; therefore I will be commanded by nobody. If I cannot lead, I will not follow." To be sure, he held this opinion in common with far too many white citizens; but the black man so deeply needs the centralization of power which would come from following one captain that it is to him especially I would commend the lesson of English obedience.

A not less important thing that is worth deep consideration, if not full imitation, is the British subject's contentment with his lot in life. I have been told that it is not contentment, but the lethargy of despair. But I do not believe it even of the lowest laborers. It is rather, a stolid, common-sense philosophy of life which says: "Let me enjoy whatever of pleasure comes to me and make the best of the inevitable sorrows." It says: "I will love my children and do the best I can to raise them to a better condition; but if I cannot leave them any other heritage, I will not leave them one of discontent and unrest." Our peasantry, if such the laboring blacks may be called, in condition is much like that of England; but in realization and acceptance of their lot, how different. The novel message of freedom has been blown into their ears with such a ringing blast that the din has for the moment confused them. Every man reads his own destiny in the stars, and sees only greatness there. He who preaches the doctrine that "They also serve who only stand and wait" is a heretic.

I know that I shall be accused of applauding, even of recommending, the stifling of honest ambition. But I do not go so far as that. What I mean is, that I prefer peace to popularity, content to a state of constant striving after ideals that cannot for many years be attained by the black race. I mean that I would have black men, who are vainly beating their heads against the impregnable wall of adverse circumstances, stop and recognize their limitations—learn a lesson of these stolid people and cease to fret away their little lives in unavailing effort. I want this for the blacks because I want them to be happy. I do not want them to continue to imbibe the dangerous draught which has intoxicated their white brothers of this Western world and sent them raving madmen, struggling for life at the expense of their fellows in the stock-markets and the wheat-pits of our great cities. I would not have black men unambitious; but I would not have them disturb the even course of their lives with feverish dreams—dreams from which but one awakening is possible. Few there are who do not know how little it has taken to make these people happy, from how small a flower they have drawn the honey of joy; but because the blossom has developed, I would not have them ravish the plant.

It would be an inestimable blessing if a number of Negroes from every State in the Union could live abroad for a few years, long enough to cool in their blood the fever-heat of strife. Here where there is so much opposition to his development, and, remember, I do not assert that is always conscious and intentional, the black man practices defense until it grows into aggression. Remove him from his surroundings, take away the barrier against which he is constantly pushing, and he will return to the perpendicular—to the upright.

England as the home for Negroes? No, a thousand times, no! Kentucky, Tennessee, Virginia, yes; even New York, Ohio, or Illinois, is better. England has her population. The Negro has a home, one which he loves and reveres. He has tilled its soil; he has felled its forests; he has digged its mines; in bitter times he has wrenched prosperity from reluctant nature; but, like an ignorant boy, I would have him go out into the school of the world and, having learned his lesson, come home and apply it. I would have him go and learn strength from a strong people, and, coming home, use that power, if it be vouchsafed him to use it in no other way, in just living and loving and being quiet.

I would not have the man who fails here go to England to succeed. Because merit is not discouraged there on account of color, neither is it taken for granted because one is black.

THE INDEPENDENT 48, Sept. 16, 1897.

OUR NEW MADNESS

We Negroes are a people who are prone to be taken by sudden enthusiasms. We fly with the swiftness of thought from one extreme to another. We are young, and we have the faults of youth and commit its errors. Age and experience, perhaps bitter, most certainly wholesome, must teach us conservatism.

We are now in the throes of feverish delight over industrial education. It is a good thing, and yet one of which we can easily have too much. There is only one point, hardly large enough, it seems, to make the basis of an article, to which I wish to call attention. It is the danger we court of going to the other extreme of educating the hand to the exclusion of the needs of the head.

The answer naturally comes back: "But industrial education means the equal training of the hand and head." Of course it does; but the danger is that the meaning may be mistaken, and the most easily appearing surface points only seized. That is, that while the high and sublime object of teaching may be to produce an able, thinking carpenter, with the power of enjoying the higher intellectual pleasures of life, is it not likely that what will be produced from this new people will be a carpenter with a steady hand—and I do not decry that—but with a mind out of which is shut all appreciation for the beauty of art, science, and literature.

You say: "But we can't all be doctors and lawyers and preachers." No, to be sure not, but let some of us be; for we cannot all of us be carpenters, tinners, and brick-masons.

There has been here, of late, too great an insistence upon manual training for the negro. He needs it. Any one who has studied his condition, either at the North or the South, cannot but admit that. But that the demands of his heart and mind call also for the most liberal and the broadest culture he can get, the earnest seeker after truth cannot deny.

The statement has been so strongly and so frequently urged that the negro should work with his hands, that the opposite of the proposition has been implied. People are taking it for granted that he ought not to work with his head. And it is so easy for these people among whom we are living to believe this; it flatters and satisfies their self-complacency.

At this late day the negro has no need to prove his manual efficiency. That was settled fifty years ago, when he was the plantation blacksmith and carpenter and shoemaker. But his intellectual capacity is still in doubt. Any attempt at engaging in pursuits where his mind is employed is met by an attitude that stigmatizes his effort as presumption. Then if the daring one succeeds, he is looked upon as a monster. He is put into the same category with the "two-headed boy" and the "bearded lady." There has not, in the history of the country, risen a single intellectual black man whose pretensions have not been sneered at, laughed at, and then lamely wondered at. If he was fair of complexion, they said that he derived his powers from his white blood. If he was convincingly black, they felt of his bumps, measured his head, and said that it was not negro in conformation. It is his intellectuality that needs substantiating.

Any one who has visited the school at Tuskegee, Alabama, and seen the efficiency of the work being done there, can have no further doubt of the ability and honesty of purpose of its founder and president. But I do fear that this earnest man is not doing either himself or his race full justice in his public utterances. He says we must have industrial training, and the world quotes him (in detached paragraphs) as saying that we must not have anything else.

A young man wants to enter a profession, and he speaks to a white man eminent in that particular work. The reply comes: "Now, what do you want to try a profession for? Why don't you take up a trade of some kind?"

"But I don't want to take a trade," says the young man. "I want to follow my own bent."

"Well, you're all wrong. It's just as your man, Mr. Washington, down there says; you people ought to be content to do manual labor for generations yet. I have always said that the colored people were too ambitious and expected too much."

"But suppose that individual inclinations—"

"You have no right to any individual feeling in the matter. You should consider your race and its especial fitness for certain kinds of work," and so on *ad nauseam*.

Now here I object. I do not believe that the individual should bend his spirit in accordance with ideas, mistaken or otherwise, as to what his race should do. I do not believe that a young man, whose soul is turbulent with a message which should be given to the world through the pulpit or the press, should shut his mouth and shoe horses; nor do I believe that this is what the best advocates of manual training would teach; but it is the interpretation which the great world is putting on their doctrine.

The incident is related that during the late war, just after the fall of a Southern city, an old colored man was seen stealing out of a lawyer's dismantled office with two volumes of Blackstone's "Commentaries" under his arm. To the question "What are you going to do with them, Uncle Ike?" he replied: "Hush, chile! I's gwine to run fu' Cong'ess."

It is just possible that the negro of the present day is not too wise to seize the most palpable tools of a strange system, and miss the deeper meaning of the whole.

I would not counsel a return to the madness of that first enthusiasm for classic and professional learning; but I would urge that the negro temper this newer one with a right idea of the just proportion in life of industry, commerce, art, science, and letters, of materialism and idealism, of utilitarianism and beauty!

The Independent 50, Aug. 18, 1898.

THE RACE QUESTION DISCUSSED

NEGRO AND WHITE MAN
(Suggested by the Wilmington, N.C. Riots)

Loud, from the South, Damascan cries
Fall on our ears, unheeded still.
No helping powers stir or rise.
Hate's opiate numbs the nation's will.
Slumbers the north. (While honor dies!)
Soothed by th' insidious breath of lies!

It would seem that the man who sits at his desk in the North and writes about the troubles in the South is very apt to be like a doctor who prescribes for a case he has no chance to diagnose. It would be true in this instance, also, if it were not that what has happened in Georgia has happened in Ohio and Illinois. The race riots in North Carolina were of a piece with the same proceedings in the state of Lincoln. The men who shoot the Negro in Hogansville are blood brothers to those who hang him in Urbana, and the deed is neither better nor worse because it happens in one section of the country or other. The race spirit in the United States is not local but general.

To the outsider, unacquainted with the vagaries of our national prejudice, the recent and sudden change of attitude of the American toward the Negro would appear inconsistent, to say the least. We are presented with the spectacle of· a people gushing, through glowing headlines, over the bravery of its black heroes. In an incredibly short space of time—almost too brief, it would seem, for the mental transition of the individual, much less the nation—we find the mouthpieces of this same people chronicling the armed resistance of the community to the Negroes in the exercise of those powers and privileges which are the glory of the country for which the colored men fought.

The drama of this sudden change of heart is incongruous to the point of ghastly humor.

The new attitude may be interpreted as saying: "Negroes, you may fight for us, but you may not vote for us. You may prove a strong bulwark when the bullets are flying, but you must stand from the line when the ballots are in the air. You may be heroes in war, but you must be cravens in peace."

It is true, as has been insistently urged, that it would be expedient for the Negro to forego his suffrage and climb to worth and to the world's respect by other means. By other means! That is the cry of the miners when they ask him out of the mines. It is the word of the whole commercial world when they ask him out of everything—the American shibboleth. Relinquish! Relinquish! And from the dust of the very lowest places, the places that grind men's souls and kill ambition, the Negroes seek to climb to places of worth and respect.

In order to cool the passions and allay the prejudices of the superior race the entire self-effacement of the Negro would be expedient—as expedient as it would be cowardly; and, say what you will of the American people, their respect is not to be won by cowardice. Let those suffering people relinquish one single right that has been given them and the rapacity of the other race, encouraged by yielding, will ravage them from every privilege that they possess. Passion and prejudice are not sated by concession, but grow by what they feed on.

The Vaudois, hiding like wild beasts in their mountain fastnesses, shot like goats upon their own hills, purpling with their blood the streams of their own valleys, France could hate, but dared not despise. The Indian himself, ground to dust under the heel of civilization, driven to death by the greed of a stronger people, will not be remembered with a sneer. But for the Negro honor is dangerous; only cowardice is safe.

The African is told that he is not yet ready to participate in government, because he has not yet learned to govern himself, and the race which preaches this proves its own right to political domination by the rioting, the rapine and the slaughter, with which for weeks past the civilized world has been scandalized. Since when was ever a psychological published with a musket?

After all, the question is not one of the Negro's fitness to rule or to vote, but of the right of the whites to murder him for the sake of instruction. Not a groan that the Romans wrung from the hearts of the conquered

Britons, but echoed and re-echoed in the sound of her own fall. Every drop of blood that France drew from her own suffering Huguenots on St. Bartholomew's Day but called its brother to the hungry sod on that awful 14th day of July. Rome sated her thirst for blood and called it civilization. France indulged her barbaric fancy and named it religion. America strides through the ashes of burning homes, over the bodies of murdered men, women and children, holding aloft the banner of progress.

Progress! Necessity! Expedience!

But why is it necessary to excuse these acts of sophistry? Is not murder murder? Is not rapine rapine? Is not outrage outrage?

The whites are stronger than the blacks. Why not then say to them openly: "We don't like you; we do not want you in certain places. Therefore when we please we will kill you. We are strong people; you are weak. What we choose to do we will do; right or no right. There is no one to wage with us a holy war in the cause of humanity."

Even the church has attempted to explain and palliate and we are told from the pulpit that the Negroes have been taught a salutary lesson: that the whites must prevail. The murderers of Wilmington are congratulated upon the effort they have made toward civilization and purer government. And some of this within a stone's throw of the nation's capitol: When the reckoning shall come, what shall such ministers say? They have not stoned martyrs but they have burned their shoulders with the coats of those who did; and every such is an accomplice dyed with the same blood of the men who stood redhanded over the murdered blacks. And yet, what else could we expect from the pulpit, when we remember that less than forty years ago with the same smug complacency, it was finding excuses for slavery in tracing out the divine intention?

The passions of the people often need a spiritual backing, and shame to say, we have a clergy always ready and willing to furnish it, whether it be when man restrains his fellow men from the exercise of his national rights or murders him for pursuing his political dues. It is a disgrace to the honor of their calling, a reflection upon the intelligences of their heroes, and an insult to the God they profess to serve.

The text for better and for different sermons might be found for those divines in Paul's first epistle to the Corinthians. It is as apt to-day as it was then, and it applies to the American people with no less strength than it did to the older race. "Take heed," said the apostle, "lest by any means this liberty of yours become a stumbling block to them that are weak."

We are comforted with the statement that the sudden enfranchisement of the Negro was a mistake. Perhaps it was, but the whites made it. The mistakes of life are not corrected in that way. Their effects are eternal. You cannot turn back the years and put ten millions of people into the condition that four millions were thirty years ago. You cannot ignore the effects that have ensued, the changes that have followed, and make the problem of today the problem of 1865. It is a different one. The whole aspect of the case has changed. The Negro has changed. Public opinion has shifted. Try as you will, though it has grown away, you cannot put the plant back into the seed. Of course you can root it up entirely; but beware of its juices.

Thirty years ago the American people told the Negro that he was a man with a man's full powers. They deemed it that important they did what they have done few times in the history of the country—they wrote it down in their constitution. And now they come with the shot gun in the South and sophistry in the North to prove to him that it was all wrong.

For so long a time has the black man believed that he is an American citizen that he will not be easily convinced to the contrary. It will take more than the hangings, the burnings and the lynchings, both North and South, to prove it to his satisfaction. He is not so credulous as he was. He is a different man. The American people cannot turn back the tide of years and make him what he was. And so it was an entirely new people with whom they have to deal. It is an entirely new problem which is presented to them for solution. Why then should it not be met with calmness, justice, breadth and manliness which should characterize a great nation?

If the problem is as much the Negro's as the white man's—and I do not say that it is not—he is doing his best to settle it. He is acquiring property. Yes he even builds churches to the religion whose servants preach his damnation. He is going forward. Such catastrophes as the Southern riots, terrible though they be, are but incidents in his growth, which is inevitable. The principle of manhood is springing to life within him. Every year men are being educated to live for it. Every year to some—to many, it seems—God gives the better grace to die for it.

TOLEDO (OHIO) *JOURNAL*, Dec. 18, 1898.

THE NEGROES OF THE TENDERLOIN

To one who sees Seventh Avenue and its environs day after day there is little or nothing in its appearance to excite comment, but go away for six months and then return to it, and one finds in the dark crowds of the Tenderloin district food for reflection.

So many of us are like parrots. Our fathers before us have made a statement or issued a dictum, and we keep on repeating it day after day and year after year, however meaningless the events of time may have made it. So we have been in the habit of saying that the South has a Negro problem, and we have looked on listlessly and wondered how she was going to solve it. Our eyes, turned away from home, did not perceive that much the same problem was creeping to our very doors. But it is so.

One looks at the crowds of idle, shiftless Negroes that throng these districts and the question must arise, what is to be done with them, what is to be done for them, if they are to be prevented from inoculating our civilization with the poison of their lives? They are not Anarchists; they never will be. Socialism has no meaning for them; and yet in these seemingly careless, guffawing crowds lies a terrible menace to our institutions. Everything in their environment tends to the blotting of the moral sense, everything to the engendering of crime. Here and there sits a weak, ineffectual little mission, doing its little best for the people around it, but altogether as inadequate as a gauze fan in the furnace heats of hell.

I look on it all, and, though I feel fear for our civilization, I must confess that the strongest emotion in my heart is pity for the poor people themselves and for their children. They are my brothers, and what touches them touches me. I can look on at the vice and degradation of Whitechapel and the Seven Dials with less emotion than I can upon the misdeeds of the Tenderloin. For the former I sorrow in the name of humanity; for the latter I grieve on account of my race, which already has so much to overcome. Do you say that this is too narrow a view, too selfish? If it is so, it is because I have been forced into it. As a race, we are thrown back upon ourselves, isolated from other Americans, and so brought into a more intimate communion one with the other. Fifth Avenue cannot feel for Cherry Hill as the better class of Negroes must feel for their degraded brethren, because the former are not so closely identified with each other. The sight of a dweller in Fifth Avenue does not suggest a denizen of Cherry Hill; but the sight of one Negro suggests a race.

It is natural to suppose that these poor people will produce offspring. Of what kind will they be? How can they run in the race of life when they are hampered from the start by the degradation of their parents? What course is open to them save one of shame and crime? I pity the children because they are being cheated out of their birthright. I pity the parents because they are blind enough to damn their own progeny. Many of them are from the small towns of the South. They have been deceived by the glare and glitter of the city streets. They are great, naughty, irresponsible children. Their highest ideal is a search for pleasure, and they think they have found it when they indulge in vice. I pity them because they have come to the city to lose so much and to gain so little. They are losing the simple, joyous natures with which God had endowed them, and are becoming hard and mean and brutal. They are losing the soft mellow voices which even slavery could not ruin. They are losing their capacity for simple enjoyment. They are growing cynical. They are losing their gentleness, their hospitality, their fidelity—all, in fact, of the good traits that distinguish them in their natural habitat. And for what? A hand-to-mouth struggle for life in a great city, and a place in the Potter's Field at last.

It is a pity to see the changes in these, my people, who, with their scant education, should be like the quaint ante-bellum type of Negro whose praises are still sung at the South. But they are not. "Chimmie

Fadden" has been grafted on to "Sambo," and the charms of neither remain.

These people have the right to the joy of life. But they are selling their birthright for a mess of pottage—and such pottage! They have given up the fields for the gutters. They have bartered the sweet-smelling earth of their freshly turned furrows for the stenches of metropolitan alleys. They have lost the step of the brawny tiller of the soil. They do not walk like clodhoppers, but they creep like vermin. Is it an improvement? They are ashamed of all the old simple delights, and cannot reach to the perfection of pure new ones. They have ceased, in great part, to play their simple melodies on the banjo, and strum out "rags" on the piano. The sensuousness that gave them warmth and glow has subsided into a hard sensuality that makes them gross. They have forgotten to laugh and have learned to sneer.

They have a right to strength and to health, but they have neither. It is the duty of the Negro especially to live for his children, to so conduct his life as to destroy in his race the defects, mental, moral and physical, placed upon them by slavery. But these people are not doing it. They are perpetuating and increasing all of his deformities, both of mind and body. The next generation of Negroes should be a better-looking one than this; they should have better brains and better souls. But is this possible with what the blacks of the Tenderloin are bequeathing to posterity?

Is it not enough to say that there are intelligent, moral, and industrious Negroes in the city? Of course there are, and about them there would be no problem. But their influence for good and for respectability cannot be fully felt as long as so large a part of the race are operating in a different direction. The man who has worked along quietly buying property, raising a respectable family, educating his sons; who has held one position for twenty years and has the respect and confidence of his employers, does not attract one-tenth part of the attention that is attracted by the "burly Negro who was beating his wife." In the public mind the race receives the odium of the latter act, but not the benefit of the former. The voice of the brute who is lynched for an unspeakable crime sounds further than the voice of the man of God who stands in his pulpit Sunday after Sunday inveighing against wrong. So if the better-class Negro would come to his own he must lift not only himself, but the lower men, whose blood brother he is. He cannot afford to look down upon the denizens of the Tenderloin or to withdraw himself from them, for the fate of the blacks there, degraded, ignorant, vicious as they may, be, is his fate.

It is probably wrong to introduce a problem and then to suggest no specific remedy, but I confess that I can see no practicable one now. The gist of the whole trouble lies in the flocking of ignorant and irresponsible Negroes to the great city. If that could be stopped, if the metropolitan could vomit them back again, the whole matter would adjust itself. But how is it to be done? For the influx continues and increases year after year. They say that they have not rights at the South; but better the restrictions there than a seeming liberty which blossoms noxiously into license.

I would not deny to these, my people, the advantages of travel and study, if they would make a proper use of them; but the majority has not yet done this. It is not their fault. They need several generations to grow into a state of calm receptivity, and it grieves me to see them elbowed to death by a civilization the genius of which they do not yet understand.

I would rather that they stayed away from the cities than that they should come only to lose purity, simplicity, and the joy of life. It would not hurt them to stay close to nature's heart for a while longer. I would fain see them happy and free, felling the forest, and tilling the field, and singing in their cabin doors at night. Until they show greater capabilities for contact with a hard and intricate civilization, I would have them stay upon the farm and learn to live in God's great kindergarten for his simple children!

COLUMBUS (OHIO) *DISPATCH,* Dec. 19, 1898.

THE HAPLESS SOUTHERN NEGRO

It was less than a year ago that I was down in the far South on a business tour and at the same time for the purpose of looking into the condition of the people themselves. I went out one sunshiny spring day, and following a red clay road for something like a mile on its tortuous course came suddenly to what struck my companion, a Southerner, and seemed also to me, a quasi Southerner, a typical Negro cabin. It was a one-roomed shanty made of unhewn logs, with a miserable stick chimney plastered with clay, coughing malarial smoke into the air. Within it lived two families numbering altogether twelve or more people. There was a bed in each corner; under the one a trundle bed and to one side a pallet. For heating and cooking purposes there was a fireplace. And here sat, slept, worked, loved and suffered a dozen beings of both sexes. To me the sight was nothing less than tragic, but the impassiveness of my friend showed me that it was a spectacle to which his residence in the South had inured him. We went in to talk to the people, and found that the husband was out working in the field. We found also that the land was worked on shares, and that year after year the head of the house found himself still in the same old rut, or deeper and deeper in debt. "What can we hope from such a condition," was my first question, "either in the way of industrial or moral advancement?"

I could not help but think of the same scene the other day as I speeded towards Denver across the wide plains of Colorado. There they lay, yellow, brown and green, great stretches, waiting the touch of a hardy hand, begging the kiss of the plough. Before me lay the mountains, with the sun turning the tops into glory, and beneath them these wide lands, which need only industry to make them blossom as the rose, and I said to myself: Colorado stands with open arms offering the store of her wealth and health to all comers. Has she nothing to give to these poor black men in the far South, who find in their little cabins and narrow mortgaged land neither? They have industry; they will work. Two hundred and fifty years of enforced labor has proved that. The whip of the overseer was not more potent a factor to draw forth their best efforts forty years ago than would be the sting of hunger now and the breezy example of their fellows in the West.

Not only could the South find relief from its congestion of unemployed Negroes, but also the larger cities of the North, whose Negro population, leaving the rural districts which they are eminently fitted to inhabit, have overcrowded.

But, says some one, we do not want these people who have already created a question in one part of the country. Let me assure you they will never create a question here. You will never get enough of them away from home for that, though the experiment is worth the trying. They have already set their seal upon the South. There is not a field or a city in that South-land that has not felt the influence of their labor. They have their idle, but they have their industrious. They have their criminal, but they have their virtuous. They have their high and they have their low. To sum it all up, they are strictly human.

Now, if this question of the South, as has been asserted, and as I am prone to believe, is a purely industrial one, will not this widening of the Negro's field, this spreading out of their district, go far towards the settlement of it? I know there will be those who will hasten to say that what the black man has done in the South he will be very apt to do in the West. But there are two things to remember. In the first place, if the black emigrant comes to the West it would be under circumstances far different from those under which the black slave went to the South. He went there under every condition making towards a destruction of his manhood. If he came here he would come with every element helping him towards a higher civilization. The West, the great and generous West, has extended her hands to every nation and said: "Come and be free." She has not refused the pauper from Europe; she has not turned back the criminal from the East. Could she then say no to her poor black brother, who has been in the family for two hundred fifty years and whose blood and whose sweat have gone to give to the South whatever wealth it possesses today? Though the Negro left the South a question he gave it wealth. Should he come to the West he will give her wealth without a question. He will go on your farms and ranches and into your mines. He will work and not weary; he will toil and be cheerful, and the mountains at night shall hear his Southern song transferred to the West. For a while, perhaps, if he comes, there will be an increase of that smelter smoke which my good friends so much abhor. But let that be; it will cease some day, no matter how. One who has seen the idle men standing thick upon the streets with drawn faces and wild eyes pleading for work; one who has seen the traffic suspended because the poor could not gain what they demanded from the rich; one who has seen the long line of hunger-stricken wretches waiting at midnight along the metropolitan street to get the few loaves of bread, stale from the day before, still sees in that smoke a banner of the vanguard of prosperity, which has for its watchword the unity of labor and capital.

DENVER POST, Sept. 17, 1899.

Negro Music

The strange, fantastic melody of the old plantation music has always possessed a deep fascination for me. There is an indescribable charm in it—a certain poetic sadness that appeals strongly to the artistic in one's nature.

The idea that art really had anything to do with this quality of negro music I never for a moment entertained. But, question as I might, I could never find out its source until passing through Midway Plaisance some weeks ago I heard the Dahomeyans singing. Instantly the idea flashed into my mind: "It is a heritage."

Perhaps this thought has already struck many others, but I must confess that it has just dawned upon me, and I am startled at its suddenness and evident plausibility.

I heard in the Dahomeyans' singing the same rich melody, the same mournful minor cadences, that have touched the heart of the world through negro music. It is the unknown something in the voice that so many people have tried to define and failed.

The Dahomeyan sings the music of his native Africa; the American negro spends this silver heritage of melody, but adds to it the bitter ring of grief for wrongs and adversities which only he has known. The Dahomeyan startles us; the negro American thrills us. The Dahomeyan makes us smile; the negro American makes us weep and smile to weep again.

If my hypothesis be correct, the man who asks where the negro got all those strange tunes of his songs is answered. They have been handed down to him from the matted jungles and sunburned deserts of Africa, from the reed huts of the Nile.

When F. J. Loudin of the Fisk Jubilee Singers told me how the people flocked to hear his troupe sing their simple old plantation songs I wondered. When I heard a college glee club or a white male quartet sing those same songs, with strict attention to every minute detail of time, attack the harmony, I no longer wondered. It is only the negro, who can sing these songs with effect. The white professional acts; the negro feels. Here lies the difference. With the black man's heritage of song has come the heritage of sorrow, giving to his song the expression of a sorrowful sweetness which the mere imitator can never attain.

Many of the old plantation hymns, rude and uncouth as they were, improvised by the negroes themselves under the influence of strong religious zeal, are models of melodic beauty. Underlined almost invariably by a strain of sadness, they sometimes burst out into rays of hope, rising above the commonplace and reaching up to the sublime.

Through them all can be traced the effect of the condition of the people. The years of depression and fear, with their intermittent moments of flickering hope, going out again in despair, and then again brightening into a hope that is almost a surety.

Even at the present day go into some of the small churches of the South and listen to their hymns. The voices of the singers assume a tone that one cannot describe. There is still that wavering minor cadence that cannot be imitated. It is that heritage of expression still there, and through it all one can hear the strain running like the theme of a symphony—the strain a supplication to God for deliverance.

It is said, and generally conceded to be true, that the negro is ashamed of his music. If it be so, it is a shame to be rebuked and one which he must overcome, for he has the most beautiful melodies of any in the world. They are his by inheritance and it is for him to make the best use of his rich legacy. Let black composers—and there are such—weave those melodies into their compositions, and to him who laughs and says that they are only fit to be played upon the banjo let them say that the banjo makes quite as sweet music as the bagpipe.

Foreign critics have said that these plantation songs were the only original music that America has produced. This is a mis-statement, for

America has not produced even these; she has only taken what Africa has given her.

If the American negro consults his best interest, he will seize upon these songs, preserve them and make them distinctively his own. It has been recently demonstrated that what he refuses to accept as a gift others will steal. Let him out with false pride and come into the heritage which is his own.

CHICAGO RECORD, 1899.

Negro Life in Washington

Washington is the city where the big ⸻ ⸻n of little towns come to be disillusioned. Whether black or white, the little great soon seek their level here. It matters not whether it is Ezekiel Corncray of Podunk Center, Vermont, or Isaac Johnson of the Alabama black belt—in Washington he is apt to come to a realization of his true worth to the world.

In a city of such diverse characteristics it is natural that the life of any portion of its people should be interesting. But when it is considered that here the experiment of sudden freedom has been tried most earnestly, and, I may say, most successfully, upon a large percentage of the population, it is to the lives of these people that one instinctively turns for color, picturesqueness, and striking contrast.

It is the delicately blended or boldly differentiated light and shade effects of Washington negro life that are the despair of him who tries truthfully to picture it.

It is the middle-class negro who has imbibed enough of white civilization to make him work to be prosperous. But he has not partaken of civilization so deeply that he has become drunk and has forgotten his own identity. The church to him is still the centre of his social life, and his preacher a great man. He has not—and I am not wholly sorry that he has not—learned the repression of his emotions, which is the mark of a high and dry civilization. He is impulsive, intense, fervid, and—

himself. He has retained some of his primitive ingenuousness. When he goes to a party he goes to enjoy himself and not to pose. If there be onlookers outside his own circle, and he be tempted to pose, he does it with such childlike innocence and good humor that no one is for a moment anything but amused, and he is forgiven his little deception.

Possibly in even the lower walks of life a warmer racial color is discoverable. For instance, no other race can quite show the counterpart of the old gentleman who passes me on Sunday on his way to church. An ancient silk hat adorns a head which I know instinctively is bald and black and shiny on top; but the edges are fringed with a growth of crisp white hair, like a frame around the mild old face. The broadcloth coat which is buttoned tightly around the spare form is threadbare, and has faded from black to gray green; but although bent a little with the weight of his years, his glance is alert, and he moves briskly along, like a character suddenly dropped out of one of Page's stories. He waves his hand in salute, and I have a vision of Virginia of fifty years ago.

A real bit of the old South, though, as one sees it in Washington, is the old black mammy who trundles to and fro a little baby-carriage with its load of laundry-work, but who tells you, with manifest pride, "Yes, suh. I has nussed off 'n on, mo'n a dozen chillun of de X fambly, an' some of de men dat's ginuls now er in Cong'ess was jes nachully raised up off 'n me." But she, like so many others, came to Washington when it was indeed the Mecca for colored people, where lay all their hopes of protection, of freedom, and of advancement. Perhaps in the old days when labor brought better rewards, she saved something and laid it by in the ill-fated Freedman's Savings Bank. But the story of that is known; so the old woman walks the streets to-day, penniless, trundling her baby-carriage, a historic but pathetic figure.

Some such relic of the past, but more prosperous withal, is the old lady who leans over the counter of a tiny and dingy restaurant on Capitol Hill and dispenses coffee and rolls and fried pork to her colored customers. She wears upon her head the inevitable turban or handkerchief in which artists delight to paint the old mammies of the South. She keeps unwavering the deep religious instinct of her race and is mighty in her activities on behalf of one or the other of the colored churches. Under her little counter she always has a contribution-book, and not a customer, white or black, high or low, who is not levied upon to "he'p de chu'ch outen hits stress." But one who has sat and listened to her, as leaning chin on hand, she recounted one of her weird superstitious stories of the night-doctors and their doings, or the "awful jedgement on a sinnah man," is not unwilling to be put at some expense for his pleasure.

The old lady and her stories are of a different cast from that part of the Washington life which is the pride of her proudest people. It is a far cry from the smoky little restaurant on the Hill, with its genial and loquacious old owner, to the great business block on Fourteenth Street and its wealthy, shrewd, and cultivated proprietor.

Colored men have made money here, and some of them have known how to keep it. There are several of them on the Board of trade—five, I think—and they are regarded by their fellows as solid, responsible, and capable businessmen. The present assessment law was drafted by a colored member of the board, and approved by them before it was submitted to Congress.

As for the professions, there are so many engaged in them that it would keep one busy counting or attempting to count the dark-skinned lawyers and doctors one meets in a day.

The cause of this is not far to seek. Young men come here to work in the departments. Their evenings are to a certain extent free. It is the most natural thing in the world that they should improve their time by useful study. But why such a preponderance in favor of the professions, you say. Are there not other useful pursuits—arts and handicrafts? To be sure there are. But then your new people dearly love a title, and Lawyer Jones sounds well, Dr. Brown has an infinitely more dignified ring, and as for Professor—well, that is the acme of titular excellence, and there are more dark professors in Washington than one could find in a day's walk through a European college town.

However, it is well that these department clerks should carry something away with them when they leave Washington, for their condition is seldom financially improved by their sojourn here. This, though, is perhaps apart from the aim of the present article, for it is no more true of the negro clerks than of their white confreres. Both generally live up to the limit of their salaries.

The clerk has much leisure, and is in consequence a society man. He must dress well and smoke as good a cigar as an Eastern congressman. It all costs money, and it is not unnatural that at the end of the year he is a little long on unreceipted bills and short on gold. The tendency of the school teachers, now, seems to be entirely different. There are a great many of them here, and on the average they receive less than the government employees. But perhaps the discipline which they are compelled to impart to their pupils has its salutary effect upon their own minds and impulses. However that may be, it is true that the banks and building associations receive each month a part of the salaries of a large proportion of these instructors. The colored people themselves have a flourishing building association and a well-conducted bank, which do part—I am sorry I cannot say the major part—of their race's business.

The influence which the success of a few men will have upon a whole community is indicated in the spirit of venture which actuates the rising generation of this city. A few years ago, if a man secured a political position, he was never willing or fit to do anything else afterward. But now the younger men, with the example of some of their successful elders before them, are beginning to see that an easy berth in one of the departments is not the best thing in life, and they are getting brave enough to do other things. Some of these ventures have proven failures, even disasters, but it has not daunted the few, nor crushed the spirit of effort in them.

It has been said, and not without some foundation in fact, that a colored man who came to Washington never left the place. Indeed, the city has great powers of attracting and holding its colored population for, belong to whatever class or condition they may, they are always sure to find enough of that same class or condition to make their residence pleasant and congenial. But this very spirit of enterprise of which I have spoken is destroying the force of this dictum, and men of color are even going so far as to resign government positions to go away and strike out for themselves. I have in mind now two young men who are Washingtonians of the Washingtonians, and who have been in office here for years. But the fever has taken them, and they have voluntarily given up their places to go and try their fortunes in the newer and less crowded West.

Such things as these are small in themselves, but they point to a condition of affairs in which the men who have received the training and polish which only Washington can give to a colored man can go forth among their fellows and act as leaveners to the crudity of their race far and wide.

That the pleasure and importance of negro life in Washington are overrated by the colored people themselves is as true as that it is underrated and misunderstood by the whites. To the former the social aspect of this life is a very dignified and serious drama. To the latter it is nothing but a most amusing and inconsequential farce. But both are wrong; it is neither the one thing nor the other. It is a comedy of the period played out by earnest actors, who have learned their parts well, but who on that very account are disposed to mouth and strut a little and watch the gallery.

Upon both races the truth and significance of the commercial life among the negroes have taken a firmer hold, because the sight of their banks, their offices, and places of business are evidences which cannot be overlooked or ignored.

As for the intellectual life, a university set on a hill cannot be hid, and the fact that about this university and about this excellent high-school clusters a community in which people, unlike many of the educational fakirs which abound, have taken their degrees from Cambridge, Oxford, Edinburgh, Harvard, Yale, Cornell, Wellesley, and a score of minor colleges, demands the recognition of a higher standard of culture among people of color than obtains in another city.

But, taking it all in all and after all, negro life in Washington is a promise rather than a fulfillment. But it is worthy of note for the really excellent things which are promised.

Is Higher Education
for the Negro Hopeless?

It is a matter of some surprise to me that the articles by Charles Dudley Warner on the education of the Negro should have attracted so much attention, for it is so evidently the work of one who speaks without authority. It might appropriately be called an essay, founded upon observation of the South from a car window.

It is a somewhat new view of the case to note the Negro considered as one of the less "sensitive" races. Heretofore we have been told, and believed, not without reason, that his character was decidedly the opposite—malleable, yielding, sensitive to impression, good or bad. The argument has been made so frequently that it has almost become axiomatic that this was the cause of so many of his faults—even of the imitativeness that made him ape the vices and the foibles of the white race.

Passing this, however, as a minor matter, another statement made by the writer that the higher education applied to the Negro in his present development has operated against his value as a worker and producer, is not borne out by the facts. Every graduate from a Negro college, it is true, does not become a Moses in the community where he is settled, but on the other hand, in every section where a Negro college is located, and where there are Negro graduates, it is proven beyond dispute, whatever detractors may say to the contrary, that the moral, social and industrial tone of the people has been raised. They have gone into districts where the people did not even know how to live, and by their own example taught the benighted the art of life, which they have learned in the schools for higher education. They have made their own homes attractive, and if by no other power than that of envy, which is prevalent in my own race, they have drawn the people about them somewhat up to their own level.

I believe I know my own people pretty thoroughly. I know them in all classes, the high and the low, and I have yet to see any young man or young woman who had the spirit of work in them before, driven from labor by a college education.

Mr. Warner makes his greatest mistake in citing New Orleans as an example. In the first place, in all but one of the schools there for higher education for the Negro, the moral training of the black race is in the hands of the whites as he recommends. And in all of them the industrial idea is insisted upon strongly and constantly. If he believes that the condition of these Negroes is lower than it was before, I am at a loss to know how he can reconcile the growth of industry, the widening out of their charitable organizations, and the larger and purer social life which is being instituted among the colored people there.

Within the last four years there have been opened two new drug stores, patronized by both races; a hospital and training school for nurses has been started by the unaided efforts of the Negro people; a free kindergarten has been set going for the black children of the city who are shut out from such advantages as the white are blessed with.

I have had the good fortune to know also some of the Negro officials whom the federal government "has imposed upon the intelligent and sensitive people of New Orleans." I have found them men of high intelligence, clean morality, and undisputed ability, and men, who, but for their race, would strive for and take place among the leaders anywhere. I say this out of no partisan or racial feeling, but because I know and think that Mr. Warner does not know or has not met these men.

If, in the Northern cities, as he says, the Negro has been crowded out of the many occupations by the more vigorous races, was it because of their vigor, or because of the prejudice which preferred the alien to the citizen? Was it the vigor of the foreign miners in Illinois that drove the Negroes from their work, or the prejudice of a narrow people which allowed it?

One more point that Mr. Warner cites is easily set aside. He brings statistics to prove the increase of Negro criminality. If he knew much about this matter I would fancy him smiling behind his hand, but I give him the benefit of believing that he is ignorant of the subject. Statistics may prove anything, but in this case especially they are inadequate. No one has the right to base any conclusions about Negro criminality upon the number of prisoners in the jails and other places of restraint. Even in the North the prejudice against the Negro reverses the precedents of law, and every one accused is looked upon as guilty until he is proven innocent. In the South it is worse. Taking into account that some of the offenses for which a white boy would be reprimanded and released would send a Negro to the chain gang or the jail, it is easy to see how the percentage of criminals is raised. A fight upon the street, picking up coal, with the accusation of throwing it off the cars, brawling generally, what with white boys would be called children's fights land the black boy in jail, and so the percentage of criminals increase, and the Northern friend of the Negro holds up his hands in dismay at the awful things he sees before him.

Criminals, yes, but how many of the Southern cities have reformatories for youthful offenders and for the punishment of youthful offenses. I know one case in a city not so far south of Mason and Dixon's line, where a boy ten years old was accused of throwing coal off the cars, arrested, convicted, and instead of being sent to a reformatory was placed in jail with the lowest type of felons and with insane people. It happened that he was placed in the cell with a madman. During the night screams were heard from the cell, but for a time were unnoticed. After awhile the keeper took his way leisurely through, and found the child horribly mutilated by the maniac. Ruined for life physically and brutalized mentally. I need not go to any one of my own race and ask for corroboration of this fact. This is what our writer terms, "A more favorable position for development than the Negro has ever before had offered him."

Mr. Warner's ill-advised article has done the Negro, who has looked to him as a friend, unutterable harm, more harm really than he knows. It is a pitiful thing, altogether. He has observed badly or been misinformed, and until he is able to strike more closely at the heart of things it were better for him to return to his easy chair.

PHILADELPHIA TIMES, June 10, 1900.

NEGRO SOCIETY IN WASHINGTON

In spite of all the profound problems which the serious people of the world are propounding to us for solution, we must eventually come around to the idea that a good portion of humanity's time is taken up with enjoying itself. The wiser part of the world has calmly accepted the adage that "All work and no play makes Jack a dull boy," and has decided not to be dull. It seems to be the commonly accepted belief, though, that the colored people of the country have not fallen into this view of matters since emancipation, but have gone around being busy and looking serious. It may be heresy to say it, but it is not the truth.

The people who had the capacity for great and genuine enjoyment before emancipation have not suddenly grown into grave and reverend philosophers. There are some of us who believe that there are times in the life of a race when a dance is better than a convention, and a hearty laugh more effective than a Philippic. Indeed, as a race, we have never been a people to let the pleasures of the moment pass. Any one who believes that all of our time is taken up with dealing with knotty problems, or forever bearing around heavy mission, is doomed to disappointment. Even to many of those who think and feel most deeply the needs of their people is given the gift of joy without folly and gayety without frivolity.

Nowhere is this more clearly exemplified than in the social doings of the Negro in Washington, the city where this aspect of the colored man's life has reached its highest development. Here exists a society which is sufficient unto itself—a society which is satisfied with its own condition, and which is not asking for social intercourse with whites. Here are homes finely, beautifully, and tastefully furnished. Here comes together the flower of colored citizenship from all parts of the country. The breeziness of the West here meets the refinement of the East, the warmth and grace of the South, the culture and fine reserve of the North. Quite like all other people, the men who have made money come to the capital to spend it in those social diversions which are not open to them in smaller and more provincial towns. With her sister city, Baltimore, just next door, the Negro in Washington forms and carries on a social life which no longer can be laughed at or caricatured under the name "Colored Sassiety." The term is still funny, but now it has lost its pertinence.

SOCIETY SUFFICIENT TO ITSELF

The opportunities for enjoyment are very numerous. Here we are at the very gate of the South, in fact we have begun to feel that we are about in the centre of everything, and that nobody can go to any place or come from any place without passing among us. When the soldiers came home from the Philippines last summer, naturally they came here, and great were the times that Washington saw during their stay. At a dinner given in honor of the officers, two Harvard graduates met, and, after embracing each other, stood by the table and gave to their astonished hearers the Harvard yell at the top of their voices. One was a captain of volunteers, and the other, well, he is a very dignified personage, and now holds a high office.

And just here it might not be amiss to say that in the social life in Washington nearly every prominent college in the country is represented by its graduates. Harvard, Yale, Princeton, Cornell, Amherst, Pennsylvania, with women from Smith, Wellesley, Cornell, Oberlin, and a number of others of less prominence.

The very fact of our being so in the way of traffic has brought about some very amusing complications. For instance, and this is a family secret, do any of you uninitiated know that there were three inaugural balls? The whites could only afford one, but we, happy-go-lucky, pleasure-loving people, had to have two, and on the same night. There were people coming here from everywhere, and their friends in the city naturally wanted to show them certain courtesies, which was right and proper. But there are cliques, and more cliques, as everywhere else, and these cliques differed strenuously. Finally, they separated into factions: one secured the armory, and, the other securing another large hall, each gave its party. And just because each tried to outdo the other, both were tremendous successes, though the visitors, who, like the dying man, had friends in both places, had to even up matters by going first to one and then the other, so that during the whole of that snowy March night there was a good-natured shifting of guests from one ballroom to the other. Sometimes the young man who happened to be on the reception committee at one place and the floor committee at the other got somewhat puzzled as to the boutonniere which was his insignia of office, and too often hapless ones found themselves standing in this midst of one association with the flower of the other like a badge upon his lapel.

Each faction had tried the other's mettle, and the whole incident closed amicably.

The War of the Social Cliques

One of the beauties and one of the defects of Washington life among us is this very business of forming into cliques. It is beautiful in that one may draw about him just the circle of friends that he wants, who appeal to him, and from whom he can get what he wants; but on the other hand, when some large and more general affair is to be given which comprises Washington not as a home city, but rather as the capital of the nation, it is difficult to get these little coteries to disintegrate. The only man who is perfectly safe is the one who cries, "The world is my clique!" and plunges boldly into them all.

Of course, there are some sets which could never come together here. And we are, in this, perhaps imitators; or is it the natural evolution of human impulse that there should be placed over against each other a smart set?—yes, a smart set, don't smile—and a severe high and mighty intellectual set, one which takes itself with eminent seriousness and looks down on all the people who are not studying something, or graduating, or reading papers, or delivering lectures, as frivolous. But somehow, in spite of this attitude toward them, the smart young and even the smart old people go on having dances, teas, and card parties and talking small talk, quite oblivious of the fact that they are under the ban.

Washington has been card crazy this year, and for the first time on record the games did not end with the first coming of summer, but continued night after night as long as there was anybody in town to play them. For be it known that we also put up our shutters and go to the mountains or seashore, where we lie on the sands or in the open air and get tanned, if our complexions are amenable to the process, and some of them are.

There are to my knowledge six very delightful card clubs, and I know one couple who for twenty-five years have had their friends in for cards on every Thursday night in the autumn and winter. If the charitable impulse overtakes us there is a run on the department stores of the city for bright new decks of cards and bisque ornaments, the latter to be used as prizes in the contests to which the outside world is invited to come and look on.

Even after the shutters are put up, when our Negro lawyers lay aside their documents, and our doctors put their summer practice on some later sojourner in town, the fever for the game follows the people to their summer resorts, and the old Chesapeake sees many a game of whist or euchre under the trees in the daytime or out on the lantern-lighted porches at night.

But let no one think that this diversion has been able to shake from its popularity the dances. And how we dance and dance, summer and winter, upon all occasions, whenever and wherever we can. Even when, as this year, we have not been compelled by the inauguration of a President to give something "socially official," there is enough of this form of amusement to keep going the most earnest devotee. There are two leading dancing clubs formed of men and one which occasionally gives a dance, but mostly holds itself to itself, formed of women. The two first vie with each other winter after winter in the brilliancy of their affairs, one giving its own especial welcome dance with four assemblies; the other confining itself to one or two balls each year.

Not the Comic Balls We Know

Do not think that these are the affairs which the comic papers and cartoonists have made you familiar with; the waiters' and coachmen's balls of which you know. They are good enough in their way, just as are your butchers' picnics and your Red Men's dances, but *these* are not of the same ilk. It is no "You pays your money and you takes your choice" business. The invitations are not sent to those outside of one particular circle. One from beyond the city limits would be no more able to secure admission or recognition without a perfect knowledge of his social standing in his own community than would Mrs. Bradley-Martin's butler to come to an Astor ball. These two extremes are not so far apart, but the lines are as strictly drawn. The people who come there to dance together are people of similar education, training, and habits of thought. But, says some one, the colored people have not yet either the time or the money for these diversions, and yet without a minute's thought there come to my mind four men who are always foremost in these matters, whose fortunes easily aggregate a million dollars. All of them are educated men with college-bred children. Have these men not earned the right to their enjoyments and the leisure for them? There are others too numerous to mention who are making five or six thousand a year out of their professions or investments. Surely these may have a little time to dance?

There is a long distance between the waiter at a summer hotel and the man who goes down to a summer resort to rest after a hard year as superintendent of an institution which pays him several thousand a year. In this connection it afforded me a great deal of amusement some time ago to read from the pen of a good friend of mine his solemn comment upon the Negro's lack of dramatic ability. Why? Because he had seen the waiters and other servants at his summer hotel produce a play. Is it out of place for me to smile at the idea of any Harriet of any race doing The Second Mrs. Tanqueray?

View us at any time, but make sure that you view the right sort, and I believe you will not find any particular racial stamp upon our pleasure-making. Last year one of the musical societies gave an opera here, not perhaps with distinction, but brightly, pleasantly, and as well as any amateur organization could expect to give it. Each year they also give an oratorio which is well done. And, believe me, it is an erroneous idea that all our musical organizations are bound up either in a scientific or any other sort of study of rag-time. Of course, rag-time is pleasant, and often there are moments when there are gathered together perhaps ten or twelve of us, and one who can hammer a catchy tune, rag-time or not, on the piano is a blessed aid to his companions who want to two-step. But there, this is dancing again, and we dare not dance always.

Indeed, sometimes we grow strongly to feel our importance and to feel the weight of our own knowledge of art and art matters. We are going to be very much in this way this winter, and we shall possibly have some studio teas as well as some very delightful at-homes which will recall the reign, a few years ago, of a bright woman who had a wealth of social tact and grace, and at whose Fridays one met every one worth meeting resident here and from the outside. The brightest talkers met there and the best singers. You had tea and biscuit, talk and music. Mostly your tea got cold and you forgot to munch your biscuit because better things were calling you. This woman is dead now. Her memory is not sad, but very sweet, and it will take several women to fill her place.

A SEASON OF LITERATURE, MUSIC, AND ART

There are going to be some pleasant times, though different in scope, in the studio of a clever little woman artist here. She is essentially a miniature painter, but has done some other charming and beautiful things; but above all that, and what the young people are possibly going to enjoy especially, she is a society woman with all that means, and will let them come, drink tea in her studio, flirt behind her canvases, and talk art as they know it, more or less. Her apartments are beautiful and inspiring. The gatherings here, though, will be decidedly for the few. These will be supplemented, however, later in the year by one of the musical clubs which is intending to entertain S. Coleridge Taylor, who is coming over from London to conduct his cantata, "Hiawatha." Mr. Taylor is a favorite here, and his works have been studied for some time by this musical club. It is expected that he will be shown a great many social courtesies.

An article on Negro social life in Washington, perhaps ought almost to be too light to speak of the numerous literary organizations here, the reading clubs which hold forth; but, really, the getting together of congenial people, which is, after all, the fundamental idea of social life, has been so apparent in these that they must at least have this passing notice.

In the light of all this, it is hardly to be wondered at that some of us wince a wee bit when we are all thrown into the lump as the peasant or serving class. In aims and hopes for our race, it is true, we are all at one, but it must be understood, when we come to consider the social life, that the girls who cook in your kitchens and the men who serve in your dining-rooms do not dance in our parlors.

To illustrate how many there are of the best class of colored people who can be brought thus together, a story is told of a newcomer who was invited to a big reception. A Washingtonian, one who was initiated into the mysteries of the life here, stood beside him and in an aside called off the names of the guests as they entered. "This is Doctor So-and-So," as some one entered the room, "Surgeon-in-Chief of Blank Hospital." The stranger looked on in silence. "The man coming in now is Judge Some-body Else, of the District." This time the stranger raised his eyebrows. "Those two men entering are consuls to Such-and-Such a place." The newcomer sniffed a little bit. "And ah!" his friend started forward, "that is the United States Minister to Any-Place-You-Please." The man who was being initiated into the titles of his fellow-guests said nothing until another visitor entered the doorway; then he turned to his friend, and in a tone of disbelief and disgust remarked, "Well, now, who under the heavens is that? The Prime Minister of England or the King himself?"

Last summer was the gayest that Washington has seen in many a year. It is true that there are hotels and boarding-houses at many summer resorts and that some of our people gather there to enjoy themselves, but for the first time there was a general flocking to one place taken up entirely and almost owned by ourselves. The place, a stretch of beach nearly two miles long with good bathing facilities, and with a forest behind it, has been made and built up entirely by Negro capital. Two men, at least, have made fortunes out of the sale and improvement of their property, and they, along with many others, are the owners of their own summer homes and cottages at Arundel-on-the-Bay and Highland Beach, Maryland. Here the very best of three cities gathered this last summer. Annapolis and Baltimore sent their quota and our capital city did the rest. It was such a gathering of this race as few outside of our own great family circle have ever seen.

There is, perhaps, an exaltation about any body of men and women who gather to enjoy the fruits of their own labor upon the very ground which their labors have secured to them. There was, at any rate, a special exaltation about these people, and whatever was done went off with éclat. There was a dance at least once a week at one or another of the cottages, and the beauty of it was that anyone who was spending the summer there needed to look for no invitations. He was sure of one by the very fact of being there at all, a member of so close a corporation. The athletes did their turns for the delectation of their admirers, and there were some long-distance swimming contests that would have done credit to the boys in the best of our colleges. There were others who took their bathing more complacently, and still others who followed the injunction of the old rhyme, "Hang your clothes on a hickory limb, but don't go near the water." Cards, music, and sailing parties helped to pass the time, which went all too swiftly, and the Isaak Waltons of the place were always up at five o'clock in the morning and away to some point where they strove for bluefish and rocks, and came home with spots. The talk was bright and the intercourse easy and pleasant. There was no straining, no pomposity, no posing for the gallery. When September came we began to hear the piping of the quail in the woods away from the beach, and our trigger-fingers tingled with anticipation. But the time was not yet ripe. And so the seal is to be set this winter upon our Maryland home by a house party, where men will go to eat, smoke, and shoot, and the women to read, dance, and—well—women gossip everywhere.

This is but a passing glimpse of that intimate life among our own people which we dignify by the name of society.

The Saturday Evening Post 174, Dec. 14, 1901.

THE NEGRO AS AN INDIVIDUAL

In a fine address upon the character of the Negro soldier which he delivered a few nights ago at the Institutional church, Brig. Gen. A. S. Burt, for more than ten years colonel of the 25th Infantry, took occasion to pay a glowing tribute to one of his faithful and well loved soldiers. He spoke feelingly of the man's courage, his loyalty, his cheerful endurance of hardship, and of his general soldierly qualities. He singled out no other soldier for such glowing special commendation. But in the after eulogy upon the whole regiment it seemed that the great body of men were seen through the halo that surrounded the head of one supremely noble fellow. Not that there were not other men equally brave, equally deserving, but the shining virtues of one individual shed unusual luster upon the deeds of his less striking comrades.

There is in this, it seems to me, a positive lesson for a race that has in the years of its freedom been attempting to lift its masses to the level of a people with a couple of thousand years the start of them. That all men are born free and equal may be true, and I, for one, have no wish to deny it. But the fellow who just allows himself to be born and stops at that can hardly expect to keep up with the game of life. The boy who was born in a log cabin next door to Booker T. Washington and is still there has no more right to be considered his equal than has a worthless vagabond to share the wealth of the hard working producer. Indeed, his only claim to consideration at all is that Booker T. Washington was born and has achieved.

For the betterment of this race of ours it is especially necessary that this exaltation of the individual be accomplished. There must be the bringing out of the few bright lights among us, and they are few, to cast some gleam into the darkness that surrounds the masses. When one seeks to consider the possibilities of the Negro he does not point to the crowds at the foot of the hill struggling up through labor and travail, but to those who walk with calmer steps near to the heights.

One black man in a community who has succeeded in gaining the confidence and respect of his neighbors is of more importance to his fellows in that particular community than a band of missionaries. John Jones may be the only decent black man among five hundred of his people, but the fact that John Jones is decent, that he is truthful, and hard working and upright, takes away everything from the shortcomings of every Negro around him. John Jones is black, and every other black man in his vicinity is invested with a moiety of his virtue. It used to be the other way round, and John would have been smeared with the mud in which the others wallowed, but the tendency to make the best of the individual is a step toward a period of right judgment.

It is not missionary work so much as individual effort that must tell for us as a race. In the backward movement of public sentiment toward the Negro which has been apparent in the last few years, what would we have done without the services of such men as Council, Wright, Du Bois, and Washington? However we may discuss their achievements, we cannot deny that it was the consideration of what they had accomplished that arrested, if it did not wholly check, the retrograde movement. They were not the old political war horses, as we used to love to call them, who, in parts of the North as well as all over the South, had been upborne by the ignorance of the mob to a factitious prominence. They were not men who were the creatures of a blind condition, but workers who had set a goal, striven for and reached it by strenuous personal effort. These were the shining examples, and the world was their community. They gained and held its respect, and in doing this gave to each of us a part of their reward.

What I mean by the value of individual success may be illustrated in a measure by the story of a man now resident in Chicago who has grown from a well kept, decent boyhood to a strong, far seeing, well to do manhood. As a boy, and his mother, a woman past eighty, tells the story, he was the only Negro with whom the white boys played. When asked the reason why one of the little Caucasians replied: "Well, you see, Rufus—it's different with Rufus—he's colored, but he ain't a nigger!" There was a world of significance in the explanation, but the moral point of it is that as Rufus had shown them the difference under a black skin they became able to recognize it when they should again meet it under similar disguising circumstances.

Few, I take it, will agree with me that the chief value of the Negro schools of the South is not in the hundreds upon hundreds of colored boys and girls which they turn out each year with more or less knowledge of the classics or the handicrafts, but the few bright particular stars which may be held up as beacons for the whole race. I count the making of ten carpenters, who merely earn their daily bread, rear their children, and die, less than the production of one especially bright man who goes into a sodden community and by the power of his example, the uprightness of his own life, leavens the whole mass. We have been dealing with questions too large for solution, with numbers too vast for manipulation. It may seem at first a hard doctrine, but it works. Aim at the individual. Somewhere the masses will be hit.

Chicago Tribune, Oct. 12, 1902.

THE FOURTH OF JULY
AND RACE OUTRAGES

Belleville, Wilmington, Evansville, the Fourth of July, and Kishineff, a curious combination and yet one replete with a ghastly humor. Sitting with closed lips over our own bloody deeds we accomplish the fine irony of a protest to Russia. Contemplating with placid eyes the destruction of all the Declaration of Independence and the Constitution stood for, we celebrate the thing which our own action proclaims we do not believe in.

But it is over and done. The Fourth is come and gone. The din has ceased and the smoke has cleared away. Nothing remains but the litter of all and a few reflections. The sky-rocket has ascended, the firecrackers have burst, the roman candles have sputtered, the "nigger chasers"— a pertinent American name—have run their courses, and we have celebrated the nation's birthday. Yes, and we black folks have celebrated.

Dearborn Street and Armour Avenue have been all life and light. Not even the Jews and the Chinaman have been able to outdo us in the display of loyalty. And we have done it all because we have not stopped to think just how little it means to us.

The papers are full of the reports of peonage in Alabama. A new and more dastardly slavery there has arisen to replace the old. For the sake of reenslaving the Negro, the Constitution has been trampled under feet, the rights of man have been laughed out of court, and the justice of God has been made a jest and we celebrate.

Every wire, no longer in the South alone, brings us news of a new hanging or a new burning, some recent outrage against a helpless people, some fresh degradation of an already degraded race. One man sins and a whole nation suffers, and we celebrate.

Like a dark cloud, pregnant with terror and destruction, disenfranchisement has spread its wings over our brethren of the South. Like the same dark cloud, industrial prejudice glooms above us in the North. We may not work save when the new-come foreigner refuses to, and then they, high prized above our sacrificial lives, may shoot us down with impunity. And yet we celebrate.

With citizenship discredited and scored, with violated homes and long unheeded prayers, with bleeding hands uplifted, still sore and smarting from long beating at the door of opportunity, we raise our voices and sing, "My Country, 'Tis of Thee"; we shout and sing while from the four points of the compass comes our brothers' unavailing cry, and so we celebrate.

With a preacher, one who a few centuries ago would have sold indulgences to the murderers on St. Bartholomew's Day, with such a preacher in a Chicago pulpit, jingling his thirty pieces of silver, distorting the number and nature of our crimes, excusing anarchy, apologizing for murder, and tearing to tatters the teachings of Jesus Christ while he cries, "Release unto us Barabbas," we celebrate.

But there are some who sit silent within their closed rooms and hear as from afar the din of joy come muffled to their ears as on some later day their children and their children's sons shall hear a nation's cry for succor in her need. Aye, there be some who on this festal day kneel in their private closets and with hands upraised and bleeding hearts cry out to God, if there still lives a God, "How long, O God, How long?"

THE NEW YORK TIMES, July 10, 1903.

PART FOUR

NOVEL:
THE SPORT OF
THE GODS

INTRODUCTION

In February 1897, Paul Laurence Dunbar arrived in England aboard the steamship *Umbria.* It was the culmination of an amazing year.

The previous February, he had been traveling through Ohio by day coach, reciting poems for pittances and peddling copies of his second book, *Majors and Minors,* trying to support himself and his ailing mother and to repay the Toledo investors who had underwritten the printing.

Meanwhile, one of those investors, Dr. Henry Tobey, sent a copy of Dunbar's book to Robert Green Ingersoll, the nation's most popular orator. There was reason to think Ingersoll would be sympathetic—in one of his most famous speeches he had declared, "To-day the black man looks upon his child and says: 'The avenues of distinction are open to you—upon your brow may fall the civic wreath. This day belongs to you.'" But Ingersoll responded more to the content of *Majors and Minors* than to the color of Dunbar's skin: "'The Mystery' is a poem worthy of the greatest [respect]," he wrote. "Dunbar is a genius . . . what can be done for him?" It was not an idle question; Ingersoll was a political wheeler-dealer. But he was a Republican wheeler-dealer, and the Democrats held the White House; there was little he could do.

Tobey also urged Dunbar to deliver a copy of *Majors and Minors* to actor/playwright James A. Herne, who was presenting his play *Shore Acres* in Toledo that spring. Again there was reason to expect a sympathetic response. Herne was an exponent of a new movement called Realism. At the time, American theater was dominated by the Aristotelian belief that "serious" drama, certainly tragedy, involved mythic events, high-born characters, and elevated language; the everyday actions and plain talk of common folk were the stuff of comedy and melodrama. Realist drama sought to reveal the pathos in the ordinary doings and sayings of "real" people. *Shore Acres,* for example, used "Down East" dialect and a Thanksgiving dinner to tell the story of two New England farmers, Nathaniel and Martin Berry, who only in old age achieve a true understanding of each other. Herne did like *Majors and Minors.* But more important, he passed the copy on to another exponent of Realism, novelist and critic William Dean Howells.

Yet again there was reason to expect a positive response. Howells was an Ohio native, and as he described himself "a poet, with no wish to be anything else," though his verses, written in the Romantic mode ("Tossing his mane of snows in wildest eddies and tangles,/Lion-like March cometh in, hoarse, with tempestuous breath"), were so awful he usually had to print them himself. He also wrote a campaign biography of Lincoln, which earned him the patronage plum of a consular post in Venice.

In Italy, Howells was introduced to "réalisme." The movement had originated with a group of French painters who converted the principles of "la Révolution" into art by portraying laborers engaged in work in all their sweaty actuality. Some found this a shocking rejection of Classic archetypes and Romantic embellishment—of the entire concept of Art. But Howells, a self-educated product of trans-Appalachian America, saw it as liberation. He abandoned Romanticism for Realism, and poetry for prose.

After returning to America, Howells became editor of *The Atlantic Monthly,* the most influential literary magazine of the day, and used his power to promote Realism and Realist writers like Bret Harte, Sarah Orne Jewett, and Mark Twain. He left *The Atlantic* in 1881 to write his own novels but continued to push the Realist agenda. He provided American Realism with its most succinct definition—"Nothing more and nothing less than the truthful treatment of material"—and issued its clarion call:

Let fiction cease to lie about life; let it portray men and women as they are, actuated by the motives and the passions in the measure we all know; let it leave off painting dolls and working them by springs and wires . . . let it not put on fine literary airs; let it speak the dialect, the language, that most Americans know—the language of unaffected people everywhere. . . .

In 1893 he had announced the discovery of a "remarkable writer" named Stephen Crane, whose self-published novel, *Maggie, Girl of the Streets,* confronted readers with the grit and vernacular of New York's East Side slums. So there was reason to think that he would appreciate a fellow Ohioan's privately printed book of poems, some in dialect.

In 1896 Howells was writing a column for *Harper's Weekly.* In the June 27 issue he praised *Majors and Minors.* Although a tad sloppy and slightly qualified—it was Howells who first misapplied the term "Minors" to the dialect poems, for which he expressed an overwhelming preference—the column included a quote that would thrill a publicist: "[Dunbar] is a real poet." The effect on sales was immediate. Dunbar, away from home when the column appeared, returned to find his mailbox overflowing with orders.

Howells's efforts on Dunbar's behalf went even further. He persuaded bookman-about-town Ripley Hitchcock to act as Dunbar's literary agent. He also recommended Dunbar to lecture agent James B. Pond, who had represented Frederick Douglass and Mark Twain. Pond brought Dunbar to New York—they met at Howells's summer home—and proposed an East Coast tour. Then Dunbar traveled to Narragansett Pier, Rhode Island, where he gave a series of lucrative readings. While there, he received word that a major New York house, Dodd, Mead, had agreed to publish a volume of his poems, with an introduction by Howells, and to pay a princely royalty. Dunbar returned to Ohio to settle his debts and to make provision for his mother, and then returned to the East, to Washington, D.C.

That journey held both hope and risk of humiliating confrontation, for to reach the nation's capital he had to travel through the Upper South, where laws mandated that Negro passengers be segregated into "Jim Crow" railroad cars. In May, the U.S. Supreme Court had ruled such laws constitutional, establishing the "Separate-but-Equal" doctrine that would subject black Americans to all sorts of segregation for the next six decades. But Dunbar, six months after the ruling, found his journey

> a very delightful one. I especially enjoyed the scenery thro' Virginia as I could look out on it from a luxurious coach all the way and did not once have to take the "Jim Crow" car.

In Washington, Dunbar came into contact with black America's best and brightest, who had been attracted by the aura of such elder statesmen as Frederick Douglass and the Reverend Alexander Crummell and the opportunity presented by Negro institutions like Howard University and M Street High School. In December, he met with Crummell and three other men to plan an American Negro Academy that would promote "Letters, Science, and Art" and perhaps extended an invitation to W.E.B. Du Bois, whom Dunbar had met when Du Bois was teaching at Wilberforce College, near Dayton. *Lyrics of Lowly Life* was published, and thanks to the Dodd, Mead imprint and Howells's imprimatur, the book enjoyed strong pre-Christmas sales. Dunbar's recitation tour proved so successful that Pond decided to send him to England. And the night before he departed, he met the love of his life.

Her name was Alice Ruth Moore. Trained as a teacher, she was acquiring a reputation as a poet and short story writer. Dunbar had seen one of Moore's pieces in 1895, as he was starting to write fiction based on recollections of plantation life shared by his kin. He had written her, demanding

> to know whether or not you believe in preserving by Afro-American— I don't like the word—writers those quaint old tales of our fathers. . . . Or whether you like so many others think we should ignore the past and all its capital literary materials.

But artistic concerns quickly gave way to less intellectual outpourings. "Let us not be literary in our letters," he wrote, and began to woo her with his words and his verses. But she was living in Boston; despite his recent East Coast travels, he had not met her in the flesh until the night before he was to sail. How much flesh was involved in that meeting is a matter of some speculation, but in mid-ocean Dunbar wrote to his mother:

You will be surprised to hear that Alice Ruth Moore ran off from Boston and came to New York to see me off.... She is the sweetest, smartest little girl I ever saw and she took everything by storm. She was very much ashamed of having run off, but she said that she could not have me gone for a year without once seeing me. Now don't laugh, but Alice and I are engaged....

And so, having crossed the Appalachians and the Atlantic, Dunbar made landfall. He had an agent, Pond's own daughter, to handle bookings and pay expenses. Howells had promised letters of introduction to British publishers, and Dunbar was no doubt expecting that within a fortnight he would be reciting before, if not royalty, then at least minor aristocracy and signing a contract with some stuffy but respectable house for the British rights to *Lyrics of Lowly Life*.

He was disappointed. Howells's letters proved useless. Miss Pond booked him—when she booked him—in halls shunned by even the petit bourgeoisie. "At one place," he complained, "I went on at midnight when half or three fourths of the men were *drunk*. Miss Pond coolly informed me that . . . I was to *tell vulgar stories*." Prospects brightened with the arrival of his American publisher, Samuel Dodd, who closed a deal for a British edition of *Lyrics* and delivered sufficient proceeds from the American edition to pay Dunbar's passage home. But Dunbar unwisely informed Miss Pond of his intention to quit London . . . and her. She promptly quit him for Paris, leaving his hotel bill unpaid. Once it was settled, he was once more stranded.

He forced himself to optimism and work. At the end of March he wrote to Alice, encouraging her to submit her own work to the *Ladies' Home Journal*, the most popular magazine in America, and reporting that

I am myself writing very hard and very steadily, the last few evenings past having seen me do sixteen thousand words in prose and about half a dozen poems.

One of those poems combined a form called lullaby, or cradlesong, with the dialect persona form to express a father's love for a "Little brown baby wif spa'klin' eyes." Dunbar thought it "the best and tenderest bit of verse that I have done since I came here." Another commented on his situation:

> Within a London garret high,
> Above the roofs and near the sky,
> My ill-rewarding pen I ply
> To win me bread. . . .
>
> Though chimney-pots be all my views;
> 'Tis nearer for the winging Muse,
> So I am sure she'll not refuse
> To visit me.

The Muse did visit, bringing both inspiration and new direction. At the end of April he wrote to Howells, "I am hard at work upon a novel." It is curious that Dunbar even mentioned his novel to Howells. Surely he recognized that Howells was an uncompromising Realist . . . and that he himself was not. He had written as much to Alice, who had apparently made a comment based on that aesthetic:

> I too believe that a story is a story and try to make my characters "real live people." But I believe that characters in fiction should be what men and women are in real life,—the embodiment of a principle or idea. There is no individuality apart from an idea. Every character who moves across the pages of a story is, to my mind, and a very humble mind it is, only an idea, incarnate. . . .

Realism abhors such symbolism. But in the novel, eventually entitled *The Uncalled,* Dunbar embraced it. Set initially in "Dexter," a thinly disguised Dayton, *The Uncalled* did, as Realism dictated, capture the details of daily life, as it told the story of an orphan named Frederick Brent who is forced into the ministry by his spinster guardian, Hester Prime. But as that homage to Hawthorne suggests, the characters incarnate a conflict between religious orthodoxy and a more forgiving and redemptive Christianity. While not exactly "painting dolls and working them by springs and wires," Dunbar does tend to manipulate the characters with an intrusive narrator—one reviewer accused him of writing like "a stage manager," a damning reference to Thackeray's "Manager of the Performance" in *Vanity Fair*—who articulates a fatalist perspective:

> "Whom the gods wish to destroy, they first make mad," we used to say; but all that is changed now, and whom the devil wishes to get, he first makes lonesome.

Like most first novels, *The Uncalled* is tinted by autobiography; Dunbar, like most intellectually oriented and dark-skinned young black men of the time, was pressured toward the ministry. But what some would consider the salient of his identity does not figure in the text; there is no indication of the characters' race. Which is not to say they are not black; only that they are not necessarily so.

Some critics have found in this evidence to argue that Dunbar had ambiguous feelings about his race. Addison Gayle, Jr., used terms such as "psychological difficulties" and even "schizophrenia." A less pathological explanation might be that Dunbar, in England, did not have to deal with American society's psychological difficulties with respect to race. What, after all, is "separate-but-equal" but legalized schizophrenia? In England, Dunbar could board a train without even looking for a Jim Crow car and could enter the British Museum to commune with the ages. "I sit with Shakespeare, and he winces not. . . . So, wed with Truth, I dwell above the veil," W.E.B. Du Bois would write in 1903. In 1897 Dunbar wrote, "when one has just gotten through looking at the 1623 folio edition of Shakespeare . . . one may be pardoned a lapse into old English."

Divorced from the phobia about "social equality" then prevalent in America, Dunbar was able to mingle with artists whose views on race and ethnicity were less rigid than the American norm. He took tea with Zionist novelist Israel Zangwell, who created the image of America as "the great melting pot." He collaborated with composer Samuel Coleridge-Taylor, the son of an African physician and an Englishwoman, who had previously been inspired by Longfellow's *Song of Hiawatha*. He may also have encountered Stephen Crane, who had settled in England to escape rumors of sexual misconduct and alcoholism. Crane was then working on a story called "The Monster," which reversed the Plantation Tale plot by depicting a white master who shows steadfast loyalty to a black retainer.

Critic Kenny Williams offers another explanation for the absence of racial referents: "Dunbar was aware . . . that 'a liberal publisher' was a misnomer." He was also aware that it had sometimes been to his advantage that some editors had not known that he was black. These awarenesses may have suggested that the novel would be more marketable were the characters not identifiably Negroes. That consideration may seem mercenary, but Dunbar considered writing prose a commercial activity. In 1893 he admitted becoming "practical enough to do a little prose work." Certainly he wanted to sell the novel; in July he wrote his mother, "still working hard upon my novel and I hope that it may bring me something soon after I get home."

Meanwhile the Republicans had taken possession of the White House—and the patronage pork barrel. Some pundits claimed the oratory of Robert G. Ingersoll was what had secured the narrow victory. In any case, after the inauguration, the party did not forget Ingersoll, and Ingersoll did not forget Dunbar. His desire to help Dunbar was realized in the form of a patronage position at the Library of Congress at a salary of $720 per year.

So Dunbar took ship for America. Before him lay respectable employment and a steady income sufficient for him to fulfill his filial duty and wed his beautiful, educated, talented, and ardent fiancée— soon, perhaps, that little brown baby in his lullaby would be a reality. He had markets for his poetry, including commissions from the *Ladies' Home Journal,* and thanks to those visits from the Muse, notes for a number of short stories and a complete draf᷏ ᷐f the novel. If ever he took station in the bows and looked ahead it must have been with wonder and gratitude. Perhaps he recalled how once he had been in such desperate financial straits that he had contemplated suicide. Perhaps he recalled the words of Andrew Marvell: "Who can foretell for what high cause / This darling of the Gods was born," or the advice of Dryden: "If the world be worth thy winning . . . / Take the good the gods provide thee." Surely he did not think of Keats's "fears that I may cease to be / Before my pen has glean'd my teeming brain," or Byron's "Whom the gods love die young," for he did not know that another visitor had come to him in his garret, or that his body still hosted it. Its name was *Mycobacterium tuberculosis.*

M. tuberculosis has been mankind's invisible companion since the pharaohs. Greek writings dating from the fifth century B.C., attributed to the legendary Hippocrates, describe a condition characterized by violent coughing up of bloody phlegm which gave off a "heavy smell" when poured on hot coals and a physical wasting so extreme it seemed the body were consuming itself. It was called "phthisis"—consumption.

In the second century A.D. another Greek physician, Galen, noted consumption's high morbidity and mortality and prescribed clean air, nourishing food, and rest. During the next sixteen hundred years other treatments appeared—garlic-and-dog-fat elixirs, smoke from burning cow dung, seaweed placed beneath the bed, a laying on of hands by whatever monarch reigned. Despite all, consumption ran rampant.

Though over the next millennium or so, other, more dramatic diseases—the bubonic plague, typhus, typhoid fever—upstaged it, consumption remained a constant, quiet killer. In the nineteenth century, cholera caused panic in the British Isles because it attacked so suddenly, killed so horribly, and seemed unavoidable—British physicians believed it lurked in the foggy, smoke-filled London air, which they called the "miasma." But even as cholera was terrifying Londoners by slaughtering six thousand in a single year, diseases caused by *M. tuberculosis* were quietly killing sixty thousand every year.

These diseases had long been known, but as separate entities, under a legion of names: scrofula, symptomized by pus-filled swellings on the neck; Pott's disease, which caused curving of the spine; lupus vulgaris, which produced painful chancres on the genitals confused with syphilis; Addison's disease, which produced fatigue, loss of appetite and body weight, vomiting, diarrhea, and emotional volatility. Improvements in microscopy allowed physicians to see that common to all were tiny "tubercles"—whence the name "tuberculosis"—which were found primarily in the lungs, but which could appear in almost any organ: kidneys, bladder, bones, blood vessels, the brain, the heart, the organs of pleasure and reproduction.

By the mid-nineteenth century, physicians understood that diseases could be linked to specific microorganisms. That understanding led to stunning victories over such diseases as rabies, anthrax, diphtheria, and gangrene. But even though tubercles were visible, *M. tuberculosis* remained invisible. Tuberculosis acquired an almost mythic quality.

In mid-nineteenth-century Britain, several charity hospitals were founded to treat the disease. One of these, the Edinburgh Royal Infirmary, produced the first famous "tuberculosis survivor," a boy named William Ernest Henley. Henley's treatment included the amputation of one of his legs and a two-year hospitalization, during which he turned himself into a poet, producing, among others, a poem called "Invictus," which includes the defiant stanza:

> In the fell clutch of circumstance,
> I have not winced nor cried aloud.

> Under the bludgeonings of chance
> My head is bloody, but unbowed.

Henley's surgery and determination appeared curative. He went on to become a poet, editor, critic, and dramatist, and the model for one of Robert Louis Stevenson's most famous characters, Long John Silver.

But on the Continent, another treatment was in fashion. In 1854 a German tuberculosis sufferer named Hermann Brehmer returned from a sojourn in the Himalayas claiming to be cured. Brehmer theorized that tuberculosis was caused by stress; he built a "sanatorium" in the mountains of Prussia where patients were treated with Galen's ancient prescription of diet, fresh air, and rest, but in a stress-free environment.

These conditions gave the body's defenses a chance against *M. tuberculosis.* Many patients did improve, sometimes long enough to be called cured. With tuberculosis the leading cause of death in Europe, sanatoriums became prevalent—and profitable. Their business boomed when it was learned that the disease did indeed lurk in the Industrial Age miasma.

That discovery was made in 1882 when a German scientist, Robert Koch, developed a stain that revealed *M. tuberculosis* to the microscope. A rod-shaped bacillus, it was tiny and so light it could be launched into the air when an infected person merely spoke or sang, and could remain suspended for hours, to be inhaled by the uninfected.

Although this prospect is disquieting, modern research has revealed that inhalation usually doesn't matter; for every three persons exposed, only one develops a "primary infection" in which the microbe lodges in the lungs and produces a detectable response. And even if there is a primary infection, the disease usually remains dormant; for every ten persons who experience a primary infection, only one develops active tuberculosis.

So what, then, divides the one from the three, and that one from the ten? The easy answer is "susceptibility," determined by many factors—degree of exposure, nutrition, medical history, level of stress.

Paul Laurence Dunbar had exposure aplenty in the months he spent breathing the London miasma. Nutrition is a trickier factor to assess. One critical factor is a deficiency of animal protein; Dunbar's infant sister died from "marasmus"—precisely that type of malnutrition. But that was in another country, and twenty years before. From

London, he reported "thriving well on English joints and ale." His medical history, however, suggests problems. He had to repeat his senior year of high school owing to absence caused by illness. He had proved too frail for his first job after high school, as a janitor at National Cash Register. Following the World's Columbian Exhibition, he wrote: "I am feeling good in mind and body, now. Would that it were always so." Stress can arise from any sudden change in fortune, good or ill. Dunbar was probably susceptible.

But susceptibility is not inevitability; it is only probability. And even the latest paradigm of medical science could have made no firm prediction about the future of the young man who might have stood at the bowsprit with poetry in his soul, genius in his brain, hope in his heart, and a pernicious pathogen in his lungs. Declares one authoritative medical text:

> the tubercule bacillus may not be the only factor in the development of tuberculosis. An individual may be exposed to a virulent tubercule bacillus, yet his constitution, his inherited or acquired immunity, as well as his physiological and psychological makeup at the time of exposure, will determine whether he will contract the disease.

In other words, what divides the one from the three, the one from the ten, what singled out Paul Laurence Dunbar, was a whim of the gods.

—

In April 1899, Dunbar was hospitalized in New York City. The event was newsworthy, for in the three years since Howells introduced him to the world, he had become a public figure, well known as a poet, a lyricist, a writer of fiction and essays.

"The age is materialistic. Verse isn't," he had observed. "I must be with the age, so I am writing prose." He turned his notes into stories which appeared in New York's *Cosmopolitan* magazine and were published in a volume, *Folks from Dixie*, by Dodd, Mead, which also published *The Uncalled* after it was serialized in Philadelphia's *Lippincott's Magazine*.

Most reviewers assumed the characters were white. Some found this a negative: *The Bookman* advised Dunbar to "write about Negroes." Others found it a positive: The Chicago *Times-Herald* said Dunbar had entered "boldly into the broader field of letters" and added: "There is no color line in letters. . . . But even if we admit . . . the existence of a color line, Mr. Dunbar stepped clean over it. . . . He should be encouraged to write more."

Publication increased the demand for recitations; Dunbar was so inundated he called this period "pouring time." His commercial success enabled him to negotiate advantageous contracts, including a "first refusal" agreement with *Lippincott's* under which the magazine got the first look at his fiction, for which the magazine paid a fee even if it rejected the piece. Some would have seen that as an opportunity to rest. Dunbar took it as an opportunity to work. "If it is only for the idle that the devil runs his employment bureau," he wrote, "I have no need of his services."

But his writing was not all work. With almost-daily letters he had pressed his suit of Alice Moore. Her family disapproved of his dark skin and his dialect poetry. Alice herself was reluctant to marry; she had a position as a schoolteacher, and the conventions of the time made married women ineligible for such posts. But in March 1898, Dunbar wrote triumphantly:

> I am married! I would have consulted you, but the matter was very quickly done. People, my wife's parents and others—were doing everything to separate us. She was worried and harassed until she was ill. So she telegraphed me and I went to New York. We were married Sunday night by the bishop but hope to keep it secret for a while, as she does not wish to give up her school. Everything is clean and honorable and save for the fear of separation there was no compulsion to the step.

Alice was forced to give up teaching. She helped manage Dunbar's recitations—she negotiated twice his usual fee for a reading in Albany—and pursued her own writing. Her first volume of stories, *The Goodness of St. Rocque,* was accepted by Dodd, Mead. In the midst of Mark Twain's Gilded Age, the Dunbars were a Golden Couple.

But if it was the best of times, it was also the worst of times. Lynchings were reported at the rate of two per week, and many went unreported. Whites routinely ran riot in Negro neighborhoods; Negroes, stripped of weapons, fled to the cities or territories. Would-be Negro voters were threatened by white "citizens councils" until state legislatures could disenfranchise them with legal stratagems which the U.S. Supreme Court upheld. Congress killed anti-lynching bills. Half a century later, historian Rayford Logan would call it "the nadir" of American racial history. Dunbar called it "the meanest, most unliterary time in America."

In February 1898, an atrocity that shocked even some white Southerners took place in Lake City, South Carolina. The state already had a virulent reputation. One of its U.S. senators, "Pitchfork" Ben Tillman, had campaigned on a promise to help lynch any black accused of assaulting a white woman; as governor, he had in fact turned one black man over to a mob. But the primary victim in Lake City was no rapist; Frazier Baker was a hard-working, church-going, family-loving black man whose only crime was accepting the patronage job of postmaster from the Republicans. At one o'clock in the morning on February 22—Washington's birthday—his home was set afire. When Baker, his wife, son, four daughters, and a babe in arms attempted to escape, they were driven back by gunfire from a mob. Baker and the baby died, and his wife and children were horribly injured; eventually they became refugees in Boston.

Lake City became a cause célèbre. Ida B. Wells demanded a federal investigation and actually got it, as government property (the post office was in Baker's home) had been destroyed. But Dunbar was too caught up in elopement intrigue to respond immediately, and after his marriage he focused on more intellectual controversy: the debate over whether the education of blacks should emphasize industrial training, as advocated by Booker T. Washington of Tuskegee Institute, or should include an emphasis on the liberal arts, as argued by Alexander Crummell, the elite—some would say effete—American Negro Academy, and W.E.B. Du Bois.

Dunbar entered the lists with an article in the *New York Independent:*

> I do not believe that a young man, whose soul is turbulent with a message which should be given to the world through the pulpit or the press, should shut his mouth and shoe horses. . . .

Booker T. Washington responded with an invitation to appear at a Tuskegee fundraiser. "What is their game?" Dunbar wondered. "Is it to destroy any future power Du Bois and I may have by bringing us before the public in the character of speakers for the very institution whose founder's utterances we cannot subscribe to?" But when in

March 1899 he appeared at Boston's Hollis Street Theatre with the first black to earn a Harvard Ph.D., it confirmed him as a public intellectual of national importance.

Shortly after, Dunbar wrote to an Ohio friend:

> I am lying in bed ill and Mrs. Dunbar is kind enough to take down my letters for me. My readings here have been very successful. . . . But they have been a little too much for me, and I am now suffering from a cold, fatigue and a bad throat.

In April, he started for Albany but collapsed in New York City. The initial diagnosis was bad: pneumonia, often fatal in those days before antibiotics. The revised diagnosis was worse: pulmonary tuberculosis.

It is difficult to say exactly what Dunbar—or Alice—was told about his condition. As Susan Sontag writes in *Illness as Metaphor:*

> it was common to conceal the identity of their disease from tuberculars and, after they died, from their children. Even with patients informed about their disease, doctors and family were reluctant to talk freely.

If his physicians were forthcoming, they most likely offered only a general—and generally depressing—prognosis. His existing pulmonary symptoms would, in the short term, probably improve, but would worsen in the long term; he would experience bouts of coughing violent enough to break ribs, expectoration of phlegm tainted by pulmonary hemorrhage, and shortening of breath as his lungs lost their ability to extract oxygen from the air; eventually he would suffocate or drown in his own blood.

He—but surely not Alice—might have been warned that he might develop tubercular masses on his neck or in his throat, failure of his kidneys, urinary incontinence, impotence or sterility, and epididymitis (pus-discharging abscesses between his scrotum and rectum). He might not have been warned about the mood swings caused by Addison's disease, but he was probably warned that he would experience a great deal of pain. He was probably not prescribed medication for pain, as there was none to prescribe. He was likely advised to drink whiskey, as it was not then known that alcohol can exacerbate the mood swings of Addison's, and whiskey-drinking, though disreputable, was preferable to taking laudanum (tincture of opium) or morphine. And he was certainly told that there was hope.

For Americans too were attracted by the image of crisp-sheeted Teutonic spas sequestered in white snow, far from the madding crowd. In 1884, a French physician opened a sanatorium at Saranac Lake, in New York's Adirondack Mountains. Saranac Lake's big success story was Robert Louis Stevenson, who was treated during the winter of 1887–88 and lived another seven years. Though he died at only forty-four, the cause of death, cerebral hemorrhage, was considered unrelated. And so, wrote Dunbar:

> After leaving the hospital my doctor insists that I must go to the Adirondacks, and stay there through October, then to Colorado. They think I am a millionaire.

Stevenson had indeed been a millionaire—the scion of a wealthy family, and a successful novelist for years. Dunbar was only recently successful, and a poet; his family was a wife and mother who were financially dependent on him. His professional income—derived as much from recitations as publications—was stabilized by the salary from his job at the Library of Congress, the duties of which he could no longer fulfill.

Dunbar did go to the mountains, but not the Adirondacks; he took up residence in the Catskills—mountains of lesser elevation in social as well as geographical terms—and on his stress-free environment intruded publishers' deadlines; he wrote one three-thousand-word article, three poems, and two stories. In September, he did go to Colorado, and accepted an ongoing commission from the *Denver Post*. One of his first pieces was "The Hapless Southern Negro," which advocated that blacks escape Southern horrors by resettling in the West.

He seems to have had little hope of escaping his personal horror. "It is something," he wrote, "to sit down under the shadow of the Rocky Mountains, even if one only goes there to die." He confronted *M. tuberculosis* and wrote that he had

> looked upon the "little red hair-like devils" who are eating up my lungs. So many of us are cowards when we look into the cold, white eyes of death, and I suppose I am no better or braver than the rest of humanity.

Settled in Harmon, Colorado, he bought a horse and completed the stories for a new collection, *The Strength of Gideon*. In crafting these stories, Dunbar relied less on the tales told by his kin than on social science and his own experience. In "The Trustfulness of Polly," a cautionary tale of a Negro from the rural South who falls prey to New York hustlers, Dunbar combined his personal observations of black life in New York, which had been the basis for an 1898 nonfiction piece, "The Negroes of the Tenderloin," with more scientific conclusions expressed by W.E.B. Du Bois in his landmark study, *The Philadelphia Negro*, published in 1899.

In "One Man's Fortunes," Dunbar fused his own experience as a recent high school graduate with that of W.E.B. Du Bois's, who, when they first met, was lamenting his inability to secure a post at a major university despite his Harvard Ph.D. The story opens with a discussion between three young men, two black, one white, who have just graduated from an integrated Midwestern college much like Ohio's Oberlin. The subject is the struggle that the blacks face to use their education in an America that denies them opportunity. One of the blacks, Bertram Halliday, offers a poem that "seems . . . to strike the keynote of the matter" and recites Henley's "Invictus." What is curious is that while Dunbar has Halliday recite the poem in its entirety and discuss Henley's career at length, he does not have Halliday mention Henley's tuberculosis nor his long-term survival, though to do so would sharpen the point and add irony to the ending, in which Halliday is forced "to do what I abhor." This suggests psychological difficulties, but they having nothing to do with race.

A similar phenomenon appears in the novel Dunbar wrote under the shadow of the Rockies, *The Love of Landry*. The plot is a romantic triangle involving Mildred Osborne of New York, an Englishman, and a cowboy, Landry Thayer, whom Mildred meets in Colorado. If *The Uncalled* suggests that Dunbar had identity problems, *The Love of Landry* provides a QED; all the characters are white except a Pullman porter, who, Kenny Williams notes,

> In a single incident . . . is used to record not only the dominant attitude of white America but also the innate feeling of the porter himself. . . . While the conversation both begins and ends from a "white point of view," clearly

the attitude of the porter is sandwiched between. Thus in one episode, Dunbar addressed himself not only to the majority of his readers but also managed to record the porter's own thoughts.

Such a covert technique was a necessity, as Dunbar wrote *The Love of Landry* under a first refusal agreement, and so had a specific publisher—*Lippincott's Magazine*—and a specific audience in mind. The main characters are not only white, but Eastern and wealthy. Even Landry, who appears as a rough-and-ready Westerner, is revealed to be related to Old Virginia stock, a frog-turned-prince symbolism to which Dunbar adds a local twist by making him also the scion of one of Philadelphia's finest families. As a further fillip to *Lippincott's* place of publication, Dunbar named a minor character, a physician, "Van Pelt," which was a hallowed Philadelphia name.

Commercial concerns dominate the novel, but social concerns are reflected in the text—it is just that many of them are not specifically racial concerns. True to his own brand of Realism, Dunbar made his characters express ideas about economics, imperialism, and what had become an essential of the American zeitgeist, the Frontier.

In 1893 Frederick Jackson Turner had found scholarly antecedent for his Frontier Hypothesis in Theodore Roosevelt's multivolume history, *The Winning of the West*. But in 1899 Roosevelt was little recognized as a scholar; he was the Spanish-American War hero and the tough New York governor, but rendered sympathetic by a bit of tragic biography. On Valentine's Day 1884, his wife, Alice, died in childbirth. His mother died later that same day. Roosevelt, devastated, and suffering from chronic asthma, had retreated with his infant daughter to a ranch in the Dakotas. It was from that restorative Western retreat that the Rough Rider had emerged.

The American public was reminded of this story in 1896, when Roosevelt's first writings about the West, sketches of ranch life, were published in volume form. Although Roosevelt himself said little of his healing, Dunbar made the theme explicit. "Some of us," says Landry,

come here to look at the great mountains and great plains and forget how little man is; to see Nature, and through it Nature's God, and so get back to faith.

And though Mildred's romance with him ends happily, that happiness is not defined entirely in terms of love. Rather, she comes to enjoy "gaiety and health, the reward one gains by living near to Nature's heart."

What is curious here is that Mildred, like Dunbar, has been ordered to Colorado for her health after she "contracted a cough." She does not suffer from tuberculosis; there is, Dunbar insists, "nothing the matter with her lungs.... Nothing, except a tendency. But a tendency ... is a thing that should always be stopped."

For Dunbar too, it seemed "living near to Nature's heart" could restore body and spirit. After a winter and spring in Colorado, and another summer in the Catskills, he returned to Washington. Although he had resigned his position at the Library of Congress, "to devote time to literary production and recitation," he purchased a home and resumed a grueling schedule of public recitations and his black bourgeois lifestyle, which Alice chronicled in a one-act play, *The Author's Evening at Home.*

But though it had been a healthful summer, it was not an easy one. In July 1900 he had written his agent, Paul R. Reynolds, discussing a new novel, *The Fanatics*, an ambitious project set in Civil War–era Ohio, in "Dorbury," another thinly disguised Dayton. The plot portrayed the conflict between white Ohioans who supported the Union and those who supported the Confederacy—the "Copperheads." Dunbar said he "would expect at least five hundred dollars, because it strikes me as a more serious work." But Reynolds was unable to sell either first serial or British rights. Also, sometime during the summer, Dunbar learned that Stephen Crane had succumbed to tuberculosis in a German sanatorium.

Nor was life in Washington golden for the Golden Couple. There was talk of public misbehavior—of angry arguments, of verbal, perhaps even physical abuse of Alice. There were rumors of alcoholism, like those which had allegedly forced Crane to England. In late autumn, Dunbar appeared, inebriated, before a large audience in Evanston, Illinois. Scandalized accounts appeared in Chicago papers. Rumor became a matter of public record.

Dunbar wrote a private apology to his Illinois host:

> The clipping you sent is too nearly true to be answered. I had been drinking. This had partially intoxicated me. The only injustice lies in the writer's not knowing there was a cause behind it all, beyond mere inclination. On Friday afternoon I had a severe hemorrhage. This I was fool enough to try to conceal from my family, for, as I had had one the week

before, I knew they would not want me to read ... so I tried to bolster myself with stimulants. It was the only way I could have stood up at all.

Though his host not only accepted the apology, but published it, the damage was done, not only to Dunbar's reputation but to his marketability.

More damage was done in December, when a musical, *Uncle Eph's Christmas*, which Dunbar wrote with composer Will Marion Cook, appeared. The piece had been commissioned by a black actor named Ernest Hogan, well known as a minstrel. Reviews implied Dunbar was responsible for the blackface style; one called him the "prince of the coon song writers."

Also in December, one of his most powerful poems of protest, "The Haunted Oak," caused controversy. Topically, it was a response to a widely reprinted newspaper story about a tree that withered after it was used for a lynching. Artistically, the poem was a rebuttal to Whitman's "I Saw in Louisiana a Live-Oak Growing." Politically, it was a response to 106 lynchings that year. Sociologically, it reflected Ida B. Wells's evidence that most lynching victims had committed no serious offense. But when Dunbar referred to the "innocence" of lynching victims, he was taken to task by some of his staunchest allies, including Toledo mayor Brand Whitlock. The day after Christmas, Dunbar felt it necessary to write to Whitlock to defend his diction.

Little wonder that when *The Fanatics* was published in March 1901, Dunbar felt great trepidation. For though the historical conflict was embedded in a romantic formula in which two "star-cross'd lovers"— the daughter of a Unionist and the son of a Copperhead—are kept apart by an "ancient grudge," the plot moved beyond "Two households, both alike in dignity," to a "new mutiny/Where civil blood makes civil hands unclean." If a single word in a poem about lynching in the South upset the mayor of Toledo, there was no telling what the response would be to a scene in a novel in which an Ohio mob threatens to lynch an innocent Negro.

In another scene, another white mob invades the black district, expecting to easily run riot over "a cowering crowd of helpless men." Instead they

found themselves confronted by a solid black wall of desperate men who stood their ground and fought like soldiers.

In the melee that ensues,

> A knife flashed in the dim light, and in a moment more was buried in the leader's heart. The shriek, half of fear, half of surprise which was on his lips died there, and he fell forward with a groan, while the black man sped from the room.

Dunbar later added that the killer "went out into the night to be lost forever," completing a scenario that surely would have alienated his white audience.

But by the time the review appeared, Dunbar was giving recitations in Jacksonville, Florida, as a guest of James Weldon Johnson, who was becoming known as a poet—his "Lift Every Voice and Sing" was already being touted as the Negro National Anthem. Decades later, in his autobiography, Johnson attributed a statement to Dunbar that would become an important part of the critical discourse about Dunbar's dialect poetry:

> I didn't start as a dialect poet. I simply came to the conclusion that I could write it as well, if not better, than anybody else I knew of, and that by doing so I should gain a hearing, and now they don't want me to write anything else.

That Dunbar was feeling this frustration at this time is corroborated by his short, bitter poem "The Poet" ("But ah, the world, it turned to praise / A jingle in a broken tongue"), which was published two years later, in *Lyrics of Love and Laughter*, in juxtaposition to the lyrical "A Florida Night." He drew on his observations in Jacksonville to write such acrid phrases as "sly convenient hell" and "This newer bondage and this deeper shame." Another powerful protest poem, "To the South: On Its New Slavery," testifies that he was also concerned with racial politics. But such concerns were surely eclipsed by another reality. From Jacksonville, he wrote to Alice:

> Both my lungs and throat are very bad, and, from now on, it seems like merely a fighting race with Death. If this be so, I feel like pulling my horse, and letting the white rider go in without a contest.

A few weeks later, from Tuskegee, Alabama, he wrote:

> I am feeling disgustingly well this morning after all my fears, although I still have the trots.

A few weeks after that, the first installment of his fourth novel appeared in *Lippincott's Magazine*. It was entitled *The Sport of the Gods*.

The Sport of the Gods is Dunbar's "blackest" novel, in several senses. Black in the sense that the plot is not romance, but tragedy; ex-slave Berry Hamilton, a hard-working, law-abiding, church-going, family-loving Southern black man, is accused of theft, and although not lynched, he is incarcerated after a sham of due process. His wife, son, and daughter become refugees in the North. Black also in a political sense, for the plot line challenges the Plantation Tradition's assumption that white former slaveholders are worthy of loyalty and reveals Southern honor as a sly, convenient sham. And black in the sense that the focal characters are black. All this blackness has earned Dunbar little credit with the most psychologically oriented critics—Addison Gayle insists that even here, Dunbar's "psychological difficulties prevented him from regarding black men as other than wards of American Society" and rendered him "incapable of viewing himself as other than the sport of the gods." More forgiving critics find in this novel the kind of bitter social condemnation they had been expecting from Dunbar.

It is perhaps inevitable, given American history and culture, that it should be so. Nor is it wrong to read *The Sport of the Gods* as a critique of American society. Hamilton and his family have shown loyalty, not only to white masters, but also to values associated with the American Protestant way of life. Nor is the critique color-blind; the story echoes the Lake City atrocity and the sociological research of Du Bois, and reiterates the words of the defeated Bertram Halliday:

> I no longer judge so harshly the shiftless and unambitious among my people. I hardly see how a people, who have so much to contend with and so little to hope for, can go on striving and aspiring.

But if one can forget race, even for a moment, one remembers something: As he wrote this novel, Paul Laurence Dunbar was dying. And he knew it. And it wasn't realism; it was simply, sadly, real.

If one can forget race, one realizes that, in a strange, sad way, *M. tuberculosis* liberated Dunbar from the category of race, changed the meaning of the term "his people" from American Negroes to the millions who, through the millennia, had truly felt his anger and his anguish. Which is not to say that Dunbar was unaffected by the knowledge that a hundred

black Americans a year fell prey to white American lynch mobs; only
that he may have been equally affected by the awareness that a hundred
and fifty thousand Americans a year, white and black, fell prey to *M.
tuberculosis*—especially as he would, some year, be one of them.

If one can maintain that realization, one can see something remarkable: Dunbar kept the novel free of even a proxied self-pity. It is about
a man untimely ripped from life and family, but it speaks little of his
suffering, focusing instead on the damage done to those from whom he
is taken.

In the text of *The Sport of the Gods*, Dunbar quotes Longfellow's *The
Masque of Pandora* ("Whom the Gods would destroy they first make
mad"), but the title comes from Shakespeare's *King Lear*. The words are
spoken by a relatively minor character, the Earl of Gloucester:

> As flies to wanton boys, are we to th' gods,
> They kill us for their sport.

At first, one wonders why Dunbar went to Shakespeare to find a
title. Then one remembers the young Dunbar, in London, contemplating the 1623 folio. Then it does not seem so strange that the most eloquent explication of *The Sport of the Gods* is found not in Dunbar
criticism, but in Shakespeare criticism, in the words of William Allan
Neilson and Charles Jarvis Hill on *King Lear*:

Shakespeare acknowledges no principle demanding poetic justice at the
end of a play in which the powers of injustice have cruelly prevailed. Even
Cordelia, whose taking off has seemed to many gratuitously wanton, must
be sacrificed, for the wickedness upon which Shakespeare meditates is a
perverse and heartless scourge. Nevertheless, Shakespeare did not con-
ceive this tragedy in a spirit of total negation... The miserable words of
Gloucester... have often been quoted as if they abstracted the spirit of the
play, in forgetfulness that Gloucester himself learned to think otherwise
and, reconciled to affliction, later cried,

> You ever gentle gods, take my breath from me;
> Let not my worser spirit tempt me again
> To die before you please.

The Sport of the Gods

CONTENTS

I

THE HAMILTONS

Fiction has said so much in regret of the old days when there were plantations and overseers and masters and slaves, that it was good to come upon such a household as Berry Hamilton's, if for no other reason than that it afforded a relief from the monotony of tiresome iteration.

The little cottage in which he lived with his wife, Fannie, who was housekeeper to the Oakleys, and his son and daughter, Joe and Kit, sat back in the yard some hundred paces from the mansion of his employer. It was somewhat in the manner of the old cabin in the quarters, with which usage as well as tradition had made both master and servant familiar. But, unlike the cabin of the elder day, it was a neatly furnished, modern house, the home of a typical, good-living negro. For twenty years Berry Hamilton had been butler for Maurice Oakley. He was one of the many slaves who upon their accession to freedom had not left the South, but had wandered from place to place in their own beloved section, waiting, working, and struggling to rise with its rehabilitated fortunes.

The first faint signs of recovery were being seen when he came to Maurice Oakley as a servant. Through thick and thin he remained with him, and when the final upward tendency of his employer began his fortunes had increased in like manner. When, having married, Oakley bought the great house in which he now lived, he left the little servant's cottage in the yard, for, as he said laughingly, "There is no telling when Berry will be following my example and be taking a wife unto himself."

His joking prophecy came true very soon. Berry had long had a tenderness for Fannie, the housekeeper. As she retained her post under the new Mrs. Oakley, and as there was a cottage ready to his hand, it promised to be cheaper and more convenient all around to get married. Fannie was willing, and so the matter was settled.

Fannie had never regretted her choice, nor had Berry ever had cause to curse his utilitarian ideas. The stream of years had flowed pleasantly and peacefully with them. Their little sorrows had come, but their joys had been many.

As time went on, the little cottage grew in comfort. It was replenished with things handed down from "the house" from time to time and with others bought from the pair's earnings.

Berry had time for his lodge, and Fannie time to spare for her own house and garden. Flowers bloomed in the little plot in front and behind it; vegetables and greens testified to the housewife's industry.

Over the door of the little house a fine Virginia creeper bent and fell in graceful curves, and a cluster of insistent morning-glories clung in summer about its stalwart stock.

It was into this bower of peace and comfort that Joe and Kitty were born. They brought a new sunlight into the house and a new joy to the father's and mother's hearts. Their early lives were pleasant and carefully guarded. They got what schooling the town afforded, but both went to work early, Kitty helping her mother and Joe learning the trade of barber.

Kit was the delight of her mother's life. She was a pretty, cheery little thing, and could sing like a lark. Joe too was of a cheerful disposition, but from scraping the chins of aristocrats came to imbibe some of their ideas, and rather too early in life bid fair to be a dandy. But his father encouraged him, for, said he, "It's de p'opah thing fu' a man what waits on quality to have quality mannahs an' to waih quality clothes."

"'Tain't no use to be a-humo'in' dat boy too much, Be'y," Fannie had replied, although she did fully as much "humo'in'" as her husband; "hit sho' do mek' him biggety, an' a biggety po' niggah is a 'bomination befo' de face of de Lawd; but I know 'tain't no use a-talkin' to you, fu' you plum boun' up in dat Joe."

Her own eyes would follow the boy lovingly and proudly even as she chided. She could not say very much, either, for Berry always had the reply that she was spoiling Kit out of all reason. The girl did have the prettiest clothes of any of her race in the town, and when she was to sing for the benefit of the A.M.E. church or for the benefit of her father's society, the Tribe of Benjamin, there was nothing too good for her to wear. In this too they were aided and abetted by Mrs. Oakley, who also took a lively interest in the girl.

So the two doting parents had their chats and their jokes at each other's expense and went bravely on, doing their duties and spoiling their children much as white fathers and mothers are wont to do.

What the less fortunate negroes of the community said of them and their offspring is really not worth while. Envy has a sharp tongue, and when has not the aristocrat been the target for the plebeian's sneers?

Joe and Kit were respectively eighteen and sixteen at the time when the preparations for Maurice Oakley's farewell dinner to his brother Francis were agitating the whole Hamilton household. All of them had a hand in the work: Joe had shaved the two men; Kit had helped Mrs. Oakley's maid; the mother had fretted herself weak over the shortcomings of a cook that had been in the family nearly as long as herself, while Berry was stern and dignified in anticipation of the glorious figure he was to make in serving.

When all was ready, peace again settled upon the Hamiltons. Mrs. Hamilton, in the whitest of white aprons, prepared to be on hand to annoy the cook still more; Kit was ready to station herself where she could view the finery; Joe had condescended to promise to be home in time to eat some of the good things, and Berry—Berry was gorgeous in his evening suit with the white waistcoat, as he directed the nimble waiters hither and thither.

II

A Farewell Dinner

Maurice Oakley was not a man of sudden or violent enthusiasms. Conservatism was the quality that had been the foundation of his fortunes at a time when the disruption of the country had involved most of the men of his region in ruin.

Without giving any one ground to charge him with being lukewarm or renegade to his cause, he had yet so adroitly managed his affairs that when peace came he was able quickly to recover much of the ground lost during the war. With a rare genius for adapting himself to new conditions, he accepted the changed order of things with a passive resignation, but with a stern determination to make the most out of any good that might be in it.

It was a favourite remark of his that there must be some good in every system, and it was the duty of the citizen to find out that good and make it pay. He had done this. His house, his reputation, his satisfaction, were all evidences that he had succeeded.

A childless man, he bestowed upon his younger brother, Francis, the enthusiasm he would have given to a son. His wife shared with her husband this feeling for her brother-in-law, and with him played the role of parent, which had otherwise been denied her.

It was true that Francis Oakley was only a half-brother to Maurice, the son of a second and not too fortunate marriage, but there was no halving of the love which the elder man had given to him from child-hood up.

At the first intimation that Francis had artistic ability, his brother had placed him under the best masters in America, and later, when the promise of his youth had begun to blossom, he sent him to Paris, although the expenditure just at that time demanded a sacrifice which might have been the ruin of Maurice's own career. Francis's promise had never come to entire fulfilment. He was always trembling on the verge of a great success without quite plunging into it. Despite the joy which his presence gave his brother and sister-in-law, most of his time was spent abroad, where he could find just the atmosphere that suited his delicate, artistic nature. After a visit of two months he was about returning to Paris for a stay of five years. At last he was going to apply himself steadily and try to be less the dilettante.

The company which Maurice Oakley brought together to say good-bye to his brother on this occasion was drawn from the best that this fine old Southern town afforded. There were colonels there at whose titles and the owners' rights to them no one could laugh; there were brilliant women there who had queened it in Richmond, Balti-more, Louisville, and New Orleans, and every Southern capital under the old régime, and there were younger ones there of wit and beauty who were just beginning to hold their court. For Francis was a great favourite both with men and women. He was a handsome man, tall, slender, and graceful. He had the face and brow of a poet, a pallid face framed in a mass of dark hair. There was a touch of weakness in his mouth, but this was shaded and half hidden by a full mustache that made much forgivable to beauty-loving eyes.

It was generally conceded that Mrs. Oakley was a hostess whose guests had no awkward half-hour before dinner. No praise could be higher than this, and to-night she had no need to exert herself to main-tain this reputation. Her brother-in-law was the life of the assembly; he had wit and daring, and about him there was just that hint of charming danger that made him irresistible to women. The guests heard the din-ner announced with surprise,—an unusual thing, except in this house.

Both Maurice Oakley and his wife looked fondly at the artist as he went in with Claire Lessing. He was talking animatedly to the girl, having changed the general trend of the conversation to a manner and tone directed more particularly to her. While she listened to him, her face glowed and her eyes shone with a light that every man could not bring into them.

As Maurice and his wife followed him with their gaze, the same thought was in their minds, and it had not just come to them, Why could not Francis marry Claire Lessing and settle in America, instead of going back ever and again to that life in the Latin Quarter? They did not believe that it was a bad life or a dissipated one, but from the little that they had seen of it when they were in Paris, it was at least a bit too free and unconventional for their traditions. There were, too, temptations which must assail any man of Francis's looks and talents. They had perfect faith in the strength of his manhood, of course; but could they have had their way, it would have been their will to hedge him about so that no breath of evil invitation could have come nigh to him.

But this younger brother, this half ward of theirs, was an unruly member. He talked and laughed, rode and walked, with Claire Lessing with the same free abandon, the same show of uninterested good comradeship, that he had used towards her when they were boy and girl together. There was not a shade more of warmth or self-consciousness in his manner towards her than there had been fifteen years before. In fact, there was less, for there had been a time, when he was six and Claire three, that Francis, with a boldness that the lover of maturer years tries vainly to attain, had announced to Claire that he was going to marry her. But he had never renewed this declaration when it came time that it would carry weight with it.

They made a fine picture as they sat together to-night. One seeing them could hardly help thinking on the instant that they were made for each other. Something in the woman's face, in her expression perhaps, supplied a palpable lack in the man. The strength of her mouth and chin helped the weakness of his. She was the sort of woman who, if ever he came to a great moral crisis in his life, would be able to save him if she were near. And yet he was going away from her, giving up the pearl that he had only to put out his hand to take.

Some of these thoughts were in the minds of the brother and sister now.

"Five years does seem a long while," Francis was saying, "but if a man accomplishes anything, after all, it seems only a short time to look back upon."

"All time is short to look back upon. It is the looking forward to it that counts. It doesn't, though, with a man, I suppose. He's doing something all the while."

"Yes, a man is always doing something, even if only waiting; but waiting is such unheroic business."

"That is the part that usually falls to a woman's lot. I have no doubt that some dark-eyed mademoiselle is waiting for you now."

Francis laughed and flushed hotly. Claire noted the flush and wondered at it. Had she indeed hit upon the real point? Was that the reason that he was so anxious to get back to Paris? The thought struck a chill through her gaiety. She did not want to be suspicious, but what was the cause of that tell-tale flush? He was not a man easily disconcerted; then why so to-night? But her companion talked on with such innocent composure that she believed herself mistaken as to the reason for his momentary confusion.

Someone cried gayly across the table to her: "Oh, Miss Claire, you will not dare to talk with such little awe to our friend when he comes back with his ribbons and his medals. Why, we shall all have to bow to you, Frank!"

"You're wronging me, Esterton," said Francis. "No foreign decoration could ever be to me as much as the flower of approval from the fair women of my own State."

"Hear!" cried the ladies.

"Trust artists and poets to pay pretty compliments, and this wily friend of mine pays his at my expense."

"A good bit of generalship, that, Frank," an old military man broke in. "Esterton opened the breach and you at once galloped in. That's the highest art of war."

Claire was looking at her companion. Had he meant the approval of the women, or was it one woman that he cared for? Had the speech had a hidden meaning for her? She could never tell. She could not understand this man who had been so much to her for so long, and yet did not seem to know it; who was full of romance and fire and passion, and yet looked at her beauty with the eyes of a mere comrade. She sighed as she rose with the rest of the women to leave the table.

The men lingered over their cigars. The wine was old and the stories new. What more could they ask? There was a strong glow in Francis Oakley's face, and his laugh was frequent and ringing. Some discussion came up which sent him running up to his room for a bit of evidence. When he came down it was not to come directly to the dining-room. He paused in the hall and despatched a servant to bring his brother to him.

Maurice found him standing weakly against the railing of the stairs. Something in his air impressed his brother strangely.

"What is it, Francis?" he questioned, hurrying to him.

"I have just discovered a considerable loss," was the reply in a grieved voice.

"If it is no worse than loss, I am glad; but what is it?"

"Every cent of money that I had to secure my letter of credit is gone from my bureau."

"What? When did it disappear?"

"I went to my bureau to-night for something and found the money gone; then I remembered that when I opened it two days ago I must have left the key in the lock, as I found it to-night."

"It's a bad business, but don't let's talk of it now. Come, let's go back to our guests. Don't look so cut up about it, Frank, old man. It isn't as bad as it might be, and you mustn't show a gloomy face to-night."

The younger man pulled himself together, and re-entered the room with his brother. In a few minutes his gaiety had apparently returned.

When they rejoined the ladies, even their quick eyes could detect in his demeanour no trace of the annoying thing that had occurred. His face did not change until, with a wealth of fervent congratulations, he had bade the last guest good-bye.

Then he turned to his brother. "When Leslie is in bed, come into the library. I will wait for you there," he said, and walked sadly away.

"Poor, foolish Frank," mused his brother, "as if the loss could matter to him."

III

THE THEFT

Frank was very pale when his brother finally came to him at the appointed place. He sat limply in his chair, his eyes fixed upon the floor.

"Come, brace up now, Frank, and tell me about it."

At the sound of his brother's voice he started and looked up as though he had been dreaming.

"I don't know what you'll think of me, Maurice," he said; "I have never before been guilty of such criminal carelessness."

"Don't stop to accuse yourself. Our only hope in this matter lies in prompt action. Where was the money?"

"In the oak cabinet and lying in the bureau drawer. Such a thing as a theft seemed so foreign to this place that I was never very particular about the box. But I did not know until I went to it to-night that the last time I had opened it I had forgotten to take the key out. It all flashed over me in a second when I saw it shining there. Even then I didn't suspect anything. You don't know how I felt to open that cabinet and find all my money gone. It's awful."

"Don't worry. How much was there in all?"

"Nine hundred and eighty-six dollars, most of which, I am ashamed to say, I had accepted from you."

"You have no right to talk that way, Frank; you know I do not begrudge a cent you want. I have never felt that my father did quite right in leaving me the bulk of the fortune; but we won't discuss that now. What I want you to understand, though, is that the money is yours as well as mine, and you are always welcome to it."

The artist shook his head. "No, Maurice," he said, "I can accept no more from you. I have already used up all my own money and too much of yours in this hopeless fight. I don't suppose I was ever cut out for an artist, or I'd have done something really notable in this time, and would not be a burden upon those who care for me. No, I'll give up going to Paris and find some work to do."

"Frank, Frank, be silent. This is nonsense. Give up your art? You shall not do it. You shall go to Paris as usual. Leslie and I have perfect faith in you. You shall not give up on account of this misfortune. What are the few paltry dollars to me or to you?"

"Nothing, nothing, I know. It isn't the money, it's the principle of the thing."

"Principle be hanged! You go back to Paris to-morrow, just as you had planned. I do not ask it, I command it."

The younger man looked up quickly.

"Pardon me, Frank, for using those words and at such a time. You know how near my heart your success lies, and to hear you talk of giving it all up makes me forget myself. Forgive me, but you'll go back, won't you?"

"You are too good, Maurice," said Frank impulsively, "and I will go back, and I'll try to redeem myself."

"There is no redeeming of yourself to do, my dear boy; all you have to do is to mature yourself. We'll have a detective down and see what we can do in this matter."

Frank gave a scarcely perceptible start.

"I do so hate such things," he said; "and, anyway, what's the use? They'll never find out where the stuff went to."

"Oh, you need not be troubled in this matter. I know that such things must jar on your delicate nature. But I am a plain hard-headed business man, and I can attend to it without distaste."

"But I hate to shove everything unpleasant off on you. It's what I've been doing all my life."

"Never mind that. Now tell me, who was the last person you remember in your room?"

"Oh, Esterton was up there awhile before dinner. But he was not alone two minutes."

"Why, he would be out of the question anyway. Who else?"

"Hamilton was up yesterday."

"Alone?"

"Yes, for a while. His boy, Joe, shaved me, and Jack was up for a while brushing my clothes."

"Then it lies between Jack and Joe?"

Frank hesitated.

"Neither one was left alone, though."

"Then only Hamilton and Esterton have been alone for any time in your room since you left the key in your cabinet?"

"Those are the only ones of whom I know anything. What others went in during the day, of course, I know nothing about. It couldn't have been either Esterton or Hamilton."

"Not Esterton, no."

"And Hamilton is beyond suspicion."

"No servant is beyond suspicion."

"I would trust Hamilton anywhere," said Frank stoutly, "and with anything."

"That's noble of you, Frank, and I would have done the same, but we must remember that we are not in the old days now. The negroes are becoming less faithful and less contented, and more's the pity, and a deal more ambitious, although I have never had any unfaithfulness on the part of Hamilton to complain of before."

"Then do not condemn him now."

"I shall not condemn any one until I have proof positive of his guilt or such clear circumstantial evidence that my reason is satisfied."

"I do not believe that you will ever have that against old Hamilton."

"This spirit of trust does you credit, Frank, and I very much hope that you may be right. But as soon as a negro like Hamilton learns the value of money and begins to earn it, at the same time he begins to covet some easy and rapid way of securing it. The old negro knew nothing of the value of money. When he stole, he stole hams and bacon and chickens. These were his immediate necessities and the things he valued. The present laughs at this tendency without knowing the cause. The present negro resents the laugh, and he has learned to value other things than those which satisfy his belly."

Frank looked bored.

"But pardon me for boring you. I know you want to go to bed. Go and leave everything to me."

The young man reluctantly withdrew, and Maurice went to the telephone and rung up the police station.

As Maurice had said, he was a plain, hard-headed business man, and it took very few words for him to put the Chief of Police in possession of the principal facts of the case. A detective was detailed to take charge of the case, and was started immediately, so that he might be upon the ground as soon after the commission of the crime as possible.

When he came he insisted that if he was to do anything he must question the robbed man and search his room at once. Oakley protested, but the detective was adamant. Even now the presence in the room of a man uninitiated into the mysteries of criminal methods might be destroying the last vestige of a really important clue. The master of the house had no alternative save to yield. Together they went to the artist's room. A light shone out through the crack under the door.

"I am sorry to disturb you again, Frank, but may we come in?"

"Who is with you?"

"The detective."

"I did not know he was to come to-night."

"The chief thought it better."

"All right in a moment."

There was a sound of moving around, and in a short time the young fellow, partly undressed, opened the door.

To the detective's questions he answered in substance what he had told before. He also brought out the cabinet. It was a strong oak box, uncarven, but bound at the edges with brass. The key was still in the lock, where Frank had left it on discovering his loss. They raised the lid. The cabinet contained two compartments, one for letters and a smaller one for jewels and trinkets.

"When you opened this cabinet, your money was gone?"

"Yes."

"Were any of your papers touched?"

"No."

"How about your jewels?"

"I have but few and they were elsewhere."

The detective examined the room carefully, its approaches, and the hall-ways without. He paused knowingly at a window that overlooked the flat top of a porch.

"Do you ever leave this window open?"

"It is almost always so."

"Is this porch on the front of the house?"

"No, on the side."

"What else is out that way?"

Frank and Maurice looked at each other. The younger man hesitated and put his hand to his head. Maurice answered grimly, "My butler's cottage is on that side and a little way back."

"Uh huh! and your butler is, I believe, the Hamilton whom the young gentleman mentioned some time ago."

"Yes."

Frank's face was really very white now. The detective nodded again.

"I think I have a clue," he said simply. "I will be here again to-morrow morning."

"But I shall be gone," said Frank.

"You will hardly be needed, anyway."

The artist gave a sigh of relief. He hated to be involved in unpleasant things. He went as far as the outer door with his brother and the detective. As he bade the officer good-night and hurried up the hall, Frank put his hand to his head again with a convulsive gesture, as if struck by a sudden pain.

"Come, come, Frank, you must take a drink now and go to bed," said Oakley.

"I am completely unnerved."

"I know it, and I am no less shocked than you. But we've got to face it like men."

They passed into the dining-room, where Maurice poured out some brandy for his brother and himself. "Who would have thought it?" he asked, as he tossed his own down.

"Not I. I had hoped against hope up until the last that it would turn out to be a mistake."

"Nothing angers me so much as being deceived by the man I have helped and trusted. I should feel the sting of all this much less if the thief had come from the outside, broken in, and robbed me, but this, after all these years, is too low."

"Don't be hard on a man, Maurice; one never knows what prompts him to a deed. And this evidence is all circumstantial."

"It is plain enough for me. You are entirely too kind-hearted, Frank. But I see that this thing has worn you out. You must not stand here talking. Go to bed, for you must be fresh for to-morrow morning's journey to New York."

Frank Oakley turned away towards his room. His face was haggard, and he staggered as he walked. His brother looked after him with a pitying and affectionate gaze.

"Poor fellow," he said, "he is so delicately constructed that he cannot stand such shocks as these;" and then he added: "To think of that black hound's treachery! I'll give him all that the law sets down for him."

He found Mrs. Oakley asleep when he reached the room, but he awakened her to tell her the story. She was horror-struck. It was hard to have to believe this awful thing of an old servant, but she agreed with him that Hamilton must be made an example of when the time came. Before that, however, he must not know that he was suspected.

They fell asleep, he with thoughts of anger and revenge, and she grieved and disappointed.

IV

FROM A CLEAR SKY

The inmates of the Oakley house had not been long in their beds before Hamilton was out of his and rousing his own little household.

"You, Joe," he called to his son, "git up f'om daih an' come right hyeah. You got to he'p me befo' you go to any shop dis mo'nin'. You, Kitty, stir yo' stumps, miss. I know yo' ma's a-dressin' now. Ef she ain't, I bet I'll be aftah huh in a minute, too. You all layin' 'roun', snoozin' w'en you all des' pint'ly know dis is de mo'nin' Mistah Frank go 'way f'om hyeah."

It was a cool Autumn morning, fresh and dew-washed. The sun was just rising, and a cool clear breeze was blowing across the land. The blue smoke from the "house," where the fire was already going, whirled fantastically over the roofs like a belated ghost. It was just the morning to doze in comfort, and so thought all of Berry's household except himself. Loud was the complaining as they threw themselves out of bed. They maintained that it was an altogether unearthly hour to get up. Even Mrs. Hamilton added her protest, until she suddenly remembered what morning it was, when she hurried into her clothes and set about getting the family's breakfast.

The good-humour of all of them returned when they were seated about their table with some of the good things of the night before set out, and the talk ran cheerily around.

"I do declaih," said Hamilton, "you all's as bad as dem white people was las' night. De way dey waded into dat food was a caution." He chuckled with delight at the recollection.

"I reckon dat's what dey come fu'. I wasn't payin' so much 'tention to what dey eat as to de way dem women was dressed. Why, Mis' Jedge Hill was des' mo'n go'geous."

"Oh, yes, ma, an' Miss Lessing wasn't no ways behin' her," put in Kitty.

Joe did not condescend to join in the conversation, but contented himself with devouring the good things and aping the manners of the young men whom he knew had been among last night's guests.

"Well, I got to be goin'," said Berry, rising. "There'll be early break-fas' at de 'house' dis mo'nin', so's Mistah Frank kin ketch de fus' train."

He went out cheerily to his work. No shadow of impending disaster depressed his spirits. No cloud obscured his sky. He was a simple, easy man, and he saw nothing in the manner of the people whom he served that morning at breakfast save a natural grief at parting from each other. He did not even take the trouble to inquire who the strange white man was who hung about the place.

When it came time for the young man to leave, with the privilege of an old servitor Berry went up to him to bid him good-bye. He held out his hand to him, and with a glance at his brother, Frank took it and shook it cordially. "Good-bye, Berry," he said. Maurice could hardly restrain his anger at the sight, but his wife was moved to tears at her brother-in-law's generosity.

The last sight they saw as the carriage rolled away towards the station was Berry standing upon the steps waving a hearty farewell and god-speed.

"How could you do it, Frank?" gasped his brother, as soon as they had driven well out of hearing.

"Hush, Maurice," said Mrs. Oakley gently; "I think it was very noble of him."

"Oh, I felt sorry for the poor fellow," was Frank's reply. "Promise me you won't be too hard on him, Maurice. Give him a little scare and let him go. He's possibly buried the money, anyhow."

"I shall deal with him as he deserves."

The young man sighed and was silent the rest of the way.

"Whether I fail or succeed, you will always think well of me, Maurice?" he said in parting; "and if I don't come up to your expectations, well—forgive me—that's all."

His brother wrung his hand. "You will always come up to my expectations, Frank," he said. "Won't he, Leslie?"

"He will always be our Frank, our good, generous-hearted, noble boy. God bless him!"

The young fellow bade them a hearty good-bye, and they, knowing what his feelings must be, spared him the prolonging of the strain. They waited in the carriage, and he waved to them as the train rolled out of the station.

"He seems to be sad at going," said Mrs. Oakley.

"Poor fellow, the affair of last night has broken him up considerably, but I'll make Berry pay for every pang of anxiety that my brother has suffered."

"Don't be revengeful, Maurice; you know what brother Frank asked of you."

"He is gone and will never know what happens, so I may be as revengeful as I wish."

The detective was waiting on the lawn when Maurice Oakley returned. They went immediately to the library, Oakley walking with the firm, hard tread of a man who is both exasperated and determined, and the officer gliding along with the cat-like step which is one of the attributes of his profession.

"Well?" was the impatient man's question as soon as the door closed upon them.

"I have some more information that may or may not be of importance."

"Out with it; maybe I can tell."

"First, let me ask if you had any reason to believe that your butler had any resources of his own, say to the amount of three or four hundred dollars?"

"Certainly not. I pay him thirty dollars a month, and his wife fifteen dollars, and with keeping up his lodges and the way he dresses that girl, he can't save very much."

"You know that he has money in the bank?"

"No."

"Well, he has. Over eight hundred dollars."

"What? Berry? It must be the pickings of years."

"And yesterday it was increased by five hundred more."

"The scoundrel!"

"How was your brother's money, in bills?"

"It was in large bills and gold, with some silver."

"Berry's money was almost all in bills of a small denomination and silver."

"A poor trick; it could easily have been changed."

"Not such a sum without exciting comment."

"He may have gone to several places."

"But he had only a day to do it in."

"Then some one must have been his accomplice."

"That remains to be proven."

"Nothing remains to be proven. Why, it's as clear as day that the money he has is the result of a long series of peculations, and that this last is the result of his first large theft."

"That must be made clear to the law."

"It shall be."

"I should advise, though, no open proceedings against this servant until further evidence to establish his guilt is found."

"If the evidence satisfies me, it must be sufficient to satisfy any ordinary jury. I demand his immediate arrest."

"As you will, sir. Will you have him called here and question him, or will you let me question him at once?"

"Yes."

Oakley struck the bell, and Berry himself answered it.

"You're just the man we want," said Oakley, shortly.

Berry looked astonished.

"Shall I question him," asked the officer, "or will you?"

"I will. Berry, you deposited five hundred dollars at the bank yesterday?"

"Well, suh, Mistah Oakley," was the grinning reply, "ef you ain't de beatenes' man to fin' out things I evah seen."

The employer half rose from his chair. His face was livid with anger. But at a sign from the detective he strove to calm himself.

"You had better let me talk to Berry, Mr. Oakley," said the officer.

Oakley nodded. Berry was looking distressed and excited. He seemed not to understand it at all.

"Berry," the officer pursued, "you admit having deposited five hundred dollars in the bank yesterday?"

"Sut'ny. Dey ain't no reason why I shouldn't admit it, 'ceptin' erroun' ermong dese jealous niggahs."

"Uh huh! well, now, where did you get this money?"

"Why, I wo'ked fu' it, o' co'se, whaih you s'pose I got it? 'Tain't drappin' off trees, I reckon, not roun' dis pa't of de country."

"You worked for it? You must have done a pretty big job to have got so much money all in a lump?"

"But I didn't git it in a lump. Why, man, I've been savin' dat money fu mo'n fo' yeahs."

"More than four years? Why didn't you put it in the bank as you got it?"

"Why mos'ly it was too small, an' so I des' kep' it in a ol' sock. I tol' Fannie dat some day ef de bank didn't bus' wid all de res' I had, I'd put it in too. She was allus sayin' it was too much to have layin' 'roun' de house. But I des' tol' huh dat no robber wasn't goin' to bothah de po' niggah down in de ya'd wid de rich white man up at de house. But fin'lly I listened to huh an' sposited it yistiddy."

"You're a liar! you're a liar, you black thief!" Oakley broke in impetuously. "You have learned your lesson well, but you can't cheat me. I know where that money came from."

"Calm yourself, Mr. Oakley, calm yourself."

"I will not calm myself. Take him away. He shall not stand here and lie to me."

Berry had suddenly turned ashen.

"You say you know whaih dat money come f'om? Whaih?"

"You stole it, you thief, from my brother Frank's room."

"Stole it! My Gawd, Mistah Oakley, you believed a thing lak dat aftah all de yeahs I been wid you?"

"You've been stealing all along."

"Why, what shell I do?" said the servant helplessly. "I tell you, Mistah Oakley, ask Fannie. She'll know how long I been a-savin' dis money."

"I'll ask no one."

"I think it would be better to call his wife, Oakley."

"Well, call her, but let this matter be done with soon."

Fannie was summoned, and when the matter was explained to her, first gave evidences of giving way to grief, but when the detective began to question her, she calmed herself and answered directly just as her husband had.

"Well posted," sneered Oakley. "Arrest that man."

Berry had begun to look more hopeful during Fannie's recital, but now the ashen look came back into his face. At the word "arrest" his wife collapsed utterly, and sobbed on her husband's shoulder.

"Send the woman away."

"I won't go," cried Fannie stoutly; "I'll stay right hyeah by my husband. You sha'n't drive me away f'om him."

Berry turned to his employer. "You b'lieve dat I stole f'om dis house aftah all de yeahs I've been in it, aftah de caih I took of yo' money an' yo' valybles, aftah de way I've put you to bed f'om many a dinnah, an' you woke up to fin' all yo' money safe? Now, can you b'lieve dis?"

His voice broke, and he ended with a cry.

"Yes, I believe it, you thief, yes. Take him away."

Berry's eyes were bloodshot as he replied, "Den, damn you! damn you! ef dat's all dese yeahs counted fu', I wish I had a-stoled it."

Oakley made a step forward, and his man did likewise, but the officer stepped between them.

"Take that damned hound away, or, by God! I'll do him violence!"

The two men stood fiercely facing each other, then the handcuffs were snapped on the servant's wrist.

"No, no," shrieked Fannie, "you mustn't, you mustn't. Oh, my Gawd! he ain't no thief. I'll go to Mis' Oakley. She nevah will believe it." She sped from the room.

The commotion had called a crowd of curious servants into the hall. Fannie hardly saw them as she dashed among them, crying for her mistress. In a moment she returned, dragging Mrs. Oakley by the hand.

"Tell 'em, oh, tell 'em, Miss Leslie, dat you don't believe it. Don't let 'em 'rest Berry."

"Why, Fannie, I can't do anything. It all seems perfectly plain, and Mr. Oakley knows better than any of us, you know."

Fannie, her last hope gone, flung herself on the floor, crying, "O Gawd! O Gawd! he's gone fu' sho'!"

Her husband bent over her, the tears dropping from his eyes. "Nevah min', Fannie," he said, "nevah min'. Hit's boun' to come out all right."

She raised her head, and seizing his manacled hands pressed them to her breast, wailing in a low monotone, "Gone! gone!"

They disengaged her hands, and led Berry away.

"Take her out," said Oakley sternly to the servants; and they lifted her up and carried her away in a sort of dumb stupor that was half a swoon.

They took her to her little cottage, and laid her down until she could come to herself and the full horror of her situation burst upon her.

V

THE JUSTICE OF MEN

The arrest of Berry Hamilton on the charge preferred by his employer was the cause of unusual commotion in the town. Both the accuser and the accused were well known to the citizens, white and black,— Maurice Oakley as a solid man of business, and Berry as an honest, sensible negro, and the pink of good servants. The evening papers had a full story of the crime, which closed by saying that the prisoner had amassed a considerable sum of money, it was very likely from a long series of smaller peculations.

It seems a strange irony upon the force of right living, that this man, who had never been arrested before, who had never even been sus- pected of wrong-doing, should find so few who even at the first telling doubted the story of his guilt. Many people began to remember things that had looked particularly suspicious in his dealings. Some others said, "I didn't think it of him." There were only a few who dared to say, "I don't believe it of him."

The first act of his lodge, "The Tribe of Benjamin," whose treasurer he was, was to have his accounts audited, when they should have been visiting him with comfort, and they seemed personally grieved when his books were found to be straight. The A. M. E. church, of which he had been an honest and active member, hastened to disavow sympathy with him, and to purge itself of contamination by turning him out. His friends were afraid to visit him and were silent when his enemies gloated. On every side one might have asked, Where is charity? and gone away empty.

In the black people of the town the strong influence of slavery was still operative, and with one accord they turned away from one of their own kind upon whom had been set the ban of the white people's displeasure. If they had sympathy, they dared not show it. Their own interests, the safety of their own positions and firesides, demanded that they stand aloof from the criminal. Not then, not now, nor has it ever been true, although it has been claimed, that negroes either harbour or sympathise with the criminal of their kind. They did not dare to do it before the sixties. They do not dare to do it now. They have brought down as a heritage from the days of their bondage both fear and disloyalty. So Berry was unbefriended while the storm raged around him. The cell where they had placed him was kind to him, and he could not hear the envious and sneering comments that went on about him. This was kind, for the tongues of his enemies were not.

"Tell me, tell me," said one, "you needn't tell me dat a bird kin fly so high dat he don' have to come down some time. An' w'en he do light, honey, my Lawd, how he flop!"

"Mistah Rich Niggah," said another. "He wanted to dress his wife an' chillen lak white folks, did he? Well, he foun' out, he foun' out. By de time de jedge git thoo wid him he won't be hol'in' his haid so high."

"W'y, dat gal o' his'n," broke in old Isaac Brown indignantly, "w'y, she wouldn' speak to my gal, Minty, when she met huh on de street. I reckon she come down off'n huh high hoss now."

The fact of the matter was that Minty Brown was no better than she should have been, and did not deserve to be spoken to. But none of this was taken into account either by the speaker or the hearers. The man was down, it was time to strike.

The women too joined their shrill voices to the general cry, and were loud in their abuse of the Hamiltons and in disparagement of their high-toned airs.

"I knowed it, I knowed it," mumbled one old crone, rolling her bleared and jealous eyes with glee. "W'enevah you see niggahs gittin' so high dat dey own folks ain' good enough fu' 'em, look out."

"W'y, la, Aunt Chloe I knowed it too. Dem people got so owdacious proud dat dey wouldn't walk up to de collection table no mo' at chu'ch, but allus set an' waited twell de basket was passed erroun'."

"Hit's de livin' trufe, an' I's been seein' it all 'long, I ain't said nuffin', but I knowed what 'uz gwine to happen. Ol' Chloe ain't lived all dese yeahs fu' nuffin', an' ef she got de gif' o' secon' sight, 'tain't fu' huh to say."

The women suddenly became interested in this half assertion, and the old hag, seeing that she had made the desired impression, lapsed into silence.

The whites were not neglecting to review and comment on the case also. It had been long since so great a bit of wrong-doing in a negro had given them cause for speculation and recrimination.

"I tell you," said old Horace Talbot, who was noted for his kindliness towards people of colour, "I tell you, I pity that darky more than I blame him. Now, here's my theory." They were in the bar of the Continental Hotel, and the old gentleman sipped his liquor as he talked. "It's just like this: The North thought they were doing a great thing when they come down here and freed all the slaves. They thought they were doing a great thing, and I'm not saying a word against them. I give them the credit for having the courage of their convictions. But I maintain that they were all wrong, now, in turning these people loose upon the country the way they did, without knowledge of what the first principle of liberty was. The natural result is that these people are irresponsible. They are unacquainted with the ways of our higher civilisation, and it'll take them a long time to learn. You know Rome wasn't built in a day. I know Berry, and I've known him for a long while, and a politer, likelier darky than him you would have to go far to find. And I haven't the least doubt in the world that he took that money absolutely without a thought of wrong, sir, absolutely. He saw it. He took it, and to his mental process, that was the end of it. To him there was no injury inflicted on any one, there was no crime committed. His elemental reasoning was simply this: This man has more money than I have; here is some of his surplus,—I'll just take it. Why, gentlemen, I maintain that that man took that money with the same innocence of purpose with which one of our servants a few years ago would have appropriated a stray ham."

"I disagree with you entirely, Mr. Talbot," broke in Mr. Beachfield Davis, who was a mighty hunter.—"Make mine the same, Jerry, only add a little syrup.—I disagree with you. It's simply total depravity, that's all. All niggers are alike, and there's no use trying to do anything with them. Look at that man, Dodson, of mine. I had one of the finest young hounds in the State. You know that white pup of mine, Mr. Talbot, that I bought from Hiram Gaskins? Mighty fine breed. Well, I was spendin' all my time and patience trainin' that dog in the daytime. At night I put him in that nigger's care to feed and bed. Well, do you know, I came home the other night and found that black rascal gone? I went out to see if the dog was properly bedded, and by Jove, the dog was gone too. Then I got suspicious. When a nigger and a dog go out together at night, one draws certain conclusions. I thought I had heard bayin' way out towards the edge of the town. So I stayed outside and watched. In about an hour here came Dodson with a possum hung over his shoulder and my dog trottin' at his heels. He'd been possum huntin' with my hound—with the finest hound in the State, sir. Now, I appeal to you all, gentlemen, if that ain't total depravity, what is total depravity?"

"Not total depravity, Beachfield, I maintain, but the very irresponsibility of which I have spoken. Why, gentlemen, I foresee the day when these people themselves shall come to us Southerners of their own accord and ask to be re-enslaved until such time as they shall be fit for freedom." Old Horace was nothing if not logical.

"Well, do you think there's any doubt of the darky's guilt?" asked Colonel Saunders hesitatingly. He was the only man who had ever thought of such a possibility. They turned on him as if he had been some strange, unnatural animal.

"Any doubt!" cried Old Horace.

"Any doubt!" exclaimed Mr. Davis.

"Any doubt?" almost shrieked the rest. "Why, there can be no doubt. Why, Colonel, what are you thinking of? Tell us who has got the money if he hasn't? Tell us where on earth the nigger got the money he's been putting in the bank? Doubt? Why, there isn't the least doubt about it."

"Certainly, certainly," said the Colonel, "but I thought, of course, he might have saved it. There are several of those people, you know, who do a little business and have bank accounts."

"Yes, but they are in some sort of business. This man makes only thirty dollars a month. Don't you see?"

The Colonel saw, or said he did. And he did not answer what he might have answered, that Berry had no rent and no board to pay. His clothes came from his master, and Kitty and Fannie looked to their mistress for the larger number of their supplies. He did not call to their minds that Fannie herself made fifteen dollars a month, and that for two years Joe had been supporting himself. These things did not come up, and as far as the opinion of the gentlemen assembled in the Continental bar went, Berry was already proven guilty.

As for the prisoner himself, after the first day when he had pleaded "Not guilty" and been bound over to the Grand Jury, he had fallen into a sort of dazed calm that was like the stupor produced by a drug. He took little heed of what went on around him. The shock had been too sudden for him, and it was as if his reason had been for the time unseated. That it was not permanently overthrown was evidenced by his waking to the most acute pain and grief whenever Fannie came to him. Then he would toss and moan and give vent to his sorrow in passionate complaints.

"I didn't tech his money, Fannie, you know I didn't. I wo'ked fu' every cent of dat money, an' I saved it myself. Oh, I'll nevah be able to git a job ag'in. Me in de lock-up—me, aftah all dese yeahs!"

Beyond this, apparently, his mind could not go. That his detention was anything more than temporary never seemed to enter his mind. That he would be convicted and sentenced was as far from possibility as the skies from the earth. If he saw visions of a long sojourn in prison, it was only as a nightmare half consciously experienced and which with the struggle must give way before the waking.

Fannie was utterly hopeless. She had laid down whatever pride had been hers and gone to plead with Maurice Oakley for her husband's freedom, and she had seen his hard, set face. She had gone upon her knees before his wife to cite Berry's long fidelity.

"Oh, Mis' Oakley," she cried, "ef he did steal de money, we've got enough saved to mek it good. Let him go! let him go!"

"Then you admit that he did steal?" Mrs. Oakley had taken her up sharply.

"Oh, I didn't say dat; I didn't mean dat."

"That will do, Fannie. I understand perfectly. You should have confessed that long ago."

"But I ain't confessin'! I ain't! He didn't——"

"You may go."

The stricken woman reeled out of her mistress's presence, and Mrs.

Oakley told her husband that night, with tears in her eyes, how disappointed she was with Fannie,—that the woman had known it all along, and had only just confessed. It was just one more link in the chain that was surely and not too slowly forging itself about Berry Hamilton.

Of all the family Joe was the only one who burned with a fierce indignation. He knew that his father was innocent, and his very helplessness made a fever in his soul. Dandy as he was, he was loyal, and when he saw his mother's tears and his sister's shame, something rose within him that had it been given play might have made a man of him, but, being crushed, died and rotted, and in the compost it made all the evil of his nature flourished. The looks and gibes of his fellow-employees at the barber-shop forced him to leave his work there. Kit, bowed with shame and grief, dared not appear upon the streets, where the girls who had envied her now hooted at her. So the little family was shut in upon itself away from fellowship and sympathy.

Joe went seldom to see his father. He was not heartless; but the citadel of his long desired and much vaunted manhood trembled before the sight of his father's abject misery. The lines came round his lips, and lines too must have come round his heart. Poor fellow, he was too young for this forcing process, and in the hothouse of pain he only grew an acrid, unripe cynic.

At the sitting of the Grand Jury Berry was indicted. His trial followed soon, and the town turned out to see it. Some came to laugh and scoff, but these, his enemies, were silenced by the spectacle of his grief. In vain the lawyer whom he had secured showed that the evidence against him proved nothing. In vain he produced proof of the slow accumulation of what the man had. In vain he pleaded the man's former good name. The judge and the jury saw otherwise. Berry was convicted. He was given ten years at hard labour.

He hardly looked as if he could live out one as he heard his sentence. But Nature was kind and relieved him of the strain. With a cry as if his heart were bursting, he started up and fell forward on his face unconscious. Some one, a bit more brutal than the rest, said, "It's five dollars' fine every time a nigger faints," but no one laughed. There was something too portentous, too tragic in the degradation of this man.

Maurice Oakley sat in the court-room, grim and relentless. As soon as the trial was over, he sent for Fannie, who still kept the cottage in the yard.

"You must go," he said. "You can't stay here any longer. I want none of your breed about me."

And Fannie bowed her head and went away from him in silence.

All the night long the women of the Hamilton household lay in bed and wept, clinging to each other in their grief. But Joe did not go to sleep. Against all their entreaties, he stayed up. He put out the light and sat staring into the gloom with hard, burning eyes.

VI
OUTCASTS

What particularly irritated Maurice Oakley was that Berry should to the very last keep up his claim of innocence. He reiterated it to the very moment that the train which was bearing him away pulled out of the station. There had seldom been seen such an example of criminal hardihood, and Oakley was hardened thereby to greater severity in dealing with the convict's wife. He began to urge her more strongly to move, and she, dispirited and humiliated by what had come to her, looked vainly about for the way to satisfy his demands. With her natural protector gone, she felt more weak and helpless than she had thought it possible to feel. It was hard enough to face the world. But to have to ask something of it was almost more than she could bear.

With the conviction of her husband the last five hundred dollars had been confiscated as belonging to the stolen money, but their former deposit remained untouched. With this she had the means at her disposal to tide over their present days of misfortune. It was not money she lacked, but confidence. Some inkling of the world's attitude towards her, guiltless though she was, reached her and made her afraid.

Her desperation, however, would not let her give way to fear, so she set forth to look for another house. Joe and Kit saw her go as if she were starting on an expedition into a strange country. In all their lives they had known no home save the little cottage in Oakley's yard. Here they had toddled as babies and played as children and been happy and care-free. There had been times when they had complained and wanted a home off by themselves, like others whom they knew. They had not failed, either, to draw unpleasant comparisons between their mode of life and the old plantation quarters system. But now all this was forgotten, and there were only grief and anxiety that they must leave the place and in such a way.

Fannie went out with little hope in her heart, and a short while after she was gone Joe decided to follow her and make an attempt to get work.

"I'll go an' see what I kin do, anyway, Kit. 'Tain't much use, I reckon, trying to get into a bahbah shop where they shave white folks, because all the white folks are down on us. I'll try one of the coloured shops."

This was something of a condescension for Berry Hamilton's son. He had never yet shaved a black chin or put shears to what he termed "naps," and he was proud of it. He thought, though, that after the training he had received from the superior "Tonsorial Parlours" where he had been employed, he had but to ask for a place and he would be gladly accepted.

It is strange how all the foolish little vaunting things that a man says in days of prosperity wax a giant crop around him in the days of his adversity. Berry Hamilton's son found this out almost as soon as he had applied at the first of the coloured shops for work.

"Oh, no, suh," said the proprietor, "I don't think we got anything fu' you to do; you're a white man's bahbah. We don't shave nothin' but niggahs hyeah, an' we shave 'em in de light o' day an' on de groun' flo'."

"W'y, I hyeah you say dat you couldn't git a paih of sheahs thoo a niggah's naps. You ain't been practisin' lately, has you?" came from the back of the shop, where a grinning negro was scraping a fellow's face.

"Oh, yes, you're done with burr-heads, are you? But burr-heads are good enough fu' you now."

"I think," the proprietor resumed, "that I hyeahed you say you wasn't fond o' grape pickin'. Well, Josy, my son, I wouldn't begin it now, 'specially as anothah kin' o' pickin' seems to run in yo' fambly."

Joe Hamilton never knew how he got out of that shop. He only knew that he found himself upon the street outside the door, tears of anger and shame in his eyes, and the laughs and taunts of his tormentors still ringing in his ears.

It was cruel, of course it was cruel. It was brutal. But only he knew how just it had been. In his moments of pride he had said all those things, half in fun and half in earnest, and he began to wonder how he could have been so many kinds of a fool for so long without realising it.

He had not the heart to seek another shop, for he knew that what would be known at one would be equally well known at all the rest. The hardest thing that he had to bear was the knowledge that he had shut himself out of all the chances that he now desired. He remembered with a pang the words of an old negro to whom he had once been impudent, "Nevah min', boy, nevah min', you's bo'n, but you ain't daid!"

It was too true. He had not known then what would come. He had never dreamed that anything so terrible could overtake him. Even in his straits, however, desperation gave him a certain pluck. He would try for something else for which his own tongue had not disqualified him. With Joe, to think was to do. He went on to the Continental Hotel, where there were almost always boys wanted to "run the bells." The clerk looked him over critically. He was a bright, spruce-looking young fellow, and the man liked his looks.

"Well, I guess we can take you on," he said. "What's your name?"

"Joe," was the laconic answer. He was afraid to say more.

"Well, Joe, you go over there and sit where you see those fellows in uniform, and wait until I call the head bellman."

Young Hamilton went over and sat down on a bench which ran along the hotel corridor and where the bellmen were wont to stay during the day awaiting their calls. A few of the blue-coated Mercuries were there. Upon Joe's advent they began to look askance at him and to talk among themselves. He felt his face burning as he thought of what they must be saying. Then he saw the head bellman talking to the clerk and looking in his direction. He saw him shake his head and walk away. He could have cursed him. The clerk called to him.

"I didn't know," he said,—"I didn't know that you were Berry Hamilton's boy. Now I've got nothing against you myself. I don't hold you responsible for what your father did, but I don't believe our boys would work with you. I can't take you on."

Joe turned away to meet the grinning or contemptuous glances of the bellmen on the seat. It would have been good to be able to hurl something among them. But he was helpless.

He hastened out of the hotel, feeling that every eye was upon him, every finger pointing at him, every tongue whispering, "There goes Joe Hamilton, whose father went to the penitentiary the other day."

What should he do? He could try no more. He was proscribed, and the letters of his ban were writ large throughout the town, where all who ran might read. For a while he wandered aimlessly about and then turned dejectedly homeward. His mother had not yet come.

"Did you get a job?" was Kit's first question.

"No," he answered bitterly, "no one wants me now."

"No one wants you? Why, Joe—they—they don't think hard of us, do they?"

"I don't know what they think of ma and you, but they think hard of me, all right."

"Oh, don't you worry; it'll be all right when it blows over."

"Yes, when it all blows over; but when'll that be?"

"Oh, after a while, when we can show 'em we're all right."

Some of the girl's cheery hopefulness had come back to her in the presence of her brother's dejection, as a woman always forgets her own sorrow when some one she loves is grieving. But she could not communicate any of her feeling to Joe, who had been and seen and felt, and now sat darkly waiting his mother's return. Some presentiment seemed to tell him that, armed as she was with money to pay for what she wanted and asking for nothing without price, she would yet have no better tale to tell than he.

None of these forebodings visited the mind of Kit, and as soon as her mother appeared on the threshold she ran to her, crying, "Oh, where are we going to live, ma?"

Fannie looked at her for a moment, and then answered with a burst of tears, "Gawd knows, child, Gawd knows."

The girl stepped back astonished.

"Why, why!" and then with a rush of tenderness she threw her arms about her mother's neck. "Oh, you're tired to death," she said; "that's what's the matter with you. Never mind about the house now. I've got some tea made for you, and you just take a cup."

Fannie sat down and tried to drink her tea, but she could not. It stuck in her throat, and the tears rolled down her face and fell into the shaking cup. Joe looked on silently. He had been out and he understood.

"I'll go out to-morrow and do some looking around for a house while you stay at home an' rest, ma."

Her mother looked up, the maternal instinct for the protection of her daughter at once aroused. "Oh, no, not you, Kitty," she said.

Then for the first time Joe spoke: "You'd just as well tell Kitty now, ma, for she's got to come across it anyhow."

"What you know about it? Whaih you been to?"

"I've been out huntin' work. I've been to Jones's bahbah shop an' to the Continental Hotel." His light-brown face turned brick red with anger and shame at the memory of it. "I don't think I'll try any more."

Kitty was gazing with wide and saddening eyes at her mother.

"Were they mean to you too, ma?" she asked breathlessly.

"Mean? Oh Kitty! Kitty! you don't know what it was like. It nigh killed me. Thaih was plenty of houses an' owned by people I've knowed fu' yeahs, but not one of 'em wanted to rent to me. Some of 'em made excuses 'bout one thing er t'other, but de res' come right straight out an' said dat we'd give a neighbourhood a bad name ef we moved into it. I've almos' tramped my laigs off. I've tried every decent place I could think of, but nobody wants us."

The girl was standing with her hands clenched nervously before her. It was almost more than she could understand.

"Why, we ain't done anything," she said. "Even if they don't know any better than to believe that pa was guilty, they know we ain't done anything."

"I'd like to cut the heart out of a few of 'em," said Joe in his throat.

"It ain't goin' to do no good to look at it that a-way, Joe," his mother replied. "I know hit's ha'd, but we got to do de bes' we kin."

"What are we goin' to do?" cried the boy fiercely. "They won't let us work. They won't let us live anywhaih. Do they want us to live on the levee an' steal, like some of 'em do?"

"What are we goin' to do?" echoed Kitty helplessly. "I'd go out ef I thought I could find anythin' to work at."

"Don't you go anywhaih, child. It 'ud only be worse. De niggah men dat ust to be bowin' an' scrapin' to me an' tekin' off dey hats to me laughed in my face. I met Minty—an' she slurred me right in de street. Dey'd do worse fu' you."

In the midst of the conversation a knock came at the door. It was a messenger from the "House," as they still called Oakley's home, and he wanted them to be out of the cottage by the next afternoon, as the new servants were coming and would want the rooms.

The message was so curt, so hard and decisive, that Fannie was startled out of her grief into immediate action.

"Well, we got to go," she said, rising wearily.

"But where are we goin'?" wailed Kitty in affright. "There's no place to go to. We haven't got a house. Where'll we go?"

"Out o' town someplace as fur away from this damned hole as we kin git." The boy spoke recklessly in his anger. He had never sworn before his mother before.

She looked at him in horror. "Joe, Joe," she said, "you're mekin' it wuss. You're mekin' it ha'dah fu' me to baih when you talk dat a-way. What you mean? Whaih you think Gawd is?"

Joe remained sullenly silent. His mother's faith was too stalwart for his comprehension. There was nothing like it in his own soul to interpret it.

"We'll git de secon'-han' dealah to tek ouah things to-morrer, an' then we'll go away some place, up No'th maybe."

"Let's go to New York," said Joe.

"New Yo'k?"

They had heard of New York as a place vague and far away, a city that, like Heaven, to them had existed by faith alone. All the days of their lives they had heard of it, and it seemed to them the centre of all the glory, all the wealth, and all the freedom of the world. New York. It had an alluring sound. Who would know them there? Who would look down upon them?

"It's a mighty long ways off fu' me to be sta'tin' at dis time o' life."

"We want to go a long ways off."

"I wonder what pa would think of it if he was here," put in Kitty.

"I guess he'd think we was doin' the best we could."

"Well, den, Joe," said his mother, her voice trembling with emotion at the daring step they were about to take, "you set down an' write a lettah to yo pa, an' tell him what we goin' to do, an' to-morrer— to-morrer—we'll sta't."

Something akin to joy came into the boy's heart as he sat down to write the letter. They had taunted him, had they? They had scoffed at him. But he was going where they might never go, and some day he would come back holding his head high and pay them sneer for sneer and jibe for jibe.

The same night the commission was given to the furniture dealer who would take charge of their things, and sell them when and for what he could.

From his window the next morning Maurice Oakley watched the wagon emptying the house. Then he saw Fannie come out and walk about her little garden, followed by her children. He saw her as she wiped her eyes and led the way to the side gate.

"Well, they're gone," he said to his wife. "I wonder where they're going to live?"

"Oh, some of their people will take them in," replied Mrs. Oakley languidly.

Despite the fact that his mother carried with her the rest of the money drawn from the bank, Joe had suddenly stepped into the place of the man of the family. He attended to all the details of their getting away with a promptness that made it seem untrue that he had never been more than thirty miles from his native town. He was eager and excited. As the train drew out of the station, he did not look back upon the place which he hated, but Fannie and her daughter let their eyes linger upon it until the last house, the last chimney, and the last spire faded from their sight, and their tears fell and mingled as they were whirled away toward the unknown.

VII

In New York

To the provincial coming to New York for the first time, ignorant and unknown, the city presents a notable mingling of the qualities of cheeriness and gloom. If he have any eye at all for the beautiful, he cannot help experiencing a thrill as he crosses the ferry over the river filled with plying craft and catches the first sight of the spires and buildings of New York. If he have the right stuff in him, a something will take possession of him that will grip him again every time he returns to the scene and will make him long and hunger for the place when he is away from it. Later, the lights in the busy streets will bewilder and entice him. He will feel shy and helpless amid the hurrying crowds. A new emotion will take his heart as the people hasten by him,—a feeling of loneliness, almost of grief, that with all of these souls about him he knows not one and not one of them cares for him. After a while he will find a place and give a sigh of relief as he settles away from the city's sights behind his cosey blinds. It is better here, and the city is cruel and cold and unfeeling. This he will feel, perhaps, for the first half-hour, and then he will be out in it all again. He will be glad to strike elbows with the bustling mob and be happy at their indifference to him, so that he may look at them and study them. After it is all over, after he has passed through the first pangs of strangeness and homesickness, yes, even after he has got beyond the stranger's enthusiasm for the metropolis, the real fever of love for the place will begin to take hold upon him. The subtle, insidious wine of New York will begin to intoxicate him. Then, if he be wise, he will go away, any place,—yes, he will even go over to Jersey. But if he be a fool, he will stay and stay on until the town becomes all in all to him; until the very streets are his chums and certain buildings and corners his best friends. Then he is hopeless, and to live elsewhere would be death. The Bowery will be his romance, Broadway his lyric, and the Park his pastoral, the river and the glory of it all his epic, and he will look down pityingly on all the rest of humanity.

It was the afternoon of a clear October day that the Hamiltons reached New York. Fannie had some misgivings about crossing the ferry, but once on the boat these gave way to speculations as to what they should find on the other side. With the eagerness of youth to take in new impressions, Joe and Kitty were more concerned with what they saw about them than with what their future would hold, though they might well have stopped to ask some such questions. In all the great city they knew absolutely no one, and had no idea which way to go to find a stopping-place.

They looked about them for some coloured face, and finally saw one among the porters who were handling the baggage. To Joe's inquiry he gave them an address, and also proffered his advice as to the best way to reach the place. He was exceedingly polite, and he looked hard at Kitty. They found the house to which they had been directed, and were a good deal surprised at its apparent grandeur. It was a four-storied brick dwelling on Twenty-seventh Street. As they looked from the outside, they were afraid that the price of staying in such a place would be too much for their pockets. Inside, the sight of the hard, gaudily upholstered instalment-plan furniture did not disillusion them, and they continued to fear that they could never stop at this fine place. But they found Mrs. Jones, the proprietress, both gracious and willing to come to terms with them.

As Mrs. Hamilton—she began to be Mrs. Hamilton now, to the exclusion of Fannie—would have described Mrs. Jones, she was a "big yellow woman." She had a broad good-natured face and a tendency to run to bust.

"Yes," she said, "I think I could arrange to take you. I could let you have two rooms, and you could use my kitchen until you decided whether you wanted to take a flat or not. I has the whole house myself, and I keeps roomers. But latah on I could fix things so's you could have the whole third floor ef you wanted to. Most o' my gent'men's railroad gent'men, they is. I guess it must 'a' been Mr. Thomas that sent you up here."

"He was a little bright man down at de deepo."

"Yes, that's him. That's Mr. Thomas. He's always lookin' out to send some one here, because he's been here three years hisself an' he kin recommend my house."

It was a relief to the Hamiltons to find Mrs. Jones so gracious and home-like. So the matter was settled, and they took up their abode with her and sent for their baggage.

With the first pause in the rush that they had experienced since starting away from home, Mrs. Hamilton began to have time for reflection, and their condition seemed to her much better as it was. Of course, it was hard to be away from home and among strangers, but the arrangement had this advantage,—that no one knew them or could taunt them with their past trouble. She was not sure that she was going to like New York. It had a great name and was really a great place, but the very bigness of it frightened her and made her feel alone, for she knew that there could not be so many people together without a deal of wickedness. She did not argue the complement of this, that the amount of good would also be increased, but this was because to her evil was the very present factor in her life.

Joe and Kit were differently affected by what they saw about them. The boy was wild with enthusiasm and with a desire to be a part of all that the metropolis meant. In the evening he saw the young fellows passing by dressed in their spruce clothes, and he wondered with a sort of envy where they could be going. Back home there had been no place much worth going to, except church and one or two people's houses. But these young fellows seemed to show by their manners that they were neither going to church nor a family visiting. In the moment that he recognised this, a revelation came to him,—the knowledge that his horizon had been very narrow, and he felt angry that it was so. Why should those fellows be different from him? Why should they walk the streets so knowingly, so independently, when he knew not whither to turn his steps? Well, he was in New York, and now he would learn. Some day some greenhorn from the South should stand at a window and look out envying him, as he passed, red-cravated, patent-leathered, intent on some goal. Was it not better, after all, that circumstances had forced them thither? Had it not been so, they might all have stayed home and stagnated. Well, thought he, it's an ill wind that blows nobody good, and somehow, with a guilty under-thought, he forgot to feel the natural pity for his father, toiling guiltless in the prison of his native State.

Whom the Gods wish to destroy they first make mad. The first sign of the demoralisation of the provincial who comes to New York is his pride at his insensibility to certain impressions which used to influence him at home. First, he begins to scoff, and there is no truth in his views nor depth in his laugh. But by and by, from mere pretending, it becomes real. He grows callous. After that he goes to the devil very cheerfully.

No such radical emotions, however, troubled Kit's mind. She too stood at the windows and looked down into the street. There was a sort of complacent calm in the manner in which she viewed the girls' hats and dresses. Many of them were really pretty, she told herself, but for the most part they were not better than what she had had down home. There was a sound quality in the girl's make-up that helped her to see through the glamour of mere place and recognise worth for itself. Or it may have been the critical faculty, which is prominent in most women, that kept her from thinking a five-cent cheese-cloth any better in New York than it was at home. She had a certain self-respect which made her value herself and her own traditions higher than her brother did his.

When later in the evening the porter who had been kind to them came in and was introduced as Mr. William Thomas, young as she was, she took his open admiration for her with more coolness than Joe exhibited when Thomas offered to show him something of the town some day or night.

Mr. Thomas was a loquacious little man with a confident air born of an intense admiration of himself. He was the idol of a number of servant-girls' hearts, and altogether a decidedly dashing back-area-way Don Juan.

"I tell you, Miss Kitty," he burst forth, a few minutes after being introduced, "they ain't no use talkin', N' Yawk'll give you a shakin' up 'at you won't soon forget. It's the only town on the face of the earth.

You kin bet your life they ain't no flies on N' Yawk. We git the best shows here, we git the best concerts—say, now, what's the use o' my callin' it all out?—we simply git the best of everything."

"Great place," said Joe wisely, in what he thought was going to be quite a man-of-the-world manner. But he burned with shame the next minute because his voice sounded so weak and youthful. Then too the oracle only said "Yes" to him, and went on expatiating to Kitty on the glories of the metropolis.

"D'jever see the statue o' Liberty? Great thing, the statue o' Liberty. I'll take you 'round some day. An' Cooney Island—oh, my, now that's the place; and talk about fun! That's the place for me."

"La, Thomas," Mrs. Jones put in, "how you do run on! Why, the strangers'll think they'll be talked to death before they have time to breathe."

"Oh, I guess the folks understan' me. I'm one o' them kin' o' men 'at believe in whooping things up right from the beginning. I'm never strange with anybody. I'm a N' Yawker, I tell you, from the word go. I say, Mis' Jones, let's have some beer, an' we'll have some music purty soon. There's a fellah in the house 'at plays 'Rag-time' out o' sight."

Mr. Thomas took the pail and went to the corner. As he left the room, Mrs. Jones slapped her knee and laughed until her bust shook like jelly.

"Mr. Thomas is a case, sho'," she said; "but he likes you all, an' I'm mighty glad of it, fu' he's mighty curious about the house when he don't like the roomers."

Joe felt distinctly flattered, for he found their new acquaintance charming. His mother was still a little doubtful, and Kitty was sure she found the young man "fresh."

He came in pretty soon with his beer, and a half-dozen crabs in a bag.

"Thought I'd bring home something to chew. I always like to eat something with my beer."

Mrs. Jones brought in the glasses, and the young man filled one and turned to Kitty.

"No, thanks," she said with a surprised look.

"What, don't you drink beer? Oh, come now, you'll get out o' that."

"Kitty don't drink no beer," broke in her mother with mild resentment. "I drinks it sometimes, but she don't. I reckon maybe de chillen better go to bed."

Joe felt as if the "chillen" had ruined all his hopes, but Kitty rose.

The ingratiating "N' Yawker" was aghast.

"Oh, let 'em stay," said Mrs. Jones heartily; "a little beer ain't goin' to hurt 'em. Why, sakes, I know my father gave me beer from the time I could drink it, and I knows I ain't none the worse fu' it."

"They'll git out o' that, all right, if they live in N' Yawk," said Mr. Thomas, as he poured out a glass and handed it to Joe. "You neither?"

"Oh, I drink it," said the boy with an air, but not looking at his mother.

"Joe," she cried to him, "you must ricollect you ain't at home. What 'ud yo' pa think?" Then she stopped suddenly, and Joe gulped his beer and Kitty went to the piano to relieve her embarrassment.

"Yes, that's it, Miss Kitty, sing us something," said the irrepressible Thomas, "an' after while we'll have that fellah down that plays 'Ragtime.' He out o' sight, I tell you."

With the pretty shyness of girlhood, Kitty sang one or two little songs in the simple manner she knew. Her voice was full and rich. It delighted Mr. Thomas.

"I say, that's singin' now, I tell you," he cried. "You ought to have some o' the new songs. D'jever hear 'Baby, you got to leave'? I tell you, that's a hot one. I'll bring you some of 'em. Why, you could git a job on the stage easy with that voice o' yourn. I got a frien' in one o' the comp'nies an' I'll speak to him about you."

"You ought to git Mr. Thomas to take you to the th'atre some night. He goes lots."

"Why, yes, what's the matter with to-morrer night? There's a good coon show in town. Out o' sight. Let's all go."

"I ain't nevah been to nothin' lak dat, an' I don't know," said Mrs. Hamilton.

"Aw, come, I'll git the tickets an' we'll all go. Great singin', you know. What d' you say?"

The mother hesitated, and Joe filled the breach.

"We'd all like to go," he said. "Ma, we'll go if you ain't too tired."

"Tired? Pshaw, you'll furgit all about your tiredness when Smithkins gits on the stage. Y' ought to hear him sing, 'I bin huntin' fu' wo'k'! You'd die laughing."

Mrs. Hamilton made no further demur, and the matter was closed.

Awhile later the "Rag-time" man came down and gave them a sample of what they were to hear the next night. Mr. Thomas and Mrs. Jones two-stepped, and they sent a boy after some more beer. Joe found it a very jolly evening, but Kit's and the mother's hearts were heavy as they went up to bed.

"Say," said Mr. Thomas when they had gone, "that little girl's a peach, you bet; a little green, I guess, but she'll ripen in the sun."

VIII
AN EVENING OUT

Fannie Hamilton, tired as she was, sat long into the night with her little family discussing New York,—its advantages and disadvantages, its beauty and its ugliness, its morality and immorality. She had somewhat receded from her first position, that it was better being here in the great strange city than being at home where the very streets shamed them. She had not liked the way that their fellow lodger looked at Kitty. It was bold, to say the least. She was not pleased, either, with their new acquaintance's familiarity. And yet, he had said no more than some stranger, if there could be such a stranger, would have said down home. There was a difference, however, which she recognised. Thomas was not the provincial who puts every one on a par with himself, nor was he the metropolitan who complacently patronises the whole world. He was trained out of the one and not up to the other. The intermediate only succeeded in being offensive. Mrs. Jones's assurance as to her guest's fine qualities did not do all that might have been expected to reassure Mrs. Hamilton in the face of the difficulties of the gentleman's manner.

She could not, however, lay her finger on any particular point that would give her the reason for rejecting his friendly advances. She got ready the next evening to go to the theatre with the rest. Mr. Thomas at once possessed himself of Kitty and walked on ahead, leaving Joe to accompany his mother and Mrs. Jones,—an arrangement, by the way, not altogether to that young gentleman's taste. A good many men bowed to Thomas in the street, and they turned to look enviously after him. At the door of the theatre they had to run the gantlet of a dozen pairs of eyes. Here, too, the party's guide seemed to be well known, for some one said, before they passed out of hearing, "I wonder who that little light girl is that Thomas is with to-night? He's a hot one for you."

Mrs. Hamilton had been in a theatre but once before in her life, and Joe and Kit but a few times oftener. On those occasions they had sat far up in the peanut gallery in the place reserved for people of colour. This was not a pleasant, cleanly, nor beautiful locality, and by contrast with it, even the garishness of the cheap New York theatre seemed fine and glorious.

They had good seats in the first balcony, and here their guide had shown his managerial ability again, for he had found it impossible, or said so, to get all the seats together, so that he and the girl were in the row in front and to one side of where the rest sat. Kitty did not like the arrangement, and innocently suggested that her brother take her seat while she went back to her mother. But her escort overruled her objections easily, and laughed at her so frankly that from very shame she could not urge them again, and they were soon forgotten in her wonder at the mystery and glamour that envelops the home of the drama. There was something weird to her in the alternate spaces of light and shade. Without any feeling of its ugliness, she looked at the curtain as at a door that should presently open between her and a house of wonders. She looked at it with the fascination that one always experiences for what either brings near or withholds the unknown.

As for Joe, he was not bothered by the mystery or the glamour of things. But he had suddenly raised himself in his own estimation. He had gazed steadily at a girl across the aisle until she had smiled in response. Of course, he went hot and cold by turns, and the sweat broke out on his brow, but instantly he began to swell. He had made a decided advance in knowledge, and he swelled with the consciousness that already he was coming to be a man of the world. He looked with a new feeling at the swaggering, sporty young negroes. His attitude towards them was not one of humble self-depreciation any more. Since last night he had grown, and felt that he might, that he would, be like them, and it put a sort of chuckling glee into his heart.

One might find it in him to feel sorry for this small-souled, warped being, for he was so evidently the jest of Fate, if it were not that he was so blissfully, so conceitedly, unconscious of his own nastiness. Down home he had shaved the wild young bucks of the town, and while doing it drunk in eagerly their unguarded narrations of their gay exploits. So he had started out with false ideals as to what was fine and manly. He was afflicted by a sort of moral and mental astigmatism that made him see everything wrong. As he sat there to-night, he gave to all he saw a wrong value and upon it based his ignorant desires.

When the men of the orchestra filed in and began tuning their instruments, it was the signal for an influx of loiterers from the door. There were a large number of coloured people in the audience, and because members of their own race were giving the performance, they seemed to take a proprietary interest in it all. They discussed its merits and demerits as they walked down the aisle in much the same tone that the owners would have used had they been wondering whether the entertainment was going to please the people or not.

Finally the music struck up one of the numerous negro marches. It was accompanied by the rhythmic patting of feet from all parts of the house. Then the curtain went up on a scene of beauty. It purported to be a grove to which a party of picnickers, the ladies and gentlemen of the chorus, had come for a holiday, and they were telling the audience all about it in crescendos. With the exception of one, who looked like a faded kid glove, the men discarded the grease paint, but the women under their make-ups ranged from pure white, pale yellow, and sickly greens to brick reds and slate grays. They were dressed in costumes that were not primarily intended for picnic going. But they could sing, and they did sing, with their voices, their bodies, their souls. They threw themselves into it because they enjoyed and felt what they were doing, and they gave almost a semblance of dignity to the tawdry music and inane words.

Kitty was enchanted. The airily dressed women seemed to her like creatures from fairy-land. It is strange how the glare of the footlights succeeds in deceiving so many people who are able to see through other delusions. The cheap dresses on the street had not fooled Kitty for an instant, but take the same cheese-cloth, put a little water starch into it, and put it on the stage, and she could see only chiffon.

She turned around and nodded delightedly at her brother, but he did not see her. He was lost, transfixed. His soul was floating on a sea of sense. He had eyes and ears and thoughts only for the stage. His nerves tingled and his hands twitched. Only to know one of those radiant creatures, to have her speak to him, smile at him! If ever a man was intoxicated, Joe was. Mrs. Hamilton was divided between shame at the clothes of some of the women and delight with the music. Her companion was busy pointing out who this and that actress was, and giving jelly-like appreciation to the doings on the stage.

Mr. Thomas was the only cool one in the party. He was quietly taking stock of his young companion,—of her innocence and charm. She was a pretty girl, little and dainty, but well developed for her age. Her hair was very black and wavy, and some strain of the South's chivalric blood, which is so curiously mingled with the African in the veins of most coloured people, had tinged her skin to an olive hue.

"Are you enjoying yourself?" he leaned over and whispered to her. His voice was very confidential and his lips near her ear, but she did not notice.

"Oh, yes," she answered, "this is grand. How I'd like to be an actress and be up there!"

"Maybe you will some day."

"Oh, no, I'm not smart enough."

"We'll see," he said wisely; "I know a thing or two."

Between the first and second acts a number of Thomas's friends strolled up to where he sat and began talking, and again Kitty's embarrassment took possession of her as they were introduced one by one. They treated her with a half-courteous familiarity that made her blush. Her mother was not pleased with the many acquaintances that her daughter was making, and would have interfered had not Mrs. Jones assured her that the men clustered about their host's seat were some of the "best people in town." Joe looked at them hungrily, but the man in front with his sister did not think it necessary to include the brother or the rest of the party in his miscellaneous introductions.

One brief bit of conversation which the mother overheard especially troubled her.

"Not going out for a minute or two?" asked one of the men, as he was turning away from Thomas.

"No, I don't think I'll go out to-night. You can have my share."

The fellow gave a hoarse laugh and replied, "Well, you're doing a great piece of work, Miss Hamilton, whenever you can keep old Bill from goin' out an' lushin' between acts. Say, you got a good thing; push it along."

The girl's mother half rose, but she resumed her seat, for the man was going away. Her mind was not quiet again, however, until the people were all in their seats and the curtain had gone up on the second act. At first she was surprised at the enthusiasm over just such dancing as she could see any day from the loafers on the street corners down home, and then, like a good, sensible, humble woman, she came around to the idea that it was she who had always been wrong in putting too low a value on really worthy things. So she laughed and applauded with the rest, all the while trying to quiet something that was tugging at her away down in her heart.

When the performance was over she forced her way to Kitty's side, where she remained in spite of all Thomas's palpable efforts to get her away. Finally he proposed that they all go to supper at one of the coloured cafés.

"You'll see a lot o' the show people," he said.

"No, I reckon we'd bettah go home," said Mrs. Hamilton decidedly. "De chillen ain't ust to stayin' up all hours o' nights, an' I ain't anxious fu' 'em to git ust to it."

She was conscious of a growing dislike for this man who treated her daughter with such a proprietary air. Joe winced again at "de chillen."

Thomas bit his lip, and mentally said things that are unfit for publication. Aloud he said, "Mebbe Miss Kitty 'ud like to go an' have a little lunch."

"Oh, no, thank you," said the girl; "I've had a nice time and I don't care for a thing to eat."

Joe told himself that Kitty was the biggest fool that it had ever been his lot to meet, and the disappointed suitor satisfied himself with the reflection that the girl was green yet, but would get bravely over that.

He attempted to hold her hand as they parted at the parlour door, but she drew her fingers out of his clasp and said, "Good-night; thank you," as if he had been one of her mother's old friends.

Joe lingered a little longer.

"Say, that was out o' sight," he said.

"Think so?" asked the other carelessly.

"I'd like to get out with you some time to see the town," the boy went on eagerly.

"All right, we'll go some time. So long."

"So long."

Some time. Was it true? Would he really take him out and let him meet stage people? Joe went to bed with his head in a whirl. He slept little that night for thinking of his heart's desire.

IX
HIS HEART'S DESIRE

Whatever else his visit to the theatre may have done for Joe, it inspired him with a desire to go to work and earn money of his own, to be independent both of parental help and control, and so be able to spend as he pleased. With this end in view he set out to hunt for work. It was a pleasant contrast to his last similar quest, and he felt it with joy. He was treated everywhere he went with courtesy, even when no situation was forthcoming. Finally he came upon a man who was willing to try him for an afternoon. From the moment the boy rightly considered himself engaged, for he was master of his trade. He began his work with heart elate. Now he had within his grasp the possibility of being all that he wanted to be. Now Thomas might take him out at any time and not be ashamed of him.

With Thomas, the fact that Joe was working put the boy in an entirely new light. He decided that now he might be worth cultivating. For a week or two he had ignored him, and, proceeding upon the principle that if you give corn to the old hen she will cluck to her chicks, had treated Mrs. Hamilton with marked deference and kindness. This had been without success, as both the girl and her mother held themselves politely aloof from him. He began to see that his hope of winning Kitty's affections lay, not in courting the older woman but in making a friend of the boy. So on a certain Saturday night when the

Banner Club was to give one of its smokers, he asked Joe to go with him. Joe was glad to, and they set out together. Arrived, Thomas left his companion for a few moments while he attended, as he said, to a little business. What he really did was to seek out the proprietor of the club and some of its hangers on.

"I say," he said, "I've got a friend with me to-night. He's got some dough on him. He's fresh and young and easy."

"Whew!" exclaimed the proprietor.

"Yes, he's a good thing, but push it along kin' o' light at first; he might get skittish."

"Thomas, let me fall on your bosom and weep," said a young man who, on account of his usual expression of innocent gloom, was called Sadness. "This is what I've been looking for for a month. My hat was getting decidedly shabby. Do you think he would stand for a touch on the first night of our acquaintance?"

"Don't you dare! Do you want to frighten him off? Make him believe that you've got coin to burn and that it's an honour to be with you."

"But, you know, he may expect a glimpse of the gold."

"A smart man don't need to show nothin'. All he's got to do is to act."

"Oh, I'll act; we'll all act."

"Be slow to take a drink from him."

"Thomas, my boy, you're an angel. I recognise that more and more every day, but bid me do anything else but that. That I refuse: it's against nature;" and Sadness looked more mournful than ever.

"Trust old Sadness to do his part," said the portly proprietor; and Thomas went back to the lamb.

"Nothin' doin' so early," he said; "let's go an' have a drink."

They went, and Thomas ordered.

"No, no, this is on me," cried Joe, trembling with joy.

"Pshaw, your money's counterfeit," said his companion with fine generosity. "This is on me, I say. Jack, what'll you have yourself?"

As they stood at the bar, the men began strolling up one by one. Each in his turn was introduced to Joe. They were very polite. They treated him with a pale, dignified, high-minded respect that menaced his pocket-book and possessions. The proprietor, Mr. Turner, asked him why he had never been in before. He really seemed much hurt about it, and on being told that Joe had only been in the city for a couple of weeks expressed emphatic surprise, even disbelief, and assured the rest that any one would have taken Mr. Hamilton for an old New Yorker.

Sadness was introduced last. He bowed to Joe's "Happy to know you, Mr. Williams."

"Better known as Sadness," he said, with an expression of deep gloom. "A distant relative of mine once had a great grief. I have never recovered from it."

Joe was not quite sure how to take this; but the others laughed and he joined them, and then, to cover his own embarrassment, he did what he thought the only correct and manly thing to do,—he ordered a drink.

"I don't know as I ought to," said Sadness.

"Oh, come on," his companions called out, "don't be stiff with a stranger. Make him feel at home."

"Mr. Hamilton will believe me when I say that I have no intention of being stiff, but duty is duty. I've got to go down town to pay a bill, and if I get too much aboard, it wouldn't be safe walking around with money on me."

"Aw, shut up, Sadness," said Thomas. "My friend Mr. Hamilton'll feel hurt if you don't drink with him."

"I cert'n'y will," was Joe's opportune remark, and he was pleased to see that it caused the reluctant one to yield.

They took a drink. There was quite a line of them. Joe asked the bartender what he would have. The men warmed towards him. They took several more drinks with him and he was happy. Sadness put his arm about his shoulder and told him, with tears in his eyes, that he looked like a cousin of his that had died.

"Aw, shut up, Sadness!" said some one else. "Be respectable."

Sadness turned his mournful eyes upon the speaker. "I won't," he replied. "Being respectable is very nice as a diversion, but it's tedious if done steadily." Joe did not quite take this, so he ordered another drink.

A group of young fellows came in and passed up the stairs. "Shearing another lamb?" said one of them significantly.

"Well, with that gang it will be well done."

Thomas and Joe left the crowd after a while, and went to the upper floor, where, in a long, brilliantly lighted room, tables were set out for drinking-parties. At one end of the room was a piano, and a man sat at it listlessly strumming some popular air. The proprietor joined them pretty soon, and steered them to a table opposite the door.

"Just sit down here, Mr. Hamilton," he said, "and you can see every-body that comes in. We have lots of nice people here on smoker nights, especially after the shows are out and the girls come in."

Joe's heart gave a great leap, and then settled as cold as lead. Of course, those girls wouldn't speak to him. But his hopes rose as the proprietor went on talking to him and to no one else. Mr. Turner always made a man feel as if he were of some consequence in the world, and men a good deal older than Joe had been fooled by his man-ner. He talked to one in a soft, ingratiating way, giving his whole atten-tion apparently. He tapped one confidentially on the shoulder, as who should say, "My dear boy, I have but two friends in the world, and you are both of them."

Joe charmed and pleased, kept his head well. There is a great deal in heredity, and his father had not been Maurice Oakley's butler for so many years for nothing.

The Banner Club was an institution for the lower education of negro youth. It drew its pupils from every class of people and from every part of the country. It was composed of all sorts and conditions of men, educated and uneducated, dishonest and less so, of the good, the bad, and the—unexposed. Parasites came there to find victims, politicians for votes, reporters for news, and artists of all kinds for colour and inspiration. It was the place of assembly for a number of really bright men, who after days of hard and often unrewarded work came there and drunk themselves drunk in each other's company, and when they were drunk talked of the eternal verities.

The Banner was only one of a kind. It stood to the stranger and the man and woman without connections for the whole social life. It was a substitute—poor, it must be confessed—to many youths for the home life which is so lacking among certain classes in New York.

Here the rounders congregated, or came and spent the hours until it was time to go forth to bout or assignation. Here too came some-times the curious who wanted to see something of the other side of life. Among these, white visitors were not infrequent,—those who were young enough to be fascinated by the bizarre, and those who were old enough to know that it was all in the game. Mr. Skaggs, of the New York *Universe*, was one of the former class and a constant visitor,—he and a "lady friend" called "Maudie," who had a penchant for dancing to "Rag-time" melodies as only the "puffessor" of such a club can play them. Of course, the place was a social cesspool, generating a poison-ous miasma and reeking with the stench of decayed and rotten morali-ties. There is no defence to be made for it. But what do you expect when false idealism and fevered ambition come face to face with catering cupidity?

It was into this atmosphere that Thomas had introduced the boy Joe, and he sat there now by his side, firing his mind by pointing out the different celebrities who came in and telling highly flavoured sto-ries of their lives or doings. Joe heard things that had never come within the range of his mind before.

"Aw, there's Skaggsy an' Maudie—Maudie's his girl, y'know, an' he's a reporter on the N' Yawk *Universe*. Fine fellow, Skaggsy."

Maudie—a portly, voluptuous-looking brunette—left her escort and went directly to the space by the piano. Here she was soon dancing with one of the coloured girls who had come in.

Skaggs started to sit down alone at a table, but Thomas called him, "Come over here, Skaggsy."

In the moment that it took the young man to reach them, Joe won-dered if he would ever reach that state when he could call that white man Skaggsy and the girl Maudie. The new-comer soon set all of that at ease.

"I want you to know my friend, Mr. Hamilton, Mr. Skaggs."

"Why, how d' ye do, Hamilton? I'm glad to meet you. Now, look a here; don't you let old Thomas here string you about me bein' any old 'Mr.' Skaggs. I'm Skaggsy to all of my friends. I hope to count you among 'em."

It was such a supreme moment that Joe could not find words to answer, so he called for another drink.

"Not a bit of it," said Skaggsy, "not a bit of it. When I meet my friends I always reserve to myself the right of ordering the first drink. Waiter, this is on me. What'll you have, gentlemen?"

They got their drinks, and then Skaggsy leaned over confidentially and began talking.

"I tell you, Hamilton, there ain't an ounce of prejudice in my body. Do you believe it?"

Joe said that he did. Indeed Skaggsy struck one as being aggres-sively unprejudiced.

He went on: "You see, a lot o' follows say to me, 'What do you want to go down to that nigger club for?' That's what they call it,—'nigger club.' But I say to 'em, 'Gentlemen, at that nigger club, as you choose to call it, I got more inspiration than I could get at any of the greater clubs in New York.' I've often been invited to join some of the swell clubs here, but I never do it. By Jove! I'd rather come down here and fellowship right in with you fellows. I like coloured people, anyway. It's natural. You see, my father had a big plantation and owned lots of slaves,—no offence, of course, but it was the custom of that time,—and I've played with little darkies ever since I could remember."

It was the same old story that the white who associates with negroes from volition usually tells to explain his taste.

The truth about the young reporter was that he was born and reared on a Vermont farm, where his early life was passed in fighting for his very subsistence. But this never troubled Skaggsy. He was a monumental liar, and the saving quality about him was that he calmly believed his own lies while he was telling them, so no one was hurt, for the deceiver was as much a victim as the deceived. The boys who knew him best used to say that when Skaggs got started on one of his debauches of lying, the Recording Angel always put on an extra clerical force.

"Now look at Maudie," he went on; "would you believe it that she was of a fine, rich family, and that the coloured girl she's dancing with now used to be her servant? She's just like me about that. Absolutely no prejudice."

Joe was wide-eyed with wonder and admiration, and he couldn't understand the amused expression on Thomas's face, nor, why he surreptitiously kicked him under the table.

Finally the reporter went his way, and Joe's sponsor explained to him that he was not to take in what Skaggsy said, and that there hadn't been a word of truth in it. He ended with, "Everybody knows Maudie, and that coloured girl is Mamie Lacey, and never worked for anybody in her life. Skaggsy's a good fellah, all right, but he's the biggest liar in N' Yawk."

The boy was distinctly shocked. He wasn't sure but Thomas was jealous of the attention the white man had shown him and wished to belittle it. Anyway, he did not thank him for destroying his romance.

About eleven o'clock, when the people began to drop in from the plays, the master of ceremonies opened proceedings by saying that

"The free concert would now begin, and he hoped that all present, ladies included, would act like gentlemen, and not forget the waiter. Mr. Meriweather will now favour us with the latest coon song, entitled 'Come back to yo' Baby, Honey.'"

There was a patter of applause, and a young negro came forward, and in a strident, music-hall voice, sung or rather recited with many gestures the ditty. He couldn't have been much older than Joe, but already his face was hard with dissipation and foul knowledge. He gave the song with all the rank suggestiveness that could be put into it. Joe looked upon him as a hero. He was followed by a little, brown-skinned fellow with an immature Vandyke beard and a lisp. He sung his own composition and was funny; how much funnier than he himself knew or intended, may not even be hinted at. Then, while an instrumentalist, who seemed to have a grudge against the piano, was hammering out the opening bars of a march, Joe's attention was attracted by a woman entering the room, and from that moment he heard no more of the concert. Even when the master of ceremonies announced with an air that, by special request, he himself would sing "Answer,"—the request was his own,—he did not draw attention of the boy away from the yellow-skinned divinity who sat at a near table, drinking whiskey straight.

She was a small girl, with fluffy dark hair and good features. A tiny foot peeped out from beneath her rattling silk skirts. She was a good-looking young woman and daintily made, though her face was no longer youthful, and one might have wished that with her complexion she had not run to silk waists in magenta.

Joe, however, saw no fault in her. She was altogether lovely to him, and his delight was the more poignant as he recognised in her one of the girls he had seen on the stage a couple of weeks ago. That being true, nothing could keep her from being glorious in his eyes,—not even the grease-paint which adhered in unneat patches to her face, nor her taste for whiskey in its unreformed state. He gazed at her in ecstasy until Thomas, turning to see what had attracted him, said with a laugh, "Oh, it's Hattie Sterling. Want to meet her?"

Again the young fellow was dumb. Just then Hattie also noticed his intent look, and nodded and beckoned to Thomas.

"Come on," he said, rising.

"Oh, she didn't ask for me," cried Joe, tremulous and eager.

His companion went away laughing.

"Who's your young friend?" asked Hattie.

"A fellah from the South."

"Bring him over here."

Joe could hardly believe in his own good luck, and his head, which was getting a bit weak, was near collapsing when his divinity asked him what he'd have? He began to protest, until she told the waiter with an air of authority to make it a little "'skey." Then she asked him for a cigarette, and began talking to him in a pleasant, soothing way between puffs.

When the drinks came, she said to Thomas, "Now, old man, you've been awfully nice, but when you get your little drink, you run away like a good little boy. You're superfluous."

Thomas answered, "Well, I like that," but obediently gulped his whiskey and withdrew, while Joe laughed until the master of ceremonies stood up and looked sternly at him.

The concert had long been over and the room was less crowded when Thomas sauntered back to the pair.

"Well, good-night," he said. "Guess you can find your way home, Mr. Hamilton;" and he gave Joe a long wink.

"Goo'-night," said Joe, woozily, "I be a' ri'. Goo'-night."

"Make it another 'skey," was Hattie's farewell remark.

It was late the next morning when Joe got home. He had a headache and a sense of triumph that not even his illness and his mother's reproof could subdue.

He had promised Hattie to come often to the club.

X

A Visitor from Home

Mrs. Hamilton began to question very seriously whether she had done the best thing in coming to New York as she saw her son staying away more and more and growing always farther away from her and his sister. Had she known how and where he spent his evenings, she would have had even greater cause to question the wisdom of their trip. She knew that although he worked he never had any money for the house, and she foresaw the time when the little they had would no longer suffice for Kitty and her. Realising this, she herself set out to find something to do.

It was a hard matter, for wherever she went seeking employment, it was always for her and her daughter, for the more she saw of Mrs. Jones, the less she thought it well to leave the girl under her influence. Mrs. Hamilton was not a keen woman, but she had a mother's intuitions, and she saw a subtle change in her daughter. At first the girl grew wistful and then impatient and rebellious. She complained that Joe was away from them so much enjoying himself, while she had to be housed up like a prisoner. She had receded from her dignified position, and twice of an evening had gone out for a car-ride with Thomas; but as that gentleman never included the mother in his invitation, she decided that her daughter should go no more, and she begged Joe to take his sister out sometimes instead. He demurred at first, for he now numbered among his city acquirements a fine contempt for his woman relatives. Finally, however, he consented, and took Kit once to the theatre and once for a ride. Each time he left her in the care of Thomas as soon as they were out of the house, while he went to find or to wait for his dear Hattie. But his mother did not know all this, and Kit did not tell her. The quick poison of the unreal life about her had already begun to affect her character. She had grown secretive and sly. The innocent longing which in a burst of enthusiasm she had expressed that first night at the theatre was growing into a real ambition with her, and she dropped the simple old songs she knew to practise the detestable coon ditties which the stage demanded.

She showed no particular pleasure when her mother found the sort of place they wanted, but went to work with her in sullen silence. Mrs. Hamilton could not understand it all, and many a night she wept and prayed over the change in this child of her heart. There were times when she felt that there was nothing left to work or fight for. The letters from Berry in prison became fewer and fewer. He was sinking into the dull, dead routine of his life. Her own letters to him fell off. It was hard getting the children to write. They did not want to be bothered, and she could not write for herself. So in the weeks and months that followed she drifted farther away from her children and husband and all the traditions of her life.

After Joe's first night at the Banner Club be had kept his promise to Hattie Sterling and had gone often to meet her. She had taught him much, because it was to her advantage to do so. His greenness had dropped from him like a garment, but no amount of sophistication could make him deem the woman less perfect. He knew that she was much older than he, but he only took this fact as an additional sign of his prowess in having won her. He was proud of himself when he went behind the scenes at the theatre or waited for her at the stage door and bore her off under the admiring eyes of a crowd of gapers. And Hattie? She liked him in a half-contemptuous, half-amused way. He was a good-looking boy and made money enough, as she expressed it, to show her a good time, so she was willing to overlook his weakness and his callow vanity.

"Look here," she said to him one day, "I guess you'll have to be moving. There's a young lady been inquiring for you to-day, and I won't stand for that."

He looked at her, startled for a moment, until he saw the laughter in her eyes. Then he caught her and kissed her. "What're you givin' me?" he said

"It's a straight tip, that's what."

"Who is it?"

"It's a girl named Minty Brown from your home."

His face turned brick-red with fear and shame. "Minty Brown!" he stammered.

Had that girl told all and undone him? But Hattie was going on about her work and evidently knew nothing.

"Oh, you needn't pretend you don't know her," she went on banteringly. "She says you were great friends down South, so I've invited her to supper. She wants to see you."

"To supper!" he thought. Was she mocking him? Was she restraining her scorn of him only to make his humiliation the greater after a while? He looked at her, but there was no suspicion of malice in her face, and he took hope.

"Well, I'd like to see old Minty," he said. "It's been many a long day since I've seen her."

All that afternoon, after going to the barber-shop, Joe was driven by a tempest of conflicting emotions. If Minty Brown had not told his story, why not? Would she yet tell, and if she did, what would happen? He tortured himself by questioning if Hattie would cast him off. At the very thought his hand trembled, and the man in the chair asked him if he hadn't been drinking.

When he met Minty in the evening, however, the first glance at her reassured him. Her face was wreathed in smiles as she came forward and held out her hand.

"Well, well, Joe Hamilton," she exclaimed, "if I ain't right-down glad to see you! How are you?"

"I'm middlin', Minty. How's yourself?" He was so happy that he couldn't let go her hand.

"An' jes' look at the boy! Ef he ain't got the impidence to be waihin' a mustache too. You must 'a' been lettin' the cats lick yo' upper lip. Didn't expect to see me in New York, did you?"

"No, indeed. What you doin' here?"

"Oh, I got a gent'man friend what's a porter, an' his run's been changed so that he comes hyeah, an' he told me, if I wanted to come he'd bring me thoo fur a visit, so, you see, hyeah I am. I allus was mighty anxious to see this hyeah town. But tell me, how's Kit an' yo' ma?"

"They're both right well." He had forgotten them and their scorn of Minty.

"Whaih do you live? I'm comin' roun' to see 'em."

He hesitated for a moment. He knew how his mother, if not Kit, would receive her, and yet he dared not anger this woman, who had his fate in the hollow of her hand.

She saw his hesitation and spoke up. "Oh, that's all right. Let by-gones be by-gones. You know I ain't the kin' o' person that holds a grudge ag'in anybody."

"That's right, Minty, that's right," he said, and gave her his mother's address. Then he hastened home to prepare the way for Minty's coming. Joe had no doubt but that his mother would see the matter quite as he saw it, and be willing to temporise with Minty; but he had reckoned without his host. Mrs. Hamilton might make certain concessions to strangers on the score of expediency, but she absolutely refused to yield one iota of her dignity to one whom she had known so long as an inferior.

"But don't you see what she can do for us, ma? She knows people that I know, and she can ruin me with them."

"I ain't never bowed my haid to Minty Brown an' I ain't a-goin' to do it now," was his mother's only reply.

"Oh, ma," Kitty put in, "you don't want to get talked about up here, do you?"

"We'd jes' as well be talked about fu' somep'n we didn't do as fu' somep'n we did do, an' it wouldn' be long befo' we'd come to dat if we made frien's wid dat Brown gal. I ain't a-goin' to do it. I'm ashamed o' you, Kitty, fu' wantin' me to."

The girl began to cry, while her brother walked the floor angrily.

"You'll see what'll happen," he cried; "you'll see."

Fannie looked at her son, and she seemed to see him more clearly than she had ever seen him before,—his foppery, his meanness, his cowardice.

"Well," she answered with a sigh, "it can't be no wuss den what's already happened."

"You'll see, you'll see," the boy reiterated.

Minty Brown allowed no wind of thought to cool the fire of her determination. She left Hattie Sterling's soon after Joe, and he was still walking the floor and uttering dire forebodings when she rang the bell below and asked for the Hamiltons.

Mrs. Jones ushered her into her fearfully upholstered parlour, and then puffed upstairs to tell her lodgers that there was a friend there from the South who wanted to see them.

"Tell huh," said Mrs. Hamilton, "dat dey ain't no one hyeah wants to see huh."

"No, no," Kitty broke in.

"Heish," said her mother; "I'm goin' to boss you a little while yit."

"Why, I don't understan' you, Mis' Hamilton," puffed Mrs. Jones. "She's a nice-lookin' lady, an' she said she knowed you at home."

"All you got to do is to tell dat ooman jes' what I say."

Minty Brown downstairs had heard the little colloquy, and, perceiving that something was amiss, had come to the stairs to listen. Now her voice, striving hard to be condescending and sweet, but growing harsh with anger, floated up from below:

"Oh, nevah min', lady, I ain't anxious to see 'em. I jest called out o' pity, but I reckon dey 'shamed to see me 'cause de ol' man's in penitentiary an' dey was run out o' town."

Mrs. Jones gasped, and then turned and went hastily downstairs.

Kit burst out crying afresh, and Joe walked the floor muttering beneath his breath, while the mother sat grimly watching the outcome. Finally they heard Mrs. Jones's step once more on the stairs. She came in without knocking, and her manner was distinctly unpleasant.

"Mis' Hamilton," she said, "I've had a talk with the lady downstairs, an' she's tol' me everything. I'd be glad if you'd let me have my rooms as soon as possible."

"So you goin' to put me out on de wo'd of a stranger?"

"I'm kin' o' sorry, but everybody in the house heard what Mis' Brown said, an' it'll soon be all over town, an' that 'ud ruin the reputation of my house."

"I reckon all dat kin be 'splained."

"Yes, but I don't know that anybody kin 'splain your daughter allus being with Mr. Thomas, who ain't even divo'ced from his wife." She flashed a vindictive glance at the girl, who turned deadly pale and dropped her head in her hands.

"You daih to say dat, Mis' Jones, you dat fust interduced my gal to dat man and got huh to go out wid him? I reckon you'd bettah go now."

And Mrs. Jones looked at Fannie's face and obeyed.

As soon as the woman's back was turned, Joe burst out, "There, there! see what you've done with your damned foolishness."

Fannie turned on him like a tigress. "Don't you cuss hyeah befo' me; I ain't nevah brung you up to it, an' I won't stan' it. Go to dem whaih you larned it, an whaih de wo'ds soun' sweet." The boy started to speak, but she checked him. "Don't you daih to cuss ag'in or befo' Gawd dey'll be somep'n fu' one o' dis fambly to be rottin' in jail fu'!"

The boy was cowed by his mother's manner. He was gathering his few belongings in a bundle.

"I ain't goin' to cuss," he said sullenly, "I'm goin' out o' your way."

"Oh, go on," she said, "go on. It's been a long time sence you been my son. You on yo' way to hell, an' you is been fu' lo dese many days."

Joe got out of the house as soon as possible. He did not speak to Kit nor look at his mother. He felt like a cur, because he knew deep down in his heart that he had only been waiting for some excuse to take this step.

As he slammed the door behind him, his mother flung herself down by Kit's side and mingled her tears with her daughter's. But Kit did not raise her head.

"Dey ain't nothin' lef' but you now, Kit;" but the girl did not speak, she only shook with hard sobs.

Then her mother raised her head and almost screamed, "My Gawd, not you, Kit!" The girl rose, and then dropped unconscious in her mother's arms.

Joe took his clothes to a lodging-house that he knew of, and then went to the club to drink himself up to the point of going to see Hattie after the show.

XI

BROKEN HOPES

What Joe Hamilton lacked more than anything else in the world was some one to kick him. Many a man who might have lived decently and become a fairly respectable citizen has gone to the dogs for the want of some one to administer a good resounding kick at the right time. It is corrective and clarifying.

Joe needed especially its clarifying property, for though he knew himself a cur, he went away from his mother's house feeling himself somehow aggrieved, and the feeling grew upon him the more he thought of it. His mother had ruined his chance in life, and he could never hold up his head again. Yes, he had heard that several of the fellows at the club had shady reputations, but surely to be the son of a thief or a supposed thief was not like being the criminal himself.

At the Banner he took a seat by himself, and, ordering a cocktail, sat glowering at the few other lonely members who had happened to drop in. There were not many of them, and the contagion of unsociability had taken possession of the house. The people sat scattered around at different tables, perfectly unmindful of the bartender, who cursed them under his breath for not "getting together."

Joe's mind was filled with bitter thoughts. How long had he been away from home? he asked himself. Nearly a year. Nearly a year passed in New York, and he had come to be what he so much desired,—a part of its fast life,—and now in a moment an old woman's stubbornness had destroyed all that he had builded.

What would Thomas say when he heard it? What would the other fellows think? And Hattie? It was plain that she would never notice him again. He had no doubt but that the malice of Minty Brown would prompt her to seek out all of his friends and make the story known. Why had he not tried to placate her by disavowing sympathy with his mother? He would have had no compunction about doing so, but he had thought of it too late. He sat brooding over his trouble until the bartender called with respectful sarcasm to ask if he wanted to lease the glass he had.

He gave back a silly laugh, gulped the rest of the liquor down, and was ordering another when Sadness came in. He came up directly to Joe and sat down beside him. "Mr. Hamilton says 'Make it two, Jack,'" he said with easy familiarity. "Well, what's the matter, old man? You're looking glum."

"I feel glum."

"The divine Hattie hasn't been cutting any capers, has she? The dear old girl hasn't been getting hysterical at her age? Let us hope not."

Joe glared at him. Why in the devil should this fellow be so sadly gay when he was weighted down with sorrow and shame and disgust?

"Come, come now, Hamilton, if you're sore because I invited myself to take a drink with you, I'll withdraw the order. I know the heroic thing to say is that I'll pay for the drinks myself, but I can't screw my courage up to the point of doing so unnatural a thing."

Young Hamilton hastened to protest. "Oh, I know you fellows now well enough to know how many drinks to pay for. It ain't that."

"Well, then, out with it. What is it? Haven't been up to anything, have you?"

The desire came to Joe to tell this man the whole truth, just what was the matter, and so to relieve his heart. On the impulse he did. If he had expected much from Sadness he was disappointed, for not a muscle of the man's face changed during the entire recital.

When it was over, he looked at his companion critically through a wreath of smoke. Then he said: "For a fellow who has had for a full year the advantage of the education of the New York clubs, you are strangely young. Let me see, you are nineteen or twenty now—yes. Well, that perhaps accounts for it. It's a pity you weren't born older. It's a pity most men aren't. They wouldn't have to take so much time and lose so many good things learning. Now, Mr. Hamilton, let me tell you, and you will pardon me for it, that you are a fool. Your case isn't half as bad as that of nine-tenths of the fellows that hang around here. Now, for instance, my father was hung."

Joe started and gave a gasp of horror.

"Oh, yes, but it was done with a very good rope and by the best citizens of Texas, so it seems that I really ought to be very grateful to them for the distinction they conferred upon my family, but I am not. I am ungratefully sad. A man must be very high or very low to take the sensible view of life that keeps him from being sad. I must confess that I have aspired to the depths without ever being fully able to reach them.

"Now look around a bit. See that little girl over there? That's Viola. Two years ago she wrenched up an iron stool from the floor of a lunchroom, and killed another woman with it. She's nineteen,—just about your age, by the way. Well, she had friends with a certain amount of pull. She got out of it, and no one thinks the worse of Viola. You see, Hamilton, in this life we are all suffering from fever, and no one edges away from the other because he finds him a little warm. It's dangerous when you're not used to it; but once you go through the parching process, you become inoculated against further contagion. Now, there's Barney over there, as decent a fellow as I know; but he has been indicted twice for pocket-picking. A half-dozen fellows whom you meet here every night have killed their man. Others have done worse things for which you respect them less. Poor Wallace, who is just coming in, and who looks like a jaunty ragpicker, came here about six months ago with about two thousand dollars, the proceeds from the sale of a house his father had left him. He'll sleep in one of the club chairs to-night, and not from choice. He spent his two thousand learning. But, after all, it was a good investment. It was like buying an annuity. He begins to know already how to live on others as they have lived on him. The plucked bird's beak is sharpened for other's feathers. From now on Wallace will live, eat, drink, and sleep at the expense of others, and will forget to mourn his lost money. He will go on this way until, broken and useless, the poorhouse or the potter's field gets him. Oh, it's a fine, rich life, my lad. I know you'll like it. I said you would the first time I saw you. It has plenty of stir in it, and a man never gets lonesome. Only the rich are lonesome. It's only the independent who depend upon others."

Sadness laughed a peculiar laugh, and there was a look in his terribly bright eyes that made Joe creep. If he could only have understood all that the man was saying to him, he might even yet have turned back. But he didn't. He ordered another drink. The only effect that the talk of Sadness had upon him was to make him feel wonderfully "in it." It gave him a false bravery, and he mentally told himself that now he would not be afraid to face Hattie.

He put out his hand to Sadness with a knowing look. "Thanks, Sadness," he said, "you've helped me lots."

Sadness brushed the proffered hand away and sprung up. "You lie," he cried, "I haven't; I was only fool enough to try;" and he turned hastily away from the table.

Joe looked surprised at first, and then laughed at his friend's retreating form. "Poor old fellow," he said, "drunk again. Must have had something before he came in."

There was not a lie in all that Sadness had said either as to their crime or their condition. He belonged to a peculiar class,—one that grows larger and larger each year in New York and which has imitators in every large city in this country. It is a set which lives, like the leech, upon the blood of others,—that draws its life from the veins of foolish men and immoral women, that prides itself upon its well-dressed idleness and has no shame in its voluntary pauperism. Each member of the class knows every other, his methods and his limitations, and their loyalty one to another makes of them a great hulking, fashionably uniformed fraternity of indolence. Some play the races a few months of the year; others, quite as intermittently, gamble at "shoestring" politics, and waver from party to party as time or their interests seem to dictate. But mostly they are like the lilies of the field.

It was into this set that Sadness had sarcastically invited Joe, and Joe felt honoured. He found that all of his former feelings had been silly and quite out of place; that all he had learned in his earlier years was false. It was very plain to him now that to want a good reputation was the sign of unpardonable immaturity, and that dishonour was the only real thing worth while. It made him feel better.

He was just rising bravely to swagger out to the theatre when Minty Brown came in with one of the club-men he knew. He bowed and smiled, but she appeared not to notice him at first, and when she did she nudged her companion and laughed.

Suddenly his little courage began to ooze out, and he knew what she must be saying to the fellow at her side, for he looked over at him and grinned. Where now was the philosophy of Sadness? Evidently Minty had not been brought under its educating influences, and thought about the whole matter in the old, ignorant way. He began to think of it too. Somehow old teachings and old traditions have an annoying way of coming back upon us in the critical moments of life, although one has long ago recognised how much truer and better some newer ways of thinking are. But Joe would not allow Minty to shatter his dreams by bringing up these old notions. She must be instructed.

He rose and went over to her table.

"Why, Minty," he said, offering his hand, "you ain't mad at me, are you?"

"Go on away f'om hyeah," she said angrily; "I don't want none o' thievin' Berry Hamilton's fambly to speak to me."

"Why, you were all right this evening."

"Yes, but jest out o' pity, an' you was nice 'cause you was afraid I'd tell on you. Go on now."

"Go on now," said Minty's young man; and he looked menacing.

Joe, what little self-respect he had gone, slunk out of the room and needed several whiskeys in a neighbouring saloon to give him courage to go to the theatre and wait for Hattie, who was playing in vaudeville houses pending the opening of her company.

The closing act was just over when he reached the stage door. He was there but a short time, when Hattie tripped out and took his arm. Her face was bright and smiling, and there was no suggestion of disgust in the dancing eyes she turned up to him. Evidently she had not heard, but the thought gave him no particular pleasure, as it left him in suspense as to how she would act when she should hear.

"Let's go somewhere and get some supper," she said; "I'm as hungry as I can be. What are you looking so cut up about?"

"Oh, I ain't feelin' so very good."

"I hope you ain't lettin' that long-tongued Brown woman bother your head, are you?"

His heart seemed to stand still. She did know, then.

"Do you know all about it?"

"Why, of course I do. You might know she'd come to me first with her story."

"And you still keep on speaking to me?"

"Now look here, Joe, if you've been drinking, I'll forgive you; if you ain't, you go on and leave me. Say, what do you take me for? Do you think I'd throw down a friend because somebody else talked about him? Well, you don't know Hat Sterling. When Minty told me that story, she was back in my dressing-room, and I sent her out o' there a-flying, and with a tongue-lashing that she won't forget for a month o' Sundays."

"I reckon that was the reason she jumped on me so hard at the club." He chuckled. He had taken heart again. All that Sadness had said was true, after all, and people thought no less of him. His joy was unbounded.

"So she jumped on you hard, did she? The cat!"

"Oh, she didn't say a thing to me."

"Well, Joe, it's just like this. I ain't an angel, you know that, but I do try to be square, and whenever I find a friend of mine down on his luck, in his pocket-book or his feelings, why, I give him my flipper. Why, old chap, I believe I like you better for the stiff upper lip you've been keeping under all this."

"Why, Hattie," he broke out, unable any longer to control himself, "you're—you're——"

"Oh, I'm just plain Hat Sterling, who won't throw down her friends. Now come on and get something to eat. If that thing is at the club, we'll go there and show her just how much her talk amounted to. She thinks she's the whole game, but I can spot her and then show her that she ain't one, two, three."

When they reached the Banner, they found Minty still there. She tried on the two the same tactics that she had employed so successfully upon Joe alone. She nudged her companion and tittered. But she had another person to deal with. Hattie Sterling stared at her coldly and indifferently, and passed on by her to a seat. Joe proceeded to order supper and other things in the nonchalant way that the woman had enjoined upon him. Minty began to feel distinctly uncomfortable, but it was her business not to be beaten. She laughed outright. Hattie did not seem hear her. She was beckoning Sadness to her side. He came and sat down.

"Now look here," she said, "you can't have any supper because you haven't reached the stage of magnificent hunger to make a meal palatable to you. You've got so used to being nearly starved that a meal don't taste good to you under any other circumstances. You're in on the drinks, though. Your thirst is always available.—Jack," she called down the long room to the bartender, "make it three.—Lean over here, I want to talk to you. See that woman over there by the wall? No, not that one,—the big light woman with Griggs. Well, she's come here with a story trying to throw Joe down, and I want you to help me do her."

"Oh, that's the one that upset our young friend, is it?" said Sadness, turning his mournful eyes upon Minty.

"That's her. So you know about it, do you?"

"Yes, and I'll help do her. She mustn't touch one of the fraternity, you know." He kept his eyes fixed upon the outsider until she squirmed. She could not at all understand this serious conversation directed at her. She wondered if she had gone too far and if they contemplated putting her out. It made her uneasy.

Now, this same Miss Sterling had the faculty of attracting a good deal of attention when she wished to. She brought it into play to-night, and in ten minutes, aided by Sadness, she had a crowd of jolly people about her table. When, as she would have expressed it, "everything was going fat," she suddenly paused and, turning her eyes full upon Minty, said in a voice loud enough for all to hear,—

"Say, boys, you've heard that story about Joe, haven't you?"

They had.

"Well, that's the one that told it; she's come here to try to throw him and me down. Is she going to do it?"

"Well, I guess not!" was the rousing reply, and every face turned towards the now frightened Minty. She rose hastily and, getting her skirts together, fled from the room, followed more leisurely by the crestfallen Griggs. Hattie's laugh and "Thank you, fellows," followed her out.

———

Matters were less easy for Joe's mother and sister than they were for him. A week or more after this, Kitty found him and told him that Minty's story had reached their employers and that they were out of work.

"You see, Joe," she said sadly, "we've took a flat since we moved from Mis' Jones', and we had to furnish it. We've got one lodger, a race-horse man, an' he's mighty nice to ma an' me, but that ain't enough. Now we've got to do something."

Joe was so smitten with sorrow that he gave her a dollar and promised to speak about the matter to a friend of his.

He did speak about it to Hattie.

"You've told me once or twice that your sister could sing. Bring her down here to me, and if she can do anything, I'll get her a place on the stage," was Hattie's answer.

When Kitty heard it she was radiant, but her mother only shook her head and said, "De las' hope, de las' hope."

XII

"ALL THE WORLD'S A STAGE"

Kitty proved herself Joe's sister by falling desperately in love with Hattie Sterling the first time they met. The actress was very gracious to her, and called her "child" in a pretty, patronising way, and patted her on the cheek.

"It's a shame that Joe hasn't brought you around before. We've been good friends for quite some time."

"He told me you an' him was right good friends."

Already Joe took on a new importance in his sister's eyes. He must be quite a man, she thought, to be the friend of such a person as Miss Sterling.

"So you think you want to go on the stage, do you?"

"Yes, 'm, I thought it might be right nice for me if I could."

"Joe, go out and get some beer for us, and then I'll hear your sister sing."

Miss Sterling talked as if she were a manager and had only to snap her fingers to be obeyed. When Joe came back with the beer, Kitty drank a glass. She did not like it, but she would not offend her hostess. After this she sang, and Miss Sterling applauded her generously, although the young girl's nervousness kept her from doing her best. The encouragement helped her, and she did better as she became more at home.

"Why, child, you've got a good voice. And, Joe, you've been keeping her shut up all this time. You ought to be ashamed of yourself."

The young man had little to say. He had brought Kitty almost under a protest, because he had no confidence in her ability and thought that his "girl" would disillusion her. It did not please him now to find his sister so fully under the limelight and himself "up stage."

Kitty was quite in a flutter of delight; not so much with the idea of working as with the glamour of the work she might be allowed to do.

"I tell you, now," Hattie Sterling pursued, throwing a brightly stockinged foot upon a chair, "your voice is too good for the chorus. Gi' me a cigarette, Joe. Have one, Kitty?—I'm goin' to call you Kitty. It's nice and homelike, and then we've got to be great chums, you know."

Kitty, unwilling to refuse anything from the sorceress, took her cigarette and lighted it, but a few puffs set her off coughing.

"Tut, tut, Kitty, child, don't do it if you ain't used to it. You'll learn soon enough."

Joe wanted to kick his sister for having tried so delicate an art and failed, for he had not yet lost all of his awe of Hattie.

"Now, what I was going to say," the lady resumed after several contemplative puffs, "is that you'll have to begin in the chorus any way and work your way up. It wouldn't take long for you, with your looks and voice, to put one of the 'up and ups' out o' the business. Only hope it won't be me. I've had people I've helped try to do it often enough."

She gave a laugh that had just a touch of bitterness in it, for she began to recognise that although she had been on the stage only a short time, she was no longer the all-conquering Hattie Sterling, in the first freshness of her youth.

"Oh, I wouldn't want to push anybody out," Kit expostulated.

"Oh, never mind, you'll soon get bravely over that feeling, and even if you didn't it wouldn't matter much. The thing has to happen. Somebody's got to go down. We don't last long in this life: it soon wears us out, and when we're worn out an sung out, danced out and played out, the manager has no further use for us; so he reduces us to the ranks or kicks us out entirely."

Joe here thought it time for him to put in a word. "Get out, Hat," he said contemptuously; "you're good for a dozen years yet."

She didn't deign to notice him, save so far as a sniff goes.

"Don't you let what I say scare you, though, Kitty. You've got a good chance, and maybe you'll have more sense than I've got, and at least save money—while you're in it. But let's get off that. It makes me sick. All you've got to do is to come to the opera-house to-morrow and I'll introduce you to the manager. He's a fool, but I think we can make him do something for you."

"Oh, thank you, I'll be around to-morrow, sure."

"Better come about ten o'clock. There's a rehearsal to-morrow, and you'll find him there. Of course, he'll be pretty rough, he always is at rehearsals, but he'll take to you if he thinks there's anything in you and he can get it out."

Kitty felt herself dismissed and rose to go. Joe did not rise.

"I'll see you later, Kit," he said; "I ain't goin' just yet. Say," he added, when his sister was gone, "you're a hot one. What do you want to give her all that con for? She'll never get in."

"Joe," said Hattie, "don't you get awful tired of being a jackass? Sometimes I want to kiss you, and sometimes I feel as if I had to kick you. I'll compromise with you now by letting you bring me some more beer. This got all stale while your sister was here. I saw she didn't like it, and so I wouldn't drink any more for fear she'd try to keep up with me."

"Kit is a good deal of a jay yet," Joe remarked wisely.

"Oh, yes, this world is full of jays. Lots of 'em have seen enough to make 'em wise, but they're still jays, and don't know it. That's the worst of it. They go around thinking they're it, when they ain't even in the game. Go on and get the beer."

And Joe went, feeling vaguely that he had been sat upon.

Kit flew home with joyous heart to tell her mother of her good prospects. She burst into the room, crying, "Oh, ma, ma, Miss Hattie thinks I'll do to go on the stage. Ain't it grand?"

She did not meet with the expected warmth of response from her mother.

"I do' know as it'll be so gran'. F'om what I see of dem stage people dey don't seem to 'mount to much. De way dem gals shows demse'ves is right down bad to me. Is you goin' to dress lak dem we seen dat night?"

Kit hung her head.

"I guess I'll have to."

"Well, ef you have to, I'd ruther see you daid any day. Oh, Kit, my little gal, don't do it, don't do it. Don't you go down lak yo' brothah Joe. Joe's gone."

"Why, ma, you don't understand. Joe's somebody now. You ought to've heard how Miss Hattie talked about him. She said he's been her friend for a long while."

"Her frien', yes, an' his own inimy. You need n' pattern aftah dat gal, Kit. She ruint Joe, an' she's aftah you now."

"But nowadays everybody thinks stage people respectable up here."

"Maybe I'm ol'-fashioned, but I can't believe in any ooman's lady-ship when she shows herse'f lak dem gals does. Oh, Kit, don't do it. Ain't you seen enough? Don't you know enough already to stay away f'om dese hyeah people? Dey don't want nothin' but to pull you down an' den laugh at you w'en you's dragged in de dust."

"You mustn't feel that away, ma. I'm doin' it to help you."

"I do' want no sich help. I'd ruther starve."

Kit did not reply, but there was no yielding in her manner.

"Kit," her mother went on, "dey's somep'n I ain't nevah tol' you dat I'm goin' to tell you now. Mistah Gibson ust to come to Mis' Jones's lots to see me befo' we moved hyeah, an' he's been talkin' 'bout a good many things to me." She hesitated. "He say dat I ain't noways ma'ied to my po' husban', dat a pen'tentiary sentence is de same as a divo'ce, an' if Be'y should live to git out, we'd have to ma'y ag'in. I wouldn't min' dat, Kit, but he say dat at Be'y's age dey ain't much chanst of his livin' to git out, an' hyeah I'll live all dis time alone, an' den have no one to tek keer o' me w'en I git ol'. He wants me to ma'y him, Kit. Kit, I love yo' fathah; he's my only one. But Joe, he's gone, an' ef yo go, befo' Gawd I'll tell Tawm Gibson yes."

The mother looked up to see just what effect her plea would have on her daughter. She hoped that what she said would have the desired result. But the girl turned around from fixing her neck-ribbon before the glass, her face radiant. "Why, it'll be splendid. He's such a nice man, an' race-horse men 'most always have money. Why don't you marry him, ma? Then I'd feel that you was safe an' settled, an' that you wouldn't be lonesome when the show was out of town."

"You want me to ma'y him an' desert yo' po' pa?"

"I guess what he says is right, ma. I don't reckon we'll ever see pa again an' you got to do something. You got to live for yourself now."

Her mother dropped her head in her hands. "All right," she said, "I'll do it; I'll ma'y him. I might as well go de way both my chillen's gone. Po' Be'y, po' Be'y. Ef you evah do come out, Gawd he'p you to baih what you'll fin'." And Mrs. Hamilton rose and tottered from the room, as if the old age she anticipated had already come upon her.

Kit stood looking after her, fear and grief in her eyes. "Poor ma," she said, "an' poor pa. But I know, an' I know it's for the best."

On the next morning she was up early and practising hard for her interview with the managing star of "Martin's Blackbirds."

When she arrived at the theatre, Hattie Sterling met her with frank friendliness.

"I'm glad you came early, Kitty," she remarked, "for maybe you can get a chance to talk with Martin before he begins rehearsal and gets all worked up. He'll be a little less like a bear then. But even if you don't see him before then, wait, and don't get scared if he tries to bluff you. His bark is a good deal worse than his bite."

When Mr. Martin came in that morning, he had other ideas than that of seeing applicants for places. His show must begin in two weeks, and it was advertised to be larger and better than ever before, when really nothing at all had been done for it. The promise of this advertisement must be fulfilled. Mr. Martin was late, and was out of humour with every one else on account of it. He came in hurried, fierce, and important.

"Mornin', Mr. Smith, mornin', Mrs. Jones. Ha, ladies and gentlemen, all here?"

He shot every word out of his mouth as if the after-taste of it were unpleasant to him. He walked among the chorus like an angry king among his vassals, and his glance was a flash of insolent fire. From his head to his feet he was the very epitome of self-sufficient, brutal conceit.

Kitty trembled as she noted the hush that fell on the people at his entrance. She felt like rushing out of the room. She could never face this terrible man. She trembled more as she found his eyes fixed upon her.

"Who's that?" he asked, disregarding her, as if she had been a stick or a stone.

"Well, don't snap her head off. It's a girl friend of mine that wants a place," said Hattie. She was the only one who would brave Martin.

"Humph. Let her wait. I ain't got no time to hear any one now. Get yourselves in line, you all who are on to that first chorus, while I'm getting into my sweat-shirt."

He disappeared behind a screen, whence he emerged arrayed, or only half arrayed, in a thick absorbing shirt and a thin pair of woollen trousers. Then the work began. The man was indefatigable. He was like the spirit of energy. He was in every place about the stage at once, leading the chorus, showing them steps, twisting some awkward girl into shape, shouting, gesticulating, abusing the pianist.

"Now, now," he would shout, "the left foot on that beat. Bah, bah, stop! You walk like a lot of tin soldiers. Are your joints rusty? Do you want oil? Look here, Taylor, if I didn't know you, I'd take you for a truck. Pick up your feet, open your mouths, and move, move, move! Oh!" and he would drop his head in despair. "And to think that I've got to do something with these things in two weeks—two weeks!" Then he would turn to them again with a sudden reaccession of eagerness. "Now, at it again, at it again! Hold that note, hold it! Now whirl, and on the left foot. Stop that music, stop it! Miss Coster, you'll learn that step in about a thousand years, and I've got nine hundred and ninety-nine years and fifty weeks less time than that to spare. Come here and try that step with me. Don't be afraid to move. Step like a chicken on a hot griddle!" And some blushing girl would come forward and go through the step alone before all the rest.

Kitty contemplated the scene with a mind equally divided between fear and anger. What should she do if he should so speak to her? Like the others, no doubt, smile sheepishly and obey him. But she did not like to believe it. She felt that the independence which she had known from babyhood would assert itself, and that she would talk back to him, even as Hattie Sterling did. She felt scared and discouraged, but every now and then her friend smiled encouragingly upon her across the ranks of moving singers.

Finally, however, her thoughts were broken in upon by hearing Mr. Martin cry: "Oh, quit, quit, and go rest yourselves, you ancient pieces of hickory, and let me forget you for a minute before I go crazy. Where's that new girl now?"

Kitty rose and went toward him, trembling so that she could hardly walk.

"What can you do?"

"I can sing," very faintly.

"Well, if that's the voice you're going to sing in, there won't be many that'll know whether it's good or bad. Well, let's hear something. Do you know any of these?"

And he ran over the titles of several songs. She knew some of them, and he selected one. "Try this. Here, Tom, play it for her."

It was an ordeal for the girl to go through. She had never sung before at anything more formidable than a church concert, where only her immediate acquaintances and townspeople were present. Now to sing before all these strange people, themselves singers, made her feel faint and awkward. But the courage of desperation came to her, and she struck into the song. At the first her voice wavered and threatened to fail her. It must not. She choked back her fright and forced the music from her lips.

When she was done, she was startled to hear Martin burst into a raucous laugh. Such humiliation! She had failed, and instead of telling her, he was bringing her to shame before the whole company. The tears came into her eyes, and she was about giving way when she caught a reassuring nod and smile from Hattie Sterling, and seized on this as a last hope.

"Haw, haw, haw!" laughed Martin, "haw, haw, haw! The little one was scared, see? She was scared, d' you understand? But did you see the grit she went at it with? Just took the bit in her teeth and got away. Haw, haw, haw! Now, that's what I like. If all you girls had that spirit, we could do something in two weeks. Try another one, girl."

Kitty's heart had suddenly grown light.

She sang the second one better because something within her was singing.

"Good!" said Martin, but he immediately returned to his cold manner. "You watch these girls close and see what they do, and to-morrow be prepared to go into line and move as well as sing."

He immediately turned his attention from her to the chorus, but no slight that he could inflict upon her now could take away the sweet truth that she was engaged and to-morrow would begin work. She wished she could go over and embrace Hattie Sterling. She thought kindly of Joe, and promised herself to give him a present out of her first month's earnings.

On the first night of the show pretty little Kitty Hamilton was pointed out as a girl who wouldn't be in the chorus long. The mother, who was soon to be Mrs. Gibson, sat in the balcony, a grieved, pained look on her face. Joe was in a front row with some of the rest of the gang. He took many drinks between the acts, because he was proud.

Mr. Thomas was there. He also was proud, and after the performance he waited for Kitty at the stage door and went forward to meet her as she came out. The look she gave him stopped him, and he let her pass without a word.

"Who'd 'a' thought," he mused, "that the kid had that much nerve? Well, if they don't want to find out things, what do they come to N' Yawk for? It ain't nobody's old Sunday-school picnic. Guess I got out easy, anyhow."

Hattie Sterling took Joe home in a hansom.

"Say," she said, "if you come this way for me again, it's all over, see? Your little sister's a comer, and I've got to hustle to keep up with her."

Joe growled and fell asleep in his chair. One must needs have a strong head or a strong will when one is the brother of a celebrity and would celebrate the distinguished one's success.

XIII
THE OAKLEYS

A year after the arrest of Berry Hamilton, and at a time when New York had shown to the eyes of his family so many strange new sights, there were few changes to be noted in the condition of affairs at the Oakley place. Maurice Oakley was perhaps a shade more distrustful of his servants, and consequently more testy with them. Mrs. Oakley was the same acquiescent woman, with unbounded faith in her husband's wisdom and judgment. With complacent minds both went their ways, drank their wine, and said their prayers, and wished that brother Frank's five years were past. They had letters from him now and then, never very cheerful in tone, but always breathing the deepest love and gratitude to them.

His brother found deep cause for congratulation in the tone of these epistles.

"Frank is getting down to work," he would cry exultantly. "He is past the first buoyant enthusiasm of youth. Ah, Leslie, when a man begins to be serious, then he begins to be something." And her only answer would be, "I wonder, Maurice, if Claire Lessing will wait for him?"

The two had frequent questions to answer as to Frank's doing and prospects, and they had always bright things to say of him, even when his letters gave them no such warrant. Their love for him made them read large between the lines, and all they read was good.

Between Maurice and his brother no word of the guilty servant ever passed. They each avoided it as an unpleasant subject. Frank had never asked and his brother had never proffered aught of the outcome of the case.

Mrs. Oakley had once suggested it. "Brother ought to know," she said, "that Berry is being properly punished."

"By no means," replied her husband. "You know that it would only hurt him. He shall never know if I have to tell him."

"You are right, Maurice, you are always right. We must shield Frank from the pain it would cause him. Poor fellow! he is so sensitive."

Their hearts were still steadfastly fixed upon the union of this younger brother with Claire Lessing. She had lately come into a fortune, and there was nothing now to prevent it. They would have written Frank to urge it, but they both believed that to try to woo him away from his art was but to make him more wayward. That any woman could have power enough to take him away from this jealous mistress they very much doubted. But they could hope, and hope made them eager to open every letter that bore the French postmark. Always it might contain news that he was coming home, or that he had made a great success, or, better, some inquiry after Claire. A long time they had waited, but found no such tidings in the letters from Paris.

At last, as Maurice Oakley sat in his library one day, the servant brought him a letter more bulky in weight and appearance than any he had yet received. His eyes glistened with pleasure as he read the postmark. "A letter from Frank," he said joyfully, "and an important one, I'll wager."

He smiled as he weighed it in his hand and caressed it. Mrs. Oakley was out shopping, and as he knew how deep her interest was, he hesitated to break the seal before she returned. He curbed his natural desire and laid the heavy envelope down on the desk. But he could not deny himself the pleasure of speculating as to its contents.

It was such a large, interesting-looking package. What might it not contain? It simply reeked of possibilities. Had any one banteringly told Maurice Oakley that he had such a deep vein of sentiment, he would have denied it with scorn and laughter. But here he found himself sitting with the letter in his hand and weaving stories as to its contents.

First, now, it might be a notice that Frank had received the badge of the Legion of Honour. No, no, that was too big, and he laughed aloud at his own folly, wondering the next minute, with half shame, why he laughed, for did he, after all, believe anything was too big for that brother of his? Well, let him begin, anyway, away down. Let him say, for instance, that the letter told of the completion and sale of a great picture. Frank had sold small ones. He would be glad of this, for his brother had written him several times of things that were a-doing, but not yet of anything that was done. Or, better yet, let the letter say that some picture, long finished, but of which the artist's pride and anxiety had forbidden him to speak, had made a glowing success, the success it deserved. This sounded well, and seemed not at all beyond the bounds of possibility. It was an alluring vision. He saw the picture already. It was a scene from life, true in detail to the point of very minuteness, and yet with something spiritual in it that lifted it above the mere copy of the commonplace. At the Salon it would be hung on the line, and people would stand before it admiring its workmanship and asking who the artist was. He drew on his memory of old reading. In his mind's eye he saw Frank, unconscious of his own power or too modest to admit it, stand unknown among the crowds around his picture waiting for and dreading their criticisms. He saw the light leap to his eyes as he heard their words of praise. He saw the straightening of his narrow shoulders when he was forced to admit that he was the painter of the work. Then the windows of Paris were filled with his portraits. The papers were full of his praise, and brave men and fair women met together to do him homage. Fair women, yes, and Frank would look upon them all and see reflected in them but a tithe of the glory of one woman, and that woman Claire Lessing. He roused himself and laughed again as he tapped the magic envelope.

"My fancies go on and conquer the world for my brother," he muttered. "He will follow their flight one day and do it himself."

The letter drew his eyes back to it. It seemed to invite him, to beg him even. "No, I will not do it; I will wait until Leslie comes. She will be as glad to hear the good news as I am."

His dreams were taking the shape of reality in his mind, and he was believing all that he wanted to believe.

He turned to look at a picture painted by Frank which hung over the mantel. He dwelt lovingly upon it, seeing in it the touch of a genius.

"Surely," he said, "this new picture cannot be greater than that, though it shall hang where kings can see it and this only graces the library of my poor house. It has the feeling of a woman's soul with the strength of a man's heart. When Frank and Claire marry, I shall give it back to them. It is too great a treasure for a clod like me. Heigho, why will women be so long a-shopping?"

He glanced again at the letter, and his hand went out involuntarily towards it. He fondled it, smiling.

"Ah, Lady Leslie, I've a mind to open it to punish you for staying so long."

He essayed to be playful, but he knew that he was trying to make a compromise with himself because his eagerness grew stronger than his gallantry. He laid the letter down and picked it up again. He studied the postmark over and over. He got up and walked to the window and back again, and then began fumbling in his pockets for his knife. No, he did not want it; yes, he did. He would just cut the envelope and make believe he had read it to pique his wife; but he would not read it. Yes, that was it. He found the knife and slit the paper. His fingers trembled as he touched the sheets that protruded. Why would not Leslie come? Did she not know that he was waiting for her? She ought to have known that there was a letter from Paris to-day, for it had been a month since they had had one.

There was a sound of footsteps without. He sprang up, crying, "I've been waiting so long for you!" A servant opened the door to bring him a message. Oakley dismissed him angrily. What did he want to go down to the Continental for to drink and talk politics to a lot of muddle-pated fools when he had a brother in Paris who was an artist and a letter from him lay unread in his hand? His patience and his temper were going. Leslie was careless and unfeeling. She ought to come; he was tired of waiting.

A carriage rolled up the driveway and he dropped the letter guiltily, as if it were not his own. He would only say that he had grown tired of waiting and started to read it. But it was only Mrs. Davis's footman leaving a note for Leslie about some charity.

He went back to the letter. Well, it was his. Leslie had forfeited her right to see it as soon as he. It might be mean, but it was not dishonest. No, he would not read it now, but he would take it out and show her that he had exercised his self-control in spite of her shortcomings. He laid it on the desk once more. It leered at him. He might just open the sheets enough to see the lines that began it, and read no further. Yes, he would do that. Leslie could not feel hurt at such a little thing.

The first line had only "Dear Brother." "Dear Brother"! Why not the second? That could not hold much more. The second line held him, and the third, and the fourth, and as he read on, unmindful now of what Leslie might think or feel, his face turned from the ruddy glow of pleasant anxiety to the pallor of grief and terror. He was not half-way through it when Mrs. Oakley's voice in the hall announced her coming. He did not hear her. He sat staring at the page before him, his lips apart and his eyes staring. Then, with a cry that echoed through the house, crumpling the sheets in his hand, he fell forward fainting to the floor, just as his wife rushed into the room.

"What is it?" she cried. "Maurice! Maurice!"

He lay on the floor staring up at the ceiling, the letter clutched in his hands. She ran to him and lifted up his head, but he gave no sign of life. Already the servants were crowding to the door. She bade one of them to hasten for a doctor, others to bring water and brandy, and the rest to be gone. As soon as she was alone, she loosed the crumpled sheets from his hand, for she felt that this must have been the cause of her husband's strange attack. Without a thought of wrong, for they had no secrets from each other, she glanced at the opening lines. Then she forgot the unconscious man at her feet and read the letter through to the end.

The letter was in Frank's neat hand, a little shaken, perhaps, by nervousness.

"Dear Brother,"

it ran,

"I know you will grieve at receiving this, and I wish that I might bear your grief for you, but I cannot, though I have as heavy a burden as this can bring to you. Mine would have been lighter to-day, perhaps, had you been more straightforward with me. I am not blaming you, however, for I know that my hypocrisy made you believe me possessed of a really soft heart, and you thought to spare me. Until yesterday, when in a letter from Esterton be casually mentioned the matter, I did not know that Berry was in prison, else this letter would have been written sooner. I have been wanting to write it for so long, and yet have been too great a coward to do so.

"I know that you will be disappointed in me, and just what that disappointment will cost you I know; but you must hear the truth. I shall never see your face again, or I should not dare to tell it even now. You will remember that I begged you to be easy on your servant. You thought it was only my kindness of heart. It was not; I had a deeper reason. I knew where the money had gone and dared not tell. Berry is as innocent as yourself—and I—well, it is a story, and let me tell it to you.

"You have had so much confidence in me, and I hate to tell you that it was all misplaced. I have no doubt that I should not be doing it now but that I have drunken absinthe enough to give me the emotional point of view, which I shall regret to-morrow. I do not mean that I am drunk. I can think clearly and write clearly, but my emotions are extremely active.

"Do you remember Claire's saying at the table that night of the farewell dinner that some dark-eyed mademoiselle was waiting for me? She did not know how truly she spoke, though I fancy she saw how I flushed when she said it: for I was already in love—madly so.

"I need not describe her. I need say nothing about her, for I know that nothing I say can ever persuade you to forgive her for taking me from you. This has gone on since I first came here, and I dared not tell you, for I saw whither your eyes had turned. I loved this girl, and she both inspired and hindered my work. Perhaps I would have been successful had I not met her, perhaps not.

"I love her too well to marry her and make of our devotion a stale, prosy thing of duty and compulsion. When a man does not marry a woman, he must keep her better than he would a wife. It costs. All that you gave me went to make her happy.

"Then, when I was about leaving you, the catastrophe came. I wanted much to carry back to her. I gambled to make more. I would surprise her. Luck was against me. Night after night I lost. Then, just before the dinner, I woke from my frenzy to find all that I had was gone. I would have asked you for more, and you would have given it; but that strange, ridiculous something which we misname Southern honour, that honour which strains at a gnat and swallows a camel, withheld me, and I preferred to do worse. So I lied to you. The money from my cabinet was not stolen save by myself. I am a liar and a thief, but your eyes shall never tell me so.

"Tell the truth and have Berry released. I can stand it. Write me but one letter to tell me of this. Do not plead with me, do not forgive me, do not seek to find me, for from this time I shall be as one who has perished from the earth; I shall be no more.

"Your brother,
"Frank."

By the time the servants came they found Mrs. Oakley as white as her lord. But with firm hands and compressed lips she ministered to his needs pending the doctor's arrival. She bathed his face and temples, chafed his hands, and forced the brandy between his lips. Finally he stirred and his hands gripped.

"The letter!" he gasped.

"Yes, dear, I have it; I have it."

"Give it to me," he cried. She handed it to him. He seized it and thrust it into his breast.

"Did—did—you read it?"

"Yes, I did not know——"

"Oh, my God, I did not intend that you should see it. I wanted the secret for my own. I wanted to carry it to my grave with me. Oh, Frank, Frank, Frank!"

"Never mind, Maurice. It is as if you alone knew it."

"It is not, I say, it is not!"

He turned upon his face and began to weep passionately, not like a man, but like a child whose last toy has been broken.

"Oh, my God," he moaned, "my brother, my brother!"

"'Sh, dearie, think—it's—it's—Frank."

"That's it, that's it—that's what I can't forget. It's Frank,—Frank, my brother."

Suddenly he sat up and his eyes stared straight into hers.

"Leslie, no one must ever know what is in this letter," he said calmly.

"No one shall, Maurice; come, let us burn it."

"Burn it? No, no," he cried, clutching at his breast. "It must not be burned. What! burn my brother's secret? No, no, I must carry it with me,—carry it with me to the grave."

"But, Maurice——"

"I must carry it with me."

She saw that he was overwrought, and so did not argue with him.

When the doctor came, he found Maurice Oakley in bed, but better. The medical man diagnosed the case and decided that he had received some severe shock. He feared too for his heart, for the patient constantly held his hands pressed against his bosom. In vain the doctor pleaded; he would not take them down, and when the wife added her word, the physician gave up, and after prescribing, left, much puzzled in mind.

"It's a strange case," he said; "there's something more than the nervous shock that makes him clutch his chest like that, and yet I have never noticed signs of heart trouble in Oakley. Oh, well, business worry will produce anything in anybody."

It was soon common talk about the town about Maurice Oakley's attack. In the seclusion of his chamber he was saying to his wife:

"Ah, Leslie, you and I will keep the secret. No one shall ever know."

"Yes, dear, but—but—what of Berry?"

"What of Berry?" he cried, starting up excitedly. "What is Berry to Frank? What is that nigger to my brother? What are his sufferings to the honour of my family and name?"

"Never mind, Maurice, never mind, you are right."

"It must never be known, I say, if Berry has to rot in jail."

So they wrote a lie to Frank, and buried the secret in their breasts, and Oakley wore its visible form upon his heart.

XIV

FRANKENSTEIN

Five years is but a short time in the life of a man, and yet many things may happen therein. For instance, the whole way of a family's life may be changed. Good natures may be made into bad ones and out of a soul of faith grow a spirit of unbelief. The independence of respectability may harden into the insolence of defiance, and the sensitive cheek of modesty into the brazen face of shamelessness. It may be true that the habits of years are hard to change, but this is not true of the first sixteen or seventeen years of a young person's life, else Kitty Hamilton and Joe could not so easily have become what they were. It had taken barely five years to accomplish an entire metamorphosis of their characters. In Joe's case even a shorter time was needed. He was so ready to go down that it needed but a gentle push to start him, and once started, there was nothing within him to hold him back from the depths. For his will was as flabby as his conscience, and his pride, which stands to some men for conscience, had no definite aim or direction.

Hattie Sterling had given him both his greatest impulse for evil and for good. She had at first given him his gentle push, but when she saw that his collapse would lose her a faithful and useful slave she had sought to check his course. Her threat of the severance of their relations had held him up for a little time, and she began to believe that he was safe again. He went back to the work he had neglected, drank moderately, and acted in most things as a sound, sensible being. Then, all of a sudden, he went down again, and went down badly. She kept her promise and threw him over. Then he became a hanger-on at the clubs, a genteel loafer. He used to say in his sober moments that at last he was one of the boys that Sadness had spoken of. He did not work, and yet he lived and ate and was proud of his degradation. But he soon tired of being separated from Hattie, and straightened up again. After some demur she received him upon his former footing. It was only for a few months. He fell again. For almost four years this had happened intermittently. Finally he took a turn for the better that endured so long that Hattie Sterling again gave him her faith. Then the woman made her mistake. She warmed to him. She showed him that she was proud of him. He went forth at once to celebrate his victory. He did not return to her for three days. Then he was battered, unkempt, and thick of speech.

She looked at him in silent contempt for a while as he sat nursing his aching head.

"Well, you're a beauty," she said finally with cutting scorn. "You ought to be put under a glass case and placed on exhibition."

He groaned and his head sunk lower. A drunken man is always disarmed.

His helplessness, instead of inspiring her with pity, inflamed her with an unfeeling anger that burst forth in a volume of taunts.

"You're the thing I've given up all my chances for—you, a miserable, drunken jay, without a jay's decency. No one had ever looked at you until I picked you up and you've been strutting around ever since, showing off because I was kind to you, and now this is the way you pay me back. Drunk half the time and half drunk the rest. Well, you know what I told you the last time you got 'loaded'? I mean it too. You're not the only star in sight, see?"

She laughed meanly and began to sing, "You'll have to find another baby now."

For the first time he looked up, and his eyes were full of tears— tears both of grief and intoxication. There was an expression of a whipped dog on his face.

"Do'—Ha'ie, do'—" he pleaded, stretching out his hands to her.

Her eyes blazed back at him, but she sang on insolently, tauntingly.

The very inanity of the man disgusted her, and on a sudden impulse she sprang up and struck him full in the face with the flat of her hand.

He was too weak to resist the blow, and, tumbling from the chair, fell limply to the floor, where he lay at her feet, alternately weeping aloud and quivering with drunken, hiccoughing sobs.

"Get up!" she cried; "get up and get out o' here. You sha'n't lay around my house."

He had already begun to fall into a drunken sleep, but she shook him, got him to his feet, and pushed him outside the door. "Now, go, you drunken dog, and never put your foot inside this house again."

He stood outside, swaying dizzily upon his feet and looking back with dazed eyes at the door, then he muttered: "Pu' me out, wi' you? Pu' me out, damn you! Well, I ki' you. See 'f I don't;" and he half walked, half fell down the street.

Sadness and Skaggsy were together at the club that night. Five years had not changed the latter as to wealth or position or inclination, and he was still a frequent visitor at the Banner. He always came in alone now, for Maudie had gone the way of all the half-world, and reached depths to which Mr. Skaggs's job prevented him from following her. However, he mourned truly for his lost companion, and to-night he was in a particularly pensive mood.

Some one was playing rag-time on the piano, and the dancers were wheeling in time to the music. Skaggsy looked at them regretfully as he sipped his liquor. It made him think of Maudie. He sighed and turned away.

"I tell you, Sadness," he said impulsively, "dancing is the poetry of motion."

"Yes," replied Sadness, "and dancing in rag-time is the dialect poetry."

The reporter did not like this. It savoured of flippancy, and he was about entering upon a discussion to prove that Sadness had no soul, when Joe, with bloodshot eyes and dishevelled clothes, staggered in and reeled towards them.

"Drunk again," said Sadness. "Really, it's a waste of time for Joe to sober up. Hullo there!" as the young man brought up against him; "take a seat." He put him in a chair at the table. "Been lushin' a bit, eh?"

"Gi' me some'n' drink."

"Oh, a hair of the dog. Some men shave their dogs clean, and then have hydrophobia. Here, Jack!"

They drank, and then, as if the whiskey had done him good, Joe sat up in his chair.

"Ha'ie's throwed me down."

"Lucky dog! You might have known it would have happened sooner or later. Better sooner than never."

Skaggs smoked in silence and looked at Joe.

"I'm goin' to kill her."

"I wouldn't if I were you. Take old Sadness's advice and thank your stars that you're rid of her."

"I'm goin' to kill her." He paused and looked at them drowsily. Then, bracing himself up again, he broke out suddenly, "Say, d' ever tell y' 'bout the ol' man? He never stole that money. Know he di' n'."

He threatened to fall asleep now, but the reporter was all alert. He scented a story.

"By Jove!" he exclaimed, "did you hear that? Bet the chap stole it himself and 's letting the old man suffer for it. Great story, ain't it? Come, come, wake up here. Three more, Jack. What about your father?"

"Father? Who's father. Oh, do' bother me. What?"

"Here, here, tell us about your father and the money. If he didn't steal it, who did?"

"Who did? Tha' 's it, who did? Ol' man di' n' steal it, know he di' n'."

"Oh, let him alone, Skaggsy, he don't know what he's saying."

"Yes, he does, a drunken man tells the truth."

"In some cases," said Sadness.

"Oh, let me alone, man. I've been trying for years to get a big sensation for my paper, and if this story is one, I'm a made man."

The drink seemed to revive the young man again, and by bits Skaggs was able to pick out of him the story of his father's arrest and conviction. At its close he relapsed into stupidity, murmuring, "She throwed me down."

"Well," sneered Sadness, "you see drunken men tell the truth, and you don't seem to get much guilt out of our young friend. You're disappointed, aren't you?"

"I confess I am disappointed, but I've got an idea, just the same."

"Oh, you have? Well, don't handle it carelessly; it might go off." And Sadness rose. The reporter sat thinking for a time and then followed him, leaving Joe in a drunken sleep at the table. There he lay for more than two hours. When he finally awoke, he started up as if some determination had come to him in his sleep. A part of the helplessness of his intoxication had gone, but his first act was to call for more whiskey. This he gulped down, and followed with another and another. For a while he stood still, brooding silently, his red eyes blinking at the light. Then he turned abruptly and left the club.

It was very late when he reached Hattie's door, but he opened it with his latch-key, as he had been used to do. He stopped to help himself to a glass of brandy, as he had so often done before. Then he went directly to her room. She was a light sleeper, and his step awakened her.

"Who is it?" she cried in affright.

"It's me." His voice was steadier now, but grim.

"What do you want? Didn't I tell you never to come here again? Get out or I'll have you taken out."

She sprang up in bed, glaring angrily at him.

His hands twitched nervously, as if her will were conquering him and he were uneasy, but he held her eye with his own.

"You put me out to-night," he said.

"Yes, and I'm going to do it again. You're drunk."

She started to rise, but he took a step towards her and she paused. He looked as she had never seen him look before. His face was ashen and his eyes like fire and blood. She quailed beneath the look. He took another step towards her.

"You put me out to-night," he repeated, "like a dog."

His step was steady and his tone was clear, menacingly clear. She shrank back from him, back to the wall. Still his hands twitched and his eye held her. Still he crept slowly towards her, his lips working and his hands moving convulsively.

"Joe, Joe!" she said hoarsely, "what's the matter? Oh, don't look at me like that."

The gown had fallen away from her breast and showed the convulsive fluttering of her heart.

He broke into a laugh, a dry, murderous laugh, and his hands sought each other while the fingers twitched over one another like coiling serpents.

"You put me out—you—you, and you made me what I am." The realisation of what he was, of his foulness and degradation, seemed just to have come to him fully. "You made me what I am, and then you sent me away. You let me come back, and now you put me out."

She gazed at him fascinated. She tried to scream and she could not. This was not Joe. This was not the boy that she had turned and twisted about her little finger. This was a terrible, terrible man or a monster.

He moved a step nearer her. His eyes fell to her throat. For an instant she lost their steady glare and then she found her voice. The scream was checked as it began. His fingers had closed over her throat just where the gown had left it temptingly bare. They gave it the caress of death. She struggled. They held her. Her eyes prayed to his. But his were the fire of hell. She fell back upon her pillow in silence. He had not uttered a word. He held her. Finally he flung her from him like a rag, and sank into a chair. And there the officers found him when Hattie Sterling's disappearance had become a strange thing.

XV

"Dear, Damned, Delightful Town"

When Joe was taken, there was no spirit or feeling left in him. He moved mechanically, as if without sense or volition. The first impression he gave was that of a man over-acting insanity. But this was soon removed by the very indifference with which he met everything concerned with his crime. From the very first he made no effort to exonerate or to vindicate himself. He talked little and only in a dry, stupefied way. He was as one whose soul is dead, and perhaps it was; for all the little soul of him had been wrapped up in the body of this one woman, and the stroke that took her life had killed him too.

The men who examined him were irritated beyond measure. There was nothing for them to exercise their ingenuity upon. He left them nothing to search for. Their most damning question he answered with an apathy that showed absolutely no interest in the matter. It was as if some one whom he did not care about had committed a crime and he had been called to testify. The only thing which he noticed or seemed to have any affection for was a little pet dog which had been hers and which they sometimes allowed to be with him after the life sentence had been passed upon him and when he was awaiting removal. He would sit for hours with the little animal in his lap, caressing it dumbly. There was a mute sorrow in the eyes of both man and dog, and they seemed to take comfort in each other's presence. There was no need of any sign between them. They had both loved her, had they not? So they understood.

Sadness saw him and came back to the Banner, torn and unnerved by the sight. "I saw him," he said with a shudder, "and it'll take more whiskey than Jack can give me in a year to wash the memory of him out of me. Why, man, it shocked me all through. It's a pity they didn't send him to the chair. It couldn't have done him much harm and would have been a real mercy."

And so Sadness and all the club, with a muttered "Poor devil!" dismissed him. He was gone. Why should they worry? Only one more who had got into the whirlpool, enjoyed the sensation for a moment, and then swept dizzily down. There were, indeed, some who for an earnest hour sermonised about it and said, "Here is another example of the pernicious influence of the city on untrained negroes. Oh, is there no way to keep these people from rushing away from the small villages and country districts of the South up to the cities, where they cannot battle with the terrible force of a strange and unusual environment? Is there no way to prove to them that woollen-shirted, brown-jeaned simplicity is infinitely better than broad-clothed degradation?" They wanted to preach to these people that good agriculture is better than bad art,—that it was better and nobler for them to sing to God across the Southern fields than to dance for rowdies in the Northern halls. They wanted to dare to say that the South has its faults—no one condones them—and its disadvantages, but that even what they suffered from these was better than what awaited them in the great alleys of New York. Down there, the bodies were restrained, and they chafed; but here the soul would fester, and they would be content.

This was but for an hour, for even while they exclaimed they knew that there was no way, and that the stream of young negro life would continue to flow up from the South, dashing itself against the hard necessities of the city and breaking like waves against a rock,—that, until the gods grew tired of their cruel sport, there must still be sacrifices to false ideals and unreal ambitions.

There was one heart, though, that neither dismissed Joe with gratuitous pity nor sermonised about him. The mother heart had only room for grief and pain. Already it had borne its share. It had known sorrow for a lost husband, tears at the neglect and brutality of a new companion, shame for a daughter's sake, and it had seemed already filled to overflowing. And yet the fates had put in this one other burden until it seemed it must burst with the weight of it.

To Fannie Hamilton's mind now all her boy's shortcomings became as naught. He was not her wayward, erring, criminal son. She only remembered that he was her son, and wept for him as such. She forgot his curses, while her memory went back to the sweetness of his baby prattle and the soft words of his tenderer youth. Until the last she clung to him, holding him guiltless, and to her thought they took to prison, not Joe Hamilton, a convicted criminal, but Joey, Joey, her boy, her firstborn,—a martyr.

The pretty Miss Kitty Hamilton was less deeply impressed. The arrest and subsequent conviction of her brother was quite a blow. She felt the shame of it keenly, and some of the grief. To her, coming as it did just at a time when the company was being strengthened and she more importantly featured than ever, it was decidedly inopportune, for no one could help connecting her name with the affair.

For a long time she and her brother had scarcely been upon speaking terms. During Joe's frequent lapses from industry he had been prone to "touch" his sister for the wherewithal to supply his various wants. When, finally, she grew tired and refused to be "touched," he rebuked her for withholding that which, save for his help, she would never have been able to make. This went on until they were almost entirely estranged. He was wont to say that "now his sister was up in the world, she had got the big head," and she to retort that her brother "wanted to use her for a 'soft thing.'"

From the time that she went on the stage she had begun to live her own life, a life in which the chief aim was the possession of good clothes and the ability to attract the attention which she had learned to crave. The greatest sign of interest she showed in her brother's affair was, at first, to offer her mother money to secure a lawyer. But when Joe confessed all, she consoled herself with the reflection that perhaps it was for the best, and kept her money in her pocket with a sense of satisfaction. She was getting to be so very much more Joe's sister. She did not go to see her brother. She was afraid it might make her nervous while she was in the city, and she went on the road with her company before he was taken away.

Miss Kitty Hamilton had to be very careful about her nerves and her health. She had had experiences, and her voice was not as good as it used to be, and her beauty had to be aided by cosmetics. So she went away from New York, and only read of all that happened when some one called her attention to it in the papers.

Berry Hamilton in his Southern prison knew nothing of all this, for no letters had passed between him and his family for more than two years. The very cruelty of destiny defeated itself in this and was kind.

XVI

Skaggs's Theory

There was, perhaps, more depth to Mr. Skaggs than most people gave him credit for having. However it may be, when he got an idea into his head, whether it were insane or otherwise, he had a decidedly tenacious way of holding to it. Sadness had been disposed to laugh at him when he announced that Joe's drunken story of his father's troubles had given him an idea. But it was, nevertheless, true, and that idea had stayed with him clear through the exciting events that followed on that fatal night. He thought and dreamed of it until he had made a working theory. Then one day, with a boldness that he seldom assumed when in the sacred Presence, he walked into the office and laid his plans before the editor. They talked together for some time, and the editor seemed hard to convince.

"It would be a big thing for the paper," he said, "if it only panned out; but it is such a rattle-brained, harum-scarum thing. No one under the sun would have thought of it but you, Skaggs."

"Oh, it's bound to pan out. I see the thing as clear as day. There's no getting around it."

"Yes, it looks plausible, but so does all fiction. You're taking a chance. You're losing time. If it fails——

"But if it succeeds?"

"Well, go and bring back a story. If you don't, look out. It's against my better judgment anyway. Remember I told you that."

Skaggs shot out of the office, and within an hour and a half had boarded a fast train for the South.

It is almost a question whether Skaggs had a theory or whether he had told himself a pretty story and, as usual, believed it. The editor was right. No one else would have thought of the wild thing that was in the reporter's mind. The detective had not thought of it five years before, nor had Maurice Oakley and his friends had an inkling, and here was one of the New York *Universe's* young men going miles to prove his idea about something that did not at all concern him.

When Skaggs reached the town which had been the home of the Hamiltons, he went at once to the Continental Hotel. He had as yet formulated no plan of immediate action and with a fool's or a genius's belief in his destiny he sat down to await the turn of events. His first move would be to get acquainted with some of his neighbours. This was no difficult matter, as the bar of the Continental was still the gathering-place of some of the city's choice spirits of the old régime. Thither he went, and his convivial cheerfulness soon placed him on terms of equality with many of his kind.

He insinuated that he was looking around for business prospects. This proved his open-sesame. Five years had not changed the Continental frequenters much, and Skaggs's intention immediately brought Beachfield Davis down upon him with the remark, "If a man wants to go into business, business for a gentleman, suh, Gad, there's no finer or better paying business in the world than breeding blooded dogs—that is, if you get a man of experience to go in with you."

"Dogs, dogs," drivelled old Horace Talbot, "Beachfield's always talking about dogs. I remember the night we were all discussing that Hamilton nigger's arrest, Beachfield said it was a sign of total depravity because his man hunted 'possums with his hound." The old man laughed inanely. The hotel whiskey was getting on his nerves.

The reporter opened his eyes and his ears. He had stumbled upon something, at any rate.

"What was it about some nigger's arrest, sir?" he asked respectfully.

"Oh, it wasn't anything much. Only an old and trusted servant robbed his master, and my theory——"

"But you will remember, Mr. Talbot," broke in Davis, "that I proved your theory to be wrong and cited a conclusive instance."

"Yes, a 'possum-hunting dog."

"I am really anxious to hear about the robbery, though. It seems such an unusual thing for a negro to steal a great amount."

"Just so, and that was part of my theory. Now——"

"It's an old story and a long one, Mr. Skaggs, and one of merely local repute," interjected Colonel Saunders. "I don't think it could possibly interest you, who are familiar with the records of the really great crimes that take place in a city such as New York."

"Those things do interest me very much, though. I am something of a psychologist, and I often find the smallest and most insignificant-appearing details pregnant with suggestion. Won't you let me hear the story, Colonel?"

"Why, yes, though there's little in it save that I am one of the few men who have come to believe that the negro, Berry Hamilton, is not the guilty party."

"Nonsense! nonsense!" said Talbot; "of course Berry was guilty, but, as I said before, I don't blame him. The negroes——"

"Total depravity," said Davis. "Now look at my dog——"

"If you will retire with me to the further table I will give you whatever of the facts I can call to mind."

As unobtrusively as they could, they drew apart from the others and seated themselves at a more secluded table, leaving Talbot and Davis wrangling, as of old, over their theories. When the glasses were filled and the pipes going, the Colonel began his story, interlarding it frequently with comments of his own.

"Now, in the first place, Mr. Skaggs," he said when the tale was done, "I am lawyer enough to see for myself how weak the evidence was upon which the negro was convicted, and later events have done much to confirm me in the opinion that he was innocent."

"Later events?"

"Yes." The Colonel leaned across the table and his voice fell to a whisper. "Four years ago a great change took place in Maurice Oakley. It happened in the space of a day, and no one knows the cause of it. From a social, companionable man, he became a recluse, shunning visitors and dreading society. From an open-hearted, unsuspicious neighbour, he became secretive and distrustful of his own friends. From an active business man, he has become a retired brooder. He sees no one if he can help it. He writes no letters and receives none, not even from his brother, it is said. And all of this came about in the space of twenty-four hours."

"But what was the beginning of it?"

"No one knows, save that one day he had some sort of nervous attack. By the time the doctor was called he was better, but he kept clutching his hand over his heart. Naturally, the physician wanted to examine him there, but the very suggestion of it seemed to throw him into a frenzy; and his wife too begged the doctor, an old friend of the family, to desist. Maurice Oakley had been as sound as a dollar, and no one of the family had had any tendency to heart affection."

"It is strange."

"Strange it is, but I have my theory."

"His actions are like those of a man guarding a secret."

"Sh! His negro laundress says that there is an inside pocket in his undershirts."

"An inside pocket?"

"Yes."

"And for what?" Skaggs was trembling with eagerness.

The Colonel dropped his voice lower.

"We can only speculate," he said; "but, as I have said, I have my theory. Oakley was a just man, and in punishing his old servant for the supposed robbery it is plain that he acted from principle. But he is also a proud man and would hate to confess that he had been in the wrong. So I believed that the cause of his first shock was the finding of the money that he supposed gone. Unwilling to admit this error, he lets the misapprehension go on, and it is the money which he carries in his secret pocket, with a morbid fear of its discovery, that has made him dismiss his servants, leave his business, and refuse to see his friends."

"A very natural conclusion, Colonel, and I must say that I believe you. It is strange that others have not seen as you have seen and brought the matter to light."

"Well, you see, Mr. Skaggs, none are so dull as the people who think they think. I can safely say that there is not another man in this town who has lighted upon the real solution of this matter, though it has been openly talked of for so long. But as for bringing it to light, no one would think of doing that. It would be sure to hurt Oakley's feelings, and he is of one of our best families."

"Ah, yes, perfectly right."

Skaggs had got all that he wanted; much more, in fact, than he had expected. The Colonel held him for a while yet to enlarge upon the views that he had expressed.

When the reporter finally left him, it was with a cheery "Goodnight, Colonel. If I were a criminal, I should be afraid of that analytical mind of yours!"

He went upstairs chuckling. "The old fool!" he cried as he flung himself into a chair. "I've got it! I've got it! Maurice Oakley must see me, and then what?" He sat down to think out what he should do tomorrow. Again, with his fine disregard of ways and means, he determined to trust to luck, and as he expressed it, "brace old Oakley."

Accordingly he went about nine o'clock the next morning to Oakley's house. A gray-haired, sad-eyed woman inquired his errand.

"I want to see Mr. Oakley," he said.

"You cannot see him. Mr. Oakley is not well and does not see visitors."

"But I must see him, madam; I am here upon business of importance."

"You can tell me just as well as him. I am his wife and transact all of his business."

"I can tell no one but the master of the house himself."

"You cannot see him. It is against his orders."

"Very well," replied Skaggs, descending one step; "it is his loss, not mine. I have tried to do my duty and failed. Simply tell him that I came from Paris."

"Paris?" cried a querulous voice behind the woman's back. "Leslie, why do you keep the gentleman at the door? Let him come in at once."

Mrs. Oakley stepped from the door and Skaggs went in. Had he seen Oakley before he would have been shocked at the change in his appearance; but as it was, the nervous, white-haired man who stood shiftily before him told him nothing of an eating secret long carried. The man's face was gray and haggard, and deep lines were cut under his staring, fish-like eyes. His hair tumbled in white masses over his pallid forehead, and his lips twitched as he talked.

"You're from Paris, sir, from Paris?" he said. "Come in, come in."

His motions were nervous and erratic. Skaggs followed him into the library, and the wife disappeared in another direction.

It would have been hard to recognise in the Oakley of the present the man of a few years before. The strong frame had gone away to bone, and nothing of his old power sat on either brow or chin. He was as a man who trembled on the brink of insanity. His guilty secret had been too much for him, and Skaggs's own fingers twitched as he saw his host's hands seek the breast of his jacket every other moment.

"It is there the secret is hidden," he said to himself, "and whatever it is, I must have it. But how—how? I can't knock the man down and rob him in his own house." But Oakley himself proceeded to give him his first cue.

"You—you—perhaps have a message from my brother—my brother who is in Paris. I have not heard from him for some time."

Skaggs's mind worked quickly. He remembered the Colonel's story. Evidently the brother had something to do with the secret. "Now or never," he thought. So he said boldly, "Yes, I have a message from your brother."

The man sprung up, clutching again at his breast. "You have? you have? Give it to me. After four years he sends me a message! Give it to me!"

The reporter looked steadily at the man. He knew that he was in his power, that his very eagerness would prove traitor to his discretion.

"Your brother bade me to say to you that you have a terrible secret, that you bear it in your breast—there—there. I am his messenger. He bids you to give it to me."

Oakley had shrunken back as if he had been struck. "No, no!" he gasped, "no, no! I have no secret."

The reporter moved nearer him. The old man shrunk against the wall, his lips working convulsively and his hand tearing at his breast as Skaggs drew nearer. He attempted to shriek, but his voice was husky and broke off in a gasping whisper.

"Give it to me, as your brother commands."

"No, no, no! It is not his secret; it is mine. I must carry it here always, do you hear? I must carry it till I die. Go away! Go away!"

Skaggs seized him. Oakley struggled weakly, but he had no strength. The reporter's hand sought the secret pocket. He felt a paper beneath his fingers. Oakley gasped hoarsely as he drew it forth. Then raising his voice gave one agonised cry, and sank to the floor frothing at the mouth. At the cry rapid footsteps were heard in the hallway, and Mrs. Oakley threw open the door.

"What is the matter?" she cried.

"My message has somewhat upset your husband," was the cool answer.

"But his breast is open. Your hand has been in his bosom. You have taken something from him. Give it to me, or I shall call for help."

Skaggs had not reckoned on this, but his wits came to the rescue.

"You dare not call for help," he said, "or the world will know!"

She wrung her hands helplessly, crying, "Oh, give it to me, give it to me. We've never done you any harm."

"But you've harmed some one else; that is enough."

He moved towards the door, but she sprang in front of him with the fierceness of a tigress protecting her young. She attacked him with teeth and nails. She was pallid with fury, and it was all he could do to protect himself and yet not injure her. Finally, when her anger had taken her strength, he succeeded in getting out. He flew down the hall-way and out of the front door, the woman's screams following him. He did not pause to read the precious letter until he was safe in his room at the Continental Hotel. Then he sprang to his feet, crying, "Thank God! thank God! I was right, and the *Universe* shall have a sensation. The brother is the thief, and Berry Hamilton is an innocent man. Hurrah! Now, who is it that has come on a wild-goose chase? Who is it that ought to handle his idea carefully? Heigho, Saunders my man, the drinks'll be on you, and old Skaggsy will have done some good in the world."

XVII

A YELLOW JOURNAL

Mr Skaggs had no qualms of conscience about the manner in which he had come by the damaging evidence against Maurice Oakley. It was enough for him that he had it. A corporation, he argued, had no soul, and therefore no conscience. How much less, then, should so small a part of a great corporation as himself be expected to have them?

He had his story. It was vivid, interesting, dramatic. It meant the favour of his editor, a big thing for the *Universe*, and a fatter lining for his own pocket. He sat down to put his discovery on paper before he attempted anything else, although the impulse to celebrate was very strong within him.

He told his story well, with an eye to every one of its salient points. He sent an alleged picture of Berry Hamilton as he had appeared at the time of his arrest. He sent a picture of the Oakley home and of the cottage where the servant and his family had been so happy. There was a strong pen-picture of the man, Oakley, grown haggard and morose from carrying his guilty secret, of his confusion when confronted with the supposed knowledge of it. The old Southern city was described, and the opinions of its residents in regard to the case given. It was there—clear, interesting, and strong. One could see it all as if every phase of it were being enacted before one's eyes. Skaggs surpassed himself.

When the editor first got hold of it he said "Huh!" over the opening lines,—a few short sentences that instantly pricked the attention awake. He read on with increasing interest. "This is good stuff," he said at the last page. "Here's a chance for the *Universe* to look into the methods of Southern court proceedings. Here's a chance for a spread."

The *Universe* had always claimed to be the friend of all poor and oppressed humanity, and every once in a while it did something to substantiate its claim, whereupon it stood off and said to the public, "Look you what we have done, and behold how great we are, the friend of the people!" The *Universe* was yellow. It was very so. But it had power and keenness and energy. It never lost an opportunity to crow, and if one was not forthcoming, it made one. In this way it managed to do a considerable amount of good, and its yellowness became forgivable, even commendable. In Skaggs's story the editor saw an opportunity for one of its periodical philanthropies. He seized upon it. With headlines that took half a page, and with cuts authentic and otherwise, the tale was told, and the people of New York were greeted next morning with the announcement of—

"A BURNING SHAME!
A POOR AND INNOCENT NEGRO MADE TO SUFFER
FOR A RICH MAN'S CRIME!
GREAT EXPOSÉ BY THE 'UNIVERSE'!
A 'UNIVERSE' REPORTER TO THE RESCUE!
THE WHOLE THING TO BE AIRED THAT THE
PEOPLE MAY KNOW!"

Then Skaggs received a telegram that made him leap for joy. He was to do it. He was to go to the capital of the State. He was to beard the Governor in his den, and he, with the force of a great paper behind him, was to demand for the people the release of an innocent man. Then there would be another write-up and much glory for him and more shekels. In an hour after he had received his telegram he was on his way to the Southern capital.

Meanwhile in the of Maurice Oakley there were sad times. From the moment that the master of the house had fallen to the floor in impotent fear and madness there had been no peace within his doors. At first his wife had tried to control him alone, and had humoured the wild babblings with which he woke from his swoon. But these changed to shrieks and cries and curses, and she was forced to throw open the doors so long closed and call in help. The neighbours and her old friends went to her assistance, and what the reporter's story had not done, the ravings of the man accomplished; for, with a show of matchless cunning, he continually clutched at his breast, laughed, and babbled his secret openly. Even then they would have smothered it in silence, for the honour of one of their best families; but too many ears had heard, and then came the yellow journal bearing all the news in emblazoned headlines.

Colonel Saunders was distinctly hurt to think that his confidence had been imposed on, and that he had been instrumental in bringing shame upon a Southern name.

"To think, suh," he said generally to the usual assembly of choice spirits,—"to think of that man's being a reporter, suh, a common, ordinary reporter, and that I sat and talked to him as if he were a gentleman!"

"You're not to be blamed, Colonel," said old Horace Talbot. "You've done no more than any other gentleman would have done. The trouble is that the average Northerner has no sense of honour, suh, no sense of honour. If this particular man had had, he would have kept still, and everything would have gone on smooth and quiet. Instead of that, a distinguished family is brought to shame, and for what? To give a nigger a few more years of freedom when, likely as not, he don't want it; and Berry Hamilton's life in prison has proved nearer the ideal reached by slavery than anything he has found since emancipation. Why, suhs, I fancy I see him leaving his prison with tears of regret in his eyes."

Old Horace was inanely eloquent for an hour over his pet theory. But there were some in the town who thought differently about the matter, and it was their opinions and murmurings that backed up Skaggs and made it easier for him when at the capital he came into contact with the official red tape.

He was told that there were certain forms of procedure, and certain times for certain things, but he hammered persistently away, the murmurings behind him grew louder, while from his sanctum the editor of the *Universe* thundered away against oppression and high-handed tyranny. Other papers took it up and asked why this man should be despoiled of his liberty any longer? And when it was replied that the man had been convicted, and that the wheels of justice could not be stopped or turned back by the letter of a romantic artist or the ravings of a madman, there was a mighty outcry against the farce of justice that had been played out in this man's case.

The trial was reviewed; the evidence again brought up and examined. The dignity of the State was threatened. At this time the State did the one thing necessary to save its tottering reputation. It would not surrender, but it capitulated, and Berry Hamilton was pardoned.

Berry heard the news with surprise and a half-bitter joy. He had long ago lost hope that justice would ever be done to him. He marvelled at the word that was brought to him now, and he could not understand the strange cordiality of the young white man who met him at the warden's office. Five years of prison life had made a different man of him. He no longer looked to receive kindness from his fellows, and he blinked at it as he blinked at the unwonted brightness of the sun. The lines about his mouth where the smiles used to gather had changed and grown stern with the hopelessness of years. His lips drooped pathetically, and hard treatment had given his eyes a lowering look. His hair, that had hardly shown a white streak, was as white as Maurice Oakley's own. His erstwhile quick wits were dulled and imbruted. He had lived like an ox, working without inspiration or reward, and he came forth like an ox from his stall. All the higher part of him he had left behind, dropping it off day after day through the wearisome years. He had put behind him the Berry Hamilton that laughed and joked and sang and believed, for even his faith had become only a numbed fancy.

"This is a very happy occasion, Mr. Hamilton," said Skaggs, shaking his hand heartily.

Berry did not answer. What had this slim, glib young man to do with him? What had any white man to do with him after what he had suffered at their hands?

"You know you are to go to New York with me?"

"To New Yawk? What fu'?"

Skaggs did not tell him that, now that the *Universe* had done its work, it demanded the right to crow to its heart's satisfaction. He said only, "You want to see your wife, of course?"

Berry had forgotten Fannie, and for the first time his heart thrilled within him at the thought of seeing her again.

"I ain't hyeahed f'om my people fu' a long time. I didn't know what had become of 'em. How's Kit an' Joe?"

"They're all right," was the reply. Skaggs couldn't tell him, in this the first hour of his freedom. Let him have time to drink the sweetness of that all in. There would be time afterwards to taste all of the bitterness.

Once in New York, he found that people wished to see him, some fools, some philanthropists, and a great many reporters. He had to be photographed—all this before he could seek those whom he longed to see. They printed his picture as he was before he went to prison and as be was now, a sort of before-and-after-taking comment, and in the morning that it all appeared, when the *Universe* spread itself to tell the public what it had done and how it had done it, they gave him his wife's address.

It would be better, they thought, for her to tell him herself all that happened. No one of them was brave enough to stand to look in his eyes when he asked for his son and daughter, and they shifted their responsibility by pretending to themselves that they were doing it for his own good: that the blow would fall more gently upon him coming from her who had been his wife. Berry took the address and inquired his way timidly, hesitatingly, but with a swelling heart, to the door of the flat where Fannie lived.

XVIII

WHAT BERRY FOUND

Had not Berry's years of prison life made him forget what little he knew of reading, he might have read the name Gibson on the door-plate where they told him to ring for his wife. But he knew nothing of what awaited him as he confidently pulled the bell. Fannie herself came to the door. The news the papers held had not escaped her, but she had suffered in silence, hoping that Berry might be spared the pain of finding her. Now he stood before her, and she knew him at a glance, in spite of his haggard countenance.

"Fannie," he said, holding out his arms to her, and all of the pain and pathos of long yearning was in his voice, "don't you know me?"

She shrank away from him, back in the hall-way.

"Yes, yes, Be'y, I knows you. Come in."

She led him through the passage-way and into her room, he follow-ing with a sudden sinking at his heart. This was not the reception he had expected from Fannie.

When they were within the room he turned and held out his arms to her again, but she did not notice them. "Why, is you 'shamed o' me?" he asked brokenly.

"'Shamed? No! Oh, Be'y," and she sank into a chair and began rock-ing to and fro in her helpless grief.

"What's de mattah, Fannie? Ain't you glad to see me?"

"Yes, yes, but you don't know nothin', do you? Dey lef' me to tell you?"

"Lef' you to tell me? What's de mattah? Is Joe or Kit daid? Tell me."

"No, not daid. Kit dances on de stage fu' a livin', an', Be'y, she ain't de gal she ust to be. Joe—Joe—Joe—he's in pen'tentiary fu' killin' a ooman."

Berry started forward with a cry, "My Gawd! my Gawd! my little gal! my boy!"

"Dat ain't all," she went on dully, as if reciting a rote lesson; "I ain't yo' wife no mo'. I's ma'ied ag'in. Oh Be'y, Be'y, don't look at me lak dat. I couldn't he'p it. Kit an' Joe lef' me, an' dey said de pen'tentiary divo'ced you an' me, an' dat you'd nevah come out nohow. Don't look at me lak dat, Be'y."

"You ain't my wife no mo'? Hit's a lie, a damn lie! You is my wife. I's a innocent man. No pen'tentiary kin tek you erway f'om me. Hit's enough what dey've done to my chillen." He rushed forward and seized her by the arm. "Dey sha'n't do no mo', by Gawd! dey sha'n't, I say!" His voice had risen to a fierce roar, like that of a hurt beast, and he shook her by the arm as he spoke.

"Oh, don't, Be'y, don't, you hu't me. I couldn't he'p it."

He glared at her for a moment, and then the real force of the situation came full upon him, and he bowed his head in his hands and wept like a child. The great sobs came up and stuck in his throat.

She crept up to him fearfully and laid her hand on his head.

"Don't cry, Be'y," she said; "I done wrong, but I loves you yit."

He seized her in his arms and held her tightly until he could control himself. Then he asked weakly, "Well, what am I goin' to do?"

"I do' know, Be'y, 'ceptin' dat you'll have to leave me."

"I won't! I'll never leave you again," he replied doggedly.

"But, Be'y, you mus'. You'll only mek it ha'der on me, an' Gibson'll beat me ag'in."

"Ag'in!"

She hung her head: "Yes."

He gripped himself hard.

"Why cain't you come on off wid me, Fannie? You was mine fus'."

"I couldn't. He would fin' me anywhaih I went to."

"Let him fin' you. You'll be wid me, an' we'll settle it, him an' me."

"I want to, but oh, I can't, I can't," she wailed. "Please go now, Be'y, befo' he gits home. He's mad anyhow, 'cause you're out."

Berry looked at her hard, and then said in a dry voice, "An' so I got to go an' leave you to him?"

"Yes, you mus'; I'm his'n now."

He turned to the door, murmuring, "My wife gone, Kit a nobody, an' Joe, little Joe, a murderer, an' then I—I—ust to pray to Gawd an' call him 'Ouah Fathah.'" He laughed hoarsely. It sounded like nothing Fannie had ever heard before.

"Don't, Be'y, don't say dat. Maybe we don't un'erstan'."

Her faith still hung by a slender thread, but his had given way in that moment.

"No, we don't un'erstan'," he laughed as he went out of the door. "We don't un'erstan'."

He staggered down the steps, blinded by his emotions, and set his face towards the little lodging that he had taken temporarily. There seemed nothing left in life for him to do. Yet he knew that he must work to live, although the effort seemed hardly worth while. He remembered now that the *Universe* had offered him the under janitorship in its building. He would go and take it, and some day, perhaps— He was not quite sure what the "perhaps" meant. But as his mind grew clearer he came to know, for a sullen, fierce anger was smouldering in his heart against the man who through lies had stolen his wife from him. It was anger that came slowly, but gained in fierceness as it grew.

Yes, that was it, he would kill Gibson. It was no worse than his present state. Then it would be father and son murderers. They would hang him or send him back to prison. Neither would be hard now. He laughed to himself.

And this was what they had let him out of prison for? To find out all this. Why had they not left him there to die in ignorance? What had he to do with all these people who gave him sympathy? What did he want of their sympathy? Could they give him back one tithe of what he had lost? Could they restore to him his wife or his son or his daughter, his quiet happiness or his simple faith?

He went to work for the *Universe*, but night after night, armed, he patrolled the sidewalk in front of Fannie's house. He did not know Gibson, but he wanted to see them together. Then he would strike. His vigils kept him from his bed, but he went to the next morning's work with no weariness. The hope of revenge sustained him, and he took a savage joy in the thought that he should be the dispenser of justice to at least one of those who had wounded him.

Finally he grew impatient and determined to wait no longer, but to seek his enemy in his own house. He approached the place cautiously and went up the steps. His hand touched the bell-pull. He staggered back.

"Oh, my Gawd!" he said.

There was crape on Fannie's bell. His head went round and he held to the door for support. Then he turned the knob and the door opened. He went noiselessly in. At the door of Fannie's room he halted, sick with fear. He knocked, a step sounded within, and his wife's face looked out upon him. He could have screamed aloud with relief.

"It ain't you!" he whispered huskily.

"No, it's him. He was killed in a fight at the race-track. Some o' his frinds are settin' up. Come in."

He went in, a wild, strange feeling surging at his heart. She showed him into the death-chamber.

As he stood and looked down upon the face of his enemy, still, cold, and terrible in death, the recognition of how near he had come to crime swept over him, and all his dead faith sprang into new life in a glorious resurrection. He stood with clasped hands, and no word passed his lips. But his heart was crying, "Thank God! thank God! this man's blood is not on my hands."

The gamblers who were sitting up with the dead wondered who the old fool was who looked at their silent comrade and then raised his eyes as if in prayer.

———

When Gibson was laid away, there were no formalities between Berry and his wife; they simply went back to each other. New York held nothing for them now but sad memories. Kit was on the road, and the father could not bear to see his son; so they turned their faces southward, back to the only place they could call home. Surely the people could not be cruel to them now, and even if they were, they felt that after what they had endured no wound had power to give them pain.

Leslie Oakley heard of their coming, and with her own hands re-opened and refurnished the little cottage in the yard for them. There the white-haired woman begged them to spend the rest of their days and be in peace and comfort. It was the only amend she could make. As much to satisfy her as to settle themselves, they took the cottage, and many a night thereafter they sat together with clasped hands listening to the shrieks of the madman across the yard and thinking of what he had brought to them and to himself.

It was not a happy life, but it was all that was left to them, and they took it up without complaint, for they knew they were powerless against some Will infinitely stronger than their own.

Bibliography

SELECTED BOOKS BY DUNBAR

Poetry

Oak & Ivy (Dayton, Ohio: United Brethren Publishing House, 1893) [actually appeared late 1892].

Majors and Minors (Toledo, Ohio: Hadley & Hadley, 1895) [actually appeared early 1896].

Lyrics of Lowly Life, Introduction by William Dean Howells (New York: Dodd, Mead, 1896).

Lyrics of the Hearthside (New York: Dodd, Mead, 1899).

Lyrics of Love and Laughter (New York: Dodd, Mead, 1903).

Lyrics of Sunshine and Shadow (New York: Dodd, Mead, 1905).

Short Stories

Folks from Dixie (New York: Dodd, Mead, 1898).

The Strength of Gideon and Other Stories (New York: Dodd, Mead, 1900).

In Old Plantation Days (New York: Dodd, Mead, 1903).

The Heart of Happy Hollow (New York: Dodd, Mead, 1904).

Novels

The Uncalled (New York: Dodd, Mead, 1898).

The Love of Landry (New York: Dodd, Mead, 1900).

The Fanatics (New York: Dodd, Mead, 1901).
The Sport of the Gods (New York: Dodd, Mead, 1902).

ILLUSTRATED BOOKS OF POETRY
Poems of Cabin and Field (New York: Dodd, Mead, 1899).
Candle-Lightin' Time (New York: Dodd, Mead, 1901).
When Malindy Sings (New York: Dodd, Mead, 1903).
Li'l Gal (New York: Dodd, Mead, 1904).
Howdy, Honey, Howdy (New York: Dodd, Mead, 1905).
Joggin' Erlong (New York: Dodd, Mead, 1906).

SELECTED COLLECTIONS OF WORK BY DUNBAR
Brawley, Benjamin, ed., *Best Stories of Paul Laurence Dunbar* (New York: Dodd, Mead, 1938).

Braxton, Joanne, ed., *The Collected Poetry of Paul Laurence Dunbar* [1913] (Charlottesville: University of Virginia Press, 1993).

Jarrett, Gene, and Tom Morgan, eds., *The Complete Stories of Paul Laurence Dunbar* (Athens: Ohio University Press, 2005).

Martin, Herbert Woodward, and Ronald Primeau, eds., *In His Own Voice; The Dramatic and Other Uncollected Works of Paul Laurence Dunbar* (Athens: Ohio University Press, 2002).

Martin, Jay, and Gossie Hudson, eds., *The Paul Laurence Dunbar Reader* (New York: Dodd, Mead, 1975).

Wiggins, Linda Keck, ed., *The Life and Works of Paul Laurence Dunbar* (Naperville, Ill.: J. L. Nichols and Co., 1907).

SELECTED BIBLIOGRAPHY OF SECONDARY WORKS, AND OF PRIMARY WORKS CITED BY AUTHORS OTHER THAN DUNBAR
Anon. *The Dream City: A Portfolio of Photographic Views of the World's Columbian Exposition,* Introduction by Halsey Ives (St. Louis: N.D. Thompson Co., 1893–1894) in *World's Columbian Exposition of 1893,* Paul V. Galvin Library Digital History Collection, Illinois Institute of Technology, http://columbus.gl.iit.edu/dreamcity/dctoc.html (accessed December 17, 2004).

Baker, Houston A. *Blues, Ideology and Afro-American Literature: A Vernacular Theory.* (Chicago: University of Chicago Press, 1984).

———. "Paul Laurence Dunbar: An Evaluation," *Black World* 21 (November. 1971), 30–37.

Bancroft, Hubert Howe. *The Book of the Fair: An historical and descriptive presentation of the world's science, art, and industry, as viewed through the Columbian Exposition at Chicago in 1893* (Chicago: The Bancroft Company, 1893).

Barrett, Paul. "Chicago's Quest for World Status" (Chicago: Paul V. Galvin Library Digital History Collection, 1999), http://columbus.gl.iit.edu/barret. html (accessed December 17, 2004).

Billington, Ray Allen. Commentary on "The Significance of the Frontier in American History" in Boorstin, Daniel J., ed., *An American Primer* [1966] (New York: Mentor Books, 1968).

Blake, William. "The Lamb" [1789] online text copyright © 2003, Ian Lancashire, for Department of English, University of Toronto, http://eir.library. utoronto.ca/rpo/display/poem181.html (accessed December 17, 2004).

Blankenship, Russell. *American Literature as an Expression of the National Mind* (New York: Henry Holt, 1931).

Blight, David. *Race and Reunion: The Civil War in American Memory* (Cambridge, Mass.: The Belknap Press of Harvard University Press, 2001).

Blount, Marcellus. "The Preacherly Text: African American Poetry and Vernacular Performance," *PMLA* 107:3 (May 1992): 582–93.

Boorstin, Daniel J. *Hidden History: Exploring Our Secret Past* [1987] (New York: Vintage Books, 1989).

Bradley, David, and Shelley Fisher Fishkin, eds. *The Encyclopedia of Civil Rights in America,* 3 vols (New York: M.E. Sharpe, 1997).

Brawley, Benjamin. *Paul Laurence Dunbar: Poet of His People* (Chapel Hill: University of North Carolina Press, 1936).

Braxton, Joanne. Introduction to *The Collected Poetry of Paul Laurence Dunbar* [1913] (Charlottesville: University of Virginia Press, 1993).

Bruce, Jr., Dickson D. *Black American Writing from the Nadir: The Evolution of a Literary Tradition, 1877–1915* (Baton Rouge: Louisiana State University Press, 1989).

Chesnutt, Charles Waddell. *The Conjure Woman* (Boston: Houghton, Mifflin and Co., 1899).

———. *The Short Fiction of Charles W. Chesnutt.* Edited and with introduction by Sylvia Lyons Render (Washington, D.C.: Howard University Press, 1974).

Cunningham, Virginia. *Paul Laurence Dunbar and His Song* (New York: Dodd, Mead, 1947).

Davis, Charles T. *Black Is the Color of the Cosmos: Essays on Black Literature and Culture, 1942–1981,* ed. Henry Louis Gates, Jr. (New York: Garland Publishing, 1982).

Dreiser, Theodore. "Nigger Jeff," *The Best Short Stories of Theodore Dreiser* (Chicago: Ivan R. Dee, 1989), 157–82.

Du Bois, W.E.B. *Black Reconstruction in America: An Essay Toward a History of the Part Which Black Folk Played in the Attempt to Reconstruct Democracy in America, 1860–1880* (New York: Harcourt, Brace, 1935).

Fishkin, Shelley Fisher. "Race and the Politics of Memory: Mark Twain and Paul Laurence Dunbar," forthcoming, *Journal of American Studies* (U.K.).

Franklin, John Hope, and Alfred A. Moss. *From Slavery to Freedom: A History of African Americans,* 8th ed. (New York: Knopf, 2000).

Fredrickson, George M. *The Black Image in the White Mind: The Debate on Afro-American Character and Destiny, 1817–1914* (Middletown, Conn.: Wesleyan University Press, 1971).

Fuller, Sara S. *The Paul Laurence Dunbar Collection: An Inventory to the Microfilm Edition* (Columbus: Ohio Historical Society, 1972).

Gates, Jr., Henry Louis. "Dis and Dat: Dialect and the Descent" in *Afro-American Literature: The Reconstruction of Instruction,* Robert Stepto and Dexter Fisher, eds., 88–117 (New York: Modern Language Association, 1969).

Gayle, Jr., Addison, *Oak and Ivy: A Biography of Paul Laurence Dunbar* (Garden City, N.Y.: Doubleday, 1971).

Goldsmith, Oliver. "The Deserted Village" [1770] online text © 2003, Ian Lancashire, for Department of English, University of Toronto, http://eir.library.utoronto.ca/rpo/display/poem875.html (accessed December 17, 2004).

Gossett, Thomas. *Race: The History of an Idea in America* [1963]. Reprint ed. Arnold Rampersad and Shelley Fisher Fishkin, eds. (New York: Oxford University Press, 1997).

Gould, Stephen Jay. *The Mismeasure of Man* (New York: Norton, 1981).

Harris, Duchess. "Negative Black American Stereotypes and Their Impact on Japanese Mindset and Behaviors," *Connecticut Public Interest Law Journal,* Fall 2002.

Harris, Joel Chandler. *Uncle Remus: His Songs and His Sayings* [1895] (New York: Appleton, 1902).

Hewetson, W. T. "The Social Life of the Southern Negro," *The Chatauquan: A Weekly Newsmagazine* (1880–1914), December 1897, 26, 3 APS.

Higginbotham, A. Leon. *In the Matter of Color: Race and the American Legal Process—the Colonial Period* (New York: Oxford University Press, 1978).

Howells, William Dean. Introduction to *Lyrics of Lowly Life* [1896] (Salem, N.H.: Ayers Company, 1992).

———. "Life and Letters" [Review of *Majors and Minors*], *Harper's Weekly* 40 (June 27, 1896), 630.

Jefferson, Thomas. *Notes on the State of Virginia* [1781], Query XIV from *Writings,* Merrill D. Peterson, ed. (New York: The Library of America, 1984), 256–75.

Johnson, James Weldon. *Along This Way* (New York: Viking Press, 1933).

———. *The Book of American Negro Poetry* [1922]. Revised edition (New York: Harcourt, Brace, 1931).

Jones, Gavin. "Paul Laurence Dunbar and the Authentic Black Voice," *Strange Talk: The Politics of Dialect Literature in Gilded Age America* (Berkeley: University of California Press, 1999).

Jordan, Winthrop D. *White Over Black: American Attitudes Toward the Negro, 1550–1812,* New York: W. W. Norton, 1977).

Keeling, John. "Paul Dunbar and the Mask of Dialect," *Southern Literary Journal* 25:2 (Spring 1993): 24–38.

Klein-Salzgitter, Irina. *The Literary Reception of the Chicago World's Columbian Exposition, 1893* [2002], www.biblio.tu-bs.de/ediss/data/20020618a/20020618a.pdf (accessed December 17, 2004).

Leja, Michael. "Progress and Evolution at the U.S. World's Fairs, 1893–1915," *Nineteenth-Century Art Worldwide,* Spring 2003, www.19thc-artworldwide. org/spring_03/articles/leja.html (accessed December 17, 2004).

Logan, Rayford W. *The Betrayal of the Negro from Rutherford B. Hayes to Woodrow Wilson* (originally published as *The Negro in American Life and Thought: The Nadir, 1877–1901*) [1965]. Reprint edition with introduction by Eric Foner (New York: Da Capo Press, 1997).

Martin, Jay, ed. *A Singer in the Dawn: Reinterpretations of Paul Laurence Dunbar* (New York: Dodd, Mead, 1975).

Matthews, Victoria Earle. "Aunt Lindy, A Story Founded on Real Life" [1893] *A.M.E. Church Review* in the Online Archive of Nineteenth-Century U.S. Women's Writings. Ed. Glynis Carr, posted Summer 2000, www. facstaff.bucknell.edu/gcarr/19cUSWW/VEM/AL.html (accessed December 17, 2004).

McFeely, William S. *Frederick Douglass* [1991] (New York: Simon & Schuster, 1992).

Metcalf, Jr., E. W. *Paul Laurence Dunbar: A Bibliography* (Metuchen, N.J.: The Scarecrow Press, 1975).

Murray, Kris. "The World's First Infomercial?" www.svcc.edu/academics/ classes/murray/hum210/wrldfair.htm (accessed December 17, 2004).

Page, Thomas Nelson. *In Ole Virginia; or, Marse Chan and Other Stories.* Introduction by Kimball King (Chapel Hill: University of North Carolina Press, 1969).

Redding, J. Saunders. *To Make a Poet Black* (Chapel Hill: University of North Carolina Press, 1939).

Reed, Christopher Robert. "The Black Presence at 'White City': African and African American Participation at the World's Columbian Exposition, Chicago, May 1, 1893–October 31, 1893" (Chicago: Paul V. Galvin Library, 1999), http://columbus.gl.iit.edu/reed2.html (accessed December 17, 2004).

Revell, Peter. *Paul Laurence Dunbar* [*Twayne's United States Authors Series,* ed. Navid J. Nordloh] (Boston: Twayne Publishers, 1979).

Riley, James Whitcomb. "We Are Not Always Glad When We Smile" in *Complete Works of James Whitcomb Riley*, vol. I, www.encyclopediaindex.com/b/01jwr10.htm (accessed December 17, 2004).

Rose, Julie K. "The World Columbian Exposition: Idea, Experience, Aftermath" (1996), xroads.virginia.edu/~MA96/WCE/title.html (accessed December 17, 2004).

Slotkin, Richard. *Gunfighter Nation: The Myth of the Frontier in Twentieth-Century America* [1992] (New York: Harper Perennial, 1993).

Stevenson, Robert Louis. "Requiem" [1900] online text © 2003, Ian Lancashire, for Department of English, University of Toronto, http://eir.library.utoronto.ca/rpo/display/poem2022.html (accessed December 17, 2004).

Stronks, James B. "Paul Laurence Dunbar and William Dean Howells," *Ohio Historical Quarterly* 67 (1958), 95–108.

Turner, Darwin. "Paul Laurence Dunbar: The Rejected Symbol," *The Journal of Negro History* 52 (January 1967), 1–13.

———. "The Poet and the Myths" from *A Singer in the Dawn: Reinterpretations of Paul Laurence Dunbar* (New York: Dodd, Mead 1975).

Turner, Frederick Jackson. "The Significance of the Frontier in American History" [1893] in Boorstin, Daniel J., ed., *An American Primer* [1966] (New York: Mentor Books, 1968).

Tuttleton, James W. "William Dean Howells & the Practice of Criticism," *The New Criterion* online 10:10 (June 1992), www.newcriterion.com/archive/10/jun92/howells.htm (accessed December 17, 2004).

Twain, Mark. *Adventures of Huckleberry Finn* [1885] [The Oxford Mark Twain] Shelley Fisher Fishkin, ed. (New York: Oxford University Press, 1996).

———. "Fenimore Cooper's Literary Offenses" in *How to Tell a Story and Other Essays* (1897) [The Oxford Mark Twain] Shelley Fisher Fishkin, ed. (New York: Oxford University Press, 1996).

———. "The Man That Corrupted Hadleyburg" in *The Man That Corrupted Hadleyburg and Other Stories and Essays* [1900] [The Oxford Mark Twain] Shelley Fisher Fishkin, ed. (New York: Oxford University Press, 1996).

———. "The £1,000,000 Bank-Note" in *The Million-Pound Bank-Note and Other New Stories* [1893] [The Oxford Mark Twain] Shelley Fisher Fishkin, ed. (New York: Oxford University Press, 1996).

———. *The Tragedy of Pudd'nhead Wilson* in *The Tragedy of Pudd'nhead Wilson and Those Extraordinary Twins* [1894] [The Oxford Mark Twain] Shelley Fisher Fishkin, ed. (New York: Oxford University Press, 1996).

———. "The United States of Lyncherdom" in *Mark Twain: Collected Tales, Sketches, Speeches & Essays, 1891–1910,* ed. Louis J. Budd (New York: Library of America, 2002).

Van Doren, Carl. *The American Novel* (New York: Macmillan, 1921).

Wagner, Jean. *Black Poets of the United States: From Paul Laurence Dunbar to Langston Hughes* (Urbana: University of Illinois Press, 1973).

Ward A. W., W. P. Trent, et al. *The Cambridge History of English and American Literature* (New York: G.P. Putnam's Sons, 1907–21), www.bartleby.com/cambridge (accessed December 17, 2004).

Warner, Charles Dudley. "The Education of the Negro" [1900] [#18 in Project Gutenberg series by Charles Dudley Warner], www.gutenberg.org/etext/3114 (accessed December 17, 2004).

Wells, Ida B. Barnett. *Crusade for Justice: The Autobiography of Ida B. Wells* [1931], Alfreda M. Barnett Duster, ed. (University of Chicago Press, 1970).

———. *On Lynchings* [*Southern Horrors,* 1892; *A Red Record,* 1895; *Mob Rule in New Orleans,* 1900] (Salem, N.H.: Ayer and Co., 1987).

———. *The Reason Why the Colored American Is Not in the World's Columbian Exposition: The Afro-American's Contribution to Columbian Literature* [1893], edited by Robert W. Rydell. (Urbana: University of Illinois Press, 1999).

Wiggins, Linda Keck. *The Life and Works of Paul Laurence Dunbar* (Naperville, Ill.: J.L. Nichols and Company, 1907).

Williams, Kenny J. "The Masking of the Novelist" from *A Singer in the Dawn: Reinterpretations of Paul Laurence Dunbar* (New York: Dodd, Mead, 1975).

Williamson, Joel. *A Rage for Order: Black-White Relations in the American South Since Emancipation* (New York: Oxford University Press, 1986).

Woodward, C. Vann. *Origins of the New South, 1877–1913* (Baton Rouge: Louisiana State University Press, 1951).

———. *The Strange Career of Jim Crow* [1955], 3rd rev. ed. (New York: Oxford University Press, 1974).

ABOUT THE EDITORS

SHELLEY FISHER FISHKIN is a professor of English and the director of American studies at Stanford University. She is the author of the award-winning books *Was Huck Black? Mark Twain and African American Voices* and *From Fact to Fiction: Journalism and Imaginative Writing in America*, as well as, most recently, *Lighting Out for the Territory*. She edited *The Oxford Mark Twain* and *The Historical Guide to Mark Twain*, and co-edited the award-winning *Encyclopedia of Civil Rights in America* with David Bradley. She is past president of the American Studies Association.

DAVID BRADLEY is associate professor of creative writing at the University of Oregon. He is the author of two novels, *South Street* and *The Chaneysville Incident*, for which he received the 1982 PEN/Faulkner Award. He has received fellowships from the John Simon Guggenheim Foundation and the National Endowment for the Arts. His nonfiction has appeared in *Esquire, Redbook, The New York Times, The Philadelphia Inquirer*, the *Los Angeles Times, The Southern Review*, and *The New Yorker*.

MODERN LIBRARY IS ONLINE AT
WWW.MODERNLIBRARY.COM

MODERN LIBRARY ONLINE IS YOUR GUIDE
TO CLASSIC LITERATURE ON THE WEB

THE MODERN LIBRARY E-NEWSLETTER

Our free e-mail newsletter is sent to subscribers, and features sample chapters, interviews with and essays by our authors, upcoming books, special promotions, announcements, and news. To subscribe to the Modern Library e-newsletter, visit **www.modernlibrary.com**

THE MODERN LIBRARY WEBSITE

Check out the Modern Library website at
www.modernlibrary.com for:

- The Modern Library e-newsletter
- A list of our current and upcoming titles and series
- Reading Group Guides and exclusive author spotlights
- Special features with information on the classics and other paperback series
- Excerpts from new releases and other titles
- A list of our e-books and information on where to buy them
- The Modern Library Editorial Board's 100 Best Novels and 100 Best Nonfiction Books of the Twentieth Century written in the English language
- News and announcements

Questions? E-mail us at **modernlibrary@randomhouse.com**.
For questions about examination or desk copies, please visit
the Random House Academic Resources site at
www.randomhouse.com/academic